A Claim *of* Her Own

Books by
Stephanie Grace Whitson

A Claim of Her Own
Jacob's List
Unbridled Dreams
Watchers on the Hill

Secrets on the Wind (3 books in 1)

Walks the Fire
Soaring Eagle
Red Bird

How to Help a Grieving Friend

A Claim of
Her Own

STEPHANIE GRACE
WHITSON

BETHANYHOUSE
a division of Baker Publishing Group

A Claim of Her Own
Copyright © 2009
Stephanie Grace Whitson

Cover design by Koechel Peterson & Associates, Inc., Minneapolis, Minnesota

Unless otherwise identified, Scripture quotations are from the King James Version of the Bible.

Scripture quotations identified NASB are taken from the NEW AMERICAN STANDARD BIBLE,® Copyright © The Lockman Foundation 1960, 1962, 1963, 1968, 1971, 1972, 1973, 1975, 1977, 1995 by International Bible Society. Used by permission. (www.Lockman.org)

Published by Bethany House Publishers
11400 Hampshire Avenue South
Bloomington, Minnesota 55438

Bethany House Publishers is a division of
Baker Publishing Group, Grand Rapids, Michigan.

Printed in the United States of America

Library of Congress Cataloging-in-Publication Data

Whitson, Stephanie Grace.
    A claim of her own / Stephanie Grace Whitson.
       p. cm.
    ISBN 978-0-7642-0512-5 (pbk.)
    1. Young women—Fiction. 2. South Dakota—Gold discoveries—Fiction. I. Title.

    PS3573.H555C63   2009
    813'.54—dc22

                                                          2008051047

DEDICATED TO THE MEMORY OF
GOD'S EXTRAORDINARY WOMEN
IN EVERY PLACE
IN EVERY TIME.

My Sincere Thanks to . . .

MR. MICHAEL RUNGE,
City Archivist, Deadwood, South Dakota, for providing maps
that enabled me to envision nineteenth-century Deadwood.

Ms. ARLETTE HANSON,
Curator, Adams Museum, Deadwood, South Dakota, for timely
answers and for putting me in touch with people
who knew the answers when you didn't.

Ms. ROSE SPIERS,
Communications Director, Adams Museum, Deadwood,
South Dakota, for your kind replies and guidance.

MR. DAN GEORGE,
aka Wild Bill Blackerby, for explaining the "how" of
Wild Bill Hickok's cavalry twist.

AUTHOR STEPHEN BLY,
for unselfishly sharing your expertise in all things Old West,

AND

ANN PARRISH:
You always make the stories so much better.
What a blessing you are!

BETHANY HOUSE PUBLISHERS:
It remains a great privilege to work for you.

THE KANSAS EIGHT:
You know who you are . . . and what you do.

RANDY ALCORN,
brother in Christ and one of the most godly men I know,
thank you for allowing me to put your words in my fictional
preacher's mouth. Thank you for your humility as you walk the
talk and for consistently challenging me to live in light of eternity.

(Readers are encouraged to seek out *The Treasure Principle*
by Randy Alcorn, which, in this author's opinion, should be
required reading for every Christian living on planet Earth.)

About the Author

A native of southern Illinois, Stephanie Grace Whitson has resided in Nebraska since 1975. She began what she calls "playing with imaginary friends" (writing fiction) when, as a result of teaching her four homeschooled children Nebraska history, she was personally encouraged and challenged by the lives of pioneer women in the West. Since her first book, *Walks the Fire,* was published in 1995, Stephanie's fiction titles have appeared on the ECPA bestseller list and have been finalists for the Christy Award and the Inspirational Reader's Choice Award, and *ForeWord Magazine*'s Book of the Year. Her nonfiction work, *How to Help a Grieving Friend,* was released in 2005. Widowed in 2001, Stephanie remarried in 2003 and now pursues full-time writing and a speaking ministry from her studio in Lincoln, Nebraska. In addition to her involvement in her local church and keeping up with her five grown children and two grandchildren, Stephanie enjoys motorcycle trips with her blended family and church friends and volunteering at the International Quilt Study Center in Lincoln, Nebraska. Her passionate interests in women's history, antique quilts, and French, Italian, and Hawaiian language and culture provide endless storytelling possibilities. Learn more at *www.stephaniewhitson.com* or write stephanie@stephaniewhitson.com. U.S. mail can be directed to Stephanie Grace Whitson at P.O. Box 6905, Lincoln, Nebraska 68506.

CHAPTER 1

And in Your book were all written
The days that were ordained for me,
When as yet there was not one of them.

Psalm 139:16 (NASB)

alking down the main street in Deadwood is like stepping onto
hell's front porch. It's frenzied and filthy, and it's the last place
on earth a man would want to bring any woman he cared about. Be
patient. I know it's hard, but you have to trust me about the timing.

Mattie had thought Dillon was just trying to scare her when he wrote that. She thought he was just making sure she didn't take a notion to follow him up here before he was ready for her. But ready or not, she was here now, slogging into town alongside a freighter's wagon piled high with goods. It didn't take long to realize Dillon wasn't exaggerating one bit when he wrote about Deadwood. "Main Street" was little more than a churning river of slops and garbage and manure. The common language seemed to be cursing, and the population 100 percent vile men who spat tobacco and smelled as if they hadn't bathed in weeks. There wasn't a real storefront for as far as she could see. At least not by her standards. Hand-painted signs improvised from old lumber or dirty sheets touted the location of laundries and stores, saloons and hotels, but most businesses were little more than large canvas tents.

Frenzied and filthy. Mattie glanced down at the mud-caked hem of her skirt. Even before arriving in Deadwood she'd encountered plenty of filth—just as predicted by the reluctant freighter she'd convinced to let her travel with the supply train. As for frenzy . . . two men across the way were screaming at each other over a promised order and a failure to supply. Saws and hammers, jangling harnesses, and rattling wagons added to the cacophony, and if that weren't enough noise, the bullwhackers were having their share of trouble getting their teams to haul through the mire.

The freighter called Swede cracked a fearsome bullwhip and called out, "Get along dere, you good-for-nuttin' flea-bitten mired-down cayoose! Almost to home now! Gee-haw!"

All up and down the long line of wagons, freighters screamed and hollered and swore and cracked their whips. Finally, with bellowed protest and lowing complaint, the teams surged ahead.

Mattie continued to take the measure of Deadwood. The business calling itself Grand Central Hotel looked like someone newly acquainted with saw and hammer had knocked it together in a few hours. She stifled a laugh. *Grand,* indeed. Giving a place—or a person for that matter—a fancy name was little more than whitewashing a rotted board as far as she was concerned, and there was obviously plenty of rot beneath the scrawled signs and piles of fresh-cut lumber lining the muddy trail called Main.

Glancing back at the towering loads of freight in Swede's three wagons, Mattie wondered who would ever want floral printed calico in a place like this. And what was the point of jet buttons and ivory combs? She stifled a cough and wished for a scented hanky. The stench of the place was getting to her. In fact—she glanced down—the stench of the place was getting *on* her in the form of more than mud clinging to the hem of her skirt and the soles of her boots.

At the sound of shrill laughter, Mattie glanced up the street just in time to see a woman clad in a rainbow of satin ruffles stumble and land on her knees in the mire. While the men around her roared with laughter, the painted creature looked up to the sky and began to bawl like a weanling calf separated from its momma. Mattie clutched at her paisley shawl and pulled it tighter around her shoulders. As the woman wailed and the men jeered, a bearded stranger exited the hotel and crossed the street to help the drunken woman get up. When she wobbled uncertainly, he put his arm around her and together they began to head up the street toward the part of town Swede had already warned Mattie to avoid.

"Dey named it after de real Badlands beyond Deadvood," Swede had explained. "It's a rough land of gulches and gorges and danger. And just like ven he is in dose Badlands, a man can get lost in dat part of town and ve never hear from him again." Swede paused. "Be sure you stay away from dere."

The sporting girl stumbled. Finally, the stranger realized she was too drunk to navigate the mess in the street, and picking her up in his arms, he hauled her off. Mattie remembered something else Swede had said about Deadwood. "Vimmen? Yah, sure. Dere's plenty of vimmen. Yoost no *ladies*."

No wonder Dillon had told her to wait in Kansas until he sent for her. She glanced behind her toward the spot where Deadwood Creek flowed into the Whitewood. If she understood his letters correctly, Dillon's claim was off up that narrow gulch somewhere. At least she wouldn't have to venture in the direction of the Badlands to find him. Again, she shivered. If she never came near a dance hall again it would be too soon.

How far would she have to climb before she found the claim? Swede had never heard the name Dillon O'Keefe. But then Swede said there were some ten thousand men swarming these hills in search of mother lodes. Mattie didn't quite believe that number. People were always exaggerating things: their wins at the faro table, the richness of their gold discoveries, the number of people rushing into a boomtown. She hoped Dillon hadn't exaggerated the richness of his placer claim.

Dillon. He wasn't going to be happy to see her. She could imagine the line between his eyebrows deepening and his dark eyes glowering with an unspoken scolding. Ah well. He'd never been able to stay mad at her for long. Today would be no exception. She'd do his laundry and polish his boots until they gleamed, and in time he'd decide he was glad she'd come. She might not even have to tell him what Jonas had done and why she'd had to run away.

An odd silence interrupted her imaginings. Mattie glanced across the backs of the oxen toward the two men who'd been arguing only a moment ago. They'd stopped now and were staring openmouthed at her. She looked away and began to walk faster. But it wasn't only those two men reacting to her presence. Pauses in hammering and sawing continued to mark her progress up the street.

Swede had warned her about this, too. "Ven dey see you, it vill cause such a stir."

Seeing Swede's prediction come true made Mattie think back to the day she'd convinced the freighter to let her come north on the Sidney-Deadwood trail. It hadn't been easy. In fact, Swede had almost refused.

"A little ting like you?" Swede laughed aloud. "You cannot mean it. No lady such as you has any business going to Deadvood." And with that, Swede turned to walk away.

"My brother's there," Mattie called out, "and if you won't take me I'll find someone who will. There's at least a dozen more bull-whackers I can ask."

Swede turned back then and with a sweep of one arm indicated the line of freight wagons waiting to pull out. "You see any seats on any of dose vagons? Ve haul *freight*. Tons and tons of freight. Ve don't haul *people*."

Mattie refused to be discouraged. "I don't expect to be hauled.

I'll walk alongside, just like you." Digging into her bag she held out a roll of bills. "I can pay."

Swede pushed the money away. "And vat about if dere is trouble from de Indians? You might not have heard, but dey don't like us settling in dose Black Hills."

Mattie would rather face Indians than Jonas Flynn. Men like Jonas didn't just let girls like her go. He'd be searching trains and stagecoaches, and she'd avoided both so far, stowing away in a farm wagon headed north out of Abilene at first and finally making her way to Sidney, Nebraska, where dozens of freighters left daily headed north to supply the mining boomtowns in Dakota.

Mattie glared at Swede, doing her best to look determined instead of desperate. "And there might be plague and blizzards and any one of a thousand other things." She lifted her chin. "And as I said, if you won't let me come with you, I'll find someone who will—but I'd feel safer with *you.*"

Swede took a long draw from the ever-present pipe, then released the smoke in a string of staccato puffs. Finally, the rough hands took the proffered roll of bills, counted out a few, and handed the rest back. "You vill need de rest for keeping body and soul until you find your brother. I von't vait for you. You must keep up."

That had been over a month and almost three hundred miles ago. Mattie walked without complaint, learning as she traveled that Swede's blustering was just that—bluster.

The sheer physical strength required to keep oxen moving along the trail was the first thing Mattie learned to admire about Swede. The tool of every freighter's trade was called a bullwhip, and Swede's sported a two-foot-long hickory handle and a fifteen-foot lash of braided rawhide. At the end of the lash, what Swede called a "popper" of thonged rawhide made a sharp cracking sound every time it was wielded by Swede's calloused hands. Even on a good day, when the freighters made eight or ten miles, the whip must be kept snapping above the oxen's heads, for as soon as it stopped, the great beasts slowed almost to a stop.

How Swede kept cracking that whip hour after hour was amazing. Mattie had tried it once. Mastering the maneuver that produced the "crack" took longer than she expected, and after only a short stint as a bullwhackeress, her back and shoulders, arms and wrists ached for hours. Swede kept it up, hour after hour, seemingly unfazed.

But there was more than physical strength to admire about Swede.

While the other bullwhackers rained down a constant barrage of foul language, Swede never swore. And though it wasn't unusual to see teams streaming with blood from whip lashes across their shoulders and flanks, Swede's whip never touched flesh.

"I paid too much for dese beasts to misuse dem in such a vay," Swede said when Mattie asked about it. "Dey are stupid and stubborn, but dey are all I have, and I vill take care of dem. I vant my own store vorse dan anyting, and if I am good to Lars and Leif and de rest, I vill have it."

Swede rested the great beasts frequently and applied a vile-smelling black ointment to even the slightest knick on leg or back. Today, as they pulled into Deadwood, Mattie could see that Swede's way of handling oxen was indeed the best. While other teams appeared to be on their last legs, Swede's twenty were in good condition. After a few days' rest they would be ready to head out again. Mattie knew that Swede hoped for three more runs between Deadwood and Sidney, Nebraska, before the next winter set in.

A cold gust of wind rattled through the gulch. Mattie glanced up at the sky, dismayed to see a bank of dark clouds moving in. Rain would make it harder to find Dillon. Swede had said Deadwood Gulch was narrow, with steep canyon walls. Every foot of it for nearly a mile had already been divided rimrock to rimrock into hundred-foot gold claims. "Dat's vere you should look first. Yah sure, dey are finding much placer gold up dere."

"*Placer* gold?"

Swede nodded. "Flakes and tiny bits and sometimes a nugget, all of it yoost vaiting for someone to come and scoop it up."

Mattie imagined Dillon crouched beside the fast-flowing creek as he panned in the frigid water. She was supposed to be back in Kansas, working hard and saving her money until he sent for her. *It won't be long now,* he'd written just last month. *Where do you want to go? Dream big, Mattie. We'll have a home of our own before too much longer.*

Thinking about Dillon wrapping his arms around her and holding her tight filled her with such peace. He'd point to the Colt revolver tucked into her waist—the very gun he'd taught her how to use—and tell her she could put it away. "I'll protect you now," he'd say. And he would.

"Ho!" Swede hollered, and with a bellow, the oxen halted.

Mattie's hand went to her midsection, where a little knot of anticipation and joy was collecting. A string of curses drew her attention back up the street toward the Big Horn Store, where two men seemed about to come to blows over the price of a pair of boots. Mattie ducked closer to one of the freight wagons. *We'll have a home of our own before too much longer.* That's what Dillon had written, and now that she'd stepped onto hell's front porch herself, Mattie decided it couldn't happen soon enough.

"Vell, don't yoost be standing dere vit your mout' hanging open!" Swede hollered at the fair-haired giant who emerged from a large canvas tent labeled Garth Merchandise. Leaning the bullwhip against the front wagon wheel, she continued scolding, "Have you never seen a lady before?"

Mattie had never heard so much affection disguised so effectively, for even as Swede tucked her pipe into her apron pocket, she pulled the blond giant into her arms and kissed him soundly on both cheeks. Then, reaching over the lower front of the first freight wagon, she lifted out her sleeping child, cradling the nine-month-old with a tenderness that belied her tough veneer.

Catching sight of his baby sister, the blond giant shrugged off Swede's withering diatribe and smiled. He shuffled near and, gazing down into Eva's face with wonder, said, "I think she *likes* freighting, Mor."

"*Likes* it?" Swede seemed offended by the idea. "She does *not* like it. She puts up vit it is all, screaming her opinion loud and long for part of every day before giving up and settling in for de ride." Swede nodded at Mattie. "Ask *her* if Eva likes freighting. She vill tell you true."

Mattie grinned. "She's feisty. Tends to declare her opinion of things."

Swede laughed. "Now dat's vat I like about *you*, Mattie O'Keefe. You say it true but you dress it up, so de bitter is not so strong." She took her son's arm. "Freddie, dis here is Miss Mattie O'Keefe. She talked me into bringing her from Sidney. She looks for her brother Dillon. I told her ve vould help her find his claim as soon as ve are set up to do business."

Freddie leaned down and muttered something in his mother's ear. She blinked a few times, then pointed at the first wagon. "Take Eva's cradle into the tent, please."

"Do you know my brother?" Mattie asked as Freddie hauled the quilt-lined cradle that had begun life as an Arbuckles' Coffee box out of the wagon.

"There's a lot of people in town," he said. "It's hard to remember all the names."

Eva woke up. Frowning, she thrust out her lower lip and, squirming in her mother's arms, prepared to yowl. But then she saw her brother emerging from the tent, screeched with joy, and reached for him. Freddie took Eva in his arms and covered her with kisses. Planting her on his shoulders, he waited for her to gather two handfuls of blond hair before taking off in a subdued gallop around the wagon train. Swede allowed one ring around the wagons before saying, "Enough," and pointing toward the coffee-box cradle now positioned just inside the tent.

Freddie deposited Eva back in the box. When Mattie went to pick up the protesting child, Swede intervened. "She cannot always have her vay. Dis she must learn." And with that, Swede went back to work as if Eva's tears were of no consequence to her.

Mattie cringed at the sound of Eva's screeching, but when both Swede and Freddie continued to turn a deaf ear to the child's cries, she relented and began to help them unload. It wasn't long before Eva was peering over the top of her "cradle," her blue eyes bright with curiosity. Every once in a while Freddie would pretend to lunge at her as he passed by with an armful of goods. Eva would giggle with delight, and before long she'd snuggled down and fallen asleep.

———

Hands on hips, Swede stood just inside the huge tent that would become her temporary store and surveyed the growing piles of boxes and bolts of cloth around her. Her real name was Katerina, but everyone called her Swede, and that was fine with her. It had not always been so. At first she had resented it. After all, what if she *was* so tall and as strong as most men? Did that mean she must have a man's name? *Swede* sounded so rough. But then she'd met Garth Jannike. He said she was "statuesque." He was glad for her strength. He called her Katerina and treated her with such tenderness that even though she was now beginning her second year of life without him, Swede's eyes still filled with tears when she thought about him. Which was why she allowed herself such moments only when she was alone. *And alone you are not. You have freight to handle and Mattie O'Keefe to help and a store to build and—* She swiped at her cheek with the back of one hand and bent to open a box.

It was seeing Freddie again that had done it, Swede realized. Every time she returned to the gulch with a load of goods, at the first glimpse of Freddie there was always that second of thinking about Garth, and with it the longing to fill the empty place in her heart. Strange how the first sight of Freddie always reminded her of Garth. Freddie wasn't even Garth's child. Strange how the adopted child had grown to be so like the man who'd taken him in and loved him as his own.

Like Garth, Freddie was tall, with shoulder-length blond hair and eyes the color of the indigo sky just when the sun had set and the last of the golden light was slipping away. He was handsome, too, in a way that made women sometimes stop and stare—until they noticed the different way Freddie carried himself, the slight shuffle in his gait, the slowness of speech. He hadn't been born that way. A high fever had done this to him, destroying not only Katerina's dreams for her child but also her first marriage. Freddie's father had left both the "damaged" child and his seventeen-year-old bride soon after the sickness passed.

But God was good. He had brought Garth Jannike into their lives when Freddie was only two years old, and with Garth came love and a future and a hope—just as the Bible promised.

Sometimes when it was late at night and Swede could not sleep because of worry or sadness, she would think on how God had brought Garth into her life just when she was most desperate. And she would tell herself to be strong, for desperation was for those who had no God. If she could last through another season of bullwhacking and freighting, good families might come to Deadwood. And if they did not come and there was no plan for a church and school, then Katerina Jannike would take her Freddie and little Eva and leave this place and they would find a home somewhere else.

As she lifted a pair of men's rubber boots out of the open box before her, Swede reached up to touch the bag of gold dust around her neck. She smiled. *Ven you sell all of dis freight you vill have even more gold. Even now you can take care of your children, vich is more dan many do.* Swede sighed as she looked around her. So much work yet to do. Oxen to tend, boxes to open, merchandise to arrange . . . Ah, but she felt old. So much older than her thirty-three years.

Freddie ducked into the tent with another box. "Three more stores opened while you were gone, Mor," he said, and set the box down in the far corner.

"Tree?"

Freddie nodded.

Swede clucked her tongue and shook her head. Three freighting contracts she had missed by being gone. So much business lost to someone else. She could almost feel the hot breath of doubt whispering in her ear. *You'll never have a real store. You'll never save enough to have a real home again.* She distracted herself from her doubt by bustling outside and yelling at a lanky passerby, "You dere! Get your hook-handed self away from my oxen—unless you like being stepped on or kicked or vorse!"

"Mor." Freddie hissed it into her ear from where he stood just behind her. "Mor, you don't want to be talking like that to that man."

"An' vy not?" Swede put her hands on her hips and whirled around. "You know Lars and Leif do not like strangers. Vat if dey should decide to cause trouble right here in de middle of Deadvood? I need no trouble from some newcomer who does not have sense to keep avay from a voman's oxen. Do I not have de right to de street de same as anyone else?"

"Of course you have the right, Mor. But—" he nodded toward the man retreating up the street—"that's Mr. English."

"And vat do I care if his name is English or Danish?"

"He's one of those three I told you about opening stores."

"Den I assume he is already contracted vit an outfit to bring in goods."

"Yes'm. He is. With you, Mor. He's contracted with you."

Swede frowned. She looked up at Freddie. "Vit me?"

Freddie's smile revealed dimples on both cheeks. "I was bringing some rabbits I trapped to sell to Aunt Lou and I saw Grover Bannister up there talking to Mr. English and I just thought Grover shouldn't get that contract. He doesn't need it as much as we do. So I quick took the rabbits in to Aunt Lou and then I hurried to Mr. English's lot and I told him that everybody knows that Grover Bannister is a cheat and marks his goods up way past what is reasonable and I told him Swede is my Mor and everybody knows she's the best freighter in the Hills and honest to boot."

"And vat did Mr. Bannister do ven you called him a cheat?"

"He called me a low-down, soft-bellied snake in the grass." Freddie glanced toward Mattie and lowered his voice. "And some other things I can't rightly say." He swallowed. "And he got real loud and doubled up his fists and came up to me, so I just helped him see he shouldn't oughta call me names and I helped him leave, and I didn't mean for him to fall but he did and he went splat right there," Freddie said, gesturing toward the middle of the street, "and everyone was laughing and that's when Mr. English asked me about our terms."

"And vat did you tell him for terms?"

"Oh, I didn't tell him terms, Mor." Freddie shook his head from side to side. "I told him I wasn't smart enough for that kind of business talk but that you'd be up to see him as soon as you got into town and you'd treat him right and honest and he said okay, he'd look for you as soon as you got back." He beamed down at her. "And he shook my hand. Just like I was a regular person." Freddie held his palm out and looked down at it and murmured, "I like Mr. English, Mor."

Swede watched the man walk down the street. "Dis Mr. English," she said, "vat is his Christian name?"

"It's Tom. Mr. Tom English." Freddie grinned. "He said for me to call him Tom. Do you think that's all right?"

Swede swallowed. Nodded. "Yah," she murmured. "If he said dat and he shook your hand—den it's all right." And without ever having met Mr. Tom English, Swede decided she liked him. Liked him and wanted to do business with him. How she regretted calling him "hook-handed." She sighed and glanced over to where Mattie had knelt beside Eva's cradle, obviously doing her best to pretend she hadn't heard a word of what Freddie had just said.

"Vell, Miss O'Keefe," she said abruptly. "It seems to me dis vould be an occasion for some kind of vord to mellow de bitter. I have just called names de man vit whom I am supposed to do business."

Swede shook her head. Sometimes life brought trouble in waves. She had missed the chance to open the first store in Deadwood. She had probably alienated a new customer before so much as meeting him. She was tired, and she missed Garth more than ever, and if that wasn't enough, as it turned out, Freddie knew exactly who Dillon O'Keefe was.

He'd helped bury him.

CHAPTER 2

The Lord is nigh unto them that are of a broken heart.

Psalm 34:18

Cephas Manning. Michael Usher. Jane Reeves. Old Man Ross. Mattie read the names someone had hand-painted on wooden crosses. Deadwood might be a new town, but violence and sickness had already reaped a fair crop of lives. Dillon's grave was unmarked. If it weren't for Freddie Jannike's being the one to dig it, Mattie would never have known which of the unmarked mounds of earth on this hillside covered over the only person on earth she loved. The only person who had ever really loved her. The only person who understood what was so funny about Mattie's distaste for horehound candy. The only person who knew "Mist-Covered Mountains" and could sing along with her. Dillon had a fine voice. She would never hear it again. How was that possible?

Sinking to her knees, Mattie leaned forward and plunged her hands into the fresh earth. He'd always had weak lungs. He never should have come here. Working in the frigid water . . . and why didn't he see the doctor at the first signs of the grippe? Picturing Dillon sick and alone on his claim . . . she let the tears slide down her cheeks. She would never hear him sing again . . . and they wouldn't be building a new life after all . . . and she was afraid.

As grief and disappointment and fear washed over her, Mattie began to rock back and forth, back and forth. She lifted her face to the gloomy skies and let her tears fall. Mam had taught her to vent quietly, and so while another woman in a similar situation might have wailed and screamed, Mattie spilled her grief softly. No one watching would know the depth of her sorrow. No one would hear her heart break in half and all the hope she'd been storing there drain away.

"What do I do now, Dillon?" she croaked. "If you can hear me, I wish you'd show me what I should do." She paused. "I'm so afraid Jonas is going to come after me. You know all that money I'd worked so hard for? He lied about it. He wasn't keeping any kind of account. And then he started pressuring me to—you know. We had an awful scene the night I left. He almost forced—" She gulped. "I slapped him and my ring cut his face. Deep. I thought he was going to kill me right there. His vanity saved me. I got away while he was at the doctor's getting his face sewn up." Her voice wavered. "I had to get away, Dillon. I couldn't wait. Don't you see?"

A breeze whipped up the hill and ruffled her dark hair. Shivering, Mattie clutched at her shawl and glanced to where Freddie Jannike was sitting on a boulder whittling at something. She looked back down at the grave. "What do I do now? I don't have much money left. There's a stagecoach, but—" She sniffed and swiped at a tear. "I avoided the train and the stage. In case Jonas decided to look for me. And besides that, I can't afford it." She answered the question she imagined Dillon asking. "No, no. I won't even consider that. I promise." She leaned forward and placed one palm on the mound of earth. "I promise on my life. My dance hall days are past."

Mattie sat for a few more minutes waiting for her heartbeat to slow and her emotions to recede. She wasn't finished crying. She would likely never finish crying over Dillon, but the daylight was waning and a storm was brewing and she had to find somewhere to sleep tonight. Her hand went to her waist. She ran her finger along the curve of the Colt's grip. A lesser woman in her situation might consider taking a fast ride to wherever Dillon was. Mattie had known girls who did that, although guns weren't the usual tool. There were quieter ways to quit life. But quitting was for cowards. And whatever she might be, whatever people might think of her, Mattie O'Keefe was no coward.

She wasn't stupid, either—except when it came to Jonas Flynn. She'd believed he would be fair to her out of respect for Mam. *Respect.* What a fool she'd been to think Jonas ever respected any woman. Mam meant nothing more to him than warmth on cold nights and a steady income from all the other men, and the minute she was dead Jonas forgot every promise he'd ever made to her to treat Mattie differently; to let her sing on stage and deal cards—and to keep her out of those little rooms upstairs.

Mattie got to her feet. "I've been a fool," she spoke to the earth. "I was stupid to trust Jonas. But I won't make that mistake again. And I'm not a coward, and I won't quit. I will make you proud of me. I promise."

As Mattie turned away from Dillon's grave, she saw Freddie close his whittling knife and put something in his pocket. He stood, waiting while she picked her way through the random arrangement of graves. When she finally got down to where Freddie was waiting, she looked up at him and asked, "Do you think your mam would agree to bring a proper tombstone for my brother's grave on her next trip?"

Swede leaned over and poured the pitcher of rainwater slowly over the back of her head to rinse out the soap. Setting the empty pitcher on the ground, she reached for the clean flour sack towel she'd tucked into the waist of her calico skirt, wrapped her hair and, with a deft twist of the towel, stood back up. Was there anything in the world that felt better than clean hair? Well, yes, she recalled with a faint smile. There was something. But her husband was gone, so there was no sense in longing for the leeks of Egypt. She had had her time of marital joy . . . and would likely never have it again. It was expecting too much to think there might be another man like Garth Jannike striding the earth.

Nearly all men wanted pretty little things with ivory skin and small waists like Mattie O'Keefe, not tall, thick-waisted women like Katerina Jannike. And now that she had calloused hands and a tanned face and muscled arms from months of wielding a bullwhip . . . Swede sighed. God had given her the miracle of Garth. Best not to appear ungrateful by hoping for yet another.

With Eva playing happily on a comforter nearby, Swede towel-dried her hair before sitting down to comb it out. She'd ignored the gathering clouds to perform her hair-washing-at-the-end-of-the-trip ritual, and she was glad. How good it felt to have these moments to herself, to feel the breeze and the warm air from the campfire move through the long silken strands of her waist-length hair. There was never a chance on the trail for much of anything beyond a quick brushing and rebraiding every few days. More than once she'd been tempted to cut it all off and be done with it. But Garth had loved her long hair so; cutting it would be another step away from him that she was not willing to take. Swede took a deep breath and closed her eyes. Clean hair was a blessing . . . and so was *sitting*.

Her feet hurt almost constantly these days. She held them straight out before her and flexed her ankles. A woman just wasn't meant to walk five hundred miles in two months, was she? *Soon. It vill be over soon.* The bag of gold with her name on it in James Woods's safe would double in size if she could sell this load of goods at the usual profit, and the tent could come down to make room for a real store on this very lot. And then—

Eva began to fuss and Swede scooped her up, unbuttoned her

chemise, and offered her breast. How she longed for a more normal life and a real home. Could that even happen in Deadwood? She didn't know anyone expecting to build a life for a family in this place. Most of the thousands of men in these hills had come to rape the land of its gold, and once that was done, they'd be gone. And unless one had arrived while Swede was on this last run, Mattie O'Keefe was the first lady in Deadwood. Oh, there was Aunt Lou Marchbanks over at the hotel, but Aunt Lou's mahogany skin prevented anyone from thinking of her when they considered the realm of *ladyship*. No, Mattie O'Keefe was probably Deadwood's official lady—and would likely be the first one to leave now that she knew her brother was dead.

What about you? Swede harrumphed at the thought. Whatever she was, she didn't think the word *lady* applied. Just the thought of Swede Jannike being invited to join a Ladies Aid Society or to have tea almost made her laugh. Or cry. She wasn't sure which. *You must stop such toughts. Dey profit you nothing.*

Perhaps she would ask around in Sidney the next time she was there and learn what was involved in homesteading on the prairie down that way. What did it cost people to build those sod houses? She'd helped Garth plow once. Surely she could break sod. She and Freddie could build a house together. If the sod road ranches she'd visited were any indication, she would want a board roof. The dirt ones leaked. Or maybe they should settle where a person could build a proper house of logs. If Freddie felled the trees, she could strip bark. Yes, Swede decided. A log house would be better.

Or maybe they should live in a town where she could buy out another storekeeper. How much money would she need for that? And what town should she choose? Looking down into Eva's sleeping face, Swede decided that yes, a town was the right choice. A town with families and a school and a *church*. How long had it been since she had set foot in a real church?

With a sigh of longing, Swede got up and retreated inside the tent, where she laid Eva in her cradle. Buttoning her chemise, she stepped back outside. The sky had cleared. *Good.* She was just settling her soup pot on the spider positioned over the fire when Freddie and Mattie O'Keefe returned.

She was an interesting girl, that one; a real beauty with very little to say about her past. Of course a young woman who kept a pistol tucked into the waist of her skirt wasn't likely to want to talk about the past. Mattie probably didn't realize Swede knew about the gun. She wore a little jacket most of the time and tied a beautiful paisley shawl about her when she didn't wear the jacket. But Swede hadn't survived in a man's world alone by taking up with strangers and inviting them on the trail without becoming a student of people. She'd known about that pistol all along, and she'd even slept with the rifle she called Old Bess beside her for several nights on the trail. But as the days wore on Swede realized that Mattie O'Keefe was just what she seemed—a beautiful woman running from an unknown past toward a promise.

Eventually Swede put Old Bess back in its place just inside the first wagon. And now that the two of them had shared so many campfires, Swede was concerned for the young woman. After all, in a few days she would be gone back up the trail and Mattie O'Keefe would be on her own in Deadwood. *Heaven help her.*

"You vill sleep in our camp tonight," Swede said. "As you have seen, Deadvood is no place for a lone woman."

"*You're* alone." Mattie glanced up at Freddie and then back at Swede. "Much of the time."

Swede nodded. "Yah. And I am six feet tall and strong as an ox. And," she said, nodding at Freddie, "in Deadvood I have my son." She motioned for Mattie to sit by the fire.

"I'm not defenseless." Mattie lifted her shawl to show the Colt at her waist.

"You are safer vit us," Swede insisted as she dished up soup.

Gunshots sounded somewhere off toward the Badlands part of town. Swede repeated, "You are safer here."

Mattie relented. "Thank you. I'll take the offer of a place to sleep. But I can't eat right now."

Swede glowered at her. "You have very big decisions tomorrow. You vill need your vits about you. So eat."

"You aren't old enough to be my mother," Mattie chided.

"But I am big enough to be your father and strong enough to bully oxen into doing vat I say, so I am not likely to give up ven it comes to knowing vat is good for you for dis night."

Mattie tasted the soup. "It's good."

"Thank you." Freddie smiled.

"*You* made this?"

He nodded. "Antelope. Got him over by Gayville."

"Freddie tracks and traps and shoots straight," Swede explained. "And he is a good cook. He is good at many more tings people do not expect of him."

"I'm not smart like some people," Freddie explained.

Mattie shrugged. "But you *are* smart—just in a different way. I'd starve if I had to hunt my food."

"I help Mor by staying here and hunting and working," Freddie said, "and I watch over Mor's town lot and live in the tent. It's important." He shook his head. "I don't tag along on the trail like a baby." He gulped down a last spoonful of soup before standing up. "More boxes to unload," he said, and headed back toward the waiting wagons.

"You must talk to de mining district recorder tomorrow," Swede said to Mattie as soon as Freddie was gone. "He vill know which claim is Dillon's. You should be ready for some offers to buy."

Freddie turned back around long enough to say, "I could help find Dillon's claim."

Swede smiled at him. "Do you know someone who vould help Miss O'Keefe vit de business dealings and not take advantage?"

Freddie chewed on his bottom lip while he thought. Finally, he nodded. "Mr. English. Tom."

Swede was doubtful. "After how I treated him earlier, Mr. English vill be in no mood to help us."

Freddie insisted. "He shook my *hand*, Mor. He looked in my *eye*. And he treated me—"

"I know, I know. But dat does not mean—"

"And let me finish." Freddie held up his hand with the index finger extended, like a child asking for permission to speak in school. "He said the best way to make money mining is to sell things to the rest of the fools who want to work in freezing cold water or burrow in the dirt. He said he figured that out on his claim over at Blacktail and he got enough out of it to set himself up in business." Freddie looked at his mother with what Mattie could only think of as a cat-that-got-the-canary look. "So he knows all about mines but he don't *want* one so he would tell Miss O'Keefe the truth and he treats me good and that means a lot." Freddie's face sobered. "You know how it is, Mor. People who treat *me* nice are nice to anybody. Even dogs."

Swede looked away quickly. She cleared her throat, then nodded briskly. "All right then." She glanced at Mattie. "Ve see Mr. English in de morning."

———

Mattie woke with a start. Had she been dreaming? *No. You really are in this awful place. And Dillon really is gone.* A dog barked somewhere. It was still dark out and oddly quiet except for the occasional rattling of spurs as someone picked their way toward the gambling houses and saloons at the lower end of town.

Maybe it was her imagination, but Mattie almost thought she could hear laughter and raucous voices and . . . a piano? She listened more carefully. Yes. There was music on the clear night air. *Well, you didn't think the piano Swede hauled up here was for a church, did you?* She hadn't let herself think about it very much when Swede said she had been paid top dollar to bring the first piano to Deadwood. The dance hall owner must have come for it while she and Freddie were at the cemetery. And someone must have tuned it. Whoever was playing it was good. Very good.

She wondered if the girl who'd been rescued from the mud this afternoon was up there right now, dancing or selling drinks to lonely miners. She wondered if the man who'd rescued her was up there, too, buying her drinks—or buying her. Just thinking about it made her shiver. She lay back down.

Someone came galloping into town, charging by only a few feet from the tent. There was gunfire and shouting, and Eva began to cry. In a flash Mattie snatched her Colt from beneath the edge of the pallet. She sat up, her heart racing. When nothing more happened, Swede began to hum softly. Eva stopped crying.

Freddie must have gotten up and checked outside. He spoke in low tones. "They went on up the street. I'm right here in the doorway. I'll take care of you. It's all right, Mor. You can go back to sleep now."

After a few minutes, Mattie put her gun back under the edge of her pallet and lay back down. She had no doubt that sweet, simple, sixteen-year-old Freddie Jannike would protect his family or die trying. But he was wrong about one thing. Things were not all right. They were not all right at all.

———

Early the next morning Freddie escorted Mattie back up the street toward Deadwood Gulch, where a huge canvas tent pitched beside a babbling brook Freddie called City Creek proclaimed *Opening soon—English Dry Goods.* When Freddie pulled back the tent flap and called for Tom, Mattie heard a pleasant voice answer, "Good morning, friend. Come right on in."

English was standing behind a counter that was little more than a few rough-hewn boards spanning the space between two upended crates. From the stacks of similar boards and crates lined up along the far wall of the tent, it appeared he had plans for quite a number of counters and shelves.

It wasn't until Freddie tied back the tent flap and morning light glinted off of Tom English's hook that Mattie's heart began to pound. As Freddie introduced her, she looked around, surveying the well-organized goods, telling herself to relax. The place smelled of freshly cut wood, spring grass, and pipe tobacco. The wiry man before her sported a neatly trimmed moustache above a warm smile. His dark eyes shone with kindness and intelligence. What with the gray flecks at his temples and the well-tailored brown pants and vest worn over the clean striped shirt, Mr. Tom English might have been a professor or a minister. And yet, Mattie recoiled from the hook. Embarrassed, she apologized.

English held it up. "Cannonball at Shiloh," he said, shaking his head in mock dismay. "Ended all my dreams of being a gunslinger." He smiled even as he flexed the long fingers of his left hand. "It took me about three years to teach leftie here to do what rightie used to do. And that was after I finally got it through my thick skull that rightie wasn't *there* anymore."

"I-I'm so sorry," Mattie said again, scolding herself inwardly, *You can't go through life flinching every time you see a man with a hook.*

"No need to apologize." English gazed down at the hook. "It is a hideous thing." He looked back at Mattie. "But it will do no harm, and I have learned to be grateful for it."

Mattie could feel her cheeks growing warm. Glancing up at Freddie, she changed the subject. "Freddie says you've some experience with mining, and—" She paused, swallowed, and then in one long breath told him how she'd arrived only to learn that her brother was "...dead...and...you can imagine my quandary," she said, and then her voice just trailed off because she couldn't go on without breaking down.

Mr. English said what society demanded. "I am so sorry for your loss."

Freddie spoke up. "I told Mattie what you said about wanting to make your money selling things to the rest of the fools while they work in freezing cold water or burrow in the dirt—"

English's eyes crinkled at the corners when he smiled. "You did, did you?"

"That's what you said." Freddie nodded.

"I suppose I did."

"And I told her you are honest and kind."

"Well." English patted Freddie on the shoulder. "Thank you for that. I couldn't ask for a better endorsement."

Mattie spoke up. "I was hoping you'd agree to be my adviser in matters concerning my brother's claim. I need help locating it, and now that he's . . . gone . . ." She cleared her throat. "I need advice. From someone who knows about prospecting and such."

English gestured around him. "But as you can see, Miss O'Keefe, I'm no longer prospecting."

"But you have experience." Mattie liked the idea that he didn't seem eager to step into the position she was clearly offering. Over-eager men made her wary.

English sighed. "Yes. I've probably been here as long as any other white man. I came in with Custer and helped a man named Gordon build a stockade a couple of years back—but then you probably don't need to hear any of that." He shrugged his bony shoulders. "By the time the army decided to usher us all out of these hills, I'd found enough color to intrigue me, so I managed to get separated from the party and 'lost.' I hunkered down and got through the winter on my own, and I imagine you've heard all of the rest of that story worth telling from Freddie."

"Everything you've just said only serves as more evidence that Freddie was right to suggest that I come to you for help," Mattie said, staring at English evenly. She wasn't above using the violet eyes that seemed to fascinate men to work a little magic on her behalf.

English stared back for a moment, then looked away. He plucked an imaginary thread off the sleeve of his shirt. Scratched his beard. Finally, he took a deep breath and said, "I had not met your brother, Miss O'Keefe, but if I had the good fortune to have a sister who cared about me, I suppose I would hope that someone honest would be willing to help her out if she needed it." He nodded. "All right. If I can be of assistance in helping you get your business settled, I'll be pleased to do what I can."

He smiled at Freddie. "Do you think you could get your mother to join us for coffee and some of Aunt Lou's biscuits? She and I have freighting business to discuss. I always like to seal my covenants over food, and I've been hankering for Aunt Lou's biscuits and gravy since I woke up this morning."

————

Mattie didn't like the claims recorder at all. She didn't like the way he looked her up and down when she came through the door of the oversized closet he called his office. She didn't like the way he made a show of shaking her hand when Mr. English introduced her and presented her case, and she especially didn't like the condescending way he waved her into a chair and addressed himself to Mr. English, almost as if she weren't even in the room.

"He left her the claim, Tom—may I call you Tom? It's as simple as that. I have it right here." He opened the middle drawer of his desk and pulled out a document. "Doc Reeves witnessed it." He pointed to the line where the doctor had testified to hearing Dillon Patrick O'Keefe's last will and testament, which left his placer gold claim and all his worldly goods to his sister, one Mattie Eileen Clare O'Keefe.

Mattie leaned toward Mr. English and said in a low voice, "How do we know this document is legal when it comes to the claim? Will it stand up in court if someone challenges the idea of a woman owning a placer claim?"

The man still didn't look at her, although he took it upon himself to answer the question she'd clearly addressed to Mr. English. "It's as legal as you're going to get, ma'am—in light of the fact that Deadwood doesn't really *exist* as far as the United States government is concerned." He pointed to the unopened envelope lying beneath the affidavit. "This is his claim certificate. Gives the exact location and records the day he filed it."

When Gates held it out to Mr. English, Mattie grabbed it. Opening it, she read, *Personally appeared before me Dillon Patrick Clare O'Keefe and recorded the undivided right title and interest to Claim Number 7, "Above Discovery" of 300 feet for mining purposes. Recorded this 9th Day of July 1875.* She handed the certificate to Mr. English, and while he read she repeated her question, "Can I be certain no one will challenge my taking ownership?"

Gates shrugged and once again addressed Mr. English. "As you know, Tom, we're operating in a rather . . . unique situation." He cast a condescending smile in Mattie's direction. "This entire territory is officially part of an Indian reservation. Now, we expect that to change in the next few months, but until such time as it does, all I can tell you is we have adopted the same time-honored practices established in California, Montana, and other regions of the country where people are engaged in the mining of precious metals." He paused. "We are confident that these contracts and practices will be judged lawful, and in the meantime there is widespread acceptance among the mining community."

"So I own my brother's claim," Mattie said.

"As soon as she signs this she does," Gates said, pointing to the transfer papers.

Mattie signed her name before asking, "And my brother's gold?"

Gates tilted his head. "I beg your pardon?"

"He was prospecting," Mattie said. "He wrote of results. I therefore assume there's gold somewhere with his name on it."

Gates shrugged. "I know nothing about any gold, Miss O'Keefe."

"But you know where he might have deposited it," Mr. English said.

"Check with James Woods. He's got a safe behind the counter of his fledgling hotel. It's not much of a bank, but a good number of the boys who came up early made deposits with him. Could be Mr. O'Keefe was among those who chose that route."

Mr. English nodded. "We can check with Miners and Merchants, too."

"Yes," Gates said. "Of course. You'd want to do that."

The claim's paying well, Mattie. It's hard work, but it's paying off. I've learned to mine with a toothpick. But lately I haven't needed the toothpick. Mattie didn't know exactly what Dillon meant, but she wasn't about to ask Ellis Gates about it. Her pulse quickened. She was the owner of a paying gold claim. Was she about to be rich? She told herself not to get her hopes up. Dillon always did paint circumstances in the best light possible. Perhaps he'd exaggerated to give her hope. She stood up. "Thank you."

"You'll be wanting to sell, I presume." Gates didn't get up.

"I'll be wanting to speak with the banks now," Mattie said, and taking Mr. English's proffered arm, she left.

"Don't mind them," Tom English said, referring to the men in the street who stared as she passed by.

"I don't."

"Some of them haven't seen a pretty *lady* in months. Maybe a year. Maybe more. They don't mean anything by it."

"I'd like to get a tombstone," Mattie said abruptly.

"A—what?"

"For my brother. The first thing I'll buy is a tombstone."

English nodded. "That's nice. You're a good sister, Miss O'Keefe."

He pointed his hook toward a building up ahead. "That's Jim Woods's." And then he asked, "Where will you go—after the tombstone's in place?"

Where, indeed, Mattie thought. Where would she finally be able to stop looking over her shoulder for Jonas—where could she finally stop being afraid? Enough to get her to that place would be all the wealth she would ever need. "I have no idea," she said.

Before long it was clear that making plans about tombstones and travel was pointless. The men at both banks offered their condolences. They agreed that her brother's claim was rumored to be a good one. But neither bank was holding so much as an ounce of gold dust belonging to Dillon O'Keefe.

CHAPTER 3

The getting of treasures by a lying tongue
is a vanity tossed to and fro of them that seek death.

Proverbs 21:6

You would have thought the miners working Deadwood Gulch had seen a ghost.

Well, maybe not a ghost. Men probably wouldn't respond to a ghost by taking off their hats and nodding as it glided by. But that's what they were all doing this Wednesday afternoon in May as Mattie followed Mr. English up Deadwood Gulch. He knew some of the men by name. Others he simply nodded at as he and Mattie picked their way along the edge of the creek that joined up with the Whitewood down below.

Yesterday she'd been too distracted by the wretched conditions in Deadwood to pay much attention to the gulch. Dillon hadn't really described the landscape in detail, and somehow, from his mention of trees and rushing water, she'd created a pleasing mental image of a babbling brook, the scent of pine, and well-ordered campsites arranged along rocky walls soaring upward toward a blue sky.

Now Mattie could see that, while the gulch had undoubtedly

had a wild appeal before the first white man noticed the glint of gold in the creek bed, mining had destroyed it. The place was a maze of brush shanties and stained canvas tents in various states of disrepair surrounded by piles of gravel and holes in the ground, all of it punctuated by strange-looking wooden contraptions Mr. English called *rockers* and *sluice boxes*.

"Mining requires water and lots of it," he explained as they paused for Mattie to catch her breath. "We had deep snow this past winter, so the creek's running fast, but once the surface gold has all been panned out, a prospector builds those." He pointed to the shallow open-ended sluice boxes on the claim above them. "See how the water's been directed to rush through? That washes the lighter gravel away while gold drops onto the baffles at the bottom—" He paused. "When you've caught your breath I'll show you."

Mattie gulped air. Finally, she nodded and followed him up toward the deserted claim he'd been pointing at. "I can't imagine Dillon doing this by himself."

"If you find sluice boxes on the claim, he definitely had help. As you've already noticed down in town, there's plenty of men hanging around allegedly looking for work."

"He never mentioned hiring help in his letters."

"Then maybe he was still getting good color from panning. Someone told me that Number 14 above Discovery has yielded $35,000 so far, and I don't think they have any special equipment up there yet."

Thirty-five THOUSAND dollars? It was more money than Mattie could imagine earning in a lifetime. She began to pepper Mr. English with questions as they climbed ever higher. From time to time he introduced her to miners. Some were half drunk and most were dirty, but all removed their hats, nodded, and gave a polite "Pleased to meet ya, ma'am." One old codger even bowed. When Mattie curtsied they shared a laugh.

Mr. English pointed out the stakes marking off the boundaries of each claim. "Those papers you see nailed to the stakes are the owner's claim papers. And miners can show some amazing creativity when it comes to naming their claims."

Mattie laughed aloud as they continued to climb and she read names like *Whizzers* and *Deadbroke*, *Wasp* and *Safe Investment*. At the latter, looking over the haphazard arrangement of sluice boxes, she observed, "I don't think Safe Investment really *is*."

Mr. English agreed. "A gully washer of a rain would probably carry it all to the bottom of the gulch—along with everything in its path—and woe to the man who's asleep in his tent when that happens."

Mattie pointed to a stake. "It's good the boundaries are marked so clearly. I imagine there'd be horrible fights otherwise."

"It certainly helps, but once a man's grubbing underground to follow promising color, it becomes extremely easy to forget about the imaginary lines on the surface."

"Then what happens?"

"Broken jaws. Gunfire." Mr. English paused. "Mining's a violent business, Miss O'Keefe."

"Is that why you quit?" She could see the corners of his mouth turn up in a sad smile as he shook his head and answered with a simple no. She tilted her head and ventured another guess. "Claim ran out?"

"No."

"Are you going to tell me?"

Instead of giving her an answer, English pointed to the claim they were just passing through. There was barely room for a lean-to shelter among the honeycomb of holes. "Once a claim is panned out, it's time to start digging. Since gold is much heavier than most dirt or gravel or rock, it's usually at the bottom of everything on what is called the bedrock. Here around Deadwood, bedrock tends to be within just a few feet of the surface, so after a prospector has panned it out of the creek bed and worked the sides of his claim, he can still keep mining without expensive equipment by digging holes down to the bedrock." He paused. "Which is what will make your brother's claim desirable to anyone really wanting to prospect. The gulch has been claimed rimrock to rimrock, so the only way to get in on the strike is to buy a claim from someone else."

"So Mr. Gates wasn't trying to take advantage of me by saying I should expect offers to buy?"

Mr. English shrugged. "Not necessarily. I imagine you'll be able to sell it without difficulty. Although he did seem a bit eager to manage things for you."

Eager is such a nice to way to put it, Mattie thought. But then, Mr. English seemed to be the kind of man who chose words carefully. Such things usually made her wary. She was surprised to realize that this man's reticence seemed more gentlemanly than anything. Realizing that her internal musings had created a rather awkward pause, she walked to the edge of one of the holes being dug on the claim at hand and peered down. "It looks dangerous."

English nodded. "I've seen claims where the bedrock is further down than it is here and they start to dig tunnels between the holes. Without bothering to shore anything up."

"That's insane," Mattie said. "If it caved in . . ." She shuddered.

"Och, see here now, me fine buckos, 'tis a hummin'bird come doon to alight in the gulch!" The voice belonged to a man with hair so red it was almost orange. He was standing just above them, his hat in his hand. "Hugh McKay, miss," he said, and with a dip of his head gave a little bow by way of greeting. He gestured at the two young men working a sluice box on his claim. "And these be me sons, Fergus and Finn. Soon as I saw ye my heart lep in me throat, knowin' it must be herself, the sister of our dear departed Dillon."

"And if I'm not mistaken," Mattie answered with a smile, "you'd be the McKays my brother wrote about." *Three Scotsmen crazy as loons and drunk most of the time, but I like them.* Happily, the McKays didn't seem drunk now, Mattie thought, but then who knew. She'd seen men play an expert hand of poker only to fall flat when they stood up to leave.

"Now, don't be believin' everything ye've been told," Mr. McKay said, then shouted for his boys to come near. "Here she is, boys, the verra picture of loveliness, just as Dillon described." When the boys only stared, their father shook his head. "You'll have to excuse me boys, miss. Hummin'birds be rare things hereabouts." He cleared his throat. "We loved your brother, Miss O'Keefe, and we mourn him sincerely." He put his hat over his heart.

Mattie felt tears gathering. She cleared her throat. "Thank you. I-I've come to see the claim," she said, nodding at Tom English as she did. "Mr. English has been describing the finer points of mining on our way up here." She looked around. "Dillon's letters make so much more sense to me now."

"Have you seen a rocker in use, miss?" Fergus McKay piped up.

"No," Mattie said with a shake of her head. She glanced at Mr. English. "Although Mr. English was kind enough to describe it on the way up here." She smiled at the young Mr. McKay. "Would you have time to explain how it works?" Now that she'd met someone who'd known Dillon, she felt inclined to delay the moment when she'd actually step onto his claim . . . face his empty tent . . . see his unused tools . . . the cot where he slept . . . the little stove that kept him warm. It was all just a few hundred feet above her now, but she didn't want to look. Not yet.

" 'Tis only another way to wash the gold out of the gravel," the brother named Finn said as they walked over to it. "One man shovels gravel in—"

"—that one bein' myself," Fergus McKay broke in, "since me brother does-nah care for the back-breakin' part of the work."

The brother in question glowered. "As I was sayin', one shovels it in here," he explained, pointing to the upper end of the rocker, which really did look a bit like a cradle, "and then chases it with water." He mimicked emptying a bucket of water into the rocker.

"Then," he said, grasping the pole attached to one side, "I rock while me brother—"

"—while I pick out the treasure." Fergus motioned for Mattie to come closer. "See those iron plates in the bottom? And the holes? As Finn is rockin'—which even a little thing like you could do if a man was to refrain from dumpin' a ton of gravel in—the gold falls through the holes and the rest gets washed out—"

"And then while Fergus keeps to the easy task of picking out the gold," Finn said, "I repeat the back-breakin' part."

"All right, you two," the elder Mr. McKay said. "See here now, boys, the bonny lass is after larnin', not hearin' you complain."

"So the rocker does the same thing as panning—only it handles more gravel faster," Mattie said. When the McKay men all nodded, she pointed back down the gulch toward another claim. "And the next step up from the rocker is those sluice boxes, and once you've gleaned all the gold from the surface, you start digging down to bedrock." Again, the McKays nodded. "Mining is hard work," she said. "A lot of hard work."

"Sure, and many there is that don't take t' it," Mr. McKay said. "But Dillon was a fine one in that regard. A fine one in the sunny lust of life," he sighed. "We miss him, lass."

Once again, Mattie barely managed the emotions roiling inside her. Mr. English intervened and, touching her arm, wished the McKays a good day and led the way toward Dillon's claim. As they climbed, Mattie regained her composure. Finally, she said, "Dillon wrote about using a toothpick. Does that mean anything to you?"

Mr. English pointed to the tent pitched atop a log frame. "If there's still a gold pan on your brother's claim, I'll show you what he was talking about."

Dillon. Mattie closed her eyes and took a deep breath, trying to fight off the threatening flood of tears.

"There now," Mr. English said quietly, and led her to a stump beside what had obviously been Dillon's campfire. "Sit for a moment," he said gently. He pulled a neatly folded handkerchief from his back pocket and handed it over.

Mattie looked around her, at the scraggly pine trees along one edge of the claim, at the brook rushing through, and up toward the rim of the gulch. Miners had cleared away most of the timber down below, but high above them pine and spruce, birch and cedar grew at strange angles out of clefts in the rock. A bird of some kind soared into view and then out again. She stared back down the gulch toward town. There was plenty of beauty here if you looked past the mining debris.

Taking a deep breath, she stood up and went to Dillon's tent. With trembling hands, she untied the canvas strips holding the flap closed, lifted the flap, and peered inside. A narrow cot to the right, a small black stove in the middle, a large coffee box to the left—larger than the one Swede was using for Eva's cradle—and that was all, save for a Dutch oven and a few other cooking utensils sitting in front of the supply box. A pile of mining equipment occupied the far back corner. Mattie motioned for Mr. English to step closer. "I think there's a pan over there," she said.

Mr. English glanced inside and nodded. "I've never seen such a well-kept claim."

"Dillon was always careful with his things. When he was a little boy he never broke a toy, never tore a page in a book." She stepped back and pointed at the log frame atop which the tent was pitched. "Why'd he do that?"

English pointed out a spike driven into one log near the corner. "If there's color to be followed, this makes it simpler to move the tent. It also helps keep the canvas dry." He gestured toward the open tent flap. "You take your time with this. I won't be far off when you're ready to talk—or leave."

Mattie watched him climb the gulch. *What a thoughtful man.* Taking a deep breath, she ducked back inside. Dillon's cot was little more than a pallet on the earthen floor. No wonder he'd ended up with pneumonia. She opened the supply box. Work pants and a worn pair of boots, two shirts, two blankets—why hadn't he used them?—some matches, and finally, at the very bottom, a cracker tin alongside a Bible and another familiar book. Mattie held the book up to the light, tracing the title with her fingertips. Dillon had read this book to her so many times when she was little she'd memorized it. But still, she begged him to read it to her again and again, simply because the sound of his voice was a comfort. A reassurance. A reminder that however harsh the world, someone loved her. Someone strong. Someone . . . gone. How could he be gone?

Oh . . . Dillon. What am I going to do now?

Closing the lid of the supply box, she sat down on the cot. *Well, here it is. All you have in the world. There's no gold. Whether Dillon was fabricating good news or someone stole what he had, you'll never know. There's no gold . . . no money . . . nothing but this tent and a claim that could very well be completely worthless.*

She was so tired. Weary to the bone. Weary from climbing the mile and a half up here, from trying to keep her footing secure in scuffed thin-soled boots, from trying to be brave and keep her composure . . . She felt worn out by life. She could bear it if Dillon were here. But facing all of this alone . . . sitting here in a dusty skirt with a tattered hem . . . with poverty just a few days away . . . with Dillon gone . . . it was all too much.

Mattie put her head in her hands and cried.

When Mattie finally went back outside, Mr. English had crossed the creek and was standing with his back to her, staring down at something in his hand. "We can go back now," she called. He dropped the rock he'd been inspecting and, splashing through the creek, came to her side. "There's no gold," she said. "There's . . ." She looked behind her. "There's nothing for me here." Her voice broke.

"I am so sorry. It's obvious you were very close to your brother."

Mattie nodded. "We were going to buy a place with his earning from this . . ." She gestured around her. "A farm or maybe a ranch or—" She broke off. "I guess it doesn't really matter." Blinking away the last of her tears, Mattie tried to imagine Dillon sitting by a campfire writing to her of his promise to send for her soon. It just didn't make any sense. If he was sending for her soon, then where was the gold?

"I said I'd show you what your brother meant by mining with a toothpick," Mr. English said. "Shall I do it now?"

Mattie shook her head. Tying the tent flap closed as she spoke, she said, "No. Thank you, but it doesn't matter."

———

Mattie and Mr. English had barely reached the first building at the edge of town when Ellis Gates came wheezing his way toward them. "I have pressing business in regard to the claim," he said to Mr. English, with barely a glance in Mattie's direction.

"Then you'd best be talking to the woman who owns it," English said, pressing Mattie forward even as he stepped back as if to leave.

"Please," Mattie said, touching his sleeve. She turned away from Gates and lowered her voice. "Please. You're the only person in Deadwood with knowledge of mining. I trust you." And just like that, she realized that she did trust him. But instead of agreeing to help her further, English was glancing up the street toward his fledgling business.

She couldn't blame the man for hesitating. After all, she'd seen the unfinished shelving and crates of merchandise waiting to be unpacked when Freddie took her over to meet him. How much business had he already missed because of her? She said quickly, "I'll help you set up your store. We can light lamps and I'll work all night if necessary. But please—" She glanced back at Gates.

English nodded. "All right."

"Thank you." Mattie squeezed his arm before addressing Mr. Gates. "What is it?"

"To my office," he blustered. "It's a matter of some importance—" he leaned close and glanced around him like a conspirator "—and requires the utmost discretion."

Nothing about the next few moments changed Mattie's initial opinion of Ellis Gates. The moment she and Mr. English were seated across from the battered desk in his minuscule office, he began to once again address English.

"Knowing of Miss O'Keefe's situation, I took the liberty of making a few inquiries on her behalf while you escorted her up to the claim." He laced his fingers together in a gesture designed to make him look relaxed, but Mattie noted his trembling hands and the fine sheen of perspiration on his forehead.

Grief and depression retreated in the face of the revolting little man's obvious assumptions that she was not only weak and defenseless, but also brainless. "How kind of you." She forced a smile. "My appreciation could only increase if you were to actually talk to *me* about *my* claim."

Gates squirmed in his chair. "Yes. Well." With a clearing of his throat, he unlaced his fingers, leaned back, and, opening the center drawer of his desk, withdrew two pieces of paper and slid them across the desktop. "What you have here, Miss O'Keefe, are two competing offers for your claim. This one," he said, tapping the one on the right with a grimy finger, "is probably the best of the two." He looked at Mr. English. "I believe you will agree, Tom, that cash is more desirable than unpredictable percentages of unknowable future findings." He raced ahead. "The cash offer is from Mr. Hardin—" he looked at Mattie—"who Mr. English will undoubtedly agree is one of the better-known miners in the area."

Gates tapped the other paper. "This one asks that Miss O'Keefe— you—accept less in cash, but it promises four percent of everything taken off the claim over the next two years. This is offered by Brady

Sloan, who has an interest in the claim just above hers—" he quickly looked at Mattie—"yours, that is." When Mattie didn't react, Gates smiled. "And I have also just spoken with another interested party who is willing to match any other offer and add a five-hundred-dollar bonus upon transfer of ownership."

Mattie reached for the cash offer. Mr. Arthur Hardin was offering two thousand dollars for Dillon's claim. Two *thousand*. And if she sold to Gates's unnamed "other party," she would have five hundred more. She pondered. How much did a nice tombstone cost? How much would Swede charge for hauling it? More important, how far from Abilene, Kansas, would what was left take her?

Mr. English cleared his throat.

Mattie glanced at him. If she read his expression correctly—and she was very good at reading men's faces—English didn't think any of this was a good idea.

"It's a promising claim," Gates said. "If these offers don't suit, you might even consider an auction. Everything decent was snapped up months ago, and plenty of latecomers will be eager to buy." Gates reached for the two offers. "I could certainly help you with that. My fees are quite reasonable."

So that's what was going on. Gates charged a flat fee. He didn't care what Mattie was paid—as long as he was the agent and as long as she sold right now, before learning any more about mining or the true worth of Dillon's claim.

Gates appealed to Mr. English. "You know how things work around here, Tom. Tell the little lady these are good offers. We all have the same thing in mind here. We want to help her out of a tough spot. There's many would say Deadwood is all thieving and whoring—begging your pardon, ma'am." Gates smoothed his lapels and straightened his string tie. "But there's plenty of us who look out for them that's less fortunate, and the truth is, Miss O'Keefe"—he almost managed an expression of sincerity—"the truth is my heart just went out to you the minute I saw you. Poor little thing, coming all this way only to find that your dear brother has passed on, saddled with all the cares of a man's world. It's not right, Miss O'Keefe. You shouldn't have to deal with it. Let Mr. English here—and me—help you out from under the burden."

The man would not shut up. The longer Mattie was quiet, the more he talked. The more he talked, the angrier she got. Finally, she silenced him with an old trick she'd learned from one of her best customers. *"It'll hush 'em up every time,"* Bill had said. And it worked. The minute Mattie pulled her gun out and set it on the desktop, Gates clamped his mouth shut. Mr. English snorted, and when Mattie glanced at him, she noted a suppressed smile. She cleared her throat, but still said nothing. Gates shifted in his chair.

"Appearances can be deceiving, Mr. Gates," Mattie finally said. "For example, you seem to think I am a 'poor little thing' in need of rescue. Now, I can see how you'd think that. My brother, Dillon, meant the world to me, and at this moment," she said, her voice wavering, "I am not at all certain how I am going to face life without him." She cleared her throat again. "But just because I am grieving does not mean I am helpless. And just because I am a 'little lady,' as you put it, does not mean I am stupid."

She folded her hands in her lap. "Let me tell you something, Mr. Gates: Life hasn't been particularly good to me. I have survived largely because of two things." She ran her finger along the top of the pistol, caressing the curve of the grip, then placing her hand over it as she said, "My friend Mr. Colt would be the first of those two things." She flashed a cold smile. "The second is a well-developed manure detector." She inhaled and, curling her lips with displeasure, looked around the tiny office. "I can usually smell it a mile away, and this office reeks of it."

Gates blustered a protest. Told her she had misunderstood. His only intention was—

Mattie stood up. Gates hushed. Mr. English rose to his feet beside her. Tucking the Colt back into the waist of her skirt, Mattie said, "Should anyone ask you, Mr. Gates, you can tell them that Number 7 Above Discovery is Mattie's Claim. When I want to sell it, I'll sell it. Right now, it pleases me to keep it. And anyone who wants to challenge that decision is welcome to mosey up the gulch and talk to me." She paused at the door and turned back. "But make sure that anyone who *does* want to discuss this knows to come in the daylight, because after dark I shoot first and ask questions later."

Just outside Ellis Gates's office, Mr. English chortled. He adjusted his hat and scratched his beard. "Mind if I ask you something?"

Mattie hoped he couldn't see how hard she was trembling as she tied her bonnet on. It had been a while since she'd had to bluff her way out of a difficult situation. She was rusty. And so she waited a minute before answering, just to be sure her voice wasn't shaking as hard as the rest of her. "Yes," she finally said, "the gun is mine. And yes, I know how to use it."

Mr. English nodded. "Now can I ask *my* question instead of the one you made up for me?"

Mattie blushed and nodded.

"Why'd you ask me to sit in on that when you already knew you were going to keep the claim?"

"I *didn't* know. Not until I realized my manure detector wasn't the only one operating in that room."

"How could you have known what I was thinking? I never said a word."

"You didn't have to say words. I could see you were thinking the same as I was."

He frowned as he looked down at her. "You could?"

"Um-hmm."

"How?"

With a sigh, she thought back. "It's hard to explain. There's a change in breathing. A slight increase in the tension. The way a man sits. The way he holds his head. You were coiling into yourself. Like a cat getting ready to pounce."

English shook his head. "If you say so."

"You do think I did the right thing not to take any of those offers?"

"Absolutely. Something's not right. You can't find any gold, and yet your brother wrote that he had had some measure of success—which is consistent with the news about town regarding that part of the gulch. It would have been premature for you to make a decision today." He paused. "I know you enlisted my help because of my experience with mining—" he glanced down at the hook that had replaced his right hand—"but I can also tell you that one often lives to regret life-changing decisions made when grief is fresh."

They had reached Mr. English's lot. He broke off and changed the subject. "I appreciate your offer to help me with the store, Miss O'Keefe, but you needn't feel obligated if—"

"Miss O'Keefe!"

It was Freddie, hurrying toward them, his face alight with excitement. "I finished it and I wanted to give it to you." He held up the result of his carving.

Taking it in her hand, Mattie swallowed. This time, she couldn't keep the tears back. As they trickled out she forced a little laugh and swiped at them. "Happy tears," she said. "It's lovely." She put her hand on Freddie's arm. "Thank you."

She cleared her throat and turned to Mr. English. "And I absolutely insist you allow me to help you with that jumbled mess you're calling a store."

Together the three stepped into the tent. Mattie paused before taking off her bonnet to inspect the masterfully carved dog. Freddie

Jannike couldn't possibly have known about Justice. As she tucked the little figure into her skirt pocket, she thanked the kind spirit responsible for sending her a sign. She'd made the right decision about the claim. *Mattie's Claim.* It had a nice ring to it.

CHAPTER 4

If I have made gold my hope, or have said to the fine gold,
Thou art my confidence . . .
this also were an iniquity. . . .

Job 31:24, 28

It was raining and Freddie couldn't sleep. Freddie could always sleep. But now he was worried. Too many things weren't right. Mor was back but she wasn't happy. She worked so hard and she was tired and now there were three other stores open in town and Mor's couldn't be first. She might not have a store at all now that Julius Talbot was gone. Julius was supposed to run the store while Mor did the freighting, but Freddie couldn't find him. His shack up on City Creek was deserted. Someone said Julius had gone to the Cricket Saloon and come stumbling out and that was the last anyone saw of him. If Julius was the kind of man who made promises and then got so drunk he forgot about them, it was better that he wasn't running Mor's store. Mor had even said she might just sell the lot. She could keep freighting and things would be fine. That's what she said but when she said it she sighed. Freddie knew that sigh. He wished he could make things better. Mor was tired of freighting. And besides . . . he missed her and Eva when they were gone.

He listened to the rain clattering against the canvas tent. When it rained hard like this City Creek ran out of its banks. Julius Talbot's shack might be washing away tonight. His thoughts turned to Tom English. City Creek ran right behind his lot. Freddie thought about the empty shipping boxes Tom had had him stack back there—as if there were already a building on the lot and he was going out the back door. Those boxes just might all wash away tonight, too.

As he worried over Mor and the store she wanted and how Tom's boxes might be floating away in the dark, Freddie smiled. Maybe he could fix things. Of course even if Mor and Tom liked Freddie's idea, that still left Miss O'Keefe to worry about.

Mattie. She'd said for him to call her Mattie tonight when they were working together helping Tom unpack all his crates. Mattie had such pretty eyes. Freddie had never seen eyes that color. He liked the way she smiled and how she was always nice to him. She didn't treat him like he was stupid. She asked his opinion and more than once she thought he had a good idea and told him so. And she let him build some shelves and put the new oil lamps on them just like he wanted. Even Tom said he did a good job with those lamps. He said folks would probably buy them all faster because of the way Freddie had them "presented." That was a new word. Stores "presented" things to people. It was a good word. People liked presents.

There was trouble with Mattie, too, though. And it wasn't because her brother was dead. Freddie was worried about the way men stared at her. He had seen her touch the gun at her side several times tonight. Just making sure it was there. Which probably meant that Mattie noticed the men staring, too. And she didn't like it, either.

Freddie worried about what Mattie was going to do. She wasn't selling Dillon's mine. Was she going to try and work it herself? *Naw. Ladies don't prospect. Everybody knows that.* But if Mattie was going to stay in Deadwood she would need a place to stay and some work to do because no one got food if they didn't work. But Freddie didn't think Mattie would want to do the only kind of work Deadwood had for women. He didn't want her to, either.

Lightning flashed. Rain poured from the sky and pounded against the tent. Baby Eva woke up and started to cry. But Freddie still smiled. After thinking really hard, he had come up with answers to all the problems. He was so excited about his answers that he wanted to wake everyone up and tell them. But people got mad when you did that. He would wait until daylight. It would be hard, but he would wait.

––––––

The morning after her meeting with Ellis Gates, Mattie knelt on a pallet just inside Swede's tent trying to change Eva's wet diaper. How did Swede do it, anyway? Mattie had watched her changing Eva dozens of times on the trail, and this morning when she'd offered to stay with Eva while Swede and Freddie took care of some business at the bank, Mattie hadn't even thought to ask about diaper changing. After all, how hard could it be? There was no reason to tell Swede she'd never done it. But obviously watching and doing were entirely different things when it came to diapers. She must be doing everything wrong, because Eva's initial grunted protests had become full-blown screams. And then, just when Mattie was ready to give up, Eva smiled and lay still, focusing on something just over Mattie's shoulder.

"Having a bit of trouble?" Mr. English's voice hinted at amusement.

"She's not much for cooperating this morning," Mattie said without looking up. "I'm just on duty until Swede gets back from the bank, but this little one—" she chucked Eva under the chin—"has a mind of her own."

"Let me try." English knelt beside her. Eva giggled. And then in nothing flat he had the diapering finished.

"Where'd you learn how to do that?!" Mattie ignored the wet diaper and picked Eva up.

"Shiloh," English said as he hooked the wet diaper and dropped it in the washtub sitting just outside.

"The same Shiloh with the cannonball?"

"The very same."

Mattie stared up at him. "Mr. English—" she sniffed—"my manure detector is working again."

"Miss O'Keefe, I have nothing to say." He grinned. "Except that I wish you'd do me the honor of calling me Tom. After all, we have now shared disdain for Ellis Gates's tactics . . . and diaper duty."

Mattie laughed. "All right, Tom. And I'm Mattie."

Tom nodded. "Mattie. Pleased to meet you."

Swede and Freddie came into view slogging through the mud from the direction of the bank. As soon as Swede was within earshot, Tom called out, "Freddie tells me his mor wants to talk to me."

"Yah, sure," Swede said.

Tom gestured around them. "You've sold quite a bit of your goods. I thought you had plans to open a store, too. At this rate, you won't need one."

"Vell," Swede said as she took Eva in her arms, "ve shall see." She motioned toward the campfire. "May I offer you coffee?"

"Thank you."

"I'll get it," Mattie said, motioning for everyone to sit down. *At least I know how to pour coffee.* Of course *making* it was another subject entirely. While Mattie was rinsing out four tin coffee mugs,

Tom was teasing Eva, reciting a rhyme while he tugged on her bare toes. Eva began to reach for him.

"Do you mind?" he asked Swede, and when Swede shook her head, he opened his arms to Eva, who literally launched herself at him. Laughing, Tom sat down and a contented Eva inserted her two middle fingers in her mouth and snuggled against him while he sipped coffee, careful to hold the tin mug out of the baby's reach.

Swede began. "I have a problem and Freddie says you can help. As it happens, de man I vas counting on to run my store has disappeared. Even if he comes back, he has revealed a weakness for drink dat makes him unsuitable." She sighed. "I have no one to vork in my store ven I am on de trail, Mr. English. And I vas hoping—" She broke off when Tom glanced at Mattie. "I thought first to ask Mattie to vork for me. But she insists she has no mind for figures."

"Mathematics is a learned skill," Tom said to Mattie, "and not at all difficult for someone with your obvious intelligence."

Mattie shook her head. "It's more than that. I want to spend some time up on the claim. Away from town." She drew in a breath. "I'm sorry, but I can't agree to working in a store." She rushed ahead before either Tom or Swede could say anything more, committing to something that had only been a whisper at the edges of her thoughts until now. "If I'm going to keep the claim, I might as well work it."

"Personally?" Tom's raised eyebrows indicated his surprise.

Yes, Mattie realized. That was exactly what she intended to do. Oh, she would be slow and inefficient, but the promise of gold had invaded her dreams. Just last night as they worked setting up his store, Tom had explained how part of the frenzy in Deadwood was every man's hope that he would be the one to find the lead—the source—of all the placer gold in the gulch. But that hope ended a month ago when two brothers found the lead a few miles to the southwest of Deadwood. Still, Tom said, that didn't mean there wasn't a good-sized vein of gold just waiting to be found. And he reassured Mattie that the frenzy for gold would continue long enough for her to decide what to do, and long enough for her to make a nice profit should she decide to sell.

Thinking about veins of gold had kept Mattie awake half the night. Dillon's tent might be pitched above a fortune just waiting to be found. Just waiting for *her* to find it. It was, after all, called *Mattie's Claim* now. She defended her plan to work it. "Freddie told me the Grand Central charges twelve dollars a week for room and board. I don't have that kind of money. I can feed myself on the claim for much less. Just this morning Freddie promised he would bring me rabbits on occasion." She glanced at Freddie and smiled. "He even said he'd show me how he makes stew."

Swede nodded. "It is your claim now, Mattie. If you vant to vork it, I say go vit God and may He bless it." She turned back to Tom. "And so I need someone to run Garth Merchandise ven I am freighting." She glanced at Freddie. "And my son says dat you are de someone I should hire."

"Do you mind my asking about the name?" Tom asked.

"Of course not. Garth vas my husband." She nodded. "Now. I vish that I pay you to see to the building of a store here on dis lot vile I bring more goods." She hesitated before saying, "Freddie has said dat your lot is not de best for a store." She gestured around them. "As you can see, mine is excellent. I propose dat you move your business to my lot."

"Well, Freddie was right about my lot," Tom said. "If he hadn't come in the middle of the night and moved them, I would have lost every packing crate." He made a sweeping motion with his good arm. "Whoosh. Who knows where they would have ended up." He peered around at Swede's lot. "And you do have a prime location."

"One of de best," Swede agreed. "If you camp on your lot and keep a store open dere for vile ve build, ve can move all the merchandise dere and take down my tent to make room for my building. You could use my tent for lodging." Eva had fallen asleep in Tom's arms while they talked. She stood up and reached for the baby. "You tink as I am putting Eva down for her nap."

Tom spoke first to Mattie. "It's only required that a claim be worked one day a week to prove possession. Is there any chance you would consider brushing up on your numbers so you could help out temporarily—just until Swede's building is finished and I can move everything in? I know enough about building to handle the project, but I can't very well oversee a building project and run a store at the same time."

"And I'm not good at figures," Freddie said.

Swede chimed in as she returned from putting Eva down. "Even a fine building can be finished in a few veeks."

"That's right," Tom agreed, and once again spoke to Mattie. "If you would help out at my present location for even part of every day we would free you up completely in three weeks' time."

"I could stay on your claim and make sure no one bothered it," Freddie offered. "Every night if you want."

"I vill pay you," Swede said.

"And I'll show you everything you need to know about panning for gold," Tom added.

"And I vill bring free of charge the finest tombstone in the territory."

Mattie looked from Tom to Freddie to Swede. What could a woman do?

———

It struck her in the middle of the night, and when Swede realized what she had done, she couldn't sleep. As soon as dawn broke, she shook Freddie awake. "You keep vatch up by his tent, and when Mr. English has avakened I must know." She brushed her hair until it shone that morning and donned a clean apron. She even put a clean dress on Eva, and as soon as Freddie reported that Mr. English was up, she put Eva on her hip and hurried up the street. The moment he answered her call and opened the tent flap, Swede blurted out, "I must to apologize."

Mr. English frowned. "For what?"

"I meant nothing by all my talk yesterday. I did not tink." She paused. Took a deep breath. "I have tought only of Garth Merchandise for so long—and you vere so kind to consider helping me. But in the night I realized dat all my talk vas as if I vas hiring you only to help. Please forgive me. My intention vas to form a partnership—not to treat you as a common laborer. And I do not blame you for being angry."

Mr. English jiggled Eva's foot and smiled when the baby giggled. "Do I seem angry?"

"No, but . . . I insulted you."

"How? By proposing a mutually beneficial business relationship?"

"The name of the store must be English and Garth," Swede said. "And you vill have a written agreement stating dat we are equal partners. Assuring dat I vill freight only for our store and ve split profits equally. I should have suggested all of dese tings. I apologize for being so concerned for my own problems and treating you—"

"Mrs. Jannike," Mr. English said abruptly, "if I may interject a word?"

Swede broke off. She nodded even as she braced herself for what was to come. He wouldn't shout. She felt certain of that. But he would most definitely take the opportunity to agree with her that she had been rude. She'd overstepped her bounds as a woman. She'd presumed on his quiet nature.

"As for the name of the store, I don't really care if my name is on it or not. I think it will be grand for Freddie and Eva to see their father's name on the store their mother built—at least partially as a tribute to him. And as for our partnership, I think we both understand exactly how it will work. You are the freighter, I am the storekeeper. You bring the goods to Deadwood and I maintain the ledger. We split the profits in half, and—" he paused—"as for a written contract, I don't think that's necessary between two honest people who respect each other."

"You—" Swede sputtered. "You aren't angry vit me?"

He shook his head. "Of course not. I'm grateful to have been rescued from the obvious problems this lot presents. And I'm honored that you'd trust me with overseeing your construction project. And," he said, chucking Eva under the chin, "I'm actually looking forward to working with you or for you, and I don't honestly care how that was worded yesterday.

"Now," he continued, "I do have one other thing I'd like to request to seal our agreement." He winked at Eva. His brown eyes crinkled at the edges as he said, "I'd like it very much if you would call me Tom."

––––––––

As Mattie climbed up to Dillon's claim on Friday morning, the sun broke through the clouds, and by the time she ducked into the tent to change into mining garb, the promise of sunshine had become reality. She opened Dillon's storage box, and as the aroma of his pipe tobacco wafted upward, she blinked back tears. *I will not cry I will not cry I will not.* She jerked a pair of pants and a shirt out and shut the box. She began to talk to herself. "You've done some shocking things in your life, Mattie O'Keefe, but this—this is an entirely new level of shocking." Her throat relaxed. She kept talking to herself. "What would the folks in Kansas say . . . Miss Mattie O'Keefe dressing like a man . . ." She stepped into the pants and bent to roll up the cuffs. "I'm going to need suspenders," she said aloud. Twine laced through the belt loops would have to do today. The wool socks were warm. She just might keep wearing those even when she donned her other clothes. She slipped into a green flannel shirt. "Thank goodness Dillon isn't . . . wasn't . . . six . . . feet. . . ." She swallowed. *Dillon isn't. Dillon was . . . but now he isn't.*

Her resolve melted. She cried again. She cried more. She sprawled on Dillon's pallet and cried until she was exhausted. Finally, she took the three steps to the "front door" in her stocking-clad feet and looked down the trail toward Deadwood.

"Tom said to tell you that he will be here soon."

With a little gasp, Mattie saw Freddie perched on a rock ledge, whittling. He gave no sign of having heard her crying. Instead, he smiled and said, "You look pretty."

As if her red eyes and runny nose didn't even exist. Bless him. "Do I look like a real miner?"

He shook his head. "You are too clean to be a real miner."

She laughed and with the laughter came release from the threat of more tears. Putting her hand atop her head, she said, "I need a hat."

Freddie jerked his off his head and sent it sailing through the air. It landed at her feet. Mattie pulled it on and they both laughed as all of her abundant dark hair and most of her head were swallowed up. She tilted her head back and looked at Freddie from beneath the brim.

"You almost disappeared there for a minute." Tom English's voice carried up the gulch from below. As he climbed toward them he said, "And I almost mistook you for Brady Sloan." He pointed to the claim above Mattie's. "He's about your size."

"Really?" Mattie handed Freddie's hat back to its owner. "Maybe he'd sell me some of his cast-offs."

"Only if you've a mind to set up a vat so you can boil them first." Tom smiled as he pointed to Mattie's bare head. "I'd suggest you see if some nice storekeeper in town would extend credit to cover the cost of a hat." He glanced down at her feet. "And rubber boots that fit."

"I didn't find a hat inside, but I can wad up some newspapers to fill the toes of Dillon's boots."

"That will work for today," Tom said, "but you'll need boots that fit before you start working in earnest. A woman who does a man's job should dress for the dance."

"All right," Mattie agreed. "I'll get some proper-sized boots soon." She ducked inside the tent and began handing out tools. "You can get set up while I resize the boots."

"Whoa," Tom said. "All you need for today's lesson is a shovel and the pan." He reached into his shirt pocket and withdrew a few toothpicks. "I've brought the rest."

As she pulled on the paper-stuffed boots, she asked, "What about something to put the gold in?"

"I truly doubt we're going to need to worry about that for today." Tom glanced up at the sky. "My aching back says the weather's turning."

"Turning to what?"

"Snow, maybe."

"In May?"

"Welcome to the Black Hills," he said with a nod. "Last year we had a two-day blizzard in June."

Mattie didn't want to think about snow. She gestured toward town. "Why do you think the gulch is so deserted today?"

Tom shrugged. "It's a rare day when every claim is being worked. Today they're all probably holed up in this saloon or that dance hall warming themselves with bad whiskey and wom—" He broke off. Cleared his throat.

Freddie spoke up. "I got something." He held out the stick he'd been whittling. It was about two inches in diameter, and before hollowing it out he'd smoothed one end so it would sit flat on a rock. "I bet it'll hold at least an ounce," he said. "And while you do the panning I'll make a lid for it." He settled back on the rock ledge and went back to work.

Tom reached for the gold pan with his hook, then pulled back and extended his left hand. "Sorry."

Mattie touched his sleeve above the hook. "Please," she said. "It's not you. It's—someone else. Someone I knew who—" She couldn't stifle the shudder. She took a deep breath. "But you're nothing like him. It's just hard to forget sometimes."

Tom nodded. "I understand."

Looking up at him, she saw palpable hurt in his dark eyes. A thread of understanding passed between them before Mattie said, "Thank you." She gestured around them. "For doing this."

Tom grinned. "We'll see if you still feel like thanking me tonight when your legs feel like they're going to fall off and your pretty little hands are red and chapped." He led the way over to the creek bed. "All right," he said and held up the pan. "First, the pan."

"It's a rusty mess," Mattie said. "I'll get a new one if that nice storekeeper who's going to extend credit for a hat and boots will allow it."

"Why would you want a new pan?"

"Because this one's all rusty."

"It's supposed to be rusty," Tom explained. "Run your fingers over the surface. Feel that? That texture will grab a lot more gold flecks than a smooth one. And since we're talking about that, don't *ever* use a gold pan for cooking. Obviously you wouldn't do that anyway with this one, but even if you had a new one, you wouldn't want it doing double-duty over the campfire. Grease would make the surface even slicker, and that would allow the gold to slip away."

"Understood," Mattie said. "Rust is good."

Tom nodded even as he crouched down by the stream. "Now take your shovel and put about a peck of gravel here," he said, pointing at the pan with his hook. Once Mattie had done that, he submerged the pan. The current in the stream stirred the gravel. "See how the dirt and silt is washing away?" Mattie nodded, and Tom brought the pan back to the surface. "Pick out the large pebbles, making sure you've rinsed them so any gold clinging to them stays in your pan." By the time Mattie was finished, her fingers were numb with cold.

"Now, this is the only part that takes a little practice." He dipped the pan back beneath the water so the sand slopped over the edge. "If there *were* any gold nuggets, you'd see them and be able to pick them out now."

"But there aren't," Mattie observed.

"No, but that doesn't mean you don't have any gold." With a flick of his wrist, Tom swirled the remaining contents of the pan in such a way that the fine gravel spread across the bottom, a crescent moon in a rust-colored sky.

"All right." Tom pointed to the far tip of the moon. "That tip has been carried over there because it's heaviest."

"And gold is heaviest," Mattie murmured, looking excitedly at the tip of the crescent. She sat back on her heels. "But there's no gold."

Tom took a toothpick and began to separate the grains of sand. Presently there were three tiny flecks of gold clinging to the side of the pan. "I'm out of practice," he apologized. "There might have been some we missed. A skilled panner could put a dozen flecks of gold the size of a pinpoint in a pan of gravel, and by the time he was finished, he wouldn't have missed a single one." He pointed to the three tiny flecks. "A lot of your gold may come in pieces just about that size."

He stood back up, grimacing with the effort. "Be forewarned. Miners who do much panning end up with sore backs and weak knees." He shrugged. "And for that reason alone, although I'm showing you how to do it, I sincerely hope you decide you don't want any part of it." Looking down at her he nodded. "And I see that look in your eyes, so just allow me to say it for you: I should mind my own business." He paused. "And henceforth I shall."

Mattie called over to Freddie, "You finished with my dust-catcher yet?" He brought it over. She looked at the three minuscule flecks of gold and wondered how to capture them. Tom moistened the end of a toothpick and, using it as a kind of "gold magnet," transferred the flecks of gold from the edge of the pan to what Mattie called her dust-catcher.

"I'd guess your little dust-catcher there will hold a couple of ounces of flecks this size. Maybe a little more. That's forty dollars worth."

Mattie considered. Forty dollars represented a lot of time crouching in that cold stream. Especially when she had routinely made more than that every night back in Abilene. *But you didn't really make that money, did you? Because Jonas wasn't really keeping an account, and he wasn't ever going to give it to you.* She forced a smile. "But you can't say there won't be any nuggets."

Tom shook his head. "No one could say that."

Freddie spoke up. "Finn McKay got a thirty-dollar nugget this morning. That's why they're in town instead of on their claim."

"So," Mattie asked, "should I follow their example and deposit every day's find in the bank?" She wasn't looking forward to the idea of a daily trek down and back.

Tom cleared his throat. "I don't think the McKays are very investment minded."

Freddie spoke up. "I saw them and they invited me to go with 'em to that new dance hall." He shrugged. "Mor would whip me good if I ever went in a dance hall." He smiled at Mattie. "Besides, I had to help Mattie." He tucked his whittling knife into his shirt pocket. "But now I gotta go help Mor," he said. "She and Eva are leaving at first light tomorrow."

"Let's get back to town," Mattie said. "Swede might need our help, too." Palming her hand-carved dust-catcher, she ducked inside the tent to change back into her town clothes while Tom and Freddie waited.

While she changed, Mattie pondered the alluring idea of finding a thirty-dollar gold nugget. If she was careful, if she was lucky, she could do well here on her claim. If she was *really* lucky, she might even get rich. Tom was right about one thing. She was going to need rubber boots that fit.

CHAPTER 5

Lay not up for yourselves treasures upon earth, where moth and
rust doth corrupt, and where thieves break through and steal: But
lay up for yourselves treasures in heaven, where neither moth nor
rust doth corrupt, and where thieves do not break through nor steal:
For where your treasure is, there will your heart be also.

Matthew 6:19–21

Lars! Leif! Gee-ho, you two-bit flea-ridden good-for-nuttin' grass-eatin'—" Swede cracked her whip and finally, with a bellow of protest, the oxen moved out, the last in a train of ten freighting outfits headed back to Sidney on another supply run. Freddie walked alongside her, Eva perched on his shoulders, laughing and giggling as Freddie did his slow-motion gallop alongside the wagons.

"Now, you mind Mr. English—Tom—and vatever he needs for de new store," Swede said.

"Yes, Mor. I already told Aunt Lou I might not be able to hunt as much."

"I put two clean shirts on top of your bedroll. You're going to be in town more, you need to stay clean."

"Thank you, Mor."

"I'm hauling for de Big Horn dis time, too, but after dis I verk just for us. So you remind Mr. English—Tom—I vill need a list ready, since I vill not be spending any time at all in town next time. I must to hurry to beat de snow on de last run."

"Yes, Mor."

They reached the part of the trail that began the ascent toward higher ground. "Be sure to check dose traps we set every day. And if you are off hunting, remind Mr. English. I'm not freighting to feed Dakota mice."

Freddie nodded.

"And try to keep an eye out for Mattie ven you can."

"I will, Mor," Freddie promised. "I'm taking her stew."

"She von't like it if she tinks ve are hovering too close."

"I won't hover. I'll just see she's all right."

Swede rattled on, reminding Freddie of this, suggesting that, until finally Freddie said, "Lars and Leif are going awful slow."

Indeed they were. The other freighters had pulled far ahead. Swede cracked the whip again. The oxen lowed in protest, but they stepped out, pulling the wagons—three empty and one full of supplies for the weeks on the trail—ever higher up and out of Whitewood Gulch. Every so often, a snowflake danced out of the sky and lighted on one broad rump or another.

"Snow," Freddie said.

"It von't be much," Swede said.

"How can you tell?"

"My bones don't ache so much as dey do right before a bad storm."

"I hate it that your bones hurt," Freddie said.

"I hate it, too. But in time my freighting days vill be over. Now dat ve have Mr. English—Tom—for a business partner, anyting could happen." *Maybe even a miracle. Like not having to make the last run of the season. Or warm weather long into the fall.*

Freddie pulled Eva off his shoulders and swooped her around

in a circle, tickling her until she giggled so hard she got the hiccups. The family reached the top of the winding trail too soon. Looking back down on the town below, Swede said, "All right, Freddie. Let me have de baby and you get back to town."

Planting a resounding kiss on Eva's cheek, Freddie deposited her back in the cradle he had anchored inside Swede's lead wagon at the first light of dawn. Swede glanced over the wagon's full complement of supplies.

"You put more shells in for Old Bess?" she asked.

"Of course," Freddie said. He put his hand on her shoulder. "Don't worry, Mor. We're going to be just fine." He leaned down and put his arms around her, and Swede inhaled his musty scent.

She closed her eyes and allowed herself one moment of being just a mother saying good-bye to her son. Tears threatened. "All right now," she said abruptly, and pulled away. Freddie blew Eva a kiss and headed back down toward town. Swede didn't dare let herself look back. If she did, she just might not be able to leave at all, and then what would they do. *A winter of roast oxen followed by a spring of starvation, that's what. Now get along, you long-faced, weak-hearted fool.*

"Mor!"

Swede turned around, but she didn't stop. She kept walking up the trail with tiny backward steps.

"I love you!" Freddie hollered.

Swede waved. She couldn't trust her voice.

———

After Mattie said good-bye to Swede and Eva, she turned her attention to helping Tom English build a few more shelves so he could accommodate Swede's goods as well as his own. While she and Tom wielded hammer and nails, Freddie moved boxes. It was late in the day before the place began to resemble anything besides a haphazard jumble of goods, but finally, things began to take shape.

"There," Mattie said, wiping her hands on her apron and standing back to survey her work. An assortment of mugs, from shaving to thunder, were now displayed to best advantage. Tom agreed, and when he complimented her display, she blushed with pleasure.

"I wish you'd reconsider and work here instead of mining," he said.

Mattie shook her head. "I have to at least try."

Tom set the packing crate in his arms down. "You're certain I can't talk you out of it?"

"I'm certain." Mattie tilted her head and smiled at him. "And you promised to mind your own business, remember?"

Tom reached into the crate Freddie had just carried in and opened it. He took out a gray felt hat with a wide brim and plopped it on Mattie's head. "All right, then, Miss Miner. I'll mind my business." He opened the account book. "I assume you've seen one of these."

She nodded. It was exactly the kind of book Jonas had shown her, pointing to the bottom number on each page to impress her with how well he was paying her and how her savings were growing.

Tom wrote her name at the top of a clean page. On the first line of the "Mattie O'Keefe" page, he entered 1 *felt hat*. "Over here," he said, indicating the right side of the page, "we enter the purchase price. In this case, forty cents. When a customer makes a payment, we weigh their gold." He pointed at the gold scales Swede had bought for Garth Merchandise. "I'll show you how the scales work in a minute, but first go pick out your boots."

"I already took the liberty." Mattie lifted the hem of her skirt just enough for Tom to see her boot-clad feet. "Does the ground *ever* warm up around here?"

"Of course it does." Tom entered her boots in the ledger, talking as he wrote. "For a minimum of a week. Then, of course, winter's back." With a smile, he opened the small drawer built into the base of the gold scale. "You put the smallest one on this side," he said, and set a cylindrical weight in the center of the pan suspended on one side of the scale. "And then you take a pinch of gold and weigh it against the standard, which is one troy ounce."

"Troy?"

"A little heavier than a regular ounce. But the standard measure for weighing gold." He paused before explaining, "Around here the miners expect twenty dollars in store credit for every ounce of gold they bring us. You'll quickly learn to get almost exactly an ounce every time you take a pinch of dust."

"What if there's a flake—or a nugget?"

English pointed to the other weights in the drawer. "Then you just combine those on the opposite side until it's balanced. Don't worry. Tomorrow's Sunday, and Sunday is typically the busiest day of the week. You're going to get lots of practice weighing gold dust. It'll all be second nature before you know it."

"Will you keep an account page for everyone?"

Tom shook his head. "Only for regular customers." He smiled at her. "So since we started a Mattie page, you can tell I'm expecting you to be a regular. Don't let me catch you over at the Big Horn." He winked.

———

The next morning, Mattie inspected the small scale again, touching the series of weights nestled in their wooden case. "It seems like there could be a lot of haggling over ounces and cents."

"If there is, I'll handle it." Tom stood back. "Ready to open for business?" He hesitated. "Oh—wait. There's one more thing." He reached into his pocket and pulled out a small buckskin bag at the end of a thin strip of leather. "This is where you put what you take in." He handed it over. "Around your neck, please. For safekeeping."

Mattie put the empty bag around her neck and tucked it out of sight beneath the bib of her apron.

"All right," Tom said. "Let's get the day started." And with that, he crossed the tent and opened for business to the resounding cheers of a group of men waiting just outside.

Did every miner in the Black Hills need a new hat? Had all their boots sprung leaks? Was there an epidemic of some kind causing shovel handles to snap and coffee mugs to rust through? Apparently so, because by noon on Sunday Tom English's mercantile was nearly out of merchandise, and still, miners kept coming in droves.

The bag around Mattie's neck grew heavy with gold and still they kept coming. And finally, she figured it out, although it took the third sale to the same stringy-haired toothless miner to confirm it. It was just a different form of Abilene, where men played poker— badly—and lost with a smile because it wasn't about the poker, it was about sitting at the table with "the prettiest dealer in town."

These miners weren't buying from Tom English because his merchandise was better. They were buying because Mattie was selling. The idea that she had come this far only to be the center of the same kind of male attention she'd had in Kansas made Mattie want to retreat to her claim and never come back to town again. *But this is different*, she told herself. *Tom is a good man. He's paying you real money. And he isn't standing over in the corner putting on airs like he's the ruler and you're some—*

"Mattie. Are you all right, Mattie?"

Tom's voice brought her back to the moment. She blinked and looked over at him. "Yes. Of course. Why?" She glanced across the counter at a familiar face and, blushing, smiled. "Hello, Mr. McKay."

Hugh McKay smiled back, clearly enjoying seeing every miner in the tent pause and look their way to see who it was Miss O'Keefe knew so well as to call him by name. "Ah, ye have done my heart good, miss, remembering an old man you've barely met."

"How can I help you today?" Mattie gestured at the depleted stock. "As you can see, we've had a good run this morning."

"Well, miss," McKay said, and leaned closer. As he spoke it became apparent he'd already patronized another sort of tent selling liquid "supplies" that morning. "It's about me boys." He hesitated. Straightened up. Glanced around. "But perhaps another time—" He turned away.

"We'd be glad to take a special order, Hugh." Tom moved to Mattie's side. "I'm in partnership with Swede now. Dependable delivery guaranteed for just about anything you need."

"No, no," McKay said, waving his hand in the air. "It's not supplies we're needing." His cheeks colored. Taking a deep breath, he continued, "What we need, miss, is a bonny lass like you. You could take your pick. Now, I know I'm older, but I'm not a bad sort. And while me boys rumble and squawk one to the other, they're gentle souls and—" he leaned close—"and they'll be well set up if the claim keeps the promise it's made. There's good color in the quartz, Miss O'Keefe. So you just think it over, now, and I'll be in town into evenin' when ye've made up yer mind. Might even have the boys attend the church meetin' today. A little religion might do 'em good. Make 'em more suitable—if a lady was to take an interest in either of 'em." He winked.

Tom cleared his throat. "Well, Hugh, now that you mention it, it is about time for me to close up and give Miss O'Keefe here a chance to attend to the reverend's sermon. So . . ." He walked around the edge of the counter and, putting his hand on Mr. McKay's shoulder, encouraged him to leave. The rest of the miners who'd been wandering from one thing to another in the depleted supply tent trickled out onto the street, and Tom pulled the tent flap down. He cleared his throat several times, and then gave up and burst out laughing.

"I don't see what's so funny," Mattie insisted, her cheeks flaming with embarrassment.

Tom did a perfect imitation of Hugh McKay. " 'What we need, miss, is a bonny lass like you. You could take your pick. . . .' " He chuckled. " 'They're gentle souls.' "

He would not stop laughing, and finally Mattie couldn't keep from joining him. "All right. I suppose it's a compliment—sort of—"

"Oh, Hugh's all right," Tom said. "And I guess you can't blame a father for trying to make a good match for his sons . . . or even for himself."

Mattie shook her head. "Dillon said those three were crazy as loons. Now I believe him."

"Men have gotten married on less than those three know about you," Tom reminded her. "I'll bet your brother talked about you all the time. And now they've seen you and you really can't blame them. After all, you're—" He paused. "You're lovely. Any father would be delighted to have one of his sons bring you home."

"Well, thank you for assuming such nice things about me." Mattie began to untie her apron. "And if you can stop laughing long enough, I'd appreciate some help gathering supplies for the claim. I'm afraid if I wait until tomorrow you'll be completely sold out. And I've been forbidden to shop anywhere else."

Tom nodded. "Thank you for helping out this morning. You're a good worker, and you caught on to the gold scale right away."

At his mention of the gold, Mattie reached up to take the bag from around her neck. "From the feel of this thing, you've got a good deposit to make. I suppose the bank is open on Sundays, too?"

"Absolutely. When we finish here, if you'd like to come with me, I'll show you how we make a deposit."

"I'd like that."

"Good. Now, you've already got a shovel and pick—"

"—and a properly rusted pan."

"Yes." Tom looked around the store. "So . . . dishes? Coffeepot? Frying pan?"

"As far as I remember it's all still there and in good shape."

"You'll need ammunition." He reached behind him and pulled a sawed-off double-barreled shotgun out from behind a sack of flour. "And this," he said as he laid it on the counter.

Mattie shook her head. "If I tried to fire that thing the kick would knock me halfway back to Sidney."

"Yes," English agreed, "right out of danger and back to someplace safe."

If only that were true. Mattie decided not to argue with him. "I can't afford it," she said. "I'll make do with the Colt." She held her hands up like two claws. "And these." She pretended to knee someone. "And this. And kicking. And screaming. I can scream really loud."

Tom didn't smile. "You can't buy the shotgun. It isn't for sale. Consider it a loan."

"Until I come to my senses and realize a mere woman has no business trying to work a placer claim?"

"There you go again, putting words in my mouth I never intended to speak. The loan is until you can buy your own. And no one said anything about you being a *mere woman.* And for the record, I consider that term an oxymoron."

"An oxy-what?"

"*Mere* doesn't describe any real woman I've ever known, so you can smooth your hackles and take the loan."

Mattie pointed at the shotgun. "What are people going to think if they see me hauling this monstrosity up to my claim tomorrow morning?"

" 'There goes a woman who is not to be trifled with.' "

When he put it that way, it made her *want* a shotgun. "All right," Mattie said and, hefting it to her shoulder, took aim.

"I take it your brother taught you about shotguns, too."

"He did." She placed it back on the counter.

Tom began to set other supplies next to it: flour and baking soda, bacon and beans, coffee and sugar, salt, pepper, and some dried apples. "If anyone comes up with eggs to spare," he said, "I'll have Freddie bring some up. You won't lack for game, thanks to him, but a piece of salt pork would be good to flavor the beans. You'll be set for flapjacks and biscuits for quite a while." He stood back and looked at the pile of provisions. "I'll add this up and put it on your account and then we can go on to the bank." He grinned. "Now all you have to concern yourself with is which McKay you'll choose."

———

If preaching didn't pay, Mattie thought the broad-shouldered man standing atop the empty crate across the street from the bank could have a promising career in the theatre. He modulated his voice like a trained actor, speaking loudly enough to attract attention from passersby and then, without warning, softening his tone so that his listeners leaned forward, straining to hear what he said. Maybe he *had* been an actor.

"Do you know him?" she asked Tom as they stood together just outside the bank.

"No, but if you ask me, he's nothing more than a skilled sales-man. That's all most preaching is. Selling religion. Or guilt. Or—if the offering plate is truly overflowing—forgiveness."

"You obviously don't have much use for men of the cloth."

Tom shrugged. "The more rabid of the Christian species get the fever to redeem the gold camps every few weeks. They come and preach and holler and tell everyone how we are all hell-bent and worthless and need salvation. After a few gullible people offer up some gold or feed 'em a few good meals, they leave. They might as well be tonic salesmen for all the good they do."

Mattie was quiet. She hadn't seen the cynical side of Tom English before, and it intrigued her. He seemed to interpret her silence as something else.

"Listen, I've got no quarrel with a man who's trying to be faithful to a sincere call. That happened to one of my friends at home, and I think it was genuine. He never took advantage of anyone and he did good until the day he died. But most of the preachers I've run into since then were little more than vultures looking for a carcass to pick clean." He motioned toward the man standing on the box.

"If you want to get all churched up, you might want to get a little closer. This one doesn't seem to be the shouting type. I prefer to watch from here."

Curious, Mattie crossed the street. The preacher's massive hands were surprisingly graceful. They reminded her of a pianist's, and that made her think of Dutch. She wondered if he was still working for Jonas. Dutch hadn't been very happy with the way Jonas treated her sometimes. With a little shiver, she returned to the moment just as the preacher began to read from the small Bible in his left hand.

" 'Wilt thou set thine eyes upon that which is not? for riches certainly make themselves wings; they fly away as an eagle toward heaven.' " Closing the Bible, the preacher surveyed the crowd.

"What a picture!" he exclaimed. "Can you imagine your bottles and bags of gold sprouting wings and flying off?"

A miner wearing a crushed top hat answered back. "I thought I saw that very thing happen just last night. But when I woke up this morning I realized it was only the whiskey talkin'."

The crowd laughed. The preacher smiled. He had a dimple in his left cheek that showed just above the line of his dark red beard. His auburn hair was sprinkled with gray. If he weren't in such desperate need of a barber, he'd be handsome. As it was, he was an odd combination of rumpled and clean.

"Sooner or later that's exactly what's going to happen—whiskey or no. All of our riches will sprout wings and fly off beyond our reach." He pointed toward the cemetery. "How much did those dear souls take with them when they died? *Nothing*. How much of their gold did they leave behind? *All of it*.

"That is why Jesus said, 'Lay not up for yourselves treasures upon earth . . . but lay up for yourselves treasures in heaven, where neither moth nor rust doth corrupt, and where thieves do not break through nor steal: For where your treasure is, there will your heart be also.' Jesus warns us, not just because wealth *might* be lost, but because wealth will *always* be lost. Storing up earthly treasures isn't just wrong. It's plain stupid. We can do better."

"By giving it to you, I expect?" someone hollered.

The preacher ignored the question. "Let us suppose that you were in the South during the war and you had accumulated an impressive stash of Confederate currency. And then one day you learned that the North was going to win the war. What do you do? Do you continue hoarding Confederate money, or do you quickly exchange what will soon be worthless for U.S. dollars?"

The grizzled miner who'd been standing in front of Mattie turned around and shouldered his way out of the crowd, swearing about the "Yankee preacher" as he went by.

"Don't you see that that is the kind of behavior mankind engages in every day? Knowing for a certainty that we are going to die, knowing for a certainty that we cannot take anything from this life into the next, we still continue to spend our lives pursuing the equivalent of Confederate money—which is any earthly treasure. Friends, that is not just unwise. As I said before, it's plain stupid.

"Now, some preachers would have you believe that Jesus was against the entire *concept* of storing up treasure. But that is not true. Jesus was not only *for* treasure, he commanded his followers to *pursue* treasure and to store it up where it will still be doing good a hundred million years from now."

"You bein' paid by the Miners and Merchants Bank?" someone joked. Laughter rippled through the crowd.

The preacher smiled. "Friends, I am here to make only one point today—"

"Well, make it and shut up," someone said back. "We've all got drinkin' to do."

The preacher nodded. "Fair enough. Here it is: you cannot take it with you, but you *can* send it on ahead." He searched the crowd, focusing first on one listener and then another. "Invest in eternity, brothers." His blue-gray eyes focused on Mattie. "Invest in eternity, sister."

Stepping down he said, very loudly, "If you want to know more, I'm not hard to find." He picked up the box he'd been standing on and put his hat on.

"Hey, Preacher," someone called, "you forgot to take up a collection."

"I have a strong back and a will to work," he said. "I'll be fine." He tipped his hat and, turning his back on the crowd, headed off up the street toward—who knew? As she watched his retreat, Mattie suddenly realized the preacher was the fool who'd helped the painted lady out of the mud the day Mattie arrived in Deadwood.

———

Late Sunday Mattie looked up from the counter in Tom's store just as the preacher ducked inside. The crowd of gawkers in the store had finally thinned. They would be closing soon, and Tom had taken the plans for Garth Merchandise over to one of the sawmills to place an order for lumber.

The preacher crossed to where Mattie stood behind the primitive counter. "Aron Gallagher," he said with a smile, "and you are the angel who listened all the way through to the end of my little talk earlier today. What did you think?"

Close up, the preacher's eyes were more blue than gray. Close up, his powerful build dwarfed her. Close up, Mattie could tell the preacher had worked some scented oil through his hair. And that was the one thing that caused her to relegate the reverend Aron Gallagher to the ranks of the preachers who had frequented Jonas's establishment—the ones who were no different from any other customers. Oh, they had a unique job, but after lecturing on Sunday they gambled on Monday just like any other low-down varmint. As far as Mattie was concerned, if there was a God, he would probably settle the score sooner or later. In the meantime, as long as they paid their gambling debts it was none of her affair.

"It was fine," she said, glancing toward the street and wishing Tom would come back. "Can I help you find something on the shelves here? We'll be closing up soon."

"Really? Did you really think it was all right? Because I'm very new at this sort of thing." He chuckled. "I don't really know what I'm doing. Could you tell?"

"If you don't know what you're doing, why do you do it?"

The preacher sighed. "I can't seem to find a way not to. I've tried running away from it and there's just nowhere to run." He looked around the store. "I was told the owner might be looking for some help with a building. . . . Is he around?"

"Mr. English should be back any moment now." Mattie picked up a rag and began to dust the mug display, blushing furiously when she realized she was wiping out a thunder mug.

"Are you Mrs. English, then?"

Freddie ducked into the tent before she could answer. "You're the preacher. I heard it was a good sermon. I didn't come because I was hunting. Aunt Lou said she listened from just inside the hotel and you did good. Are you going to build a church? Deadwood needs a church." Without waiting for the preacher to answer, Freddie took it upon himself to make introductions. "I'm Freddie Jannike and this is Mattie O'Keefe. She's going to be a miner. Mr. Tom English is building the store. He's partners with my mor. She's gone now with the freighters. Did you want to buy something?"

Expecting to see the preacher's expression change the way others' sometimes did when Freddie rambled enough to reveal his child-like mind, Mattie was surprised when instead the preacher shook Freddie's hand and introduced himself. "I'm Aron," he said. "Aron Gallagher. And it would be wonderful to have a church someday, but I wouldn't expect folks to hire a street preacher they didn't know to pastor a church." He smiled. "Actually, I was looking for Mr. English in hopes he'd hire me to help with his building."

Freddie looked the man over. "Do you know anything about building stores?"

"I do," the preacher said with a nod.

"Then you should come with me and talk to Tom," Freddie said. "Our store is going to be big. With an upstairs for Mor and me and Eva. Tom can show you the drawings." He glanced at Mattie. "But first I have to help Mattie close up." The preacher offered to help and it wasn't long before the merchandise they'd had stacked just outside the tent flap was all back inside.

"Thank you," Mattie said as she grabbed the account book. She glanced at Freddie. "If you want to go with the reverend—"

"I'm not a reverend, ma'am," the preacher broke in. "I'd be much obliged if you'd just call me Aron."

If it weren't for that scented oil in his hair, she'd have been inclined to think the preacher was an honest and humble man looking for a real job. As it was, she couldn't bring herself to trust him, and she certainly was not going to call a stranger by his given name. She cleared her throat and spoke to Freddie. "If you'd want to help Mr. Gallagher find Tom, I'll turn the lamps down and close up."

"I promised Mor I'd set some traps," Freddie said. "She said she isn't hauling freight to feed the mice."

"I can set the traps," Mattie said.

"But you were going to come and eat with Tom and me at the hotel," Freddie protested. "I wanted you to meet Aunt Lou."

Gallagher broke in. "That's perfect. Aunt Lou offered to share leftovers with me later." He raked his fingers through his hair. "I tried to unrumple myself a bit, but I don't think I succeeded very well."

"Aunt Lou doesn't mind rumpled people," Freddie said. "And besides that, you look fine." He glanced at Mattie. "Doesn't he?"

Mattie wasn't about to answer that. "You know, Freddie, I really do want to meet Aunt Lou, but I'm exhausted. I think I'm just going to have a cup of that stew you put on this morning and call it a day." She glanced at Gallagher and nodded. "Good evening." And with that, she began to turn down the lamps.

It was the preacher who caught on. "Good evening, ma'am," he said, and together he and Freddie headed for the sawmill.

———

Ladling some of Freddie's stew into a bowl, Mattie settled by the campfire with a contented sigh. They hadn't moved Swede's tent off her lot yet, and it was good to be tucked back here behind it, free from ogling eyes—and marriage proposals. She chuckled, wondering what Fergus and Finn McKay would think of their father's plan. Overall, it had been a satisfying day. She'd earned an honest wage, and she hadn't even minded setting the mousetraps, although she was glad Freddie would be handling them from now on. This time tomorrow she'd be up on her claim. How much gold would she pan the first day?

Just as she was thinking of turning in early, voices heralded the arrival of Freddie, Tom, and Mr. Gallagher. Apparently the preacher knew more than a little about building. So impressed was Tom by the man's understanding of carpentry that he seemed to have forgotten all about his earlier opinion of preachers.

"It looks as though I really can have the store finished before Swede gets back," Tom said to Mattie as he poured a mug of coffee and handed it to Mr. Gallagher. "Aron looked over my drawings and came up with ways to build faster—and better."

Mr. Gallagher took a sip of coffee without sitting down. He was already looking the lot over. "We've still got some daylight left," he said. "Why not get started?"

The two men began measuring and pounding stakes, and by nightfall the outline of a building had appeared on Swede's lot.

"We'll have to take the tent down tomorrow," Tom said to Mattie at one point. He nodded toward a broken-down wagon at the back of the lot. "What would you think of setting up a room in that wagon for when you need to stay over in town? I know it doesn't—"

"It'll be fine," Mattie said. "Not much different from a claim tent, as far as I can tell."

"You're sure?"

Mattie smiled. "I'm sure." She stood up. "In fact, I'll move in tonight so you men can work as long as you like. I would appreciate it, though, if Freddie could stand watch. Not so much for me as to protect the last of the merchandise we haven't moved yet."

Tom nodded. "Done. And thank you."

"You're welcome." Mattie poured the dregs of her coffee on the ground and crossed to the wagon, happy when there was no evidence of it being inhabited by anything other than dust. *No need for mousetraps up here.* She spent the last hour of daylight cleaning, and by nightfall when she spread out her bedroll and realized she would be able to see the moon and stars through the opening at the back, she decided she liked the new setup. If it rained she could draw the canvas together and close the opening. As for deep snow and winter's cold, she would be able to sleep in the finished store long before that became a concern. How good it was to have Tom and Freddie looking out for her. Dare she think of them as friends? The idea felt right. She could not, however, say the same for Tom's hired man.

Earlier in the evening Mattie had scolded herself for thinking badly of Mr. Gallagher because of his scented hair oil. When it turned out that he was just trying to get cleaned up to eat with Aunt Lou, she felt guilty for suspecting he had designs on her. Still, as the evening wore on, she had become increasingly uneasy until finally she thought she had it figured out. It was the way Gallagher moved, the way he watched people, the way he used his hands. Especially the hands. He might be charming. He might be a good carpenter. He might be calling himself a preacher today. But Mattie would have bet her first gold nugget that Aron Gallagher would be more comfortable dealing faro than he was preaching or pounding stakes at a building site.

Aron Gallagher was a gambler.

CHAPTER 6

In her tongue is the law of kindness.

Proverbs 31:26

It's the brother. *The sniveling, overprotective weakling of a brother.* Jonas Flynn sat in the Kansas City hotel lobby looking down at the newspaper in his lap and wondering how he could have missed it. Now that he'd realized it, he could think back to a dozen times when he should have made the connection. But he hadn't. Not until just this moment reading the article bemoaning the lack of concern for the miners up in Dakota, decrying the "Indian problem," and opining what the United States government and Generals Crook and Merritt should be doing about it.

Flynn laid the newspaper aside and stood up. Crossing the hotel lobby, he took the stairs two at a time up to the second floor. Once in his room, he stared out over the city, wondering at his stupidity. He'd assumed that, wanting to get away as quickly as possible, Mattie would jump aboard the first train to roll out of Abilene. He'd spent weeks tracing her supposed eastern route, doubling back, stopping at every town along the way, checking every saloon, every dance hall, every gambling establishment. Even if the conductor or the ticket agent didn't remember a brunette beauty with violet eyes, he still combed the town. Just to be sure. And now here he was in Kansas City. He'd spent time in places that made even *him* sick, and nothing. Not one trace of the thieving witch named Mattie O'Keefe.

He usually didn't stop the hunt until so late at night that he dropped right off to sleep, and he hadn't read a newspaper in days. But today . . . today he'd felt defeated and so out of sorts he'd paused long enough for a good cigar and a newspaper. And that's when it hit him. Mattie O'Keefe hadn't run away from *him* as much as she had run *to* her brother.

And where else would Dillon O'Keefe have headed than the rich gold fields in Dakota Territory? After all, their mother had raised her brats on fairy tales about the gold fields of California, where she'd hooked up with a young Jonas P. Flynn.

As he stared out the window, Jonas could imagine the O'Keefe siblings plotting against him: Dillon would leave Abilene, thereby lulling Jonas into thinking he'd finally succeeded in running him off. Mattie would stay for a while, charming Jonas into a sense of false security. And all the while she was just waiting to rob him and run. Jonas swore under his breath. He should have killed Dillon O'Keefe when he had the chance. And when he finally caught up with them, maybe he'd kill them both—just as soon as he got his money back.

A man in his position couldn't let one of the girls get away with stealing. Now that he thought about it, he realized that he couldn't kill Mattie. At least not until after he'd dragged her back to Abilene and made an example of her. The minute she'd left, a couple of the other girls had started looking at him with a certain glint in their eye. Especially the redhead. Maybe Flo was stealing from him, too. He hadn't been able to prove it before leaving to chase Mattie down, but once the chase was over, once Flo saw what happened to girls who crossed Jonas Flynn—*that*, Jonas vowed, would be the end of *that*.

Mattie O'Keefe had been trouble for as long as he'd known her.

He'd let her get away with things another girl would have been sacked or beaten for. *"My voice is for sale,"* she'd said. *"My body isn't."* The minx. As if she were something special. Jonas closed his eyes, and there she was in his imagination, her perfect hair tumbling over silken ivory shoulders . . . and those eyes . . . she was the tantalizing prize he couldn't have . . . hadn't had . . . yet. . . . And the way she danced just out of his reach had fueled his longing until at times he felt half mad with desire.

For a while he'd been content just to listen to her sing, to watch her sit at the high-priced table and deal cards and rake in the money for him. For a while it had been enough knowing that as far as anyone else was concerned, Mattie O'Keefe was the property of Jonas P. Flynn, and that after the other fools who'd slobbered all over her throughout the evening staggered out the door, Mattie came upstairs to his room. As far as anyone else knew, the door that connected his quarters with her room was always open.

Eventually, Jonas told himself, things would go according to his will. After all, in spite of his age, in spite of the loss of a hand and the need for a prosthetic hook, Jonas P. Flynn possessed the ultimate aphrodisiacs: money and power. And he had time. He'd let her sashay about and promote his business. He'd even created a false account to show her how much money she was earning. But that was all over now.

He'd been patient . . . so patient. And yet Mattie had remained unwilling to accept the realities of life: that what she earned on paper didn't become *real* until she took that last step into his bed. And when he'd finally made it clear to her naïve brain, she'd actually believed she could say no.

Remembering the final scene between the two of them, he grimaced and swiped an open palm across his perspiring forehead. Turning away from the window, he crossed to the mirror hanging above the bureau and fingered the angry red line running along the ridge of his left cheekbone. He looked down at the ring she'd left behind—the ring he wore on his little finger as a reminder. He snorted. The ring was nothing. What mattered was his reputation. Half the girls in the place had heard them fighting. He could still imagine them with ears pressed to their doors, listening. If he let Mattie get away with this, every girl in the place would think she could talk back and choose what she would and would not do. A man couldn't run a business that way.

Standing back from the mirror, Jonas admired the neatly trimmed gray beard, the impeccably tailored vest, the posture that said, *THIS is a man of substance. A respectable businessman.* Well, he was about to make certain that never changed. Packing quickly, he descended to the hotel lobby and checked out. At the train station a helpful ticket agent explained the route to the gold fields of Dakota. North to Omaha, then west to a place called Sidney, Nebraska.

"Now, I don't know about how a gentleman gets north from Sidney," the ticket agent said. "Of course there's all kinds of freight being moved, but as for passengers—I know there was talk of a stage line, but whether it's in service yet, I have no idea. I suppose a man in a hurry with the means to do so would just buy a good horse and head north. But with all the Indian trouble, I don't know as that's advisable."

Jonas bought the ticket to Sidney. One way. As the train rolled out of the station and headed north along the Missouri, he leaned his head back and closed his eyes. He hated Kansas City. Give him Abilene any day. Abilene, where he'd built a small but lucrative kingdom, where justice was cheap and women knew their place. *Except for Mattie O'Keefe.* Jonas smiled. That was about to change.

———

Mattie waded into the creek and, crouching down, sunk the pan of gravel into the frigid water. Before she could attempt any kind of move like Tom had demonstrated, the strong current in the creek caught the pan, flipped it over, and threatened to wash it away. She stumbled around, rescued the pan, and then lost her balance, nearly falling flat in the middle of the creek.

"You!" someone shouted. "What d' you think yer doin'! Is it a dead man's gold yer after!" Swearing and hollering, redheaded Finn McKay came stomping toward her. When Mattie looked up at him he stopped in mid-obscenity. Again he said, "You!" only this time the tone was surprise laced with wonder. "You were mindin' the store for Tom."

Mattie nodded. "Yes, but most of his goods have already been sold and he's hired that preacher to help him with the building. He decided he could manage without me, so here I am." She tugged on the brim of her hat. "I don't know what I'm doing yet, but from your reaction I must at least *look* like a miner now."

Finn shook his head. "Well, now, I wouldn't say so. Yer not like any miner *I've* ever seen. 'Tis more like as if an angel has come t' live among us."

"Trust me," Mattie protested. "I am about the furthest thing from an angel you will ever meet."

Fergus McKay was next to show up, belching and scratching his backside as he climbed out of his tent hollering all the while about a terrible headache and that cheating card dealer at the Green Front. Dressed only in a set of filthy long johns—the back door dangling open—Fergus walked up beside his brother. Mattie had trouble not laughing aloud when Fergus recognized her and, with a quick reach behind, closed the gaping flap and with a "beggin' yer pardon, miss," backed his way across the claim toward the tent. He bumped into the rocker on his way, stumbled, and nearly fell. In the process he lost hold of his "back door" and Mattie was witness to something she hoped wouldn't haunt her dreams.

"I thought you was a claim-jumper," Finn sputtered.

"Well, I'm grateful to know you've been keeping an eye out."

"We can be a foul bunch of bandits, but those of us who've been here since the first tend to watch out fer each other."

"I may be new to the gulch, but I'll certainly do my part to keep an eye on your claim when I'm up here."

"It's true then—you intend to work it . . . with your own lovely hands?"

"I do, although at the moment the claim is working me. How long does it take to get the hang of panning? Tom made it look so easy."

"It depends," Finn said. "I never could do much with a pan." He looked back toward the tent. "If Fergus don't die of embarrassment first, he might could give you a lesson or two."

"You've got your own claim to work," Mattie said. "I wouldn't want to impose."

"It's not imposin'," Fergus called as he ducked back into view. He was dressed this time, and as he fastened the last button on a ragged flannel shirt, he said, "I'll do it for the gold in the first pan."

"There might not be any."

"Well, now, that's just a chance I'll have to take."

————

It was late in the afternoon before Mattie finally managed to create a crescent shape of fine sand and gravel in her gold pan. True to his word, Fergus had crouched down beside her and patiently shown her the very same things Tom had demonstrated. He was willing to stay as long as she wanted, but after filtering through two pans and finding a respectable-sized flake of gold with which to thank him, Mattie said she was a slow learner and would do better without her teacher watching her every move.

Fergus retreated back to the McKay claim and Mattie breathed a sigh of relief. He was a nice enough fellow and not a bad teacher, but he needed a bath. Taking a deep breath of fresh air, she went back to work and by the end of the day had added a dozen tiny flecks of gold to her hand-carved dust-catcher.

Freddie arrived just at sunset. Mattie watched carefully as he built a fire, grateful she didn't have to reveal how little she knew about cooking and campfires. She'd managed to hide her ignorance from Swede by tending to Eva on the trail, but she'd need to know about such things if she was going to survive up here on the gulch.

With two dressed rabbits, an onion, and a few pinches of seasonings he said were "one of Mor's secrets and he couldn't tell," Freddie cooked a succulent stew. Later, as she settled down for her first night on the claim, Mattie wondered how long she could make the stew last . . . and how often she could count on Freddie's cooking.

––––––

Tom English was right. Panning for gold was backbreaking work. The water was frigid and the air was cold. Mattie's hands were chapped, her entire body was sore, and her feet would likely never be warm again. She probably wasn't going to get rich, either. It was going to be a while before she could pan with any efficiency at all. In her first week of mining full time, she had added only seven flakes of gold to the dozen specks collected on her first day. And yet, on days when the sky was blue and the gulch was relatively quiet, when the rest of the miners were either sleeping off their whiskey or going on a binge in town, when birds swooped across the gulch and the creek sang, Mattie rejoiced in being a free woman.

When the men working their claims began to turn in and the night grew quiet, Mattie pulled her tired feet out of her rubber boots and lit the lamp inside her tent. As she settled back on her cot and tucked her pistol just beneath the edge of the comforters, she was content. She'd never really had a specific dream of a home, but if she had, it would never have been a canvas tent on a placer claim. And yet, given a choice between this tent and her room back in Abilene, Mattie would gladly call her tent home.

She'd always loved to watch the pink-tinged Kansas dawns before she turned in. Often she'd managed to slip away from the gaming tables and take a break just around sunset, too, marveling at the way every single one was different and wishing she could somehow preserve them. Here in Dakota it was practically noon before much daylight shone down into the gulch. Mattie saw no pink-tinged dawns and no spectacular sunsets. The sun dropped quickly, shadows gathered, and night fell. It was a quick three-step as opposed to a slow waltz. But she didn't mind. Her time was her own, and if she wanted to sit by the fire and drink half a pot of coffee, no one was telling her to "get dressed and get downstairs."

She didn't even mind that the cold was hanging on so long people had begun to mutter and wonder if it was "fixin' to snow right smack in the middle of summer." Such talk only encouraged her imaginings of frosting on the boulders and pine tree branches. How pretty that would be, and how clean everything would seem when dusted with new-fallen snow.

There was still plenty to make a person think of Deadwood as a hellish place. And yet, she could already name four people she could almost call her friends. And, she reminded herself with a smile, she'd already had a proposal of marriage.

Of course, for the few good people Mattie knew, there were dozens of the other kind. But mostly they didn't bother her. She stayed to herself when she was in town, and up here on the gulch, between Freddie's frequent visits and the McKays keeping watch, she was beginning to feel less afraid even without Dillon to protect her.

She was almost happy at times. But then she'd think of Dillon and how she wanted to tell him something or show him something, and missing him would hurt all over again. Sometimes the pain was so sharp it was as if she'd just found out he was gone.

Grief was ever present, the work was hard, and it would likely be a long time before she stopped looking over her shoulder for Jonas. But, she told herself, she really didn't have to be afraid anymore. All things considered, Mattie loved her new life.

When Freddie got too busy helping build his mother's store to hunt, and her supplies ran low, Mattie realized that if she didn't figure out how to make flapjacks and biscuits fairly soon, she was going to go to bed hungry on a regular basis. And so, on the Monday that would begin her second week on her claim, Mattie rose early and dressed for town, descending the gulch just as gray light was beginning to filter down toward the creek. She picked her way quietly past claims, smiling to herself at the snores and snorts coming from various tents and claim shacks.

When the skeleton of the building that was to become Garth Merchandise came into view, Mattie could see that it was going to be a fine store. As soon as he saw her, Freddie insisted that Mattie go with him to view the sign Mr. English was having Judd Morgan paint. *Garth & Company Merchandise*, it said.

"Tom says he doesn't care if his name is on it," Freddie said. "It's just like I told Mor and you—he's a really good man." He pointed to the stylized outline of a red horse at either end, the noses of the animals pointed toward the lettering like artistic bookends. "That's a Dala," Freddie explained. "Mor will like that." He held his hands apart as he said, "We had one this high on the mantel at home. Mor packed it away after Garth died. When we move in above the store, I bet she brings it out again."

"I imagine she will," Mattie agreed. "And she's going to be very pleased to see what you've done for her with the sign."

Freddie reached into his pocket and pulled out a piece of wood he'd been carving.

"I'm making Eva her own Dala," he said, and then, as Mattie was beginning to realize he often did, Freddie changed the subject, asking Mattie what supplies she needed.

"Oh, I don't need anything just yet," she said. "I was wondering, though . . . would you mind introducing me to Aunt Lou? I need her advice about something."

———

Peering through the screen door, Mattie saw a willow-thin woman with smooth mahogany skin and snow-white hair at work in the hotel kitchen. She was rolling out dough on the kitchen table, but at Freddie's knock she glanced up, smiled, and called out a cheerful greeting. "And how is Mr. Jannike today?"

"I'm fine, Aunt Lou," Freddie said as he opened the door and motioned for Mattie to step inside. "This is my friend Mattie. The one I've been telling you about."

Aunt Lou looked Mattie up and down. "Ah yes, the prettiest little lady in the gulch." She winked. "I heard about you." She motioned toward a small crock atop the table. "Shove that lard over here to Aunt Lou, won't you, honey?"

Mattie scooted the crock within Aunt Lou's reach and watched, fascinated, as one dark hand made a well in a bowl of flour, added lard and water, along with a little salt, and mixed it all—without any measuring.

Aunt Lou talked while she worked. "When you gonna bring me some more game, Freddie?"

"I've been helping build Mor's store. I haven't had time to hunt very much. And when I got two rabbits I made stew for Mattie." Freddie paused. "I been helping her some, but she said she needs to talk to a lady about something, and so here she is."

Aunt Lou glanced Mattie's way again, then smiled and nodded. "Well, all right, then. Don't mind if I say I've been lonely for lady-talk myself here lately." She turned to Freddie. "Don't you worry, I'll save you a big slice of this here pie when it comes outta the oven."

As soon as Freddie left, Mattie asked, "How do you know that crust will work? I mean, you didn't measure anything."

Aunt Lou shrugged. "Same way I know you ain't here to talk about pie," she said. "Practice and experience, honey, practice and experience." When she looked up Mattie saw nothing but kindness in Aunt Lou's hazel eyes. "Freddie talks about you all the time, Miss Mattie. Now, what can Aunt Lou do for you today?"

Mattie blurted it out. "I need to learn how to make flapjacks and biscuits."

The rolling pin ceased its progress across the pie dough as Aunt Lou tilted her head and looked up, one eyebrow arched, doubt on her kind face. "You need to learn *what?*"

Mattie swallowed. "I've never done it before. Tom English loaded me up with supplies, and so of course he assumed—and I wasn't about to admit it. I thought I could figure it out. How hard could it be? I thought. But I can't make it work. All I've managed is rocks and flat cakes that taste like—well, I don't know what they taste like, but I'm tired of pretending I know what I'm doing."

Aunt Lou was looking at her as if she'd just crawled out from beneath a rock. "Everybody knows how to make biscuits and flap-jacks, honey. Now, how 'bout you sit down there at Aunt Lou's table and tell me what's *really* on your mind. You lonely for some beau back home? You feelin' sad about Dillon?" She went back to rolling out pie crust and in nothing flat had three pie pans lined. She rolled out the leftover crust, sprinkled it with cinnamon and sugar, cut it into strips, and rolling them up, popped them into the oven. "Been a long time since I had a child around to eat the leavings for me." She smiled. "Freddie just loves my pinwheels. You don't mind bein' a child this morning, do ya, Miss Mattie?" She took a towel off a crockery pitcher on the counter and, pouring a mug of milk, set it in front of Mattie.

Aunt Lou's kitchen was filled with warmth and the aromas of roast beef and bacon grease, bread dough and cinnamon. Taking a sip of milk, Mattie leaned back in the rickety chair. "No, ma'am.

I don't mind. But I really did come up here to ask you to teach me about biscuits and flapjacks."

Aunt Lou gently reached down to cup Mattie's face in one hand. Lifting her chin, the old woman looked down into her eyes. When she next spoke, her voice was gentle. "I gotta make biscuits for supper and you can help. Flapjacks don't take near as much fuss. I can tell you how to do that, and long as you got a fryin' pan you'll be fine."

"Dillon had a frying pan," Mattie said.

"You got a Dutch oven?" Aunt Lou asked. Mattie nodded. "All right," she said. "You'll be able to bake up a nice batch of biscuits with that. There's a few tricks to doin' it over a campfire." Aunt Lou motioned toward a clean apron hanging on a hook by the door. "Just put that on and we'll get started. You don't by chance want to know how to make chess pie, too?"

Mattie got up to don the apron. "I'd *love* to," she said. "What's chess pie?"

"Lordy, lordy, what's the world comin' to," Aunt Lou grumbled. "Girls growin' up into women that don't know how to make flapjacks or biscuits and never heard of chess pie." Aunt Lou kept grumbling, but she was smiling.

———

"You got a gift, honey," Aunt Lou said at the end of Mattie's first day of lessons. "I never saw a gal take to dough and bakin' as quick as you."

"Thank you," Mattie said. "I'll keep that in mind if the claim doesn't pan out."

Aunt Lou put her hands on her hips and stared at Mattie. "So what I been hearing is true. You're workin' that claim by yourself."

"I am."

With a shaking of her head, Aunt Lou turned away. Opening

the oven door, she removed a batch of cinnamon pinwheels and slid them onto a plate. "You want some coffee?"

"No thank you," Mattie said as she took one of the cinnamon pinwheels. The flaky crust, and just the right amount of spice, made for a mouthwatering combination. "You should make these and sell them," Mattie said. "The miners would buy them by the sacks full."

"I expect you're right," Aunt Lou said. "But I don't sell my pinwheels, honey. I give 'em away."

"But why?"

Aunt Lou smiled. " 'Cause sometimes a body just needs a little morsel of love to encourage 'em, and Aunt Lou's love ain't for sale. She gives it free."

The proclamation of love produced a warm glow, but at the same time it made Mattie feel uncomfortable. No one except Dillon had ever said they loved her unless they wanted something. This woman didn't seem to be that kind of person, but you never knew.

Aunt Lou shoved a bowl across the table at Mattie. "All right, honey," she said. "Time to see if you can do it without any help from Aunt Lou."

———

It was long after dark when Mattie finally said good-night to Aunt Lou and headed across Main Street to Swede's lot, thankful that Tom had her set up in the broken-down wagon. It was late, and she was too tired to even think about finding her way up the gulch. She reached into the pocket of her dress and felt the piece of paper where she'd written Aunt Lou's instructions for both biscuits and flapjacks.

She would likely still make a few mistakes, but at least now she wouldn't be gnawing on rocks and trying to swallow leathery discs of barely palatable fried dough. She was almost looking forward to having Freddie show up with a rabbit or a squirrel for the stew pot now. Maybe she should get another Dutch oven so she could bake biscuits while he made stew.

It was a typical night in Deadwood, which meant that drunken men were stumbling along the street and any minute now there would likely be gunfire somewhere. Her hand went to the Colt in her pocket, and just as she crossed the street, someone stepped out of the shadows and called her name. Someone with a gray beard. Her heart lurched. She was pointing the gun at the shadowy figure when a voice called out, "Whoa, don't shoot! It's me. Judd Morgan. The sign painter."

Aron Gallagher hurried over from the direction of Swede's lot. "Everything all right?"

Mattie tucked the pistol back into her pocket. "I'm sorry. I thought—" She broke off. "Never mind. I'm sorry."

"Freddie thought you'd want to see the finished sign," Morgan said. "I was just headed over to the Cricket for a drink and saw you coming out of the hotel. I didn't mean to scare you."

"I'd love to see the sign," Mattie said. "How about if I stop by on my way back up to my claim tomorrow?"

"That'd be just fine," Morgan said. He glanced at Aron Gallagher. "Came darned near needing you to preach at my funeral." He nodded toward Mattie. "Dangerous woman. Better keep an eye on her."

As he tugged on the brim of his hat and said good-night, it was impossible to tell if Morgan was angry, impressed, or a little of both. Gallagher, on the other hand, made no attempt to hide his reaction, which was concern. For her. "What are you so afraid of?" he asked once Morgan was out of earshot.

Mattie snorted. "I'm not afraid of anything," she said, hoping she sounded convincing. "Any woman would be a fool not to—"

"—shoot first and ask questions later?"

"Exactly."

Gallagher's voice was gentle as he said, "That could end badly for you someday."

"It's more likely to end badly for any varmint lying in wait to prove his manhood by taking advantage of the weaker sex."

"Sounds like the voice of experience."

"Every woman alive has had an experience or two with varmints," Mattie said. "The only difference between me and them is I'm not one to wait around for somebody in pants to rescue me."

CHAPTER 7

Let them be turned back and brought to confusion
that devise my hurt.

Psalm 35:4

L ook, mister, if you want to provide the red devils with a new scalp, you just go right ahead. But I'm telling you the best way to Deadwood is to hook up with a string of freighters and share their campfire." The balding livery owner planted his feet and hooked a thumb behind his holster buckle. "Either way, yer gonna have to buy a horse outright instead of renting from me, and that bay ain't fer sale." He nodded toward the first stall. "He's the best horse I've got, and I owe him better than to send him where I know he's gonna end up crow bait on account of some idiot who won't listen to reason."

Jonas grabbed a handful of the man's worn shirt and gave it a twist. With his hook he snatched the gun from the man's holster and tossed it toward the corner of the barn, where it landed in a pile of fouled hay.

"Now, you listen to me," he said, enjoying the sound of the cretin's vain struggle to breathe. "I understand your reluctance.

Really, I do. But I'm convinced that if you think about it for just one minute more you'll see how misguided it is for a businessman such as yourself to refuse to sell that horse. Why, I looked him over carefully, and I can tell you that bay is very nearly at the end of his usefulness." He smiled at the question in the man's eyes. "What you may not understand is that I have an uncanny ability to evaluate horseflesh, and that bay has a look about him. Just think how you'll feel tomorrow when you find he's foundered or got in the way of a stray bullet. Think how you'll regret missing the chance to make some money off him." Jonas held on a little longer, and just at the second when the man's eyes began to roll back in his head, he let go.

The man gagged, coughed, bent over, gasped, then staggered backward and dropped onto a stack of hay bales, his hand at his throat. He glanced at his gun, now resting atop the manure-laced hay. "Forty-five dollars," he croaked.

"I'll need the whole outfit," Jonas said. "Saddle, bridle, saddle blanket."

"Forty-five dollars," the man repeated, waving his hand toward the barn door. "Just take what you want—and go."

Jonas peeled forty-five dollars off the money roll in his pocket, then made a ceremony of raining bills over the man's head. As they drifted to the ground, he said, "See there? I knew we could come to an agreement if we really tried." He headed for the door. "I'll be back in an hour. Have my horse saddled and ready." He didn't bother to look back. After a while it got boring watching weak men tremble.

————————

Mattie had been staying on her claim for nearly three weeks when she woke one night to the realization that someone—or some*thing*— was snooping around her claim. She could hear them—or *it*—circling the tent. Her stomach clenched. An owl hooted. Closing her eyes, she listened. Wouldn't there be some kind of animal sound if it was one of those mountain lions? What did bears do in a camp? Did they just come crashing through the canvas or would she have some warning? Could whatever it was smell her fear? Almost holding her breath, she leaned down and felt around in the dark for the shotgun Tom had loaned her. When at first she couldn't feel it, her heart sank. Would the Colt be enough?

Someone cleared his throat. Instantly she thought of Jonas, but just as quickly she knew it wasn't him. Jonas was stealthier than a snake. He'd never make a mistake that warned his prey.

She was about to have her first encounter with a claim-jumper, and all of a sudden she wished she'd loaded Bessie II with something besides Tom English's homemade rock salt cartridges. It didn't help that Fergus McKay had an entire complement of stories about claim-jumpers and loved telling them around her campfire. *Well, here you go, Fergus. Hopefully this will give you another story I'll live to hear.*

She lay back with the shotgun pointed at the tent flap. Whoever was out there was fumbling around at the opening now. She'd always felt like those ties weren't enough. But—a *hand*. Someone was sticking their *hand* inside.

Mattie pulled the trigger. As the claim-jumper roared with pain, she dropped the shotgun, grabbed her pistol and, leaping up, ripped the tent flap open. "You'd better lay still," she said as she pointed the pistol. "If I pull *this* trigger it'll do a lot more damage than wadding and a few pellets of rock salt."

The intruder stayed put, moaning and rolling from side to side in agony while Mattie tried to think what to do. She should probably tie him up, but to do that she'd have to put her gun down. He might be playacting about how badly he was hurting.

The McKays were still in town or they would have come running by now. The two men supposedly working the claim just above her hadn't actually been *on* their claim since she'd arrived. Apparently there was some rule that a miner could put in his work on a road or a trail around here and it still counted as working a claim. At any rate, there didn't seem to be anyone nearby.

Finally someone from down below shouted, "Ho there, what's happened?"

"Shot a claim-jumper on Mattie's Claim," she hollered back.

"Is he dead?"

The claim-jumper tried to sit up and hollered, "No, I'm not dead!"

Mattie kicked his boot. "You shut up," she snapped. "Whatever you were up to, it was no good and you deserve whatever you got, you good-for-nothing—" Just when she'd spouted some of the most colorful terms from her Abilene days, she noticed a half-dozen lanterns coming up the hill. *Let them hear it. Maybe it would make the point that she wasn't some little lady to be taken for a fool.* And so she kept up the swearing about everything from the cold stream to the worthless claim to low-down varmints who tried to take advantage. Although she had much more useful words than *varmint* in her vocabulary.

"Are you really all right, Miss O'Keefe?"

Great. Just great. In the light of the lanterns she could see concerned faces, and among them the preacher. When she felt a flush of embarrassment creeping up her neck, it made her angrier still. After all, she didn't even think he was a *real* preacher.

"I'm fine," she snapped. "What in tarnation are *you* doing up here?" She glanced at the others and recognized more than one face. "I didn't know you boys were in the habit of holding prayer meetings." Of course they weren't. But they all played cards and gambled around their campfires. And if her suspicions about him were correct, Gallagher had probably been winning.

Gallagher knelt beside the intruder.

"It's just rock salt," Mattie said. "I didn't use the pistol—yet."

Gallagher held the lamp up to the man's face. "Brady? Brady Sloan? Is that you?" He sounded surprised.

Recognizing the name, Mattie blurted out, "He wanted to buy my claim!" She looked at Gallagher. "Ellis Gates had his offer all written out the same day I got into town." She kicked Sloan's boot again. "Decided to just help yourself to what wasn't for sale?"

Sloan moaned and tried to sit up. "I didn't mean anything by it," he said. "I just wanted to borrow—"

"—some sugar? Coffee? Tea?" Mattie leaned down and yelled, "*GOLD?*"

"No!" Sloan protested, but he was in no condition to explain any more. Hugging himself, he began to moan again.

Gallagher called to the men who were with him. "Let's get him down to the doctor." He turned around to face Mattie. "We'll need a blanket."

"Check Mr. Sloan's shanty," Mattie said, but then something in the way Gallagher looked at her—as if he was disappointed in her—made her grab one of Dillon's extra blankets from inside and hand it over. Two men she'd never seen before rolled Sloan onto the blanket and, with a man grabbing each corner, hoisted him off the ground and headed down the gulch with two others holding lanterns to light the way.

As soon as they were a few feet away, Mattie sat down abruptly on one of the tree stumps she used as camp seats. She saw Gallagher say something to one of the stretcher-bearers and head back her way. She began to tremble. *Here we go again. Just like always. Near to fainting as soon as the crisis passes.*

"Give me the gun," Gallagher said gently and held out his hand.

Mattie handed her pistol over. Gallagher ducked into her tent and emerged with another blanket, which he draped around her shoulders before stirring up the fire. Removing the lid to her coffeepot, he peered in, inhaled, and made a face. "Care if I dump this?"

"What? You don't like my coffee?" She swiped at a tear.

Gallagher made a fresh pot, set it on the fire to heat, and sat down. Mattie sniffed and dabbed at her cheeks with a corner of the blanket. Gallagher was at least polite enough to appear not to notice. All she needed was for him to think she needed some kind of maudlin comforting. She'd really fall apart then. "You don't have to stay," she said. "I'm a little shaky, but I'll be fine."

"I'm quite certain you will be fine," he replied. "I just thought I'd hang around and make sure Sloan was acting alone."

She hadn't thought about that. *What if Sloan wasn't acting alone? What if his partner was out there somewhere watching them right this very minute? What was the partner's name again? It had been on that bogus offer Ellis Gates had worked up.* She couldn't remember. She glanced at Gallagher. He was unarmed. She wished he hadn't taken her Colt into the tent.

Clutching the blanket around her shoulders, she peered up toward the top of the gulch. "There's a ledge up there," she told him. "Finn McKay was up there the other day. Said he found a vein of quartz."

Gallagher followed her gaze but said nothing.

"He used a rope to lower himself down to it." Mattie shivered involuntarily. "I hope he pulled it back up after he did whatever it was he was doing."

"I'm sure he did," Gallagher said.

They sat quietly while the coffee brewed and Mattie regained most of her composure. When it was ready, Gallagher poured them each a cup. Mattie kept her palms curled around the tin cup after taking her first sip. The warmth felt good. She finally stopped shivering. "Good coffee," she said.

"Thank you." Gallagher picked up a stick and poked at the fire. A shower of sparks flew up.

"I-I'm grateful you and your friends came to the rescue."

"I'm glad someone was around, too." The edges of his mouth

turned up in a little smile. "I guess the word will get out now that Mattie O'Keefe shoots first and asks questions later."

Feeling defensive, she answered, "I suppose you would have turned the other cheek and all that."

He took a sip of coffee. "I don't know what I would have done. But I'm glad you did what you did. There's already one too many O'Keefes in the cemetery as far as I'm concerned." He cleared his throat. "Saying words over your brother wasn't easy. He was a good man."

"You knew my brother?"

Gallagher nodded. "He caught my attention because he didn't heckle when I preached." He smiled. "Although he did ask some of the darndest questions." He looked across the campfire at Mattie. "Your brother was a hard case when it came to the things of the Lord."

"He had reason to be."

"That's exactly what he said." The preacher poured the remaining coffee out of his cup into the fire and stood up. "I'd best be getting down to the doc's and see if Brady Sloan needs praying over."

"You think he's hurt that bad?" Mattie's heart thumped. Now that she'd had time to calm down, she wasn't sure she liked the idea of mortally wounding a man, even if he was trying to steal from her.

"Not physically. But if his conscience is bothering him, he might be open to a word or two of the gospel. I've seen the Lord use things like what just happened to haul a black sheep into the fold."

" 'Repent, sinners, for now is the hour of salvation,' " Mattie said in a sonorous voice. When Gallagher looked her way with surprise, she smiled ruefully. "Why yes, Brother Gallagher, I've heard it all many times before."

"Apparently not from anyone who lived the message."

"Is that what you do, Reverend Gallagher? *Live* the message?"

He shook his head. "As I've said before, I don't qualify for the title of 'reverend.' I've never been to seminary. And as to living the message, I do try, but sometimes it seems that the harder I try the more I fail."

Mattie was about to ask him why, if he was a failure, he kept climbing up on that box and telling other people how to live. But just then a skittering of rocks tumbled from right above where they were sitting. Mattie yelped and jumped so high she nearly unseated herself.

"Don't be a-scared," Freddie said, gasping for breath as he stepped into the campfire light. He'd been running and could barely talk, but from what he did say Mattie gathered he had heard about her encounter with Brady Sloan and come sneaking up the gulch along the opposite side of the creek—making sure there weren't any more varmints on the prowl, as he put it. The idea that Freddie had run to her rescue made Mattie want to get up and hug him. But she didn't. She wasn't the hugging type.

"You should pray with Aron," Freddie said. "It will make you feel better. I pray a lot, and it always makes me feel better. Like when I'm worried over Mor and Eva when they are gone." Freddie sat down on the vacant stump near the fire and, sitting up straight, put one hand on each knee and waited. When Gallagher didn't speak up, Freddie said, "Okay. We're ready."

Gallagher looked at Mattie with an unspoken question. When she shrugged and nodded, he sat down again and bowed his head. "Heavenly Father. Thank you for Mattie's courage. Thank you for giving her a brother who loved her. Thank you for keeping her safe tonight. Thank you for listening when we talk to you, for loving us, and for promising eternal life. Thank you for Jesus. Amen."

Freddie spoke up. "I'll stay and sleep by the campfire tonight, Mattie. If you want me to."

"You don't have to do that."

"I know I don't have to," Freddie said. "I *want* to."

"Then thank you. I appreciate it."

Freddie looked at Gallagher. "I know what you said in that prayer is right. About God keeping Mattie safe," he said. "But don't you think sometimes God likes it when *people* protect people, too?"

"Absolutely." Gallagher stood up. "And between you and the good Lord, I believe Miss O'Keefe is in good hands." He moved the coffeepot off the fire, tipped his hat, and headed off down the gulch.

————

Wagon master Red Tallent had a crooked nose and a thick beard that reached almost his waist. Swede liked him and Eva adored him, at times treating him like her own personal pet to be alternately cuddled and pummeled according to whim. Red seemed to delight in either one, and Swede would have almost allowed herself to like him a great deal if only Red weren't in the habit of drinking himself into a stupor at the end of every run.

Still, the man insisted that his wagons were loaded properly, so as to make the hauling as easy as possible on the oxen. More than once he'd saved fragile cargo by suggesting a better way to stack things, and he was not above shouldering a crate of goods and working alongside the teamsters. Swede had seen Tallent negotiate between two drivers about to come to blows over something that happened on the trail, and had learned to trust his judgment about campsites. She respected the man and had thought he respected her. Until now.

"*Cats?!*" Tallent nearly spit the coffee out of his mouth as he sputtered the word. He stared across the campfire at Swede in disbelief, swallowed his coffee, and leaned forward as he repeated, "Did you just say you're thinking of hauling *cats* to Deadwood?" He pointed at the black pup cradled in Swede's arms. "You starting one of them zoological parks?"

Swede stroked the pup's head even as she glowered at the burly German. "Vat I am starting is a campaign to keep my store free from mice," she said, "and to make some money in de doing."

"Well, you're starting with the wrong critters," Red said, pointing at the dog.

He was right, of course. There was no good reason for rescuing the half-starved puppy she'd found cowering beside a chicken coop back in Sidney. She didn't need the extra mouth to feed. She didn't need the worries. She didn't need the distraction. And yet, she could no more have left the black-as-coal puppy to the elements than she could let her own oxen suffer. When the man who owned the chickens joked about shooting the black "wolf" hanging around his hens, Swede asked if the dog was for sale. That man, too, had looked at her as if she were crazy, although he was more than willing to accept the half-dollar she offered for the pup.

Ah well, Swede thought as Red made fun, he would eventually think over what she had said and perhaps be willing to help her. For the moment, though, he didn't see the potential. He was, in fact, looking around to see who would share the joke. Eva distracted him by crawling too close to the fire. Tallent swept her up and, with a chuckle, said, "Did you hear your mama, little one? She's talking crazy."

If she could have somehow given her oxen wings, Swede would have done it right then—first to escape Red's teasing, but also because she was impatient to see her new store. Other than the unusual addition of a puppy to the freight, life on the trail these past weeks had been uneventful. No one got sick. Everyone kept their wagon wheels greased and in good repair. Each noon and evening they gathered in groups of four around campfires and took turns cooking. The men had even begun to toss scraps the puppy's way. God had provided unusually good weather, abundant grass, and plenty of fresh water along the way. And yet, it was difficult to be patient with the plodding oxen. Swede wanted to see her new store, to see her cargo arranged on shelves she owned, to see the proof that *Doubt* was mistaken—she *could* provide her family with a home of their own.

She had more calico. Thousands of yards of it. All hideous as far as Swede was concerned, but it was cheap and she would take a chance. Miners and town dwellers alike could use it instead of paper to line walls, and it would help keep the wind, the dust, and the bugs at bay. In addition to the calico piled high against the six-foot sides of the wagons, Swede had bolts of wool shirting, bib overalls and hats, fur-lined boots, long johns, and more than one box of fine cigars. She was reluctant to haul liquor, but tobacco was another matter. Her one vice was enjoying her pipe, and while she knew many who frowned upon the use of tobacco, she did not think the good Lord would begrudge a hardworking woman a small indulgence. Of course it wasn't exactly feminine, but then how would femininity benefit her? In the world in which she lived and breathed, to be feminine was to be weak and vulnerable to all kinds of evil.

Hundred-pound sacks of flour lined the bottom of another wagon. Thanks to one Joseph Murphy of St. Louis, the man who'd designed freight wagons with seven-foot-high wheels, sixteen-foot beds, and strong axles, she could stockpile hundreds of pounds of flour before winter.

Up front on the light wagon where Eva rode, five chickens squawked in a makeshift cage perched atop the barrels of goods lining the smaller wagon bed. The four hens and one rooster were for Aunt Lou, a thank-you for looking after Freddie while she was gone. The chickens had given her the idea about cats. If she could haul chickens, why not cats, and wouldn't it be wonderful to have help controlling the mice and rats in Deadwood? She could not think why God would have created creatures whose sole aim in the world seemed to be the destruction of goods she worked so hard to acquire.

Cats. How much would people pay for one? And would she be able to stand the yowling all the way to Deadwood? Or would they eventually settle down and endure the journey without complaint? These were questions Swede had planned to discuss with Red tonight, now that the other teamsters had turned in and it was only the two of them sitting by the fire. But Red's reaction changed her mind.

Swede looked away. She set the puppy down and fiddled with her pipe while Red played with Eva. And she decided she would wait to discuss the matter of cats with Tom English, a man with some ability to think beyond what everyone else had always done.

Maybe Tom would want the dog.

"Look at that," Tallent said. He set Eva on the ground only to have her pull herself up and stand, wobbling as she clung to his knee. "Won't be long and she'll be walking."

Swede nodded. "Yah." Only yesterday Eva had gripped the edge of her coffee box and pulled herself up on her sturdy little legs. Wobbling and bobbing her head, she'd screeched with joy and called out, "Mor-mor-mor" as she pumped her little legs up-down, up-down, up-down. It wouldn't be long, Swede realized, and she would have to improvise some way to keep the little doll from tumbling out on her head. So many children were lost beneath the wheels of wagons. Swede did not think she would survive such a horrible thing happening to her Eva.

Drawing on her pipe, Swede pondered the future. Perhaps Tom English could help her devise a way to keep Eva safe. And a way to haul cats. Red Tallent might think the idea cause for laughter, but he'd been a drifter all his life. He knew nothing of making a home. He'd never battled mice in his pantry, never had to fish a dead one out of a crock of sourdough starter, never had a wife to teach him a different view of life. She didn't know if Tom English had ever made a home or battled mice in a pantry or had a wife, but for some reason she felt that he would understand. And even if he didn't understand about rescuing starving puppies and hauling cats . . . he wouldn't laugh at her.

CHAPTER 8

As ye would that men should do to you,
do ye also to them likewise.

Luke 6:31

"G-g-good morning," Freddie said as he sat beside a roaring campfire clutching a blanket around him.

Mattie stepped out of her tent onto ground that was white with snow. She looked up at the gray sky and two tiny pinpricks of cold bit her face as fresh snowflakes drifted down. "Oh, Freddie," she said, putting her hand on his shoulder, "you're half frozen. I'm glad you stayed that first night, but it's been a couple of days now and I'm fine. You didn't have to stay through a snowstorm!"

"Well s-s-sure I did, Mattie," Freddie said through his shivers. "I s-said I would."

The boy's simple sincerity brought tears to her eyes. She'd never met anyone like Freddie Jannike. When he said he would do something, he did it, and whether it was difficult or whether it inconvenienced him just didn't seem to matter. How ironic that of all the men in Deadwood who swaggered down the street flaunting their six-shooters and bragging about their finds and their conquests, simpleminded Freddie Jannike, the kid they ignored and made fun of, was more of a man than any of them. She patted his shoulder. "Well, come in and warm up."

Perched atop Mattie's closed supply box, Freddie was soon not only warm, but hungry. Mattie made flapjacks atop the small camp stove. And then made another batch. And then another. "You must have a hollow leg," she teased.

"No," Freddie said, holding up one leg. "But Mr. Tuttle at the hotel does. He showed me."

"What?"

"He has a wooden leg and one time I was bringing in a deer I shot and Mr. Tuttle was sitting on the back stoop with his leg off and when he went to put it back on I saw it was hollow and he had some money hidden in it." Freddie smiled. "It might be good to have a hollow leg."

"For money?"

"Naw." He shook his head. "I don't need money. Mor takes care of that for me. And gold dust just makes people mean. Besides, gold weighs too much to hide it in a hollow leg." He thought for a moment. "I know." He smiled. "*Candy*. That's what I'd keep in a hollow leg."

"What kind?"

"All kinds." He stood up abruptly. "I got to go now, Mattie, but thank you for breakfast."

"Thank you again for protecting me," Mattie said. "I think you just might be my hero, Freddie Jannike."

He turned bright red. Ducking out of the tent, he headed up the gulch.

Mattie called after him. "Aren't you going back into town?"

Freddie turned around. "Not until I check around," he replied. "I'll look for stepping in the snow. If there's no stepping and Brady Sloan is shot then you don't have to be afraid anymore."

"Have you heard how Mr. Sloan is doing?" She was surprised

at how often over the last couple of days she'd thought about that, alternately thinking she'd go into town herself and then talking herself out of it. After all, she'd acted in self-defense. But it still bothered her when she thought about Sloan's suffering. She was glad Tom English had given her rock salt instead of something more lethal, and she wondered if she would ever actually be able to shoot anyone with her pocket pistol. Hopefully she would never have to find out. Hopefully the incident with Sloan would be sufficient to make whatever point needed to be made so that everyone left Matt the Miner alone.

"Yesterday when he was working on the store, Aron said Mr. Sloan will be all right. It took the doctor a long time to get all the salt out of him but once he did and washed him up he felt a lot better. He still has that big hurt where the wadding hit him and he's moving really slow but he'll be all right."

Mattie nodded as Freddie turned to check for footprints. "Thank you again for staying up here until things settled down," she said. Maybe she would give him whatever gold she found today as a way of saying thanks. And she'd tell him to get himself some candy.

But then she found her first pea-sized nugget.

I am going to be rich. It really is happening. Mattie didn't know if her hands trembled from the cold or from the excitement of finally finding her first nugget. It snowed off and on for another day and night after Freddie went back into Deadwood, but Mattie remained resolute, panning for gold several hours a day in spite of the cold and rejoicing in the discovery of more nuggets. She was finally seeing the possibilities of the claim.

She imagined digging test holes down to the bedrock and wondered if Freddie would be willing to help. If her luck held she'd be able to pay him. Then Freddie could buy his own candy and contribute to Swede's savings without combing the hills for game. She would discuss it with Swede first, as soon as the freighters got back into town at the end of June. In the meantime, she was thrilled with her success. But still, her angst over Dillon's missing gold would not die.

As she worked her claim, she remembered snippets of things Dillon had said in his letters. If only she'd kept them. But it was important for Jonas to believe Dillon was gone for good, so Mattie had paid the postmaster to keep her mail a secret, she'd never read Dillon's letters at Jonas's, and she'd destroyed each one as soon as she'd read it.

The claim is giving us more than I ever dreamed, he'd written. *If it keeps up we are going to be rich.* Alone on her claim, Mattie began to wake up in the middle of the night, transitioning from a dream about gold into a memory or a question.

What was it Brady Sloan had said? *"I only wanted to borrow . . ."* She could not put the suspicion to rest that Sloan had something to do with the disappearance of Dillon's gold. She couldn't let him get away with it. It was too bad Deadwood didn't have a sheriff she could appeal to.

What about Aron Gallagher? The night of the shooting, Gallagher had left her campfire on his way to talk to Sloan about his eternal soul. Maybe, Mattie thought, just maybe Sloan had confessed. And what if that confession included information about Dillon's gold?

It was time to head back into town.

When Tom English said he could have Swede's store finished in a matter of weeks, Mattie hadn't believed him. But he'd done it. Swede's once-empty lot now boasted a solid two-story building with merchandise displayed behind the windows and an *Open* sign hanging above the front door.

Stepping inside, Mattie surveyed the unfinished interior. Tom, wearing a sturdy shopkeeper's apron while he sanded a substantial counter, waved hello even as he spoke to the two men watching him. "Swede will be back by the end of the month, and we'll have everything you need. And yes, we will meet the competition's price. Be sure to come down for opening day. Aunt Lou is overseeing an outdoor pig roast."

"Free beer?" one of the men asked.

Tom stopped sanding. "Now, you know what Swede thinks of strong drink. But we'll have cold lemonade, and there has been talk of *ice cream*."

With a grumbling comment about teetotalers, the men nodded at Mattie and exited the store.

"Well, if it isn't Matt the Miner," Tom said. Taking one last swipe at the counter, he laid the sandpaper down and ran his hand along the grain, nodding with satisfaction. He patted the smooth surface. "I've been hoping to get everything varnished before Swede gets back. And I just might make it." He motioned around the huge space. "Think Swede will be pleased?"

"She'll be thrilled," Mattie said. "It's a fine store."

"Glad to see you survived the snow up in the wilderness."

"It wasn't bad," Mattie said. "The little stove in the tent does a good job of keeping things warm. Poor Freddie about froze out by the campfire, though."

"I heard."

"He seems to think it's his sacred obligation to be my guard dog. I feel terrible about it. I didn't even know it snowed until I opened the tent flap and there he was, shivering. I hope he doesn't get sick."

"Freddie's as healthy as a horse and none the worse for wear."

"Thank goodness." Mattie opened the bag she'd carried into town and pulled out her wooden dust-catcher.

English took the lid off and whistled low. "Someone had a good week on the claim."

"Can you tell me what it's worth?"

"Of course." He paused. "But you can trust the bank, you know.

They'll weigh it before you deposit it and give you a receipt so you have proof of exactly how much you put in the safe."

Mattie shook her head. "I just need to learn how to estimate weight and value so I can keep my own accounting." She pointed at the dust-catcher. "Those flakes are bigger than anything I've taken in at the store."

Crossing to the opposite side of the store, Tom emptied the gold onto one side of the scale sitting atop another counter and began to set weights on the empty pan. Presently he looked up, smiling. "Well, Miss O'Keefe, at seventeen dollars an ounce you're looking at about forty-five dollars. Which is very good work for an inexperienced miner."

She couldn't hide her disappointment.

"Wages around here average a couple of dollars a day for everyone but skilled miners. So if you had a paying job, you'd be looking at maybe thirty dollars every couple of weeks. You're way ahead mining. Assuming, of course, there's more gold to be had on Mattie's Claim." He opened a drawer and pulled out the same soft leather drawstring bag she used when she worked in the store. "Even if you want to keep using Freddie's dust-catcher, you should still have insurance in case the lid he carved comes off. You can put the whole thing in here."

"What do I owe you?" Mattie asked as she put the bag around her neck.

"Another beautiful smile," Tom said, pouring her gold back into the wooden dust-catcher and handing it over.

Mattie tucked the leather bag inside her chemise before asking, "Is there any chance you'd know where Aron Gallagher is?"

"I haven't seen him this morning. He's been staying pretty close to Doc Reeves's recently. I think he's hoping to reel in a lost lamb."

"*Thievin' varmint* is more like it," Mattie said. When Tom didn't comment she continued, "I'm grateful I had that shotgun, by the way."

"Do you need more rock salt?"

Mattie shook her head. "I doubt anyone's going to try that again."

Tom smiled. "You've got a point there. But just the same—"

A group of miners came in the front door. They were laughing and joking and cursing about something one of them had just said, but the minute they caught sight of Mattie all speech stopped. One of the younger ones nudged the one standing next to him and muttered something under his breath. "Ma'am," they all said, and took off their hats and stood to one side of the door.

Mattie nodded and, with a glance at Tom, left the store. She hesitated just outside the front door. *Forty-five dollars.* For hours and hours of backbreaking work. Once again, Dillon's letters came to mind. As did the reminder of her nightly earnings in Abilene.

She glanced up the street toward the Badlands. At a dollar a dance she could easily bring in several hundred dollars in three weeks. Of course she'd have to put up with being pawed and— *No.* With a little shiver, she put the thought out of her mind.

She stepped into the street and headed for the Grand Central Hotel. Aunt Lou would be busy in the kitchen. Maybe she would want some help. Aron Gallagher would likely show up there before the end of the day, and with a belly full of Aunt Lou's cooking, maybe he'd be more inclined to talk about Brady Sloan.

A few days out of Sidney, the lone stranger who'd been traveling alongside the freighters invited himself to join the men sitting around Swede's campfire. She'd noticed him before, but he'd spent his time around other campfires, and she was fine with that. There was something about him that made her uncomfortable, and it had nothing to do with the hook that had at some point in the past replaced the man's left hand. No, it was something else. Something less tangible. As she watched him, Swede realized the man never looked relaxed astride his fine bay gelding, but Swede didn't think it had anything to do with his ability as a rider.

The horse was spirited, but the stranger didn't seem to have any particular trouble controlling him. Still, he rode leaning slightly forward, as if by doing so he could make them all go faster. Swede would not have been surprised if the stranger had simply kicked his horse to a gallop and disappeared into the distance one day. That would have been foolish, but fools were not in short supply out here in the West.

Today, as the bullwhackers all the way down the freight line shouted to their teams to stop for their midday break, the stranger dismounted and walked with Red toward Swede's campfire.

The closer Tallent got, the louder Eva babbled and the more energy she put into her latest little "up-down" routine while she grasped the edge of her cradle. As for the pup, he positioned himself between Swede's wagon and the approaching men and began to bark. It was odd behavior. The pup had never barked at Tallent.

"Shoosh," Swede hollered, even as she bent down to swoop the pup into her arms. He lay quietly, except for a barely perceptible growl as he watched Tallent and the stranger head to the wagon. When Tallent picked Eva up, the stranger said something to Eva and chucked her under the chin. She smiled at him but leaned into Red in a sudden and uncharacteristic bout of shyness.

When the puppy began to wriggle to be put down, Swede set him alongside Eva's cradle in the wagon. Immediately he raised up on his haunches and, bracing his front paws against the wagon-box sides, barked again. It took more than a little scolding to settle him.

Finally, Tallent introduced the stranger as Mr. James Saddler. Swede was obliged to invite him to share the midday meal around her campfire. It was her turn and she was not about to be openly rude to a man just because the puppy didn't seem to like him and she didn't like the way he sat a horse.

"I'm afraid I've been caught unawares with the length of the journey," Saddler said. "Mr. Tallent thought you'd be open to the idea of boarding me the rest of the way. I hope he's right."

Swede shrugged. "Two dollars a day vould do it," she said. It was more than they charged in town and she knew that, but this wasn't town and she was hoping Saddler would turn her down. He didn't, and so Swede determined to make the best of it, reminding herself that God was bringing some unexpected income her way, that she should be thankful, and that perhaps she was wrong about the stranger.

"Thank you," Saddler said.

"Tak oo," Eva echoed, and everyone laughed.

After the meal everyone headed back up the line to get things moving again, and Saddler went after his horse. Swede watched him remove the hobbles and climb aboard. He was an elegant man with impeccable manners and plenty of money. And she did not like him one bit.

CHAPTER 9

Moreover He said to me, "Son of man, take into your heart
all My words which I will speak to you, and listen closely.
And . . . speak to them and tell them, whether they listen or not,
'Thus says the Lord God.'"

Ezekiel 3:10–11

Mattie didn't have to wait for Aron Gallagher to show up at Aunt Lou's. As she made her way along the side of the hotel toward the back door, she caught a glimpse of him through a screened window. He was spreading jelly on a biscuit while Aunt Lou talked.

"Now, don't you think that way," the old woman was saying. "Some of the hearts in this place are so stony, why, I doubt they'd listen if the Lord Jesus himself climbed up on that box to preach."

"I know you're right," Gallagher said, "but I still can't help thinking—" He paused in midsentence and turned around, following Aunt Lou's gaze to where Mattie stood on the back stoop, feeling more than a little like an eavesdropper.

"How's them biscuits bakin'?" Aunt Lou called, and waved her inside.

Mattie nodded at Gallagher, who had jumped to his feet the instant she stepped into the kitchen. She untied her bonnet and hung it on one of the hooks inside the back door as she talked. "All right, I guess. The McKays are about to eat me out of tent and flour sack. If that's any indication, you taught me well." She motioned for Gallagher to sit back down. "Actually, I've been looking for you. I wanted to ask you something."

Aunt Lou plopped a mug of coffee on the table. "Set yourself down, honey."

Mattie hesitated. "Only if I can help you with something while I sit."

Aunt Lou handed her a bowl of garden peas. "Didn't think they'd grow, but they did. You can shell 'em while you and the reverend talk."

"Please, Aunt Lou. You know I'm not ordained." Once again, Gallagher honestly seemed embarrassed by the title.

"Well, of course you're ordained," Aunt Lou insisted. "Ordained by God, and that oughta be good enough for any man."

Gallagher shook his head and smiled at Mattie. "You'd think I'd have learned by now that it's no use arguing with Aunt Lou." He reached for his own cup of coffee. "You wanted to talk to me?"

Mattie nodded. "About Brady Sloan."

"It'll be a while before he's completely healed, but he'll be able to work again in a few days. It's good of you to ask after him."

"I'm not asking *after* him," Mattie said. "I'm asking *about* him. Has he confessed to what he was doing at my claim the other night? I've come to believe that he didn't know I was there that night. All that means, though, is he wasn't attacking a defenseless woman, which is little comfort. If you know what he was really up to, I'd appreciate—"

Gallagher's blue-gray eyes twinkled. He was grinning.

"Have I said something amusing?"

"I think so." He pointed at her. "Defenseless woman? *You?*"

"Of course I'm not defenseless," Mattie retorted. "I didn't say I was defenseless. I said Sloan might have thought of me that way. Assuming he was after me—which I don't think he was. But that begs the question—what, exactly, *was* he after in my tent?" She paused. "He must know something about my brother's gold. And I'd like to know what it is." She met Gallagher's gaze. "Will you ask him about it? For me?"

She hadn't spent years smoothing ruffled feathers and convincing men to gamble more for nothing. She knew exactly how to look at a man to entice him into doing what she wanted, and she used it on Aron Gallagher. Full strength.

Gallagher leaned back in his chair. He rubbed his chin. Tugged on one earlobe. Cleared his throat. "An honest man doesn't talk behind people's backs, Miss O'Keefe. If you have questions for Brady Sloan, you need to be the one asking them." He stood up slowly, stretching as if the conversation were over and he was contemplating a nap. He reached for his hat and set it on his head, tugging on the brim until it came down over his gray eyes. No, blue. His eyes were blue. She couldn't decide. It didn't matter. *Get ahold of yourself. You're letting him get away.*

"What kind of preacher just walks away when a lady asks for help?"

"Well, I guess by the way you said that, the right answer would be a worthless one." He smiled again. Shrugged. Nodded at Aunt Lou. "See, Aunt Lou? Just what I was saying when Miss O'Keefe here came knocking. I'm worthless as a preacher."

Aunt Lou crossed the kitchen and, placing both her palms on Gallagher's shoulders, looked up into his eyes. "Don't you be calling yourself worthless, young man. I won't stand for it." She patted his broad chest. "You got the heart of a man who loves God. You remain faithful and He will do mighty things. You think that little shepherd boy named David could figure how God was gonna get him outta that field and onto a *throne?*"

Gallagher bent down and kissed Aunt Lou on the cheek. "I'd like to think my mother was like you, Aunt Lou."

A flustered Aunt Lou slapped Gallagher on the shoulder. "Now, you go on," she said. "It's Sunday and God expects a good word for His side of the street today." She shooed him toward the door. "I'll keep you a piece of my chess pie for later."

At the door, Gallagher turned back to Mattie. "I won't interrogate Brady for you, but I will walk you down to Doc Reeves's office if you want to talk to him yourself."

———

Mattie and the preacher were not twenty feet from Dr. Reeves's small building when the air filled with curses and a barrel-shaped man across the way threw a pile of rags into the middle of the street. As it turned out, the rags were attached to a human. When the human lifted his mud-caked face and stared back at the building he'd just been dragged out of, Mattie couldn't help but wonder how anything that underfed and filthy could have done something so heinous as to get tossed out of a saloon as pathetic as the one called the Cricket.

The raggedy man blinked his eyes a few times and looked around. Most people in the street were simply walking around him as if they encountered such events often. Which, Mattie supposed, was not far from the truth. But suddenly the man in the street called to Gallagher.

"Aronnnnnn . . ." He swore an apology. "I shouldn'ta gone in there. . . ." He hiccuped, then tried to get up, but was clearly too drunk to manage.

"Oh, Brady." Gallagher almost whispered the name, but the tone of sadness and disappointment was undeniable. "Excuse me," he said to Mattie. Touching the brim of his hat by way of taking leave, he headed over and hauled the drunk up to help him out of the street. The effort was in vain. Sloan was too drunk to even stumble along beside him.

When he fell forward onto all fours and vomited, then fell face first into it, Mattie backed away. Gallagher, on the other hand, knelt beside the drunken sot and, pulling a kerchief out of his own pocket, wiped the man's face. Grabbing Sloan's arms, he lifted him into a sitting position, then crouched down and hefted him over his shoulder. He glanced over at Mattie. "I'll take him back to the doc's," he said, "but I don't imagine he'll be fit to talk to anyone until sometime tomorrow. Maybe even the next day."

Mattie watched as the preacher staggered toward the doctor's small building and pounded on the door. It opened, and he disappeared inside with his foul burden.

———

"Slow down, honey," Aunt Lou said. "You just *knead* the dough. Ain't no call to beat it to death."

Mattie paused. "I'm sorry." She went back to kneading, and in a few minutes had formed four loaves of bread.

"You gonna tell me what the matter is?"

"I already told you," Mattie said. "Brady Sloan's passed out drunk. If I want to talk to him, I'll have to make another trip down from my claim in a couple of days."

"Oh, I heard what you said. But that ain't what's the matter."

Mattie pursed her lips. She shook her head and huffed around the kitchen for a few more minutes, washing out the bread bowl, scraping the table clean, hauling a bucket of kitchen slops out to the hogpen in the back. Finally, when she got back inside, she blurted it out. "I just don't understand him. He's a darned fool if he thinks he's going to make some kind of heroic difference in the world hauling sporting girls back to the Badlands and standing on a box preaching to the likes of Brady Sloan."

Aunt Lou flipped the meat in her giant frypan before saying, "You know anyplace that needs changing more than Deadwood?"

"You can't change these people," Mattie said. "Even the ones who *seem* nice are usually just waiting to gain everyone's trust so they can make their move on the rest of us."

"Aron Gallagher," Aunt Lou insisted, "is a good man tryin' his best to do good work here."

"Hmph," Mattie grunted. "Show me a good man, and I'll show you a good actor."

Aunt Lou stared at Mattie, her expression changing gradually from frustration to gentleness and a compassion that was harder to stand than disapproval. "I don't know what kind of man you've known who called hisself a preacher, honey, but whoever it was—" She broke off. "I have seen *this* reverend give the last penny in his pocket to someone who was hungry. He chops wood to pay for the meals he eats in my kitchen, and he's never once left off choppin' before there was a stack of wood twice as high as what we agreed on. I know for a fact that he's already given away every cent your Mr. English paid him for buildin' that store—because he brought it to me and asked me to do it for him so no one would know he was doing it." Aunt Lou paused.

"And as for making a difference for the folks here in Deadwood, it may be hard, but it is *not* impossible. Not with God. The Good Book says that." Aunt Lou walked over and patted her hand. "You're not really so angry with the reverend, honey. You're angry because you've been done wrong—by more than just Brady Sloan, if I know anything."

"I have a right to know what Sloan was up to sneaking around my tent," Mattie insisted. "And whether that preacher helps me or not—" She broke off. How could she say the things she suspected about Gallagher when Aunt Lou had just given witness to the man's good deeds? She shook her head. "All I'm saying is if a woman doesn't stand up for herself, there are plenty who will take advantage. And that's a lesson from the past I can't just forget because some good-looking preacher does a few good deeds."

"I understand what you're saying. But just under the surface of that common sense of yours is a layer of somethin' that—" Aunt Lou's voice was gentle as she continued, "Honey, if I was to take out on this here city what's been done to me in the past, I'd be slittin' white men's throats left and right. And you know what? That wouldn't do a thing to change the fact that I was done wrong, and the men that done it are still walkin' the face of this earth and likely forgot it ever happened. I can't change the past and you can't, either. Maybe you can't help feeling angry about it. But you *can* stop punishing the good men in your life today because of the bad ones in the past. And you *can* learn to trust again. With the good Lord's help."

Mattie only nodded. Aunt Lou had witnessed the preacher's good deeds. She couldn't argue with that. And Aunt Lou was right about something else—she *was* suspicious of men in general. What Aunt Lou didn't realize, however, was that her suspicions about the preacher were based on years of living with and around cheats, gamblers, and pretenders. What Aunt Lou didn't realize was that before showing up in Deadwood, Aron Gallagher had almost certainly been one—or all—of those things. Of course Mattie couldn't say *that* without revealing her own past . . . so she kept quiet, finished helping Aunt Lou, and left the hotel no wiser about what Brady Sloan had been up to than if she'd stayed up on the gulch prospecting.

Mattie had no intention of listening to another sermon as she rounded the back corner of the hotel building and headed toward the street. But then she heard Gallagher's voice asking, "Do any of you here in Deadwood think you have *enough?*" She stopped short of the street, out of sight of the Sunday crowd gathered to hear the preacher. She relaxed against the rough board walls of the hotel exterior and listened.

The preacher repeated his question. "Do any of you here in Deadwood think you have *enough?*"

"Enough what?" someone said.

"Enough of anything."

"Well," the same voice replied, "I've already had about enough of you."

People laughed.

Gallagher began to read. " 'He that loveth silver shall not be satisfied with silver; nor he that loveth abundance with increase.' " He paused. Mattie could imagine him staring over the gathered crowd as he said, "One of the wealthiest men in history learned that when a man's goal is earthly treasure, he never has enough. That man left his wisdom for us in his writings in the Bible in hopes that future generations would learn that seeking wealth is just so much striving after wind. But Solomon wasn't the only one to say that. The disciple Matthew was even more blunt about the topic of earthly possessions. He said that we should not be concerned with laying up treasures on earth. He said we should be looking to eternity."

"I don't know where I'm gonna spend next Friday night," someone hollered. "I got no time to be worryin' over eternity."

"No one has to *worry* over it," Gallagher replied. " 'These things,' John says, 'have I written unto you that believe on the name of the Son of God; that ye may *know* that ye have eternal life.' "

The words rankled at first. How could anyone be so cocksure of something as mysterious as life after death? And yet, as she peeked around the corner of the building, Mattie saw no hint of arrogance in the preacher. She thought back to his rescuing the whore from the street . . . his kneeling in the filth beside Brady Sloan. If he was scamming Deadwood, it was a strange sort of scam. Especially in light of what Aunt Lou had just said about Gallagher giving all his money away. What made a man willing to do something like that?

As for his comment about people never having enough, maybe that was true of some folks, but she wasn't like that. She'd never been a greedy person. She'd know when she had enough. In fact, if her claim kept paying out, *enough* wasn't far in the future.

———

When it began to rain in the night. Mattie woke with a start, but as the gentle shower pattered against her claim tent, she snuggled back beneath her blankets, comforted by the murmuring of a gentle wind, dreaming of spring flowers and warm breezes. When morning came and it was still raining, she used the few sticks of wood inside the tent to build a fire in the little stove and make coffee. Once the coffee was ready, she tied the tent flap back as far as possible to let in the daylight while she cooked flapjacks on the tiny stove.

She had just closed the supply box and perched atop it to eat when the wind came up and rain began to fall in earnest. Closing the tent flap, Mattie lit a lamp and wondered what she would do all day. If only she had a book. In Abilene she'd spent countless pleasant hours reading. But there were no books up here on the claim. Maybe she should slip and slide her way into town again and make another attempt to talk to Sloan. No, it was probably best to stay put. Tom wouldn't have enough customers in this weather to need her help, and Sloan wasn't going anywhere. She could wait for dryer weather. After holding her plate and fork outside the tent flap long enough for the rain to rinse them off, she set them down. Returning to the cot in the corner, she lay back down and dozed.

When the rain didn't let up, Mattie donned Dillon's rubber slicker and, rolling up the sleeves, pulled on her boots and hat and headed outside. The creek was running deep and fast. On the claim below hers, the McKays were mucking about, cursing the rain for filling the holes they'd dug. After a few minutes, the three of them threw their shovels down in disgust and prepared to head down the gulch and into town. Finn hollered an invitation for Mattie to join them. A day in one saloon or another seemed to be the McKays' antidote for every trouble. Wondering if they had ever mined for a complete week, Mattie hollered back, "Thanks, but no."

Not long after the McKays left, she realized it was almost impossible to do any panning wearing the oversized slicker. She finally gave up and, stomping back to her tent, huddled inside drinking coffee. Early in the afternoon the rain began to let up. Freddie slid down the gulch from higher up with a deer carcass slung over his shoulder. Hanging it from a tree growing near the rock wall of the gulch, he dressed it, burying the entrails and cutting away a generous portion of meat for Mattie before showing her how to rig a tarp over her campfire so she could cook.

"Now you know why I made you stack some wood inside," he said as he built a fire with her dry wood and set the deer meat to cooking.

Mattie nodded at the stew pot. "I'll be able to eat for a week off that. Thank you."

After Freddie had slung what was left of the deer over his shoulder and made his way down toward town, Mattie kept busy tending her fire. She tried digging a test hole to see what it would be like "digging to bedrock," but everything she dug silted back in immediately. By what she imagined was about suppertime, she had given up on getting anything accomplished. After dishing up a small portion of venison stew for her supper, she slapped the lid back on the pot and settled it down in the coals to let it simmer through the night.

Closing her tent flap, she huddled in her tent rereading the letters she'd written to Dillon—he'd saved them all—and reliving the past, which was a terrible way to spend a rainy evening. She began to hum to herself. Finally, she gave the melody words and launched into one of the songs she and Dillon used to sing together. That night, she cried herself to sleep.

CHAPTER 10

Labour not to be rich . . . for riches certainly make themselves
wings; they fly away as an eagle toward heaven.

Proverbs 23:4–5

Swede's yellow braids trailed down her back and felt like two sodden ropes, flapping against her slicker as she grabbed a shovel out of her wagon and slowly, methodically, began to scrape at the ring of mud so thick it was threatening to clog up the wheel mechanism. She'd seen axles break at times like this, and she could not have that. She stood up straight and took a deep breath, thinking how her back hurt, how her shoulders burned from the constant battle to keep the wagons moving, how it was still so far to Deadwood.

Eva whimpered softly. Swede had tried to rig a tarp to keep the baby dry, but the wind was not cooperating and Eva's good spirits had been washed away by the incessant rain. Even the pup had been affected by the weather. Today he was hunkered down in the wagon box next to Eva.

Gloom hung over the long line of freighters thicker than the clouds in the skies above them. Making time on the trail was often the difference between a successful season and a dismal one, and they were going to land in Deadwood at least a week behind schedule. It was already June 6, and if winter came early, the last run of the season next fall might encounter snow.

Taking another swipe at the mud caked on the wheel, Swede pulled away another layer of gumbo. The world needed rain, but it would be so much better if the rain could have waited another week. Once she was back in Deadwood she would be so busy setting up her new store she wouldn't care if it rained every day.

Yes, Swede thought, it would be good to get home, even if Deadwood was to be only a temporary home for her family. She took another stab at a clod of mud, scolding herself aloud. "Stop thinking about selling vat you have not even seen and verk on getting yourself unstuck from dis rain-soaked mud-caked miserable-excuse-for-a-territory called Dakota."

Hearing Eva giggle, Swede looked up to see Red Tallent headed her way, shovel in hand.

"You have your own troubles," Swede said. "You don't have to bother vit mine."

"I'm not botherin'," Red said, and attacked the mud on the wheel opposite the one Swede was trying to clear. "I'm belly-achin'." At Swede's look of surprise, Tallent explained, "Mr. James Saddler has apparently decided he's had enough of our company. He rode out this morning with not so much as a fare-thee-well."

"Why does dat concern you?"

"Well, it don't, really," Tallent said. "I guess I shoulda known by the way he was dressed he wasn't the type to pick up a shovel and help dig us all out. But I'm missin' a sack of jerky and a bag of oats. And that's just not neighborly."

Swede shook her head. She worked at the wheel for a while. Finally, she said, "I never liked dat man." She looked off to the north, wondering what bad business James Saddler might have in the Black Hills. If James Saddler was really his name.

Rain, rain, and more rain transformed the Deadwood Gulch landscape into a morass of mud that clung to Mattie's boots so that after walking only a few yards she felt like she was dragging a ten-pound weight around each foot. And there was no just shaking it off. Oh no. It had to be *scraped* off. Hugh McKay warned her that if she didn't get it off before it dried, she'd have boots "set in hardened mortar."

By Thursday, when the rain still hadn't let up, Mattie decided to try to talk to Brady Sloan again. Knowing the mud would essentially ruin her only skirt, she didn't bother to change out of her Matt the Miner clothing, but slipped and slid down into town dressed like a man. The streets were clogged with slicker-clad men sloshing their way into this saloon or that. It was almost cheering to hear the music emanating from the Green Front as Clyde Fellows pounded the keys of the only piano in town. Mattie went straight to Doc Reeves's, but Sloan wasn't there.

"I don't think he's in Deadwood anymore," the doctor said. "The last thing I heard him say was that he was too weak to resist the temptations of this place and he needed to get away from it."

Mattie's next stop was the tiny office where Ellis Gates was huddled smoking and trying the age-old ninety-proof way to keep warm. He wasn't drunk, but neither was he helpful. "Don't know a thing," he said, all the while eyeing the pocket where Mattie had secreted her Colt.

"Didn't you tell me he had a partner?" Mattie asked, and slipped her hand in the pocket Gates was watching just in case it would convince him to tell her anything.

"I told you," Gates said. "I don't know a thing. Haven't heard from or seen either of those boys since you shot Sloan."

"What was the partner's name?"

"Will Browning. And as I said, I haven't heard from or seen him." Gates belched.

"I thought a miner had to represent work on his claim to keep it."

"That's right," he said with a nod. "At least a day of pick and shovel every week—or so."

"But I haven't seen anyone up there, and I've been on my claim every day since about the eighth of May," Mattie protested. "Today is June eighth. Seems to me that claim above me has been abandoned." And did that mean she could get her hands on a second claim? Maybe Sloan's tomfoolery would work to her advantage.

Gates shrugged. "Don't know nothin' 'bout that," he said. "Maybe they've been working the public roads. That stands for 'representing work' just as well."

She'd forgotten about that. "What road would they be working?"

"Well, certain parties keep mining away the Deadwood-Gayville road looking for placer gold. There's always work needed to keep that one passable. Maybe the boys' claim wasn't paying and they decided to work for grub."

Gates was being polite, but it was obvious he didn't know any more, or if he did, he wasn't going to share it with her. Leaving his office, Mattie picked her way through mudholes and rivulets of running water to Swede's store. She smiled the instant she was through the front door. The place was no longer an empty room. Tom had installed all the shelving and finished another counter since Sunday. He'd assembled the stove and was standing atop a ladder shoving a section of flue through a hole in the ceiling, where it would apparently pass through the upstairs hall and on up to the roof. Glancing up, Mattie could see the hole itself was bordered with metal flashing.

Tom paused in his maneuvering of the stovepipe long enough to glance down at her. "What brings Matt the Miner to town on such a day?"

"Rain," Mattie replied. "Rain and gumbo, rain and boredom. And more rain. And I was hoping to talk to Brady Sloan."

"I assume by the way you just said that, you've been disappointed." After adding another section to the flue, Tom braced the stovepipe against the highest step of the ladder and began to climb down.

"You'd be right," Mattie said. "And can I help with that?" She pointed up at the stovepipe.

"Well, I've a bit more work to do on this upstairs. Could you mind the store?"

"Glad to," she said. "I hope Freddie isn't out hunting in this weather. He'll catch pneumonia."

"Well, aren't you just the little mother hen," Tom teased. "No. In fact, he'll probably be back before too long. I sent him to see if he could find Aron to help me finish this." Just then Gallagher and Freddie stomped in. Greeting Mattie, Gallagher followed Tom upstairs while Freddie climbed the ladder and maneuvered the stovepipe as directed by the two men waiting upstairs to extend it up and through the roof.

While the men worked, Mattie went to stand behind the counter by the gold scales. She could hear Gallagher and Tom talking and laughing. How different they were from the McKays, who blustered and hollered and swore their way through most workdays. Thinking about it, Mattie realized she'd never heard Tom or Gallagher say a harsh word, much less a swear word. They had an easy kind of friendship in spite of the fact that Tom displayed no interest in the religion Gallagher seemed eager to share with everyone in Deadwood.

Mattie's musings were interrupted by the arrival of several miners, more in search of a place to stay out of the rain than merchandise. She didn't know them, and their reaction to a woman dressed in overalls made her feel more like a circus act than a storekeeper. But apparently they recognized her.

"You must be the one that shot Brady Sloan full of rock salt," one said.

Mattie shrugged. "He's lucky it was only salt."

"Knocked him clean out of mining and into church from what I hear." The man's smile revealed a mouth crowded with crooked yellow teeth.

Mattie snorted. "The last time I saw him he was dead drunk in the middle of Main Street."

"I heard about that, too," the man said. He looked at his companion. "That preacher dragged him back to Doc's and paid the bill. Bought Sloan a horse so he could go home." He glanced outside. The rain had let up and the men headed back out the door.

Gallagher helped Brady Sloan leave town? Without so much as telling me? Without so much as giving me a chance to—

"Got it!" Gallagher's voice boomed from upstairs. Freddie climbed down the ladder as Tom and the preacher clomped back downstairs.

When Tom said something to Freddie about "seeing how she draws" and commenced to fiddling with the new stove, Mattie went to Gallagher. "So you bought Sloan a horse." He nodded. "And he's left town." When he nodded again, she bit her lip to keep from swearing even as she glared at him. Finally she said, "You—you knew I wanted to talk to him. You knew that."

"I did, but when a man wants to start fresh and he's already fallen away once, when he's ready to acknowledge his weakness, it's best to make a way for him to do the thing he needs to do before he—"

Mattie held up her hand. "Save it," she said. "Save it for some of your other churchgoing friends, *Reverend*." She spat the title out as if it were a swear word. "I thought maybe, just maybe, you were—" She broke off. "Never mind."

"There!" Tom English called out, and Mattie turned around to see the smile on his face as he looked down at the stove and then up toward the ceiling. "Draws fine." He patted Freddie on the back. "Thank you for your help. You, too, Aron. How about that game of checkers now?"

"You're on," Gallagher said. "In just a minute—soon as I make us some coffee," and with that he motioned for Mattie to follow him back into the combination storeroom-kitchen.

Mattie marched after him.

"A couple of good men I know were leaving town, and Brady was willing to go with them," Gallagher said. "He was hanging by a slim thread of hope, and I wanted to help him get out of town before he let go. So I bought him a horse and gave him a little Testament and sent him on his way."

"Well, now, isn't that just so sweet of you," Mattie snapped. She headed for the back door. "I'll be seeing you."

Gallagher's arm placed across the doorframe kept her from opening it. "If you'll let me finish, I'll—"

"You'll what?"

"I'll tell you how Brady reacted when I asked him what he was after up at your claim that night."

Mattie dropped her hand from the door handle.

"That's better. I know I told you I wouldn't do it, but the situation changed. He needed to leave and there was an opportunity, but there wasn't time to climb the gulch and retrieve you . . . so I asked him about that night and I believe what he told me."

"Which was—?"

"That he was so drunk he thought he was at his own tent. That all he was thinking about was falling into his bedroll and he had no intention of making trouble for anyone."

Mattie glowered. "And did he seem drunk to you that night?"

"Well, no," Gallagher said. The dimple in his cheek showed, although he managed not to smile as he continued, "But then a barrelful of rock salt would likely blow the liquor right out of any man." He cleared his throat. "You don't have to take my word for any of this." He reached into his shirt pocket and withdrew a smudged envelope. "I've been carrying this around since he left, waiting until I saw you." He handed her the envelope.

Mattie opened it and read. *I am sory for what I done. I wuz drunk.*

I didn't mean no harm and I don't blame you for shooting. Keep that rifle handy so you are ready in case innyone bothers you. I am sory.

"Well," Mattie said, and cleared her throat. She looked toward the front of the store. "I guess I owe you—and Sloan—an apology."

"I should have brought the note up to you," Gallagher said.

Mattie shrugged. "Can't blame you for not wanting to climb the gulch in this weather." She finally met his gaze just as Freddie's voice sounded from the doorway.

"Are we playing checkers or not?"

"You are," Mattie said abruptly and, stuffing Sloan's note in her pocket, nudged past Gallagher toward the huge stove dominating what would soon be Swede's kitchen at one end of the storeroom. She shooed Gallagher out without looking at him. "Go. I'll make your coffee before I leave for my claim." As soon as Gallagher and Freddie had retreated to the checkerboard, she looked around the room, noticing for the first time that Tom English's organizational abilities were evident here, too. He'd stacked three boxes on their sides to create a kitchen cupboard. He'd even hung an advertising calendar over the small kitchen table. The place was becoming downright cozy.

Laughter rang out from the front room as the men settled in. Something about that sound made Mattie think of Dillon. Swiping at the threatening tears, she considered how Swede and Freddie and little Eva were going to have themselves a nice home here in Deadwood—what with this new store and the sleeping quarters upstairs and with friends like Tom English and Aron Gallagher helping run the store and coming by to play checkers. She was glad for them all. So glad she almost cried. Again.

———

Back up at her claim, Mattie woke the next morning as suddenly as if a rooster had flown into her tent and crowed. For a moment she lay with her eyes closed thinking she'd probably only dreamed that the rain had stopped. And then when she realized it wasn't a dream, she waited, expecting that the silence wouldn't last for long. False hopes had been raised several times over the past week, when clouds split to show a strip of blue sky, only to gather again and pour down rain with a vengeance. She got out of bed, full of hope, and by noon the sky was a startling shade of blue, the sun was shining, and the birds were singing.

With the lifting of her spirits, Mattie decided it was time to make the tent her own. With Freddie's help she'd hauled a few empty boxes up to the claim, and with a little work she could make some sense of the jumble of things inside the tent. While she'd managed to keep her bedding mostly dry, thanks to the way Dillon had created his bed—building a wooden frame and tacking a tarp to it as a liner before adding a straw-filled tick and other bedding—everything still smelled musty. She began to haul things outside, spreading blankets and comforters and towels on the rocks and bushes bordering the claim. She dragged all the paraphernalia in Dillon's supply box outside and, using the closed box as a workbench, hammered some empty cracker boxes together to create a cupboard like the one Tom had built for Swede.

She hauled pail after pail of water from the creek and scrubbed surfaces that hadn't seen a scrub brush probably since Dillon moved onto the claim. And then, in a burst of enthusiasm, she decided to haul the bed frame out, too. It wouldn't hurt to rinse off the rubber liner and air out the straw tick. Getting it outside took some doing, but she managed and, leaning the frame against a tree, went to work rinsing the tarp. While it dried she went back inside. That's when she saw the round stove lid resting on the dirt beneath where the cot had been.

Reaching for the handle that had come with the camp stove, she knelt down and, inserting it into the notches in the lid, slid it over to reveal . . . a hole filled with water. But not only water. Five small bottles nestled against one another at the bottom. She reached for the clear one first. Dillon had melted what looked to be candle wax around the cork, and it had worked to keep the flakes of gold inside dry. With a little shiver, Mattie set the clear bottle down and pulled out the others—one green, two blue, one amber—each one heavy, each one sealed with wax, each one full. Gold dust. Gold flakes. Gold nuggets. Her heart pounding, Mattie sat back on the damp earth.

Dillon. Oh . . . Dillon.

———

By evening Mattie had rearranged everything in her tent except the location of the bed. Sleeping over the cache was an excellent idea. Besides that, the cot was positioned to give her a clear shot at anyone who dared intrude. Did anyone suspect the cache beneath Dillon's bed frame? She would have to be more careful than ever. Careful to keep the Colt with her and careful to keep Bessie II not far away. Maybe she should reconsider loading the shotgun with something besides rock salt.

Mattie had contemplated all of this while she moved her newly scrubbed belongings back into the tent. The cracker box cupboard fit fine just to the left of the tent flap, where Dillon had kept his supply box. She shoved that all the way to the far back corner, where the top of it could serve as a dressing table or a desk. She would buy a mirror on her next trip into town and ask Swede to bring her some books on the next supply run. Then she'd be prepared to stay on the claim the next time it stormed. Maybe even through the winter if she could get Freddie to cut and stack a mountain of firewood.

As the day waned Mattie ducked back inside her tent, propped up the bed frame on a couple of sticks, and inspected the bottles by lamplight. She ran her fingers along the curve of the bases and peered at the contents, reminding herself they were real. It wasn't a dream anymore. She might be rich. The puzzle was *how* rich. Without weighing what was in those bottles, she couldn't know. But she couldn't just sashay into the bank and dump it all onto a scale.

Word would spread and she would be a target for every two-legged varmint in the area.

No, Mattie thought as she returned the bottles to the cache, slid the iron stove lid into place, and lowered the bed frame. *At least for now, no one must know.*

CHAPTER 11

*Deliver me, O Lord, from the evil man: preserve me from the
violent man; which imagine mischiefs in their heart.*

Psalm 140:1–2

She could afford a new life now. All the next week after finding
Dillon's cache, Mattie lay awake at night planning just how she
would handle it all, how she would have it valued, where she would
go, what she would do. It was a challenging week. The rains had
apparently washed new placer gold onto several of the claims. Hoots
and hollers went up from time to time about pea-sized nuggets and
newly discovered color in the quartz. All the while, Mattie crouched
in the cold stream and swirled sand into crescents, more often than
not finding gold at the tip of the moon in her pan. She smiled to
herself even as she thought, *No one must know.*

The McKays below her were having the time of their lives,
whooping about their good luck and shouting encouragement to
Mattie not to give up, that her turn would come. She did nothing to
keep them from feeling sorry for her. Poor Mattie O'Keefe, working
her brother's claim, coming to Deadwood expecting Eldorado and

finding her brother dead and no gold on deposit in the banks, no gold in the stream, nothing but a tent and a few basic tools.

And so, Mattie decided, it must remain. If anyone found out about Dillon's bottles, who knew what would happen? A lone woman the only thing standing in the way of a man and—how much?

How much? That was the question. How much was the gold in those bottles worth?

No one must know. Aunt Lou was too good at reading faces. Mattie would have to wait a few days before visiting her. Tom English was just too smart. He'd figure out something was up. And from what she'd heard him preach about, Aron Gallagher might try to convince her she should give it all away.

And so it was nearly a week after Mattie found Dillon's cache before she ventured into town, and when she did she carried only the dust-catcher Freddie had made inside the bag around her neck. Instead of going to the bank, Mattie asked Tom to weigh the gold, drumming her fingers on the counter as he set tiny weights on the scale.

"Well," Tom finally said when the pans were evenly suspended in the air above the base of the small scale. "I see why you're excited. That's about three hundred dollars." He looked up at her, his dark eyes serious. "And please tell me you aren't going to keep it up on the gulch."

"I'm not."

Tom smiled at her. "You're not?"

Mattie shook her head. "But I don't want word getting out that Mattie's Claim is paying well." She reached across and touched the back of Tom's hand. "You keep it. And credit my account."

"That's—crazy." Tom frowned. "Even if we did sell everything you'll ever need, it's too much money—"

"What could I possibly need that I can't get at Garth and Company Merchandise?"

Tom rattled off a list that ended with milk, eggs, and butter.

"I'm bartering with Aunt Lou for those things. She said she could use some help getting ready for the crowds on Sundays, so I'm going to come into town on Saturdays and help her and she'll pay me in eggs and butter. In fact, I'm headed over there just as soon as—" She steered the conversation away from herself and her gold. "Have you considered building a chicken coop out back? And a shelter for livestock? Swede could bring chickens and a couple of milk cows on her next run. I bet you'd sell all the butter and eggs they could produce."

"I'm sure you're right," Tom agreed. "Except I don't see myself milking cows," he said, holding up his hook, "and it wouldn't be fair to tie Freddie down to milking twice a day. He's a hunter at heart and always will be." He paused. "Actually, I have been thinking about something along those lines, though. There are acres of good grazing on the Belle Fourche north of here. Someone so inclined could start themselves a homestead, and Deadwood merchants would pay premium prices for everything they could raise. Of course that assumes the situation with the Sioux settles down." He shrugged. "I don't know if it'll work at all. But I've been thinking on it a lot lately. If we could partner with someone who'd supply fresh produce and meat, I think we could turn a very respectable profit—for both parties."

"I think Swede will love the idea," Mattie said, "and speaking of her, when do you think she'll pull back into town?"

Tom gazed toward the street. "Sooner than later, I hope. It seems like she's been gone for months. We talked about a grand opening on July Fourth. But if it rained south of here like it's been raining in Deadwood, the entire freight train will be mired down. Who knows when they'll finally get here."

"Well, she's got a wonderful surprise awaiting her," Mattie said. "You've built her a fine place."

"Couldn't have done it without Gallagher's help."

"Of course you could have. It just would have taken longer." As if he'd been waiting offstage to hear his name, Gallagher came in through the back door. He greeted Tom with, "Got that wood cut you wanted," before turning to Mattie. "When I had breakfast this morning Aunt Lou said you'd agreed to help her on Saturdays."

"She's seeing that I get paid in eggs and butter. I couldn't turn that down."

"I'll walk you over there if you—" Gallagher stared past Mattie toward the front door.

And just like that, the past Mattie had fled strode into the store.

———

She would have recognized him anywhere. Even if he'd cut the brown hair that hung in ringlets around his broad shoulders. Even if he'd stopped wearing the long, heavily embroidered buckskin coat or abandoned his gleaming ivory-gripped pistols—always worn butt out. In fact, Mattie would recognize Wild Bill Hickok if all she could see was his hands, because she'd spent more hours than she could count dealing cards to those hands down in Kansas, both before and after Bill's short stint as the sheriff of Abilene.

She shouldn't be surprised to see him here. After all, like so many of his kind, Bill was a rolling stone of a man who'd become famous by not putting down roots, by getting involved in startling situations that created fodder for news-hungry reporters fascinated by the breed of men who were part of the legendary and quickly disappearing Wild West. Deadwood was just the kind of place to attract a man like Wild Bill Hickok, and here he was, staring from her to Gallagher and back again, taking the measure of the situation before saying a word. Finally his thin lips curved upward in a smile and his mellow voice called her name. "Mattie." He nodded. "Good to see you."

Mattie could feel the blush rising to her cheeks even as she answered. "Hello, Bill." She glanced to where the woman who'd come in with Bill slouched, her hand resting lightly atop the butt of the gun resting in the holster slung around her narrow hips. Although Mattie had never met her, there was no mystery as to the identity of the trail-worn raggedy buckskin–clad woman the world knew as Calamity Jane. Mattie nodded at her even as Bill addressed the preacher.

"Aron," he said, "still on the straight and narrow, I presume."

"Doing my best, Bill," Gallagher said. And then they all just stood there staring at one another.

The uncomfortable silence was broken when Calamity Jane blustered, "Aron? Did he say *Aron?*" When Gallagher nodded, she continued. "Well, it's high time this hellhole got itself a man of the cloth. I heard about you from this son-of-a-straight-flush. You preachin' hereabouts on Sundays?"

"Yes, I—"

"Got yourself a proper church?"

"No, but—"

"Well, get ready to build one, 'cause we're gonna fix that. I'll pass the hat a time or two, and if the boys don't cough up enough, I'll draw on 'em."

"You don't have to—"

"Aw, I was just funnin' with ya," Calamity said. "I won't really force 'em at gunpoint. But I do like a good sermon. What time do you usually preach?"

"It depends," Gallagher said. "Sometimes midmorning, some-times—"

"Why so goldurned early?" Calamity interrupted. "Folks that need preachin' most ain't up till noon on Sunday." She slapped him on the back. "You make it after lunch and you'll get a better crowd." She winked at Mattie. "You tell him I'm right, ma'am. A man always listens to his wife—at least when she's as pretty as you."

Mattie could feel the color creeping back into her cheeks. "I'm not— We're not married."

"Well, why in tarnation not?" Calamity squinted up at Gallagher. "You stringing her along? That ain't gentlemanly."

Mattie spoke up again. "I'm a miner, Miss . . . Jane . . . uh . . . Calamity."

"Aw now, honey, nobody calls me 'Miss' anything. It's just Calamity." She looked Mattie up and down. "A miner, huh?" She slapped Mattie on the shoulder. "Good for you, honey." She looked at Bill. "I'm thirsty enough to drink the Whitewood dry, Bill."

"You go on, then," Hickok said, nodding toward the door. "I'll find you after I have a word with the storekeeper here."

With a wave at them all, Calamity headed for the door.

"I'll walk as far as the hotel with you," Mattie called after her. She glanced at Tom. "Aunt Lou's expecting me." It was as good an excuse as any to get out of there and avoid talking about how it was she and Wild Bill Hickok were on a first-name basis. She needed time to think this through . . . and besides, Aunt Lou *was* expecting her, although maybe not this early in the day.

"All right," Calamity said. "Maybe you can tell me where the good dealers are—and, more important, where they don't water the whiskey down."

Mattie didn't know how to respond to that. Calamity obviously assumed that if Wild Bill knew her, she would know something about the seamier side of Deadwood. Tom and Gallagher would be thinking the same. She could feel them watching her as she followed Calamity Jane outside. So much for leaving the past behind.

———

In spite of the lateness of the hour after she finished at Aunt Lou's, Mattie decided to climb back up to her claim. Whatever Tom and Gallagher decided to do about the earlier scene in the store, she needed time to think things through. Time alone. Time away. Bunking in the wagon on Swede's lot would threaten both. So here she was, hunching over her makeshift table in the dim glow of her lantern, staring down at the mound of gold she'd just poured out of the first of Dillon's five bottles, pondering the day's events.

She'd never forget the look on Tom and Gallagher's faces when Bill called her by name. Of course, there'd been a bit of a surprise in Bill's knowing Gallagher, too, but the preacher had never claimed to be anything more than a reformed sinner. And besides, men were given allowances society never extended to women. As she stirred the pile of gold flakes, Mattie wondered if now was the time for her to leave Deadwood. If she headed east, the past would be less likely to catch up to her. How far east was the question.

She wondered anew over Bill's talking to Aron Gallagher as if they were old friends. Bill associated Gallagher with "the straight and narrow," but the way he'd said it, it was obvious there was more to their relationship than sermons.

Calamity Jane was certainly a woman cut from an entirely different kind of cloth than Mattie had ever known. Mattie had heard about her, of course. Who in the West hadn't? But the reality of Calamity Jane was even more fascinating than the legend. She was loud and profane, and yet if a person bothered, they'd see other qualities beneath the rough veneer. Good qualities.

As the night wore on, Mattie's thoughts kept circling back to Wild Bill's knowledge of her past. He had to be wondering what she was doing all the way up here. Should she seek him out and explain why she'd run out on Jonas? Or just let the past lie behind the curtain of the present and trust Bill to do the same? Wild Bill never had liked Jonas. In fact, they'd had words one night, and the thin line of tolerance between them had nearly been shattered by gunfire. But on that occasion, Bill had left Jonas's place instead of drawing his weapon.

No, Mattie finally decided. She would trust Bill. If he stayed in town for long, she might seek him out for a private talk, but even then she'd have to trust him. After all, a person couldn't go through life never trusting anyone . . . could they?

Aron Gallagher, on the other hand, was a concern. He might have protected Brady Sloan, but Mattie had never known a preacher who could keep his mouth shut. She could almost imagine Gallagher talking to Aunt Lou, suggesting they should pray for Mattie now that her sordid past had come to light. Poor Mattie O'Keefe, a scarlet woman trying to start fresh. The idea made her want to . . . *run. You want to run.* It was true. Running was her first thought. But it had been followed quickly by the realization that a new part of her wanted to put down roots here in Deadwood near Swede and Freddie and Eva and Tom.

Tom. Would today change his willingness to trust Mattie to work in the store? Would he talk to Swede about it? Mattie gulped. Everything might be different now. And all because of a few words spoken by a blue-eyed gambler. *"Mattie. Good to see you."*

With a sigh, Mattie moistened her fingertip and picked up a flake of gold. *You can go anywhere you want to go.* Except she wasn't ready to leave her claim. Not yet. There was more gold, and she wanted it.

Returning the flake of gold to the little mound before her, she practiced snatching her Colt pistol off the table and pointing it at the tent flap. When she was satisfied that she could do it and be ready to fire in under a second, she did the same with Bessie II. Tom's sawed-off shotgun was no longer loaded with salt. Anyone who dared come in her tent uninvited would earn a spot in Ingleside Cemetery.

"You didn't really think I was going to fund your leaving me, did you?" Even now, settled in her tent on her own claim, well defended and enjoying the beginnings of friendships with good people, Mattie was terrified by the memory of Jonas snarling those words. She'd been able to suppress all of that for weeks now, but seeing Bill Hickok changed everything. It might even change her budding friendships with good people.

It was long past midnight before Mattie returned Dillon's gold to his cache and turned down the lamp. She fell into a fitful sleep with her hand on Bessie II.

————

When the light inside Mattie's tent finally went out, Freddie rose from his hiding place behind a boulder. She had refused his offer to walk her up here earlier tonight, and he didn't want to make her mad, so he'd let her go and then followed at a respectful distance just to make sure no one bothered her. Stretching and rubbing a stiff shoulder, Freddie made his way toward home.

Just as he passed Tom English's lot, a lone rider came trotting into town. Freddie stopped to watch the horse. It was a beautiful bay, but it had been ridden hard. Its coat was flecked with sweat, and when, just outside of Usher's Livery, the rider yanked back on the reins, foam flew from the bit. When the man dismounted and banged on the closed livery door, Freddie trotted toward him.

"Mr. Usher closes at sundown," he said. "Now it's dark."

Even in the moonlight Freddie could tell that this was one of those people who would treat him bad. Which made sense from the way he had treated his horse. "I'll take care of your horse if you want," he offered. "He's a pretty horse. I'll be real good to him. I like horses. He could founder or drink too much. I'll walk him until he cools down and—" The man didn't let him finish. Instead, he reached in his pocket, pulled out a wad of paper money, and stuffed a bill in Freddie's hand.

"Do it," he said. "And take the bedroll and the saddlebags to . . ." He looked up the street. "A hotel? A *decent* hotel?"

"That'd be the Grand Central," Freddie said. "It's just before you get to a big new building going up. You'll see it. That's going to be Mr. Jack Langrishe's new theatre. He's gonna have plays and music and concerts and—" Freddie paused. "There won't be girls like the ones . . . like the ones farther on down Main." He cleared his throat. "You'll like the Grand Central. It's real nice. And Aunt Lou—"

The stranger didn't even wait to hear about Aunt Lou's cooking. "Grand Central," he growled. "Take care of it." And without even waiting for an answer, he marched off up the street.

Freddie looked down at the paper money. He glanced toward the stranger, who was striding toward the swath of golden light spilling out of the nearest saloon. Folks in Deadwood didn't want paper money. They wanted gold. In fact, things cost more if paid in paper money. But the stranger probably wouldn't believe him even if Freddie told him. He'd find out soon enough.

"Come on, boy," he said, speaking gently to the animal, which at first shied away from his uplifted hand, but then submitted to being petted. Freddie walked the horse up and down the street in front of Mor's store until he was breathing normally. Then he led him over to the Whitewood Creek and let him drink, but only a little. Then he walked him some more. Finally, he took the horse around to the back of the store.

After lighting a lamp and setting it in the storeroom window to help him see, he took the saddle and the soaking wet blanket off and brushed the horse down until all traces of dried sweat and mud were gone. He cleaned his hooves and discovered that, while the horse had been skittish at first, he really was a good old boy and willingly lifted each hoof to be cleaned. He didn't try to bite or kick at all.

"Good boy," Freddie said as he worked. "Good boy." Finally, he let the horse drink again. He had some old hobbles from when he'd owned a roan pony. The pony was long since dead, but Freddie held on to the hobbles in hopes that someday soon he'd come into new wealth and maybe own a horse again. For now, he would use the hobbles on the stranger's bay.

While he worked, Freddie talked aloud, asking the horse where it had come from and wishing he didn't belong to a man who treated him this way. "I know," Freddie said. "He's just a strange one, isn't he. I saw him come out of that first saloon when you and me came back from the creek the first time. I thought he would come to check on you, but he just barged across the street and into another place. I guess he didn't like the first one. What's he up to? What's he so mad about? Is he mad at you for making him fall? Is that where he got that scar?"

————

As the village idiot tended his horse, Jonas took the measure of Deadwood: businesses that were little more than unadorned boxes, most of them without so much as a permanent sign, one long cesspool where there should be a street, and that cursed gumbo everywhere. If Dillon O'Keefe was raping the earth for gold in any of the valleys or gulches near here, if this was where Mattie had run to, she had to be sorry she'd ever left Abilene. Maybe he should rethink his intentions. Convince her he only wanted his money back. She might be ready to beg him to take her back. The idea opened up all kinds of new possibilities for making an example of Mattie O'Keefe that the girls in Abilene would never forget.

From what he'd seen so far, there wasn't a man in Deadwood who knew the first thing about how to run a gambling hall or a saloon. Not a single one of the places he entered was worth the cost of the lumber it'd been built with. Only one had so much as a piano. Most were furnished with a haphazard arrangement of chairs and beat-up tables Jonas wouldn't have cut up for firewood, much less used to furnish a place he owned. Some didn't even have real tables. Rough-cut boards balanced atop barrels served in those hovels. After a while Jonas stopped even going in those. Mattie O'Keefe would starve before she'd work in a place like that.

A person sometimes learned more by listening than by asking questions, and Jonas was a good listener. As the night wore on, he learned a lot about the area just standing at the bar drinking whiskey in several different saloons and dance halls. The lead was southwest of here at a place called Homestake. Bobtail was taking five dollars an hour. Claims in some of the side gulches were averaging five dollars a pan. Everywhere Jonas went he heard about the wealth found in the next gulch, the quartz with a promising vein, the miner who'd struck it rich. Apparently it was not uncommon for a man to own several claims. More than a few seemed eager to sell out, and from what Jonas could see, none were half as eager to work as they were to drink and gamble.

It took most of the night, but Jonas finally admitted that, with all its exposed brutality, Deadwood had its allure. Time after time he saw a prospector toss a bag of gold dust on the bar. Time after time he saw the bartender pinch out fifty cents worth for a drink. It was impressive to see men dressed in rags with bags of gold hanging around their necks. Appearances aside, Deadwood appeared to be primed for a man who knew how to run an entertainment palace.

What they needed was women. Beautiful women, not the aging cow billed as the Fascinating Danseuse, who gyrated through a pathetic series of supposedly seductive moves at the Bella Union. He couldn't bear to watch for long.

Turning away, he ordered another drink and pondered the idea of how, with his polished veneer and Mattie's charm, the two of them could have the miners of Deadwood literally throwing money at them every night. He'd only heard one singer tonight and she could hardly carry a tune. Mattie could have anyone in the room eating out of the palm of her sweet little hand after one verse of "Annie Laurie."

Sweet. There hadn't been anything sweet about Mattie's hand the last time he'd seen her. He touched the scar on his face. Ah well, all cats had claws, didn't they? He should have known she'd bare them sooner or later. They'd been playing a game of cat and mouse for months with him pushing and her dancing away. He'd let that go too far, letting her think she was far too independent for far too long. All that talk of "keeping accounts" and "planning for the future." As if she could choose a future. As if she could just up and walk away after all the imported brandy and stunning gowns he'd provided. As if she didn't owe him for teaching her about the finer things in life.

As he leaned against a bar in one of the older establishments — he couldn't even remember the name—and looked around him, Jonas could not believe that Mattie O'Keefe would have willingly stayed in Deadwood. *Unless her brother had actually found some gold and bought her a place of her own.* That was something to ponder.

Turning around, Jonas sipped his drink. Now that he thought about it, he could see Mattie using what she'd learned from him to rejuvenate a place like this. With enough money she could own the jewel of the Black Hills. And she'd left Abilene with his three thousand dollars.

There was a staircase at the back of this place. Was Mattie up there right now, lounging in one of those rooms, waiting to come down later and play the role of the queen of Deadwood? Maybe that was it. Maybe she wasn't *working* one of these dives. Maybe she *owned* one.

He couldn't just go from place to place asking about her, though. That would tip his hand. And the brother might be a problem. Again. And even if he didn't think caution was wise for those reasons, the idea of just showing up had provided endless enjoyment on the way up here. He loved envisioning the surprise in those violet eyes, the barely masked panic. She would go pale. She might even faint. If he couldn't make her believe he just wanted her back . . . if her worthless brother was working with her . . . he would do whatever it took. First, to get his money back. But almost more important than the money was the need to drag Mattie back to Abilene and show the others what happened to trollops who thought they could run out on Jonas Flynn. If she wouldn't cooperate, he'd threaten to kill the brother. It had worked once when he needed to keep her in line. It could work again.

Once he had the upper hand, he would appear to be generous. He might even offer the brother a job. He'd gain Mattie's trust again, and then a terrible accident would befall Dillon. Something like that *should* have happened in Kansas long ago. He wouldn't make that mistake again.

Jonas took his pocket watch out. He'd given this place enough of his time. He was tired and he wanted to get at least some of the grit and grime off him. Stepping out into the street, he headed for the Grand Central Hotel. What a name. *Grand.* If he opened a place here that's what he'd name it. The Grand. And it *would* be grand compared to the rest of these dives. As he made his way back to the hotel, he wondered if the imbecile who'd offered to tend his horse had remembered to take his bedroll and saddlebags to the hotel and get him a room.

Gunfire broke out up the street. No one dodged for cover except a Chinaman with a deer carcass slung over his shoulder. Which reminded Jonas of another way to find Mattie. Opium dens. Dillon O'Keefe had had his problems in that regard. Find him and Mattie wouldn't be far away.

The village idiot had done what he was told. Jonas's bedroll and saddlebags were waiting at the hotel desk, and for the first time since he'd arrived in this town, Jonas smelled something that didn't make his eyes water and his stomach roil. The man behind the desk noticed when Jonas inhaled.

"That's the promise of tomorrow, sir," he said with a smile. "The Grand Central offers the finest dining experience in Deadwood, courtesy of Aunt Lou Marchbanks, the best cook in Dakota. Maybe the best cook in the West."

Jonas only grunted. *Best?* He'd be the judge of that. Of course if Aunt Lou was a proper mammy he supposed she had learned a thing or two about cooking. At least that's how things had worked where he came from.

Up in his room, Jonas undressed and washed thoroughly, hoping he could sleep without battling the vermin that often mounted a full attack on hotel guests in places like this. Happily, when he stretched out on the lumpy mattress, it became clear that he was the only living resident in the bed. Good.

He would spend tomorrow in Chinatown, and if he didn't find any trace of either O'Keefe, he'd head to some of the other camps. Sonny Manning could be trusted to keep things going at the place back in Abilene for at least a little while longer.

Jonas fell asleep reviewing his plans for Mattie. One of the things he'd realized on this journey was that he'd failed to frighten her properly. That mistake would have to be corrected. A woman's fear could be useful. Jonas liked it when terrified women did what he told them to do. There was a raw pleasure in it that he couldn't quite experience in any other way.

CHAPTER 12

You turned out to be an easy man to find." Mattie plopped down beside where Wild Bill Hickok sat leaning against the back wall of the Grand Central Hotel.

At the sound of her voice, Hickok lifted his head, squinted at her, and closed his eyes again. Groaning, he took off his hat and put his hand to his head. "What day is it?"

"Sunday," Mattie said. "And I came down the gulch hoping we could have a talk. A private talk."

Bill moaned, "Sunday? Sunday *morning*? Please tell me I didn't black out before I got to my room."

"Well, I can't tell you much of anything, seeing as how I just got into town," Mattie said. "Thought I'd help Aunt Lou with breakfast—and earn my own—then look for you early this afternoon. But here you are. And I'd say, based on the evidence, that what you don't want to hear is exactly what happened. You blacked out before you got to your room."

Bill opened his eyes a little wider and tilted his head to look her way. "Coffee?"

Mattie stood up. "Coming right up."

Aunt Lou was bustling around the kitchen with more than her usual energy. When Mattie asked for a cup of coffee for Wild Bill, she poured it, but while she was pouring she scolded. "I don't care how famous that man is. He still don't have no right to bring his drunken self to my back door."

"You are absolutely right, ma'am." Bill stood in the doorway and invited himself into the kitchen, sliding into one of the chairs at the table. "I apologize for my uninvited presence. I didn't mean to frighten you. But I sincerely hope you'll put up with me until I can get a cup of strong coffee in me."

Aunt Lou glared down at the man slumped at her kitchen table. "You didn't frighten me," she said, and proceeded to turn the flap-jacks cooking on the stove. "At least not much. After I realized you was just sitting there on the ground—that you wasn't *dead*." She continued to rattle pans and clank lids as she worked, sending the message that she was busy and this was her kitchen.

Mattie set a mug of steaming coffee in front of Bill. He took it with a grateful sigh before addressing Aunt Lou. "I am beholden to you for the best cup of coffee I've tasted in many a day, ma'am." He laid a gold coin on the table. "Is there any chance you would consider feeding me breakfast before I go upstairs to my room?"

"Breakfast is served in the dining room starting in about fifteen minutes," Aunt Lou said without turning around.

"I—" Mattie cleared her throat. "I need to talk to Bill, Aunt Lou. And I'd rather do it back here. If you don't mind too much."

Aunt Lou turned around. She looked with surprise from Mattie to Bill and back again. Mattie's heart thumped as she realized that she cared very much what this good woman thought of her.

Good women crossed the street to the other side rather than come face-to-face with gambling hall girls like Mattie O'Keefe. Good women assumed such women were prostitutes, and unless they were the rare woman who held out a helping hand to the girls trying to escape that life, good women did not speak to, did not smile at, did not acknowledge the existence of gambling hall girls. These were the facts that had continued to haunt Mattie the day before, when Bill had walked into Swede's store and greeted her by name. These were the facts that would not let her simply hope for the best when it came to Wild Bill and his knowledge of her past.

And so Mattie cast a smile in Aunt Lou's direction and said, "Yes, ma'am. I know Wild Bill Hickok. Pretty well, in fact. You see, Aunt Lou, I'm a—"

"She's a prospector," Wild Bill interrupted. He smiled at Aunt Lou. His most charming smile. "A prospector and a good woman." Bill nodded. "I'd say that about sums it up."

"I followed Dillon here because I want a *respectable* life," Mattie croaked, wiping her clammy palms on her skirt.

Aunt Lou put a hand on Mattie's shoulder and gave her a gentle shake. "Calm down, honey. Not a soul in Deadwood doesn't have something in their past they'd like to forget. Shoot, there's not a person *alive* doesn't have *something* in their past they'd like to forget. As far as Aunt Lou's concerned you are a sweet girl who has faced a terrible loss and is working hard to make good. Anything else doesn't matter. Not one bit." Aunt Lou pulled another chair out. "Now, you sit down and calm yourself."

Mattie plopped down, and Aunt Lou set a mug of coffee before her. For a few minutes she and Bill drank in silence. Finally, she mentioned Jonas. "I've been worried he might come looking for me. Worried he'd see *you* and start asking questions."

"You know what I think of that snake in the grass," Wild Bill said. "It's good you're free of him." The glint of hatred in his eyes faded. His voice gentled as he said, "I was mighty sorry to hear about Dillon."

"How'd you learn about Dillon?"

"Aron told me. He felt compelled to try and save my soul last night. Calamity's, too." Bill took another sip of coffee. He leaned close. "And he's wondering about you, same as you are about him." He sat back. "But you know the code." Bill was talking about the code of silence that reigned in a gambler's world, where past lives were counted dead and a man who asked too many questions could end up the same way. "So while I didn't say much about you to him, and I can't say much about him to you, I will tell you that I'd trust Aron Gallagher with my life on any day of the week. You have nothing to worry about from him, especially now that he answers to an even higher power than Winchester and Colt." He paused. "And as for Jonas Flynn—" he swept his coat back behind the pistols at his side—"I'm happy to keep an eye out for you."

While they talked, Aunt Lou had been alternately growing a mountain of flapjacks, cracking eggs into her giant iron frypan, and cooking bacon. Hearing Bill say he'd keep an eye out for Mattie, Aunt Lou turned about and, beaming kindness and approval, asked, "Now, how do you like your eggs, Mr. Wild Bill?"

When he'd finished his breakfast, Wild Bill reached for his hat and stood up and, with a little nod at Aunt Lou, said, "Thank you for sharing your kitchen with me, ma'am. I won't impose on your hospitality again." He headed for the door leading toward the front of the hotel.

"You're welcome in Aunt Lou's kitchen any time you need it, Mr. Wild Bill."

Hickok thanked Aunt Lou as he settled his hat on his head. "I'm gonna head upstairs and sleep the night off," he told Mattie. "It'll likely take all day." He winked at her. "I'd be honored to buy you dinner later, though. If you're hereabouts come sundown."

"Thank you," Mattie said, "but I just came into town to talk to you. As soon as I help Aunt Lou get caught up here, I'm headed back up to my claim."

Bill nodded. "I think you've started yourself a good life up here, Mattie O'Keefe. I always thought you were too fine a lady to be dealing cards to drunks and gunslingers." He rested one palm on the butt of a gun. "Now, don't you forget what I said earlier. If Jonas Flynn comes sniffing around Deadwood, I will live up to my reputation." And with that, he was gone. Mattie could hear his spurs rattle as he mounted the stairs leading up to his room.

As soon as Wild Bill was gone, the silence in Aunt Lou's kitchen grew heavy with unspoken words. When Mattie reached for an apron, Aunt Lou interrupted her. "If you want to get back on up to your claim, I can manage here."

"That's good of you, Aunt Lou, but we interrupted your morning, and I'm thinking you could use some help to get caught up." Without another word she donned the apron and went to work making biscuits. Boots clomping down the hotel stairs and voices in the lobby signaled the expectation of breakfast, and while Aunt Lou served up her bacon and eggs, flapjacks and biscuits, Mattie set great platters of food on trays and shuttled them into the dining room.

The two of them were elbow deep in dirty dishes before Mattie returned to the topic that had brought her back into town. After telling Aunt Lou how Wild Bill and Calamity Jane had come into the store and how Wild Bill had greeted her and Gallagher by name, she asked, "Do you think I should say something to Tom before I leave town? He has to be wondering about me. I-I don't want to lose his friendship."

Aunt Lou considered. Finally she said, "Like I said before, honey, there's not a living soul that don't have something in their past they'd just as soon others didn't know about. I imagine that even Mr. Tom English—fine man that he is—has left a thing or two in the shadows of the past." She squeezed Mattie's shoulder. "The good Lord takes us where He finds us, honey. And good *people* do the same. You don't owe Mr. English or me or anyone else an explanation of where you've been. We see where you *are*, and we like you just fine."

He'd never seen anything like Sunday in Deadwood. Thousands surged through the streets in a wave of palpable lust, and as Jonas moved along with them, he understood the lure of Deadwood even more completely. Any caste of human being was welcome here as long as they had gold. No vice was unattainable, and there was no law to interrupt either the pursuit of pleasure or the fulfillment of desire. Once again he thought of how much money a man could make here with the right kind of place. Once again he regretted the loss of Mattie O'Keefe.

He reconsidered his strategy of not asking about Mattie by name. If she didn't turn up soon, perhaps he'd show the daguerreotype around. He could pretend to be a concerned family member looking for a runaway. It rankled that he'd likely have to pretend to be Mattie's father if he took that route. But for now, he still preferred the advantage of surprise. If she got wind of his looking for her, she might run again. No, he'd keep her name to himself. Sooner or later she would turn up.

As planned, he skipped breakfast at the hotel and spent most of Sunday searching opium dens, but there was no trace of Dillon O'Keefe. By the end of the day he left Chinatown and returned to the Badlands, finishing his search of the various dives there. Finally he asked the desk clerk at the hotel to draw a map of the area. Montana City and Elizabethtown. Blacktail and Terraville. Gayville and Central City, Anchor, Pluma, and Peck Garden were all within a few miles of Deadwood. He would check them all.

The imbecile named Freddie had taken his horse to the livery the morning after he arrived. He was glad to know he hadn't ruined the creature spurring it toward Deadwood. Haste hadn't been necessary after all. In fact, it was looking like he would be in these hills for a while. He couldn't so much as telegraph Manning back in Abilene as to when he would be back. The telegraph hadn't reached Deadwood yet and the Indians were doing their best to see that it never would. So be it. Manning would run the place well in his absence, and if he didn't, he'd be sorry.

Late Monday morning Jonas climbed into the saddle. He'd do Splittail Gulch camps first, then circle back and follow Deadwood Creek toward Gayville. Along the way he'd encounter plenty of miners and plenty of camps. He might even ask about Dillon O'Keefe by name. He could pretend to be *his* brother.

———

"She's coming!" Freddie yelled as he hurried in the door of Garth and Company Merchandise. "There's a whole string of freighters headed down from Splittail and I can see Mor's outfit. I know it's hers. You want me to run up and walk with her like I usually do? If I don't run up there she might think something is wrong. We don't want her to think anything's wrong. Or she might guess a surprise. We need to hurry and get the canvas up."

He charged toward the back of the stairs, up to the second story, and was nearly out the window that looked out on the porch roof before Tom caught up. "Slow down, Freddie," he said. "If you fall off the roof, it will be a *bad* surprise."

"I won't fall," Freddie said. "I climb around up on the gulch all the time. There's a ledge and—"

"All right, all right." Tom smiled and motioned for Freddie to climb out the window.

Tom followed him and together they crept across the roof of the porch and, grasping the corners of the piece of canvas rolled up behind the sign, unfurled it so the sign itself was covered.

Once back downstairs, Tom surveyed the inside of the store with a critical eye.

"You don't have to be worried," Freddie said.

"I'm not worried."

"Yes you are. You have that look on your face people get when they are worried. Why are you worried, Tom?"

"Well," Tom sighed. "We changed things quite a bit in here. I hope she isn't upset with us."

"She won't be upset," Freddie said. "She's going to be happy. She likes lemonade." Freddie gestured toward the cooler. "It will make more people come, just like you said. And we want more people." He headed for the door. "You'll see. She's going to be so happy about everything you won't believe it." He set off up the trail at a gallop.

———

"Gee-ho!" Swede cracked her whip. "Get on dere, Lars, you four-legged candidate for de slaughterhouse. You're almost to pasture and a few days off, so give it another pull and let us get dis vagon to home." She was actually hoarse. All that rain and damp, she supposed. Tired, too. More tired than she'd ever been. But she'd be fine once she had a good night's rest in her own place. *Her own place.*

She wanted to be excited but kept trying to tell herself that a million things could have happened to keep Tom English from making good on his promise to have the store finished when she got back. Oh, sure, the saw mills were running and buildings going up fast, but mills could break down, and if that happened up here it could take weeks to get them up and running again. With all the thousands of men roaming the area in search of gold, one would think that laborers were easy to find. Such was not true.

There might be little more than a wooden shell. Tom English was a good man, and he could do more with that hook than a lot of men could with two good hands, but he wasn't going to set any records at building. Freddie was strong, but when it came to hammering nails he was slow. Swede worried that Tom wouldn't have understood that. Freddie knew he was different and he felt bad about it sometimes. She should have told Tom about Freddie's problems with things like hammering nails.

Eva screeched, "Free! Free! Free!" and practically threw herself out of the wagon with excitement.

Freddie galloped up and scooped her out of the wagon, beaming with joy. "She said my name, Mor!" He kissed Eva's cheek.

"That she did," Swede agreed, as surprised as Freddie. Eva had been muttering "Free" for most of one of those rainy days. Could she have been wishing for her brother to play with her?

Swede wanted to ask about the store, but Freddie kept babbling about everything that had happened since she left. He spent most of his time talking about Mattie O'Keefe shooting Brady Sloan. Mattie bringing gold into town. Mattie insisting on carrying a big credit on the store ledger. Mattie staying on her claim even in all the rain. Mattie having "grit" and earning the name Matt the Miner from the McKays and others in the gulch. Mattie not liking Aron Gallagher. And Mattie wanting to help unload the freight and get first chance at whatever Mor was bringing into Deadwood this trip.

"I'm supposed to let her know when you're back," Freddie said.

"Well, I'm back," Swede said. "So you can go after her."

"I will," Freddie said, but he didn't let go of Eva.

Swede cracked her whip above the heads of her team. "It vill take you about as long to get up dat gulch and get back down as it vill take me to get dese oxen down de trail," Swede said. "So yoost go."

"Not yet," Freddie said.

Swede frowned. "Is someting wrong?"

He shook his head.

"Mr. English isn't hurt? Or sick?"

Freddie shook his head again. Finally he blurted out, "It's a surprise. I can't go until you get your surprise."

So the store is finished. Swede smiled. "Ah," she said. "So my store is finished?"

"It's a surprise," Freddie repeated. "And you shouldn't ask, because then it's not a surprise."

Swede nodded. Tom English had finished her store while she was gone. What a good man he was. What a blessing. What would she do if he decided to leave Deadwood?

Katerina Ingegard Jannike. Stop borrowing tomorrow's troubles. Didn't God provide you Garth when Freddie's father ran off? And won't He provide again if Mr. English must go? Why do you always spoil today's joy with worry? Why must the sky always be about to cloud over for you?

Well, she didn't know the answer to that. Except that life was so hard, and that's just how it had always been ever since Garth died. *Count the blessings.* Ah. So many blessings. Twenty of them right here with her, lumbering along pulling all these tons of freight and not one of them sick. *And isn't that a small miracle in itself?* It was. She was thankful. But, God forgive her, how she longed to part from these particular four-legged blessings, to lay down her bullwhip and not look back. And how she wished that she had time to wash her face and tend to herself a bit.

————

The closer Swede got to town, the more nervous Tom English felt. He'd been stupid to think he could change any of Swede's plans and not raise her ire. Who did he think he was, anyway? Oh, she called him her partner, but people did that until a disagreement came along. Then you found out the truth. They'd been thinking of you as a paid employee all along, and now that you'd exercised your own opinions in such a blatant way— *Stop worrying. If she doesn't want the ladies' geegaws at the back of the store, you'll move the displays. If she doesn't want to give away free lemonade, so be it. You've done good work here, and she'll acknowledge it.*

Inspiration struck. As Swede's train inched its way into town and he caught sight of the yellow bonnet she always wore, Tom went back inside just long enough to grab a tin mug and fill it with lukewarm lemonade. He wished they had ice. Something to think about. Maybe a small icehouse out back.

Finally he heard her voice. Tom went back out to greet her. She was looking up at the sign with a puzzled expression on her face. Freddie had Eva perched on his shoulders. She smiled and raised both hands and shouted, "Ta-ta!"

"Hello, little angel," Tom said, smiling.

"Ta-ta!" Eva repeated.

Tom frowned. "Is she—?"

Swede said hello and nodded. "Freddie is 'Free.' I believe you have been christened 'Ta-Ta.' "

Tom reached up to take Eva's hand. He felt strangely moved at the idea that little Eva would learn his name as part of her first words. Swede was staring at the store. Tom let go of Eva's hand. "We have a little surprise," he said, and handing Swede the mug of lemonade, he cupped her elbow in his hand and guided her to step back away from the store.

"All right, Freddie," he said. "Do the honors."

Freddie pulled first one and then the second rope that released the canvas covering the sign. The mug of lemonade dropped to the ground and both Swede's hands came up to her mouth as she read, " 'Garth and Company Merchandise.' "

"Dala," she croaked through her hands.

"Freddie's idea," Tom explained. "He said you always had one on the mantel in your home. I hope you're pleased."

Swede blinked rapidly. She made a strange half-choking sound as she tried to clear her throat.

"Ah," Tom said and put his hand on her shoulder. "You approve. I'm so glad." He hesitated. "I made some changes inside. I hope you won't be too upset. We can go back to what you planned if—" He never finished that sentence. Swede lost the battle to control her emotions. First, she leaned against her wagon and hid her face in her hands to cry. And then, as Tom and Freddie patted her and tried to bring comfort, Eva started to cry.

Freddie took Eva off his shoulders. "There, there," he cooed. "It's all right. Mor's happy. Aren't you, Mor?"

Swede nodded, but she didn't stop crying. So Tom did what any gentleman would do. He offered a clean handkerchief. And then he offered his shoulder. And then he held Swede in his arms.

CHAPTER 13

A talebearer revealeth secrets:
but he that is of a faithful spirit concealeth the matter.

Proverbs 11:13

Mattie grunted as she hefted a flour sack onto one shoulder. She almost staggered beneath the weight but still managed to get it inside the store before yelling, "Help!"

Tom came running. "We're already impressed with Matt the Miner," he scolded. "You don't have to hurt your back proving how hard you can work." Easing the sack onto his own shoulder, he headed for the combination storeroom and kitchen at the back of the building.

"You listen to him," Swede agreed as she came through the front door carrying several bolts of calico. "Leave dose sacks for Freddie and Tom." She slid fabric onto the shelves along one wall before asking, "Vat do you tink?"

Mattie didn't want to say.

"Come now," Swede insisted. "Really. Vat do you tink?"

"Bright colors. Cheerful, I suppose."

Swede stood back and surveyed the pile of goods. "I vas tinking more . . . hideous dan cheerful." She laughed. "Vich is vy I paid only five cents per yard. Ve charge ten cents and de miners who have cabins or brush shanties have a cheap cover for de insides. Much better dan paper."

"I hope it sells," Mattie said. The stuff really was awful. She touched one particularly ugly sample. Garish tones of yellow and green outlined unrecognizable shapes on muddy-colored back-grounds far too reminiscent of the color of gumbo mixed with a liberal amount of manure.

"Ve have a few tousand yards. I suppose I can use it to paper de valls upstairs if I can't sell it."

Freddie grimaced. "Do we have to, Mor?"

Everyone laughed.

A few minutes later, as Mattie and Swede added the last of the fabric to the shelves, Freddie came from the back holding a black furball in his arms. "Mr. Tallent said he's ours." When he put it down, the furball uncurled and stood up. It was a gangly black puppy with intelligent dark eyes.

As everyone looked on, Swede explained. "He vas cowering behind de chicken coop ven I vent to get de hens for Aunt Lou. No one seemed to know vere he vas coming from. He vas so tin and frightened," she said. "Mr. Tallent said I vas crazy to take him along, but den on de vay here, he vas not so sure." Swede chuckled. "De pup vas vit him for most of de last veek, and as you can see, he is not so tin now."

"Doesn't Mr. Tallent want him?" Freddie asked.

Swede shook her head. "I vas hoping, but he says no." She sighed. "I don't know vat kind of dog he vill be—other dan big, from de look of dose paws."

The puppy cocked his head and sniffed the air. He gamboled over to Mattie, sniffed at her shoes, grabbed the hem of her skirt in his teeth, and gave it a tug, all the while wagging his tail so fast it was little more than a dark blur.

"He looks like the dog I carved," Freddie said.

Mattie swallowed. "Yes. He does." She glanced at Swede. "He's a Newfoundland. He'll be about so high," she said, holding her hand out even with her waist. "And he'll defend his owner—" her voice cracked—"with his life." When she bent down and scooped him up, the pup licked her chin with enthusiasm before settling back with a contented sigh. Mattie looked at Swede. "I have plenty of credit on the books to pay whatever you want."

"Vell," Swede said. "For all my trouble, Eva is a bit afraid of him. And vit Freddie gallavanting all over da countryside hunting, he is hardly in a position—"

"Mattie should have him," Freddie said.

Tom chimed in. "I'm not much of a dog lover."

"It's settled, den," Swede said. "The dog is yours. For *friendship*, Mattie. Not for money."

Clearing her throat, Mattie croaked her thanks. She pried opened her past just a bit. "Dillon had a dog like this. His name was Justice."

"What happened to him?" Freddie asked. "Dillon didn't have a dog here. Unless he ran off."

Mattie shook her head. "No. Justice died a few years ago. Actually, someone shot him. Someone very evil." She swallowed. "It'll be nice having company up at the claim." She kissed the dome of the puppy's head and set him down. Instantly, he spread his legs and peed on the floor.

"Name him Whizzer," Tom said, and everyone laughed.

———

A whining puppy lured Mattie outside her canvas home long before dawn the morning after Swede's return to Deadwood, but she'd been awake since midnight thanks to the cannon the miners were firing to salute Independence Day. She'd lost count at about ten. According to the McKays, a hundred volleys were planned.

Snuggled with her dog above her cache of gold, Mattie listened to the sound reverberate through the hills for quite a while, but when Justice began to squirm, she abandoned any hope of celebrating the holiday by sleeping late.

"Ow," she said as she climbed out from beneath the covers. She looked down at Justice. "Apparently unloading wagons uses different muscles than prospecting." She groaned as she got to her feet and tried to stretch. "In fact, apparently unloading wagons can pull just about every muscle a body has." She lifted the tent flap and let Justice outside to do his business while she got dressed for town. As soon as she stepped outside, he came tearing back. Just the sight of him bounding over the rocks made her smile.

Fergus McKay hollered good morning and pointed at the dog. "Won't y' look at it, lass!"

Mattie scooped the pup up. "This is my new guard dog," she said. "What do you think?"

Fergus yawned and scratched his backside. "Be the look of it he's a bit young to be guardin' the keep." He glanced at Mattie's campfire. "No biscuits today?"

"As many as you can eat—in town," Mattie replied. "Today's Garth and Company's grand opening. I'm helping and they're serving up roast pig and biscuits."

"I'll be doon directly," McKay said, and stumbled back into his tent.

———

Justice sat just inside her closed tent flap while Mattie dressed and put up her hair. She reached for her bonnet, fingering the tattered ribbons used to tie it on. "I'm about due for a new one," she said, and glanced over at Justice. "Think I can get a new bonnet without attracting too much attention from the kind of folks I don't want wondering where I got the money?" When Justice tilted his head as if trying to understand her, she smiled. "It might not be wise to flaunt the success of Mattie's Claim." With a sigh, she put the old bonnet on and got up. "We'll just make do, Justice." The puppy yapped agreement and loped ahead of her as she descended into Deadwood dressed and decorated for the Fourth of July.

Today even the most wretched hovels had found a way to display red, white, and blue. Bunting draped the Grand Central Hotel sign. The owners of the Big Horn Store had erected a liberty pole and sent up an assortment of homemade flags. Mattie suspected the lace-edged banner painted with blue stars hanging outside the peanut vendor's stall had begun life as a petticoat.

Justice had stayed close all the way down the gulch, but with the crush of people in town, Mattie worried he'd be stepped on or run over. Picking him up, she carried him with her to the hotel, where a crew of men had undertaken the prodigious task of leveling out the street with shovels in preparation for laying down a dance floor.

Deadwood would have its first official ball that evening. There were only a handful of women in town—Mattie, Aunt Lou, and Swede—unless she counted the sporting girls from the Badlands. She wondered if any of them would come to the ball. *That* would certainly make for an interesting dance. And then of course there was Calamity Jane, and there had to be a dressmaker or milliner, because, although Mattie had never met her, she'd seen a new sign on Main touting "the latest styles." Working the claim prevented her knowing much about any new arrivals in town.

Aunt Lou exclaimed over the pup, "I do wish he was a cat, though. I declare, my pantry is just about overrun with mice." Crossing to the stove she lifted a lid off a pot and fished out a huge bone. "Look what Aunt Lou's got for you," she said to Justice, who yapped and wagged his tail.

Mattie put puppy and bone together on the back stoop, then donned an apron and began to roll out dough and cut biscuits while Aunt Lou mixed a second batch. While they worked they chatted about the grand opening of Garth and Company Merchandise and the other festivities planned for the day ahead.

"The reverend and Tom got the pig to roasting right at dawn," Aunt Lou said. "I stayed long enough to slop on some of my good sauce and left them to tend it. The reverend's readin' the Declaration later, and there'll be lots of other speeches. Someone's got up a petition to ask the government for protection from the Indians."

"Tom English says that's not likely to happen anytime soon," Mattie replied. "Since we're all lawbreakers and illegals anyway."

Aunt Lou *hmphed* a response and pulled another pan of biscuits out of the oven. "There," she said. "That's two baskets ready to go on over to Swede's. I need those baskets back, though. You tell Swede I'll keep bakin' until she says stop." She pointed to the special edition of the *Pioneer* lying on her table. "Take that over, too. The ad is right there on the front page. Just like Mr. English wanted." While Mattie got ready to leave, Aunt Lou said, "Things are gonna be crazy with that pup chasing around. You want me to keep him over here for the day? He seems happy with that bone."

Mattie glanced outside. Justice had the bone between his forepaws and was contentedly gnawing away. "If he gives you one second of trouble, you send someone to tell me."

"He'll be all right," Aunt Lou said. "I can tell he's a good dog. Ain't ya, boy?" At the sound of the word *dog*, Justice looked up. "Ain't ya, boy?" Lou repeated. Justice yapped at her and wagged his tail. "See?" She bustled out of the kitchen into the small adjoining room that served as her living quarters. When she came back into the kitchen, she had a raggedy comforter in hand that she tossed on the floor and tucked beneath her table. "He can sleep right there. Don't you worry a thing about him."

Mattie grabbed the paper and the two baskets of biscuits and headed for the store. When Justice moved to follow her, Aunt Lou grabbed the bone. "Now, you stay here with Aunt Lou. Mattie'll be back directly." The pup hesitated, looking up at Mattie.

"Go on," Mattie said, and Justice bounded into the kitchen.

———

Garth and Company Merchandise was decked out for the holiday with an American flag just to the right of the front door and a banner to the left announcing a *PIG ROAST* and other *GRAND OPENING SPECIALS,* among them *a selection of the finest calico at only ten cents a yard.*

Mattie caught up with Tom English just inside and held out the newspaper. "The ad looks wonderful," she said. "It's right where you wanted it. Bottom right corner of the front page. Aunt Lou says hello and she'll keep baking biscuits until you tell her to stop." She set the two baskets on the counter. "And she needs the baskets back." Mattie pulled out the plank of wood they would be using as a serving tray and pointed to the bolts of calico. "All right with you if I cut off a length of fabric to cover the tray? Might be a good way to advertise it." Tom nodded and Mattie went to work while he glanced over the paper.

When Swede came downstairs Tom held the paper up for her to see. "You should be proud," he said. "You've done it."

"I am proud." Swede smiled at Tom. "Proud and tankful. None of it vould be vitout your help, Mr. English."

"Acknowledged and appreciated, Mrs. Jannike."

Swede blushed.

He read aloud, "Claims in the area are yielding a thousand dollars a day. The famous Number 2 owned by W. P. Wheeler and Company has run two sets of sluice boxes and taken out about $43,000. Bobtail picked up a nugget at the end of a day's run last week that was worth $44.50." He glanced up. "Not to make you jealous or anything," he said to Mattie. "Your claim's doing real well."

You have no idea. Mattie shrugged. "Well enough," she said, and headed off to return Aunt Lou's baskets and to check on Justice. On her way back to the store, she lingered in front of the dressmaker's window, smiling to herself at the strangeness of such a business even existing in Deadwood. The display contained a number of creations obviously intended for the girls who lived at the opposite end of Main Street, but there was a smart lavender bonnet with blue trim that Mattie loved. A hat like that would turn heads all the way from here to Bobtail. She stepped away. What was she thinking? She shouldn't be turning heads in Deadwood. She needed to hunker down, pan for gold, and leave before word spread that Matt the Miner had struck it rich.

Just as she was about to cross the street and head for the store, the door to the dress shop opened and two women stepped out calling after her. "Saw you admiring my bonnet," one said, and turned to the other. "I told you the trim was a good idea." She extended a hand and smiled. "Lyra Berg," she said. "And this," she nodded at her twin, "is my sister Vina."

"Hmph," Vina said. "It wasn't that little purple thing at all. It was my creation." She squinted at Mattie. "Wasn't it? You'll be a veritable Lady Liberty." She pointed at another hat in the window, an amazing platter of red, white, and blue ribbon and feathers worthy of the Badlands if ever a hat was. The very thought made Mattie so uncomfortable she could feel herself blushing.

"Now look what you've done," Lyra scolded. "She's a lady, Vina. She wouldn't be caught dead in something one of our other girls would want."

"Actually," Mattie interrupted, "I was admiring the one with the blue trim." She glanced at the other sister. "Although yours is definitely worthy of a Lady Liberty . . . it's just not . . . me."

Vina didn't miss a beat. "Well, that's fine," she said. "I understand. Aren't you the lady miner we've heard so much about?"

"Of course she is," Lyra said. "Who else would she be? We've met every other female in town." She smiled at Mattie. "We admire you immensely, Miss O'Keefe. Standing up for yourself in a man's world and making a way for yourself up on the gulch."

"Clearly I'm not the only female in Deadwood making a way for herself," Mattie said, pointing at the storefront. "My congratulations. Opening your own business in this town takes courage." She pointed toward Swede's store. "Have you met Mrs. Jannike?"

"The bullwhackeress?" Lyra asked. When Mattie nodded, she said, "Not yet. We will today." She waved toward her shop. "This is just a way to keep ourselves sane while our husbands entertain their own golden follies."

"They have a claim?"

"Three," Vina grumped. "All worthless. If it weren't for this shop and the girls from the Badlands buying our wares, we'd all be starving."

"Now, Vina," Lyra scolded, "have a little faith in the boys."

"I'll have faith when I see some results."

"Goodness me," Lyra said, and made a face. "We're going to drive away one of our first customers with all this squabbling."

The sisters might squabble, but Mattie almost wondered if it was a sales tactic, for as they talked, they had expertly maneuvered her through the door of their shop.

Lyra reached for the lavender bonnet. "Here you are." She pressed Mattie toward the mirror. "No charge to try it on," she said with a smile.

At the same time as Lyra was enticing Mattie to try on a bonnet, Vina emerged from behind a dressing screen with a blue dress in hand. "They'd look lovely together. Won't you at least try it on?"

Lyra joined in. "You'd be doing us a favor if you'd just wear it to the ball, and when you get complimented, tell everyone where it came from." She glanced at her sister. "Promotion, Vina. Promotion by a beautiful live model."

Vina didn't miss a beat. "Please," she wheedled, "wear our dress. We'll give you a discount on the bonnet. And we extend credit."

And so Mattie found herself standing behind the Berg sisters' dressing screen in the corner of their tiny shop trying on the blue dress. As she pulled it over her head and the hem of the skirt cascaded to the floor, she couldn't help but appreciate the softness of the cloth. It had been a long time since she'd had a proper dress. The skirt and waist she'd worn all the way from Kansas were nearly worn out. Maybe she *would* buy the dress. But when she stepped out from behind the screens and looked in the mirror her hand went to her waist. "I'm sorry." She shook her head. "But I can't."

"Of course you can," Lyra crooned. She stepped up behind and gazed at Mattie in the mirror. There's a seam right here," she said, indicating the side seam of the generously cut skirt. "I can easily insert a little pocket. Just the right size. And the line of the skirt is perfect to conceal it. No one will have any idea." The woman smiled knowingly, and when she stepped back she patted her own skirt and in one easy move withdrew her own pocket pistol. "You see? If you like it well enough to buy it, you can. You'll be safe as ever walking up the gulch dressed in a creation from the Berg sisters." She chuckled.

Vina handed her the lavender bonnet. "It's a lovely ensemble," she said. When Mattie finally left the shop—dressed in her worn bonnet and old clothes—she had agreed to return in time to don the Berg sisters' ensemble for the Independence Ball.

———

Aron Gallagher was the center of attention as he stood on the platform erected near the flagpole and read the Declaration of Independence. Hundreds of people were hanging on his every word. And from where she stood just outside Garth and Company's front door, all Mattie could do was stare at his clean-shaven jaw and the way it had changed his looks. If she wasn't mistaken he was wearing a new suit and a freshly pressed shirt. *Tarnation*, but he was a handsome man. And she didn't want to notice. Didn't want to think about how

Bill said Gallagher could be trusted, how Aunt Lou admired him, how those blue-gray eyes twinkled when he laughed.

She retreated inside the store under the guise of checking to see if she could make more coffee or lemonade . . . or perhaps make another run to the hotel for something. But Gallagher's voice rumbled after her.

" 'When in the course of human events, it becomes necessary for one people to dissolve the political bands which have connected them with another . . .' " Mattie went to the window of the now empty store and looked out on the crowd. They were a motley collection of people, but every single one of them was standing with his eyes locked on Gallagher, who Mattie realized for the first time wasn't *reading* the Declaration of Independence. He was reciting it. Like an actor on a stage. Like a *gifted* actor on stage. He gestured as he spoke and made eye contact with the crowd. And he *did* have a nice voice. Not a golden voice . . . but a nice one.

" 'We hold these truths to be self-evident, that all men are created equal, that they are endowed by their Creator with certain unalienable Rights, that among these are Life, Liberty and the pursuit of Happiness. . . .' "

Whether it was the words themselves or the way they were delivered—or the man who delivered them—Mattie sensed a moment when the entire crowd stood as if suspended in time. They were hushed, soaking up Gallagher's offering like parched soil welcoming the rain.

From where she stood inside the store, Mattie noticed something else about the audience. One of the women in attendance appeared to be particularly entranced by Aron Gallagher. Or was it the speech? She was young and had an abundance of blond hair twisted into a bun at the nape of her neck. She was standing, her arms wrapped around herself, her lips slightly parted, her eyes fixed on Gallagher. The towheaded girl at her side was probably her sister. And the older woman who glanced around nervously and seemed bent on keeping the two girls within inches of her protective sphere had to be their mother. Apparently a *family* had come to Deadwood.

" '. . . we mutually pledge to each other our Lives, our Fortunes, and our sacred Honor.' "

The second Gallagher had finished his recitation, a cheer went up from the crowd.

Gallagher mopped his brow and stepped down. He hadn't taken three steps when he was surrounded by the three females Mattie had been watching. As the older girl smiled up into Gallagher's face, Mattie turned away. *Lovely girl. All-fired lovely.*

———

After the speeches ended, the crush of humanity in the streets got worse as the afternoon progressed, until finally Mattie began to have trouble getting back and forth to Aunt Lou's kitchen to replenish the biscuit supply. Freddie began going instead, and Mattie stayed behind to work in the store with Swede while Tom served up roast pig out back. They ran out of lemonade and had to substitute water. No one seemed to mind. Most customers were quenching their thirst in other ways anyway.

The June 25 massacre at the Little Big Horn was the main topic of conversation among customers for most of the afternoon. Deadwood had received the news via the founder of Gayville, whose wife was Indian and had heard it from an Indian runner on his way to Spotted Tail Agency. It didn't seem possible that the great General Custer and hundreds of troops could have been so thoroughly wiped out. Throughout the day men discussed and rehashed what was known and surmised what was unknown. Discussion of Indian battles led some of the old-timers to reminisce about other battles at places like Shiloh and Manassas, Vicksburg and Gettysburg. Mattie noted that Tom had nothing to say—even when the topic was Shiloh.

Late in the afternoon as she was helping him clean up around the fire pit out back, Mattie asked Tom if he agreed with everyone who seemed to assume the next logical place the Indians would try their hand at murder would be the Black Hills. As he and Mattie stepped inside, Tom spoke to Swede, who was standing by the stove heating water for coffee. "Mattie here's been asking me about the situation with the Indians. I told her you should both sign that petition asking the government for protection." He paused, waiting for Swede to turn around. When she did, he added, "And I think you should consider putting off your next freighting run until things quiet down a bit."

"I vill sign de petition," Swede said. "We need peace so dat more families will come. So ve can build a church and a school." She paused. "But ve also need more of everyting before snows block de trail. I von't have us going hungry all vinter because I vas a coward." She turned back to the coffeepot. "I vill leave as planned."

While Swede and Tom talked—or was it arguing?—Mattie went back to work behind the counter. She sold a surprising amount of ugly calico. She smiled to herself. How relieved Freddie would be that his mor wasn't going to tack any of it to the walls upstairs. And she smiled, wondering how long it would be before Tom and Swede realized how much they cared for each other.

———

As daylight faded someone lighted the torches planted in the dirt along the street, the fiddler took up his bow, the pianist from the Bella Union sat down—several burly men had hauled the piano up the street earlier in the day—and with the sound of an arpeggio across the ivories, the music began. An odd assortment of couples crowded the dance floor, most of them male with one partner sporting the red armband that designated him as the one who followed while the other led. It didn't matter to anyone, least of all the dancers. It was Independence Day, and nothing short of rigor mortis would have kept folks from celebrating.

The Berg sisters accompanied Mattie back into the fray once

she'd changed into their blue dress. Mattie met timid Lydia Underwood, the mother of the young woman she'd noticed listening to Gallagher's speech earlier, and wife of the proprietor of a new hardware store going up on a corner lot. Mrs. Underwood thought the store was much too close to "the other part of town" and expressed a litany of fears and concerns about Deadwood that began with the need for a decent church and ended with a sincere wish that "Mr. Underwood would see the light and sell his business before something horrible happens."

Mrs. Underwood's fears seemed to center around her daughters, and it wasn't long before Mattie could see why she was worried. Blond-haired Kitty Underwood was lovely, flirtatious, and naïve in a city where naïveté could get a woman in serious trouble.

Mattie danced and reeled until she was almost as tired as she was after a day of prospecting. She'd almost forgotten how much she enjoyed dancing . . . and how nice it was to have a new dress. She couldn't help but notice Kitty Underwood's eyes grow large with surprise—and envy—when Wild Bill Hickok took off his hat and bowed, calling Mattie by her given name and asking for "the favor of a dance with the prettiest gal in town."

When Bill spun her away, Mattie smiled up at him. "I'd forgotten. You aren't a bad dancer."

"You aren't a bad dancer yourself, Miss O'Keefe." He grinned and whirled her around the floor. When the pace slowed a bit, he leaned close. "Thought I should tell you I may not be in town that much longer. I wanted to remind you that you can count on Aron, should you need an extra gun."

Mattie leaned back in his arms and looked up at him with a little frown. "In case you haven't noticed, he doesn't *carry* a gun."

Bill smiled. "I didn't mean that exactly literally," he said. "What I meant was—"

"It's all right," Mattie interrupted him. "Let's just enjoy the dance."

When the song ended, Bill bowed and stepped off the dance floor. "Now, don't you forget what I said about Aron. If he's got your back, you don't have any worries." He winked, then touched the brim of his hat. "You look real pretty tonight, Mattie. I'll enjoy the memory." He headed off up the street toward the Number 10, a hovel that, for some reason, Bill had favored almost exclusively since arriving in Deadwood.

CHAPTER 14

The word of God is quick and powerful, and sharper than
any two-edged sword, piercing even to the dividing asunder of soul
and spirit, and of the joints and marrow, and is a discerner
of the thoughts and intents of the heart.

Hebrews 4:12

It was nearly midnight. Aunt Lou was out on the dance floor laughing and having a wonderful time as miner after miner bowed and nearly fought over the next dance. Little Eva was asleep in her room over the store, and Freddie was finishing the pig roast cleanup out back, chopping up the carcass for Aunt Lou, who wanted every morsel for flavoring beans. And Tom English and Swede were dancing. With a happy sigh, Mattie plopped down on one of the benches beside the front door of the store, leaned her head back, and closed her eyes.

Justice, who'd been curled up at her feet, moved and gave a little puppy growl just as a now-familiar male voice said, "I expect you've about danced your feet off tonight." When Mattie opened her eyes, Aron Gallagher was offering her a mug of root beer. He nodded at Justice. "Call your dog off, ma'am, so he doesn't take off my hand."

As she took a sip of root beer, Mattie glanced down at the pup and laughed. She patted him on the head while she said, "It's all right, Justice, but you are a good boy to take note of strangers that way." With a sigh, Justice settled between them. Mattie nodded toward the dance floor. "I've never had a dance card quite so full." She held her feet out in front of her. "My feet are still there, but I can't say as I really feel 'em anymore."

"Well, I'm sorry to hear that," Gallagher said. "I was hoping you'd grant one more dance." He paused. "Do you mind if I sit down?"

"Of course not," Mattie said, and motioned for him to join her.

Gallagher sat quietly for a long time, sipping his own root beer and watching the dancers. Finally he spoke up. "You and Bill had a nice waltz or two."

"We did," Mattie said. "He always was a good dancer. And a gentleman. At least to me."

Gallagher glanced her way. "I was helping some men haul the remains of the speaking podium away when I saw him. He said you two had a talk about—things. Me being one of them."

"You were mentioned," Mattie said. "In the context of 'watching my back' and 'an extra gun.' " She sighed. "Bill's thinking of leaving town, and he seemed to feel a need to appoint a guardian to take over for him."

"So he told me. I would imagine that annoyed you."

Mattie shrugged. "Not really. It did confuse me a bit."

"Why?"

"Well—and don't take this as an insult—if I did need protecting I'd want someone who was a gunman first and a gambler second—not the other way around."

Gallagher chuckled softly. "Well said. And reassuring in a way. Obviously my past doesn't show, which makes it less likely some

drunken fool will draw on me someday just to see how fast I am."
He paused. "Especially since I don't even shoot my own game
anymore."

Mattie shifted her weight so she was turned more toward him.
He met her gaze evenly. *He used to be a gunslinger? A good enough
one to earn Wild Bill's respect?* Mattie forced what she hoped was a
matter-of-fact tone into her voice even as she allowed a little smile.
"I take it you're a good shot."

"I was. When I had to be." He reached down to pet Justice.
"Bill seemed to think you might need someone around like that. I'm
happy to oblige—in your case—but I do hope you won't make my
past common knowledge."

"You don't have to worry about me expecting you to take up
arms on my behalf," Mattie said. "I know Bill meant well, but he
shouldn't have said anything. I think I've proven I can take care of
myself."

Gallagher nodded. "I should also admit that, once he brought
your name up, I asked Bill about you . . . and your . . . story." With
a final pat to Justice's head, he leaned back. "I was hoping he'd be
able to shed some light on what I did or said that made you dislike
me so much."

"I don't—" When Gallagher looked her in the eye, Mattie broke
off. Shrugged.

"I'm only asking because if it's something I can fix, I'd like
to. First, because it would make things easier and less awkward
when we're with our mutual friends, and second," he said, forcing
a grin, "because it'd make it more likely that I'll get *my* chance to
dance with the prettiest girl in town tonight." He flashed a smile
that brought the dimple back to his cheek and crinkled the corners
of his eyes.

All right, Mattie thought. *So you have a certain charm.* And try
as she might, Mattie realized she was softening a little toward the
preacher. Especially now—when he'd opened up about his past. She

gave a little shrug. "It's not you personally. It's every preacher I've ever known. They all acted the part pretty well during the day, but then when the sun came down they'd come to me. To my faro table at the place in Abilene where I worked. As a dealer." She lifted her chin. "Not as *anything* else."

He waved his hand, batting the revelation aside as if it were no more than a bothersome fly. "I believe you. Please go on. About the preachers you've known."

"They'd show up to gamble and they were just like all the other customers. No difference." She took a deep breath. "I knew one who could roll Scripture off his tongue like he'd memorized the whole book. He never treated me badly. But with the upstairs girls?" She shuddered. "My employer finally banned him from the place."

Gallagher's voice was gentle as he said, "I don't suppose it'd do much good to tell you that if that's the only kind of preacher you've ever met . . . you don't know *my* kind."

"*Hmpf.*" Mattie gave a little chortle. "That's exactly what Aunt Lou said when I told her I didn't like . . . uh . . . trust you."

"She did?"

With a nod, she went on. "She says you give away the money you collect on Sunday. And you do all kinds of good things you don't want anyone to know about. To hear Aunt Lou tell it, you're a saint."

"Well"—Gallagher stretched his legs out in front of him and leaned back—"I guess that just goes to show that on occasion even someone as wise as Aunt Lou can be wrong." He folded his arms across his torso. "I'm probably the biggest sinner in Deadwood. The only difference between me and anyone else in town is—" He broke off.

"What?"

He thought for a moment before saying, "You read the Bible much?"

She shook her head. "Never had a reason." Justice got up and headed off toward the back lot. "I'd better make sure he doesn't wander off," Mattie said, and moved to follow him. Together they walked around the building to the back of the store, where they could just see Justice meandering about in the golden light shining through the back window.

As the two of them stood watching the dog, Gallagher said, "I never read the Bible, either. Not for most of my life, anyway. But you know about Jesus, right? The crucifixion and the three crosses on the hill—how He died with a criminal on either side of Him."

"Everyone knows that story."

He nodded. "One of the criminals made fun of Jesus and one defended Him—said Jesus didn't deserve to die, and asked Jesus to remember him." Gallagher paused. Cleared his throat and murmured, "The way I see it, every man is one of those or the other. *I'm* the one who doesn't have a thing to offer and just hopes Jesus will remember him." He broke off and apologized, "But here I am sermonizing again."

Mattie forced a joke. "Well, I'd rather listen to you sermonize than go back out there and have to dance with the rest of Deadwood." She opened the back door to the store. "Let's see if we can find something to eat. It feels like a year ago since the pig roast." She called Justice to follow them inside. In a few minutes they were seated at Swede's small table. Mattie left the door open, and as the street music filtered in, Justice sprawled across the threshold and fell asleep. "So," Mattie said, prying the lid off a tin of biscuits and starting fresh coffee. "Finish the sermon, Preacher."

Taking a deep breath, Gallagher began. "There was a toothless old codger who used to come to the jail—"

"Jail?"

He nodded. "He never once preached. All he did was sit outside the cell and read to us. At first we all made fun of him. But he kept coming. And at some point I started looking forward to his visits. And then I started listening. I thought Jesus had to be the craziest person who ever walked the face of the earth. But eventually I started to see it different. And finally, I decided what the h—" He broke off and gave an embarrassed little laugh before continuing. "I decided I didn't have anything to lose. Why not throw myself at Jesus like that man on the cross and see what happened."

"What happened?" Mattie reached for a biscuit and took a bite while she waited for the answer.

"Nothing at first. Nothing I could feel, anyway. But the next time Jerry came to read to us, the Bible made more sense. Somewhere along in there I started wanting to be a better man. So I asked God to help me with that." He moistened his lips and glanced her way, almost as if he were nervous about what he was about to say. "I was in jail for a long time, Mattie. I had plenty of time to listen while Jerry read. When I walked out of that place I was a different man. I couldn't go back to the other life."

"And you wanted to be a preacher."

"No, I've never wanted to be a preacher. It scares me nearly spitless every time I climb up on that box."

"Then why do you do it?"

"Because there's nobody else in Deadwood willing. Everyone's trying to get rich, thinking it'll make 'em happy. When all money does is help them cover over the real problem."

"The real problem." Mattie frowned. Most of her problems would be solved quite well by money. *Then why don't you cash out the gold and solve them?* She wouldn't think about that now.

"Humans were created for a life beyond this one. For a relationship with God. Some of us murder, some of us lie, some of us are pretty good people who only do little things that are wrong. But every wrong breaks the relationship we were meant to have with God, and we end up trying to fill the resulting emptiness with other things. Here in Deadwood, it's gold. Women. Whiskey. But the emptiness won't go away unless we ask the man on the cross to bridge the gap for us." He broke off and sat back. "Whew. I've been talking for at least an hour. Why didn't you tell me to shut up a long time ago? I'm sorry, I—"

"It's all right," Mattie said. "I *asked* for a sermon this time."

"How'd I do?"

"Not bad. To be honest, I've never heard anyone talk about religion like that before."

"To be honest, I never had anyone *listen* like you before. You didn't heckle once."

Mattie laughed.

Gallagher nodded toward the front of the store and the street where the dance was still in full swing. "So what d'ya say, Miss O'Keefe? Mind taking a spin with a varmint-turned-preacher?"

Mattie didn't mind. Ordering Justice to stay, she closed him into the storeroom and followed Gallagher back outside. At some point—maybe it was the second or third dance, she wasn't sure—Mattie began to think that Wild Bill and Aunt Lou were right about Aron Gallagher. He could be trusted. He was a decent man. For all her blustering and claiming she could take care of herself, she also realized it never hurt to have a good man on your side. And if that good man turned out to be a saint who knew how to use a gun, so much the better.

———

She began to sing again. She hadn't even realized she was doing it until one morning in mid-July when she looked up and saw that the McKays had stopped their own mining to listen. When she broke off, Hugh called out, "Please, Matt. Bless us with another." And so she did, and little by little Mattie began to realize that grief and fear were beginning to loosen their grip on her. Oh, she still slept with Bessie II nearby, and she was grateful for Justice and what he would become, but she stopped slipping her pistol into her pocket every morning on the claim, and when Aron Gallagher climbed the gulch one day to see how she was, she let down her guard and allowed herself to enjoy his company.

Gallagher climbed the gulch every few days after that. Through him, Mattie learned the news. Charlie Utter and a partner had established a pony express between Deadwood and Fort Laramie. The plan was for it to make weekly trips. The Lawrence County Commission had voted a reward of twenty-five dollars for every Indian brought in, dead or alive. Tom English was doing a brisk business while Swede was freighting. Later in the month the *Pioneer* published an extra with the "full details of the butchery of General Custer and his forces." Mattie learned all of it through Aron Gallagher or Freddie, although the latter had begun to hunt more than he checked on Mattie. And that was all right. Aron was good company.

———

It was July 20 before Mattie ventured into Deadwood again. At Garth and Company she found Tom English bent over the newspaper he'd spread out on the counter with a worried expression on his face. "What's wrong?"

With a sigh, he shook his head and stood up. He pointed to the article he'd been reading. "General Merritt's left Fort Robinson down in Nebraska. He's headed to meet up with General Crook and march north. With Terry's troop coming from the east, and Gibbon's forces from the west, they're trying to surround Crazy Horse and the rest of the marauding Sioux with a three-pronged attack." He paused. "There's talk of forming a militia to protect the camp. Captain Jack Crawford's got up three companies plus cavalry. They're calling themselves Custer's Minutemen."

"Well, nobody's going to expect you to join them, I hope," Mattie said.

English shook his head. "No. But I would if I thought it would keep the Sidney-Deadwood trail safe."

"You think Swede's in danger? I thought it sounded like all the trouble was to the north of us."

"After reading this"—he tapped the paper with his hook—"I don't know what to think. It doesn't seem like a very well-planned campaign, and from what I've heard, Sheridan has nothing but contempt for the Sioux. Which means he's probably underestimating them."

"The weather's been fine since the freighters left Deadwood this last time," Mattie reminded him. "I bet they're at least halfway to Sidney. Surely that's far enough south to be out of danger." Tom didn't look any less worried, so Mattie tried harder. "Even if the Sioux were inclined to attack a freight train, don't you think they'd be after the ones headed this way so they could cause as much damage as possible? I mean, what's the point in going after empty wagons?"

"Everything you're saying is logical," Tom said. "But you and I both know that no matter the color of their skin, men aren't logical when they're fighting for their survival. And if I were Sioux, I'd be desperate and more than willing to attack anything that represented the whites whose presence was threatening my way of life."

"All right," Mattie said. "I see your point. But don't forget how long Swede has been freighting with Mr. Tallent as the wagon master and how smart they both are. If there's trouble on the trail, they'll lay over in Sidney until things quiet down." She forced a laugh. "Or maybe raise their own militia down there and blast their way back home. I could see Swede doing something like that."

Tom didn't laugh. "I wish they'd get that telegraph strung. Freddie's so worried he can hardly sleep."

"From what I can see, Freddie isn't the only one who isn't sleeping for worry," Mattie said. "You know . . . the whole camp depends on those supplies. Maybe you should organize some men to guard the trail going south." She walked over to the paper calendar hanging on one wall. "She left on Friday after the Fourth . . ." She looked back at Tom. "How long does it take with empty wagons? About a month?"

"Twenty-two or three days if they make twelve miles a day. But that assumes no rain and a smooth, dry trail."

"So . . ." Mattie turned back to the calendar. "Let's say it didn't rain. That means she'll land in Sidney . . . Saturday. The twenty-ninth. With two days to load they all head back north on the thirty-first." She dropped her arm. "You have plenty of time to make your case and gather a troop to ride with you. You could meet the train on its way back. Shoot, if you hurry you could provide an escort for nearly the entire way. Am I right?"

"You are, but—" He looked around him at the store.

"If you don't mind my closing up one day a week so I can work my claim and keep anyone from challenging its status as an active operation, I'll mind the store." *What are you saying? Right when you're finding good color . . . and enjoying having time to yourself. . . .* Part of her wanted to pull the words out of the air and stuff them back inside. But it was too late.

Tom was smiling. "You'd do that?"

The look on his face . . . Ah well. It wasn't like her gold was going anywhere. She was likely going to be here for the winter anyway. What was a month more or less. "Of course I would. The McKays would watch over things for me, and as long as I can work it a day a week I've 'shown interest'—right?"

Tom nodded. "We could ask Freddie to sleep up there— if you aren't comfortable with making arrangements with the McKays."

"Freddie would want to go with you, and I think you should let him. He's a good shot. There's no reason to leave him here worrying."

"You've got a point." Tom looked back down at the newspaper and murmured, "I just wish I knew she was all right."

"You've become quite fond of Swede."

He hesitated before answering. "I admire her" was all he said.

"So do I," Mattie said. "But I'm not climbing on my trusty steed and going out to rescue her."

"If I do this, don't you dare describe it that way to Swede. Ever. She's not the kind of woman who wants a man to come running to the rescue."

Mattie smiled. "You might be surprised, Mr. English. You just might be surprised."

———

It happened on his way back toward Deadwood. Jonas had camped early and just gotten a fire going, glad for the peace and quiet. Needing time to think about what to do next. Weeks of combing these gulches and mining camps for some trace of Mattie O'Keefe and nothing. He was sick of it. Sick of the filth and the stink. Sick of half-rotten food and drunken miners. Sick of the hysteria about what Crazy Horse did or didn't do and what Spotted Tail did or might do. And, interestingly enough, Jonas realized he was just about out of anger. In fact, if it weren't for the three thousand dollars he was missing since Mattie ran off, he would just pack it up and head home.

"Help me. Please, somebody. Help me."

Jonas sprung up and looked around. Had he really heard that? He looked to the trees above him, followed the rocky terrain all the way to the rim of the gulch. Nothing. Not so much as a rustle in the trees. *You have to get out of this place. It's making you crazy.*

He hobbled his horse and then pulled off the bedroll and saddlebags and finally the saddle. It would be good to get some rest in a place where there wasn't gunfire or a street fight or some drunk screaming profanity at the top of his lungs every few minutes. Not that Abilene was tame. But it was familiar. And a man could see where he was. See the horizon, know what was going on. He felt claustrophobic in these hills. Too closed in.

He positioned the saddle so he could use it like a pillow. Spreading his bedroll out, Jonas lay back and stared up at the sky. The only thing left to try was going back through Deadwood with Mattie's picture, posing as a worried father looking for a runaway daughter. Could he play that part? He'd just about decided he was better off without the little witch. If this Godforsaken country was what she wanted, so be it. All she had to do was give the money back.

He'd just closed his eyes when he thought he heard something again. Not a voice really, but there was definitely the sound of rock skittering down the side of the gulch. Snatching his pistol, Jonas leaped to his feet and searched the rocks above him again.

Over at Bobtail today all they could talk about was how Custer was killed and Crook was beaten and the next fight would be right here in these mining camps. Afraid to go out on the plains, freighters were delaying their departures. Some of the freighters on the way in were turning back toward Sidney and Pierre, Fort Laramie and Cheyenne.

Imagining a hunting party of Sioux on the rocks above him, Jonas decided enough was enough. Maybe Mattie was in these hills and maybe she wasn't. Either way, it wasn't worth getting scalped to find out. He'd stop at the newspaper office in Deadwood and put a notice in about his "long lost daughter." He'd write something so sappy and emotional that every bleeding heart who read it would want to help him. And if that didn't turn her up in the next few days, so be it. He'd consider it a lesson learned and never again let a little vixen like Mattie O'Keefe flit around his place setting limits on what she would and would not do.

Now that he thought about it, that one saloonkeeper down in Deadwood had a pretty good idea. He was advertising in the papers back East for hotel maids and singers, paying their way to Deadwood, and then introducing them to the real world. Swearengen said he mostly got innocents without kin. Desperation made such women more pliable. Especially if you were nice to them at first. As far as Jonas could tell, it was working out all right for Swearengen. Oh, he'd had one girl who couldn't take it, but so what. As the man's wife said, some girls just didn't work out. Nothing you could do about that.

The Swearengens had plans for a new place. They were going to call it the Gem. Two stories, with a balcony right on Main Street where the women could "take the air." Swearengen said he'd be taking in five thousand a night inside of a year or close up shop and move on. He was the right kind of man for Deadwood. Just past being openly brutal. His own wife had a black eye and was walking with a limp. Not Jonas's style at all. To his way of thinking, if you had to get physical, you were careful not to leave a mark where people could see it. No, he wouldn't operate a place using Swearengen's tactics, but he might try recruiting for Abilene through the newspapers. What did he have to lose?

He glanced around him and decided he was overreacting about a few rocks sliding down the gulch. The horse was grazing quietly, and that surely wouldn't be the case if Sioux were lurking on the ridge above. He lay back again. He had to get out of this place and back to Abilene. People who thought his part of Kansas was uncivilized didn't know what they were talking about. *You want to see uncivilized?* he'd say when he got back where he belonged. *Take the trail north to Dakota Territory.*

"Help . . . anybody . . . please."

Jonas grabbed his gun again and barked, "Show yourself!"

"Can't. So . . . sick."

The voice seemed to be coming from up above him somewhere. Was it a trick? He peered up into the trees again, searching for even

the smallest movement that would give the owner of the voice away.
Nothing.

Trick or no, he'd be a fool to camp here tonight. Not after whoever or whatever had made their presence known. It was getting
dark, but he could still follow the creek down through the camps
and back into Deadwood.

He doused the fire and began to pack up. Just as he was saddling
the bay, another pile of rocks slid down from above, only this time
the rocks were accompanied by a man-size lump of humanity falling,
rolling, crawling down toward his campfire.

The man—he was white, that much Jonas could tell—held up
his hand. "Please. Help. Need a doctor."

"You been shot?" Jonas laced the girth strap through the saddle
ring and pulled it tight. He lifted the stirrup off the saddle horn and
reached for his bridle.

"Fever . . . everywhere . . . hurt . . . awful." The man tried to sit
up. Failed. Dropped his head back to the earth and lay still.

Jonas saw the bag around the unconscious man's neck. No way to
know if it was empty. At least not from here. He glanced around. It
could still be a trick. He bridled the horse and took off the hobbles.
In the failing light it was hard to know if someone was up there on
the ridge or not. He waited.

One thing you could count on in these hills. Shadows gathered
quickly, bringing on the night. The unconscious man coughed once,
twice, and lay still again. Dead or not, it was all the same to Jonas,
who was busy rolling up his bedroll and tying it in place behind his
saddle. The only noise in the gulch right now was an owl hooting
somewhere off to the southwest. The bay's ears twisted to check on
it but he remained calm. That was a good sign. Nothing to worry
about.

Walking over to where the man lay motionless, Jonas bent down
and cut the bag away from around his neck. It was heavy. Jonas

smiled. Maybe his luck was turning after all. Just as he was tucking the bag into his vest pocket, the man roused.

He gasped and grabbed Jonas's foot. "Keep gold . . . just . . . help me . . . please." This time he coughed so hard he gagged.

Jonas jerked his foot away. He put his gun to the man's head. No. The noise might draw attention. Easier to just knock him unconscious and get out of there.

CHAPTER 15

Father, forgive them; for they know not what they do.

Luke 23:34

Freddie hunkered behind a shelf of rocks and peered down into the gulch. He'd seen some tracks over this way last week, and if he could get that buck, Aunt Lou would be so pleased. Freddie liked making Aunt Lou smile. He liked seeing Mattie smile, too, and she was doing more of it lately. She wasn't so sad and she wasn't afraid as much. She'd stopped carrying that pistol when she was up on her claim. He would tell her she should keep it in her pocket when she was in town minding Mor's store.

Mor. Tom was worried about her, and it made Freddie worry. He'd never worried before, but things were changing everywhere. The stage was bringing more people into town every day now. Normal people like storekeepers and women. Deadwood wasn't going to be just miners and bad men anymore. But now—

Ah. *There.* Finally some morning light was beginning to filter into the gulch. Freddie stood up slowly, smiling when he saw that even in the moonlight he'd been right about the tracks. There they were, leading all the way down to the— *Whoa.* What was that? *Who* was that?

Ducking behind the rock again, Freddie listened carefully. Nothing but birdcalls broke the morning calm. He peered over the rim of the boulder and a chill went up his spine. Whoever it was down there wasn't moving. He looked around again, then, satisfied that no one lingered in the gulch, he picked his way down to the still form.

"Hey, mister," Freddie said. Crouching down he reached over to— *No need.* The stiffness told him that whoever— *Brady Sloan.* Freddie sat back and stared at the contorted face. Assuming Sloan must have been shot, he searched for evidence, but Sloan's clothing, while filthy, was free of bloodstains.

Freddie looked back up the gulch. Brady had been up there somewhere and slid down here to the trail. You could tell that by the wide path of scattered rocks and the marks and tears in Sloan's pants. Finally Freddie understood. Poor Brady Sloan had gotten drunk and taken a fall that killed him.

Freddie took a long time going over the campsite. From what he could read from the tracks, Sloan had been headed back to Deadwood from the direction of Blacktail. That didn't make much sense, seeing as how he'd been headed south away from Deadwood the last time anyone had heard from him. And he'd been with two other men Aron trusted to keep Brady away from whiskey. But Freddie knew enough about people to know they didn't always keep their promises. Brady Sloan had promised Aron Gallagher to get a fresh start. He'd promised he wouldn't drink again. Aron was going to be sad. Bending low, Freddie shouldered a different kind of carcass than the one he had been hoping for and headed for town.

Justice barked his best puppy-defender bark and bounded out of the tent. Grabbing Bessie II, Mattie stepped to the doorway just in time to see the pup splash through the creek and paint the front of Aron's pants with wet paw prints.

"Some watchdog," he laughed as he pointed down at the pup's wagging tail. He glanced at Bessie II and nodded. "But I see you have a backup."

Mattie set the rifle down and stepped through the tent flap. "I was just about to make some flapjacks," she said. "Care to join me?"

"Thanks, but Aunt Lou filled me up earlier." He nodded up the gulch. "I'm headed to Elizabethtown to preach."

"What about Deadwood?"

"Oh, I'll bother Deadwood later in the day."

"I didn't know you did services in the other camps."

"I haven't until today." He shrugged. "I've been thinking I should be willing to spread the net a little wider. But I've been resisting."

"Well, if you want to procrastinate," Mattie said, "you're welcome to my terrible coffee while I mix up my breakfast." She pointed to the coffeepot on the campfire.

"Thanks."

"I'll be right out." Mattie ducked back inside to mix her batter. In the past two weeks of prospecting she'd had plenty of time to ponder the things Aron had talked about that night at the ball. To think about what Wild Bill had said about him. And to consider Aunt Lou's opinion. While she was no closer to understanding Aron's religion, Mattie had decided to believe Wild Bill and Aunt Lou and to stop worrying over Aron's past and his knowledge of hers. Which made some things easier . . . but did nothing to explain just why her hands were trembling this morning with Aron standing there at the open tent flap drinking coffee and watching her mix flapjack batter.

She'd just poured three dollar-sized flapjacks on the hot griddle positioned over the campfire when Justice let out a yelp and darted down the gulch. "That's Freddie headed this way," she said. "I thought he was hunting for Aunt Lou." She frowned. "He's in an awful hurry." She set the bowl of batter down. "Something's wrong."

"I-I came for Aron," Freddie gasped as soon as he was within earshot. He bent over to catch his breath. "It's Brady. Brady Sloan. I found him. I was hunting over toward Blacktail. There was a track of a big buck and I thought I could get him for Aunt Lou and—"

Aron put his hand on Freddie's shoulder. "It's all right now. Just calm down. What about Brady?"

Freddie gulped. "He's dead. I found him this morning. I brought him back to the doc's." He shuddered.

"Dead how?" Mattie asked.

"He was up high and I guess he fell and hit his head." He paused. "I'm sorry, Aron. He musta got drunk again."

Mattie glanced at Aron, surprised to see him blinking away tears. Justice padded over and nuzzled at his hand. When he didn't react, the pup went to the other hand, nuzzling first and then licking. Finally Aron bent down to pet him, swiping tears away with the back of his hand before standing back up.

"Well," he said, clearing his throat, "guess I'll be making funeral arrangements instead of preaching in Elizabethtown today."

Mattie didn't have any kind thoughts for Brady Sloan, but for Aron's sake she felt bad. "Did he have any family hereabouts?"

"I don't know."

"What about his partner?" She nodded toward the claim above her.

"No one's seen anything of him since before you arrived in the gulch." Aron's voice wobbled as he said, "Poor Brady." He took a deep breath. "It won't be much of a funeral, I expect, but I'll do one anyway."

"I'll help," Freddie said.

Their kindness surprised her. Sloan might have claimed to get religion, but obviously it hadn't taken. She would have expected Aron to resent being duped into paying Sloan's doctor bills and buying him a horse, only to have this happen.

"I think I know what you're thinking," Aron said to her, his voice gentle. "I'm just trying to do unto others, if you know what I mean."

Mattie shook her head. "Honestly, no. I don't understand why you'd be in any hurry to pay your respects to someone who did nothing to earn it."

"Like I said, because the Bible says I should do to others what I'd like them to do to me. Maybe he's got family somewhere. In any case, I'll always think of him as *my* brother in the spiritual sense, and I'd be grateful if someone took care of my brother if I wasn't around to do it. Even if it only meant a proper burial."

———

Mattie rattled around her claim for most of the afternoon after Aron and Freddie left, trying to understand the preacher's obvious grief over a drunk, who as far as she was concerned might not have been bent on stealing her gold but had certainly stolen a horse and money from Aron Gallagher. And yet Aron was paying for a funeral.

As she thought back over the things they'd discussed the night of the Independence Ball, Mattie went inside and took Dillon's Bible out of his supply box. It was well used, although Mattie couldn't remember ever seeing Dillon read a Bible. No matter. She wanted to read about the man on the cross next to Jesus. The one Aron seemed to relate to. That story would be in one of those first New Testament books. She didn't know much about the Bible, but the poker playing preacher had made her curious enough to learn how things were set up. Old Testament. New Testament. The Jewish people. The Christians. The part about Jesus dying would be in the new part.

She started with Matthew and read about both criminals insulting Jesus. When she realized that the next book was about Jesus' life, too, she read it through. Again, both criminals insulted Jesus. Instead of reading all of Luke, she skipped to the end. There it was. The change of heart that resulted in a promise of Paradise. Mattie read the account over and over again. She wondered if Aron had really done all that much blaspheming in his day—enough to identify with the two men crucified alongside Christ. And she wondered what it was about Jesus on the cross that had spoken so loudly to that one thief, when so many other people around him that day just kept hurling insults. And what about the Roman soldier who said, "Truly this man was the Son of God"? How was it that he believed Jesus was special when most of Jesus' own people screamed for the Romans to crucify him?

Something amazing leaped out at her as she read. *Jesus prayed for the people who were killing him. "Father, forgive them, for they know not what they do."* The idea that anyone could be dying like that and care about the very people who were torturing him was unfathomable. What kind of man did that? It was a kind of forgiveness Mattie had never seen, and it made Aron's willingness to preach Brady Sloan's funeral look insignificant by comparison.

Maybe that's how he looks at it, too. All the time I've been thinking he was doing so much for someone who didn't deserve it. . . . Maybe Aron was thinking about Jesus and thinking preaching Sloan's funeral wasn't anything special. But Aron had paid for Brady Sloan's medical care. Aron had picked Sloan out of the mud and wiped the vomit off his face, and never given up hope that Sloan was changed. And now he was making arrangements to have the man buried and paying for it out of his own pocket.

Setting the Bible down, Mattie began to dress for town. Sloan might not deserve a proper burial, but she was going to do what she could to help Aron give him one. After all, it couldn't hurt to follow the example of a man who wanted to be like Jesus.

———

Could anything else possibly go wrong in this hellish place? A thrown shoe had forced Jonas back to Blacktail, and a drunken blacksmith had made it necessary to wait in that Godforsaken hole an entire day before the bay could be attended to. Now he was once again riding the trail back to Deadwood. There was no sign of the drifter, but Jonas wasn't worried about being identified. The shadows had been long that evening. Stand the two of them face-to-face in a court of law—which as far as Jonas knew did not exist up here anyway—and he had no doubt he could convince anyone the drunk had fingered the wrong man. Even so, he would take precautions.

He'd lamented the condition of his trail-worn suit, but now it might prove to be a boon. Tonight when he camped he'd take it off and beat it over a boulder to make it look even worse. Bending down, he dragged his fingers through the dirt, collecting grime beneath his nails. He'd stop shaving and get rid of his carpetbag. That should complete the look and separate him thoroughly from the possibility of ever being connected with the image of a well-appointed gentleman mounted on a handsome bay gelding.

The horse was another matter. He'd have to get rid of it. Removing his saddlebags and bedroll, he backed away lest the creature lash out at the sudden noise, pulled his gun from its holster, pointed it toward the sky, and pulled the trigger. With a terrified scream the bay charged away. Jonas watched it go with a satisfied smile. Who knew where that horse would end up. It was a fine animal. Anyone who found it would be likely to keep it and hope no one came looking.

Tossing his carpetbag behind an outcropping of rocks, Jonas picked up his bedroll and his saddlebags and headed for Deadwood. He'd get a room, place the ad about Mattie in the *Pioneer*, and lie low while he waited to see if anyone responded. There'd been a new arrival at the Green Front when he had been in there before looking for Mattie. A petite brunette with an air of innocence about her. He hadn't had any feminine company in far too long. The brunette would do.

"You can do this, Mattie," Tom said, and closed the ledger book they'd been poring over. "It's not hard. Just be patient with yourself about the ciphering and check your numbers each night after you close." He paused. "And here in town I think you should consider taking the Colt out of your pocket and tucking it at your waist again. In plain sight. Especially when you walk over to make the bank deposit at the end of the day. Make a deposit *every day*, and don't be shy about being seen. We want it known there's no gold kept in the store overnight. Ever."

Mattie nodded. "I understand, but I still don't like the idea of just locking the place up and heading off to my claim. What would you say to my asking one of the McKays to help out while you're gone? Not as a storekeeper—just as a guard of sorts. I'd have them sleep in the storeroom."

"That won't be necessary. I've already asked someone to keep an eye out for you." He glanced toward the street. "And here he is now."

Mattie frowned. Why wasn't Aron going with Tom and the others? He was likely the best shot in town except for Wild Bill— but then, Tom probably didn't know that. Clearly Aron hadn't volunteered the information, either. And if he wasn't going to ride out with Tom and the others . . . then why couldn't *he* mind the store and leave her to work her claim? "If Aron can mind the store," she said to Tom, "you don't need me."

"Aron's taken work enlarging the living quarters behind Underwood Hardware. I knew Swede would be relieved to know that someone was guarding both the store *and* the temporary storekeeper." Tom smiled at her. "And, frankly, so am I."

Mattie wanted to protest. Wanted to say she didn't need guarding. But the truth was, if she wasn't going to be up on her claim and out of the public eye most of the time, maybe she did. It had been three months since she'd left Abilene, and part of her wanted to believe that Jonas would have turned up by now if he'd followed her. But she couldn't be sure. The old tightness still returned to her midsection sometimes, and even though it wasn't the grip of fear she'd arrived with, she realized that knowing that someone trustworthy was still in town when everyone else was leaving was comforting. Aron was more than just a trustworthy man. He knew how to handle a gun. And, if she let herself admit it, the idea of his watching over her wasn't all that unattractive for other reasons, too. Reasons she didn't want to think about right now.

———

Tom and Freddie and a band of about two dozen other riders left Deadwood on the last day of July. If all went well, they'd meet up with Swede's wagon train on their return trip and be back in Deadwood at the end of August.

"Thank you for suggesting this," Tom said to Mattie as he and Freddie mounted up. "And for making it possible by offering to keep the store open."

"You're welcome."

"Be sure and check all the locks before you go upstairs every night."

"I will."

"And don't forget to deposit—"

"—the day's earnings in the bank every day." Mattie nodded. "And check and recheck my work on the ledger. I know."

"And don't forget that those sacks of flour at the back of the storeroom—"

"—are part of the stock you'll need this winter, so don't sell it."

Freddie spoke up. "Stop worrying, Tom. Mattie is smart."

Tom blanched. "I'm sorry. I just—"

"I understand. This place is important to you. I'll do my best with it until you and Swede get back."

"I know you will. I just want Swede to be pleased with what she finds when that finally happens."

"As I said, I'll do my best. Now go." She shooed him toward the trail. "Be a hero. Deadwood could use one." As the men rode away, Mattie smiled, picturing Swede's expression when she saw Tom riding toward her. Swede was going to light up like a heroine in a novel being rescued by her prince.

———

He'd always been strong, able to fight off anything, but this time—this time Jonas barely had the strength to lift his head off the mattress. He couldn't stop shivering. The fever must be high. He hadn't had anything to eat today, but that was all right, because starting yesterday he hadn't been able to keep anything down. He didn't care about finding Mattie anymore. He didn't even care so much about the missing money. He cursed her and her thieving ways. He cursed the sick lowlife he'd encountered out on the trail—who'd likely given him whatever this was. He cursed Deadwood and the Black Hills and the lumpy mattress and the threadbare blankets. As he lay shivering, all Jonas wanted was to get back to Kansas.

But another day passed, and still he didn't feel better. He kept shivering and vomiting, and then, sometime in the middle of the second night of this infernal sickness, the pain woke him up. Pain like he'd never felt before. Pain as if a strong hand with a hammer were working over his joints. As for his back, that was more like an entire crew of carpenters pounding nails. His groaning finally roused the ire of whoever was in the next room. Someone called for the doctor. Jonas was too sick to care what the man said as long as he got some relief. But then the doctor said *smallpox*.

CHAPTER 16

*The secret things belong unto the Lord our God: but those things
which are revealed belong unto us and to our children for ever,
that we may do all the words of this law.*

Deuteronomy 29:29

Mattie had dug a hole halfway to the bedrock and was rejoicing over her progress when Justice yapped and tore off
down the gulch, his tail wagging. The surprising surge of joy she
felt at the sight of Aron climbing the gulch toward her abated as
soon as he was close enough for her to read his expression. Setting her shovel down, she pulled her gloves off and waited. When
he was close enough that she didn't have to shout, she swallowed
hard and said, "Somehow I don't think you walked up here to have
afternoon tea."

"Afraid not." He motioned toward the campfire. "Let's sit down
for a minute."

Swede. Tom. Freddie . . . Indians! She searched his eyes, troubled
by the depth of sorrow she saw there, and blurted out the question.
"Who? I'll sit down in a minute. Just tell me who."

"Wild Bill."

225

Dumbfounded, Mattie just stared at him. She could read the rest of it in his eyes even as she croaked, "Dead?" When he nodded, she gave a little cry of disbelief and stumbled to one of the logs by the fire to sit down. Justice whined and came to sit beside her. He leaned close, his tail flopping once or twice in the dust as he looked up into her face. When she absentmindedly reached out to the dog, he snuggled closer. In spite of the animal's warmth she could feel through her work pants, she shivered. "How? Who?"

Aron sighed and sat down beside her. "Shot."

Mattie shook her head. "Wild Bill couldn't have been shot. He was too good. Too fast."

"It wasn't exactly a fair fight. The way I hear it, a drifter with some sort of grudge sneaked up behind him while he was playing poker at the Number 10."

"You and I both know that can't be what happened. He always sat with his back to the wall."

Aron nodded. "Except for today. Today one Jack McCall walked up behind him and—"

The two of them sat quietly for a few minutes. Finally Mattie muttered, "I hope he didn't suffer."

"Doc says he probably never knew what happened. One second here—the next in the afterlife." He paused. "Charlie Utter claimed the body. There'll be a service tomorrow. I've been asked to say a few words."

"Poor Calamity," Mattie said. "She'll be devastated."

"She's tearing around town like a wild woman screaming for vengeance and saying they don't need a trial, everyone knows who did it and McCall should be hanged by sundown."

"Western justice," Mattie murmured. Thinking she'd said his name, Justice yipped softly and licked her hand. Mattie patted his head. "Do you think Mr. Utter would mind if I sang something— for Bill?"

Aron cleared his throat. "Bill isn't the only reason I'm here.

There's a sickness down on North Main. Seems to have started with a drifter holed up at the Green Front. It's spreading. The doc thinks it's smallpox."

Just the words sent a chill through Mattie. She'd had a regular customer once who'd survived his encounter with the dreaded disease. He was one of the gentlest men Mattie had ever met, and yet, even knowing the man beneath the mass of pits and scars that formed his face, it took effort to look at him without shuddering with revulsion. Jonas had had to pay the girls extra to entertain him.

"So," Aron said, "while I understand your wanting to be at the funeral, I'm thinking it would be better if you stayed up here on your claim for now."

"But the store—"

"The store can be closed until the town decides what to do. Many of the businesses have closed up already. Swede and Tom will understand."

"What's to be done but ride it out?"

"Well, if it's really smallpox, we'll put up a pest tent. Quarantine the sick. Try to keep it from spreading."

"A pest tent? For how long?"

He shrugged. "The doc doesn't know. He says no one can. It runs its course, and until it does—"

"But Tom trusted me to take care of things. And Swede needs the money."

"Folks can be contagious before they even know they have it," Aron said, "and you can catch it just by taking a breath within ten feet of a victim." He paused. "Swede wouldn't want you doing business when any customer could end up giving you a life-threatening disease." His voice was gentle as he pleaded, "Please, Mattie. Just stay up here and work your claim. I'll see that you get supplies."

"But what about you? If it's so contagious—"

"I've been around it before. Apparently I have an immunity."

"You don't have any scars."

"I don't know why. I just didn't get it." He reached over and touched the back of her hand. "I know Bill meant a lot to you. It's a terrible thing to have him go this way. I'll make it a good service. I promise."

She stood up. "I know you will. And I'll sing."

At least he didn't try to order her to stay put. Instead, he tried a different argument. "You want *everyone* to know he was your friend? That's going to cause folks to talk."

"Then they'll talk. It can't be helped." She forced a smile. "Besides, Bill said you had my back, remember?"

"I can't protect you from smallpox."

"Then help me protect the store. You can't just put a Closed sign on the door and expect people to honor it. Especially if things get really bad. Someone has to make sure no one breaks in." She was making sense and Aron knew it. She could see it in his eyes. "I'll stay off the streets if that'll make you feel better. As soon as I sing for Bill." She paused. "He was my friend once at a time when no one else had the guts to—" She shook her head. Tears threatened as she said, "I'm coming to show my respects. Please don't fight me on this."

Aron's expression softened. He nodded. "All right. I won't fight you. But I *will* walk you there, and I *will* expect you to stay behind closed doors at the store for at least a few days after that. You may not realize it, but you have friends who care about you now. And they'd never forgive me if I didn't do everything in my power to keep you safe."

As she changed for the trip into town, Mattie considered Aron's words. She wasn't used to having people tell her what to do because they *cared* about her. She wasn't used to it . . . but she could learn to like it.

> Died in Deadwood, Black Hills, August 2, 1876, from the effects of a pistol shot, J. B. Hickok (Wild Bill) formerly of Cheyenne, Wyoming. Funeral services will be held at Charlie Utter's camp, on Thursday afternoon, August 3, 1876, at 3 o'clock P.M. All are respectfully invited to attend.

Charlie Utter's notice in the newspaper had invited "all," and as far as Mattie could tell, "all" had come, from sporting girls and gamblers to business owners and their families. Hundreds of miners turned out, and as they filed by Bill's open coffin with their hats in their hands, Mattie saw more than one swipe tears away. Even the Underwoods were there, although it was obvious Mrs. Underwood did not approve. She walked past Bill's coffin without a glance at the famous man's body. When her daughter Kitty paused to stare, her mother positively yanked on her arm, forcing her to keep moving.

Mr. Utter began the service by thanking everyone for coming. And then he nodded at Aron, who began, "If there is anything we can learn from this tragic event, it is that none of us knows the hour when we will find ourselves on the other side of the thin veil that separates this life from the next. Who among us would have expected such an end for such a man?" Aron paused for a moment. "When a man named John wrote his version of the life of Jesus, he said that he was writing so that folks who read it could know that they would have eternal life.

"I think it's fair to assume that a lot of us here today have been shaken by what's happened to our friend Bill Hickok. But among all the feelings of anger and shock, if we just listen to what John said, this horrible event can result in a lot of good for a lot of people."

He looked down at the coffin. "The Bible says that 'it is appointed unto men once to die and after this the judgment.' And when it comes right down to it, the only question we really have to know the answer to is this: what happens when *we* stand before the Judge?" He looked over the crowd. "You can *know*. God promises eternal life to all who believe in His Son. He promises eternal death to all who refuse to believe." He held up his Bible. " 'These things have I written unto you that believe on the name of the Son of God; that ye may know that ye have eternal life, and that ye may believe on the name of the Son of God.' If my friend Bill Hickok could talk to us right now, I'm pretty sure he'd have one thing to say to us all, and that would be to get things settled right now about where we'll be when it's *us* in that box and it's *our* friends and family gathered to say good-bye."

Abruptly, Aron closed his eyes and began to pray. "Father God. Thank you for my friend Bill and for the way you are using him on this day to give us all a moment to reflect on our own situation. May we all do just that. Thank you for sending Jesus to make a way for us to get to heaven. Thank you for having John write it down so we could know it. Help us to pay attention. Amen."

Six men stepped forward. The coffin was closed and the men hoisted it to their shoulders and began the trek to Ingleside Cemetery. At the grave, Mattie began to sing as they lowered Bill's coffin into the earth. She only knew one hymn, and she didn't know all the words to that one, but she did her best. " 'Amazing grace, how sweet the sound, that saved someone like me. I once was lost, but then got found. Once blind, I now can see.' "

It didn't seem enough, somehow. One verse of one song for such a famous man. Dillon's grave was only a few feet away. Mattie hesitated, but then she thought, *Why not?* Bill had known Dillon, too. Had even stood between him and Jonas once and saved Dillon a beating. And so while hundreds filed past, some scooping up a handful of earth and scattering it across the coffin, Mattie launched into "Mist Covered Mountains," barely making it through the line that went, "they'll give me a welcome the warmest on earth . . . in the sweet-sounding language of home." When her voice wavered,

Aron took her hand and squeezed it. She held on until she'd finished the song.

When the crowd was finally gone and Mr. Utter and the pall-bearers were shoveling the last of the earth atop the grave, Mattie said to Aron, "I hope there was someone over there saying welcome home to him." She gazed over at Dillon's grave. "To *them*."

"So do I, Mattie. So do I." Aron dropped her hand. Together, they made their way back into town. Justice was waiting inside the back door of the store, tail wagging, puppy kisses abounding. Mattie declined Aron's invitation to join him in Aunt Lou's kitchen for a meal. Croaking a hasty good-bye, she closed the door behind her, sat down on the floor, scooped Justice into her lap, and let the tears fall.

———

Angels. Jonas listened carefully to the singing. Not something he would have expected to hear when he crossed over. Likely he was hallucinating as they carried him toward the pest house. He wasn't the only one suffering. At least half a dozen lay moaning around him. Did they hear the angel, too? He opened his eyes.

The man next to him had already broken out with the rash. It didn't look that bad. He didn't seem to feel all that bad, either. He was just lying there, waiting. Pale. Eyes closed. At one point he opened his eyes and turned to look at Jonas. "Beautiful music, isn't it," he said. "Sounds like an angel."

Jonas was hurting too much to talk. Hurting . . . angry . . . and afraid. He'd always been considered handsome. But now—the specter of the scarred face of a regular customer down in Abilene would not fade.

The fever returned. And the pain . . . oh . . . the pain.

———

Red Tallent laughed. "You mean you still want to do this?"

Swede glowered as she hung the sign on the side of one freight

231

wagon that read *Wanted: Cats. All kinds. Paying 25 cents each.* "I am doing it" was all she said to the wagon master as they stood on Sidney's main street.

A boy stopped to read the sign. He pointed at it. "You mean that?"

"I do," Swede said.

"How many you want?"

"How many can you bring?"

The boy thought for a moment, then extended the fingers of one hand. "Five?"

"Den you vill have earned over one dollar."

"Cash?"

"Yah, sure," Swede nodded. The boy tore off up the street as if chased by a mad dog. She turned to Red. "Now vill you help me build dis cage I am needing or should I ask elsevare?"

Red chucked Eva under the chin. "Your mother," he said, "has gone plumb crazy."

"Yah," Swede agreed. "Crazy from fighting to keep de mice and rats from eating vat I vork so hard to bring to Deadvood. Crazy to find a solution." She paused. "Every voman in Deadvood vill vant one. You vill see. Next trip *you* vill be buying up cats."

"But what if they don't sell? You will have taken up all that space in a wagon—and earned nothing."

Swede planted her feet and put her hands on her hips. "Dey vill sell."

Tallent shook his head. "It's the craziest thing I ever heard of." He sighed. "But I guess that's to be expected. Who ever heard of a woman bullwhacker to begin with?" When Swede opened her mouth to defend herself, Tallent raised both hands in the air. "All right, all right. I'll help." He walked away muttering to himself. Presently he stopped and called back to her, "How big does this cage need to be?"

"Vat do you advise?"

"How would I know? I'm not a cat-hauler."

Swede pondered. "Pretend it is chickens. Big ones."

"So how many big chickens are you hauling to Deadwood?"

"Forty." When she said the number aloud, even Swede was tempted to laugh. But if she could sell them for ten dollars each . . . "Four hundred dollars and ve paid only ten, baby girl," she muttered to Eva as she smoothed the baby's downy hair into place. "So much vould build a good church. Or maybe a school. Vich do you tink is most important?" Eva babbled a response. Swede laughed.

How she loved this child. How she longed to be the kind of mother Eva needed. A storekeeper, not someone who wielded a whip and shouted at oxen. *Or a storekeeper's wife, even.* The thought came uninvited and Swede apologized to God at once.

Forgive me. I am grateful for vat you have done. For vat you have given. And I am content. She paused and looked up at the sky. Feeling guilty, she corrected her prayer. *All right. Maybe not so much content. But I am trying. And I vill see to the building of a church if you vill help me to sell some cats.*

———

He was going to live after all, and he was glad. He'd wished to die more than once during the first few days of the disease. Now, as Jonas lay in the pest tent with the other victims all around him, he began to think that maybe everything would be all right. The fever, which had raged for days, was finally gone, and the interminable severe backache was nearly gone, too. Good things. And yet he was weak. So weak that just holding up his head to take a drink was a challenge. As for eating, chewing was too much work.

He despised being weak like this. Being at the mercy of others was the worst part about being sick now. He lifted one arm and inspected the rash. It wasn't all that bad. Maybe he would be spared the worst.

Dropping his arm, he lay still, wishing he could get out of there. Now that he felt better, he found the noises in the pest tent annoying. Groans. Retching. Pleas for help. Ramblings from a delirious patient on the opposite side of the tent. The longer he lay there the more he hated it. The more he wanted to get away.

The famous Calamity Jane was helping in the pest tent. Jonas had heard stories about her back in Abilene, about her tender streak for children, how she surprised folks by giving away money or nursing the sick. None of that made him inclined to see her as anything but a revolting excuse for a woman. She had rough hands and a weathered face framed by snarled hair. She was making her way toward him now. He could feel her stinking breath on his face as she leaned down to help him lift his head and take a drink.

He pulled away. "I can get my own water," he said, and managed to sit up. The effort made him break out in a sweat, but still he held on lest she think him feeble.

Calamity was not impressed. "You listen up," she said. "You'd best be taking any help you can get and saving your energy, because you're just at the start of this here thing. The fever's down and you're feeling a little better, but it ain't gonna last. You need to save your strength because you're still facing a couple of weeks of hell. If you know what's good for you, you'll lay back down and take this." She shoved the water back at him.

Jonas drank. It was lukewarm and tasted like the bottom of someone's washbasin. Maybe it was, for all he knew. He lay back down. The patient next to him had died yesterday after two days of moaning and groaning that nearly drove Jonas crazy. All he cared about now was getting out of there. Surviving and going home to Abilene, where beautiful women fawned over him and his clientele respected him.

The truth of what Calamity Jane had said began to reveal itself the very next day. The rash was only the beginning of sorrows. Over the next couple of weeks it spread. The lesions became tiny pits filled with vile liquid. They tore open and leaked, and at one point Jonas nearly suffocated when ulcerating lesions in his throat began to leak, and he couldn't make himself either swallow or bring it up for the pain. As he sank into an abyss of incomprehensible agony, he cursed God. He even tried a kind of prayer, intoning whatever powers might answer, *Let me die. Let me die. Let me die.*

———

Mattie expected the people of Deadwood to be angry at God over the smallpox. She even wished that Aron would forgo a Sunday sermon for a week or two until things had settled down. What with the upheaval over Wild Bill's death and the subsequent trial—the killer was set free because he claimed Bill had killed his brother—what with the creeping threat of disease, Mattie imagined more heckling than ever. In fact, she and Aunt Lou worried that someone might take their anger out on the preacher in ways stronger than words. But none of those fears were realized. The people of Deadwood not only flocked to hear Aron preach, they *listened*. And so did Mattie.

"Why smallpox? Why here? Why now? Why does this one die and that one live? *Why?*" Aron paused and looked out over the crowd before saying, "I've had the same questions. I've had the sleepless nights and the anger at God. I've had the bitterness and the rage. I've held someone I loved in my arms and tried to hold back death only to hear that one I loved breathe their last." He broke off for a moment before continuing. "I know more about this disease and the pain our town is feeling than most. I know, because smallpox took my brother and sister and parents and then played a trick on me and left me whole. And I will go to my grave wondering why."

Aron's revelation fell on Mattie like a cold rain. She shivered and rubbed her arms to dispel the prickles. As she looked around, she could tell that more than one listener had been impacted the same way. To have a preacher sermonize about how folks should react to the fear of smallpox and the threat of death was one thing. To know that preacher had lived through it was entirely another. There were no hecklers now. There was only a common yearning to be comforted and a new willingness to hear what the preacher had to say.

"But even though I still don't have the answer to that question 'Why?' in time I came to understand that the God who did not abandon Adam when he sinned in the garden, who did not abandon Peter when he denied Jesus, had not abandoned me. For all my anger and all the horrible things I did after my family died, God never once let go of me. And when I was finally ready to listen, He opened my heart and my mind and helped me understand how much He loved me." Aron smiled. "And He'll do that very same thing for every single person in Deadwood who turns to Him for help."

Aron glanced Mattie's way. She nodded. *We want to hear more.*

"This world is full of trouble," Aron continued, "but we can have hope through our Lord Jesus Christ, who promises that *nothing* can separate us from Him; not smallpox or death or life or gambling debts or drunken binges or desertions or any other earthly thing. Jesus loves us. This we can know because the Bible tells us so." He paused. "Just Jesus, folks. That's the only answer I have for all the questions. But I stand here this morning to tell you, both because the Bible says it and because I've experienced it: He is enough. Always and forever, He is enough."

Mattie folded her arms and studied the ground, no longer willing to meet Aron's gaze as she tried to reconcile her own questions with Aron's experiences and the idea that Jesus was enough. She wasn't certain about that part of the message, and yet she could feel herself being drawn toward it. One thing *was* certain: Aunt Lou had been right when she said that Aron Gallagher wasn't anything like the preachers Mattie had known before. He was sincere. He didn't quote the Bible on Sunday and then forget everything he'd said on Monday. He didn't just spout easy answers, either. He shared things he knew because he'd lived them.

Someone called out, "Pray for us, Reverend." The crowd murmured their agreement. And for one miraculous moment, Deadwood turned its collective face toward heaven.

CHAPTER 17

Jealousy is cruel as the grave: the coals thereof are coals of fire,
which hath a most vehement flame.

Song of Solomon 8:6

ust on the horizon. Swede's heart leaped. She tried to calm
herself. It could be anything. Another freight train ahead of
them. *But ve were first to leave Sidney headed to Deadvood.* A company
of soldiers. *But they have all gone yet further north past Deadvood.* A
string of settlers' wagons. *Except most are waiting until vord comes*
that the Indians are defeated.

Swede clutched her bullwhip and gave it an extra crack. Leif
bellowed in protest. Eva whimpered. Up ahead, Red Tallent was
moving into a familiar pattern. Circle the wagons. Which meant that
he had seen the dust on the horizon and was worried, too.

Dear God . . . are ve to be massacred?

Her heart pounding, Swede guided her own team into position.
Finally, when everyone had moved into position, accomplishing the
only defensive move possible, Tallent dismounted and hurried over
to Swede. She stood beside Eva's cradle, aiming Bessie at where,

sooner or later, human forms would emerge from the approaching cloud of dust.

"If anything happens to me—" Red began, but Swede would not listen.

"Noting vill happen. Ve have freighted together dese three years and noting vill happen. It must not."

"But if it does, I've got a sister back in Virginia." Red pressed a piece of paper into Swede's hand. "Would you write and tell her I—"

Even as she tucked the piece of paper into her apron pocket, Swede shook her head. "I vill not have to do dis. But someday ven I meet your sister I vill tell her how her brother is my good friend." She blinked tears away.

Foolish old man, giving her such a task to do. A task she could not accomplish, because there was a pistol inside her supply box, and if that cloud of dust was Indians, she would see to it that neither she nor her precious Eva became entertainment for savages. She trembled as she prayed. *Please, God. A miracle. Let there be no killing.* Even so, as Red walked away to check on the other drivers, she leveled Bessie at the oncoming . . . *white* men! Thanks be to God. Not enemies, for they had no guns drawn.

"Don't shoot!" Swede called out to Red. "Do you see dem? Don't shoot!"

"I see!" Tallent hollered back. He hurried to her side, a broad smile barely visible beneath his thick moustache and beard. "Looks like you won't be needing that address after all," he said, and held out his hand.

Swede reached into her apron pocket and handed it back. And just at that moment Eva began to jump up and down, clapping and calling out, "Ta-ta! Free! Ta-ta! Free!" and there were Tom English and Freddie riding toward her at the head of an entire company of armed men. Tom. Come to rescue her.

Swede's heart swelled with love—and then—then she looked

at her hands, calloused and gnarled from hard work. She swiped at her tears and felt leathery skin tanned from all her time in the wind and the sun. She looked down at her apron, stained with mud from the trail and tattered at the hem. She greeted Tom and Freddie with tears, and no one knew that it was not for joy that she was crying, but for a broken heart. For no man as handsome and refined and kind as Tom English would ever love such a woman as her.

———

"Doc says the worst is over now," Calamity said as she walked past Jonas's cot. "Thought you might like to hear that."

What did she expect? A *thank you*? A *praise the Lord*? Jonas nodded and turned his face to the canvas wall of the pest tent. He was too exhausted to speak. Wrung out with fighting through pain and tired of seeing what was happening to his body. God help him—if his hand and arms looked like this, what had happened to his *face*? *God.* Purely a turn of phrase. Anyone who believed someone in someplace called heaven cared for humanity was a blind fool.

By afternoon Jonas had thought of something he did want to know, and it seemed to take hours for anyone to get close enough for him to ask. Swallowing, he croaked when Calamity Jane came near, "What day of the week is it? What date? How long have I been here?"

"It's Tuesday. August. The twenty-ninth, I think." Calamity held out a glass of water. "I don't know as I can say how long you've been here. There's been too many to keep track of things like that."

Jonas drank the water and handed the glass back. "I'm hungry," he said.

"That's a good sign." Calamity nodded. "I'll see what I can do for ya."

The hunger grew until it was a pain deep in his gut. And still, no one brought food. His bedroll. His money. Where were they? Probably gone. He was too sick to have noticed or cared. But no, they were both still tucked beneath his cot. He sat up and looked around. *Empty cots.* So Calamity Jane had told the truth. Things were getting better. But where was she? How long was he going to have to wait for something to eat?

They said everyone should stay put until every pustule dried up. Until the scabs were completely gone. That was the only certain way to prevent giving it to someone else. His stomach growled. Grabbing his bedroll, he crept outside. He'd find something to eat if he had to challenge a boar for its slops. He'd have to stay out of sight, though. Anyone who saw him would force him back to the pest tent. So be it. He would stay out of sight, but he was finished with depending on others. Finished with thirst and hunger.

———

"I don't know what it's gonna take to get that man to listen." Aunt Lou shook her head. "He's killin' hisself, plain and simple." She poured herself a cup of coffee and sat down at the kitchen table opposite Mattie. "Barely eating, up at the pest house, down at the lumberyard, out in the street preaching, and all the time he's mourning the dead while he tries to save the living." She tore a hunk of bread off the loaf she'd placed in the middle of the table and popped it in her mouth.

Mattie looked down at the dinner plate Aunt Lou had piled high with mashed potatoes and roast something, then covered over with milk gravy. She shared some of Aunt Lou's frustrations with Aron Gallagher, but not primarily because she was worried about Aron. Mostly she wanted to see more of him because . . . well, just because. She'd torn down the last of the wall of suspicion she'd kept between them, and now that it was gone, she realized she liked being around Gallagher. She liked it a lot.

"He doesn't even stop by for supper these days," Aunt Lou said, shaking her head.

"Let's make him a picnic," Mattie suggested. "I'll find him before

I turn in for the night and refuse to leave until I see him *eat* it." If Aron needed an annoying sister to nag him into eating, she could do that. Dillon always said she had a talent for annoying. She smiled. *Dillon.* How good it was to remember him without dissolving in tears. How good it was to have Aunt Lou provide an excuse to check in with a certain preacher.

She reached over and squeezed Aunt Lou's hand. "This town is so lucky to have you in it." She gestured at her plate. "And I appreciate your inviting me to have supper with you. I like the solitary life up on my claim, but here in town there is absolutely no charm in staring at four walls and eating alone." She took her first bite of potatoes.

Aunt Lou waved the praise away. "Ain't nothin' to setting an extra plate, honey. I'm glad for the company—and an ear to listen to my worrying over that reverend of ours. He seems to have forgotten that the Lord Jesus hisself took a rest now and then."

Mattie smiled. "Well, maybe you should deliver the meal and remind him."

"Maybe I will," Aunt Lou said with a nod. "We can go together."

And so, basket in hand, Aunt Lou and Mattie made their way up the street toward the job site at the Underwoods', intent on seeing to it that Aron Gallagher ate a decent meal. As they approached the Underwoods' back door they heard laughter, and looking in through one of the nice new windows gracing the west wall of what was obviously the dining room, they saw that the reverend was already eating a decent meal. With the lovely Kitty Underwood on one side and her twelve-year-old sister, Pearl, on the other.

"Guess he don't need a picnic supper after all," Aunt Lou murmured.

"Apparently not," Mattie said, surprised at just how disappointed she was.

The two women did an about-face and returned to the hotel. Once there, Mattie agreed with Aunt Lou that it was wonderful that the reverend had finally stopped working long enough for a good meal. She even agreed that it was nice to see him smiling and enjoying himself.

Bidding Aunt Lou good-night, Mattie stepped out on the back stoop. She looked up at the sky, reveling in the cool breeze on this late August night. If she were back in Abilene right now, she'd likely be sweltering, patting her cheeks with a dainty hanky and hoping to transform the beads of sweat collecting on her brow and upper lip into a feminine glow.

A chicken squawked. Mattie slipped her hand in her pocket and grasped the butt of the Colt as she peered at Aunt Lou's half-empty coop. She regretted leaving Justice up at the claim with the McKays. What had she been thinking? *You were thinking you didn't have time to housebreak a dog and run a store.* Which was true. Still, as she tried to see into the darkness, she decided to retrieve Justice. *As soon as you can convince Aron Gallagher to tear himself away from Kitty Underwood and watch the store while you climb the gulch.*

Aunt Lou came to the back door. "Everything all right out there?"

"Everything's fine," Mattie said. "The hens were squawking. Seems all right now." As she bid Aunt Lou good-night and made her way toward the store, Mattie began to hum.

———

Jonas sat back abruptly, wincing when his backside hit the earth and hoping against hope no one was on their way out here to check on their squawking chickens. Gasping for breath, he stumbled to the corner of the hotel. He moved along the edge of the building . . . looked around the corner . . . trying to see—*there!* There she was! Finally. There was no mistaking that hair or that voice. It was Mattie O'Keefe he was watching as she unlocked the door to some business. He sat down in the shadows of the building and waited. Eventually he saw what he needed to see. Lamplight appeared in an upper-story window.

He was as weak as a kitten. His legs trembled with the effort he'd made just to follow her this far. Forcing himself back to his feet, Jonas stumbled toward the hillside that rose behind the hotel. He crawled the last few feet to the hiding place he'd found behind an outcropping of rocks. After all he'd been through, and the minx had been right here in Deadwood all along. Obviously she'd learned some tricks from all the years working for him. Building a general merchandise store was a wise move for someone like her. Someone with money to spend and a past to hide. Who, he wondered, was the *Garth* of Garth and Company Merchandise?

Jonas's mind raced even as his body reeled from hunger and exhaustion. Wonderings and imaginings wove together until, when he finally fell asleep, he dreamed of hideous smallpox-scarred women and platters of succulent food, of pest tents and gambling halls, of bags of gold dust and emerald rings, all of them part of the endless quest for Mattie O'Keefe.

———

Freddie was sick of yowling, spitting cats. He'd been helping his mor out on the trail for over a week and couldn't wait to get back to Deadwood. The fuss the cats put up every time he fed them was almost scary. He sure hoped no one he knew in Deadwood ever found out that he'd gone hunting so he could feed a bunch of cats. People already made fun of him enough.

"Tom," he said as they were riding together one day, "do you think those cats are a good idea? All the other freighters are laughing at Mor. Even Red Tallent thinks she's crazy this time."

Tom didn't answer right away. Instead, he raised his rifle to his shoulder, took aim, and fired at a jackrabbit. Fired and missed. With a shake of his head, he lowered the rifle. They rode along for a few more minutes before he finally said, "Well, Freddie, it's like this: Your mother isn't like any other woman I've ever known. She's strong. Determined. And smart. She was right about that ugly fabric. I didn't think we'd sell any of it, but there isn't so much as enough left to make a comfortable." He smiled without looking over. "So if I was a betting man—which I am not—I would bet on Katerina Jannike every time."

Freddie had almost forgotten Mor had a name besides Swede. Katerina was a nice name.

Tom chuckled. "Maybe she'll trade in Swede for a new name."

"What kind of name?"

"Kat," Tom laughed. And with that, he nudged his horse into a lope.

————

"You got yourself a problem with them cats, Swede." Red Tallent hitched his thumb toward the wagon he'd helped Swede transform into a cage.

"Vat kind of problem?" Wrinkling her brow, Swede got up from the campfire and walked over to inspect the load. For once the cats were quiet. Most were asleep. Others were grooming themselves.

"That one." Red pointed at an undersized tabby. "Ain't gittin' enough to eat is what."

"It vill be fine," Swede said. "Ve are almost to Deadvood."

Tallent fiddled with his long beard. Finally he muttered, "I could watch over it fer ya."

Swede bit her lower lip to keep from smiling. "Yah, sure. Only mind you don't lose five trying to get de one out."

By sundown, Red was lying on his back by his campfire with a contented smile on his face. His brawny forearms were marked with scratches, but he didn't seem to mind. As for the undersized tabby, it lay curled up on its new owner's chest, Red's thick beard serving as a pillow.

Tom leaned over and nudged Freddie. "You think those cats were a good idea?"

Freddie smiled. Red had insisted on paying Mor *twelve* dollars for the cat he was calling Schatz, which Tom said was German for "dear." Freddie nodded. "Yes. The cats are going to work out just fine." And maybe Tom and Mor would, too.

————

Aron Gallagher let himself in the back door of Garth and Company just as Mattie was sitting down to eat her breakfast.

"Have you eaten?" she asked. When Aron said he hadn't, she pushed her plate at him and stood up. "Help yourself. I haven't touched it yet. I'll make myself some more."

"How about you sit and eat, and I'll make my own?"

Mattie sat back down. "There's coffee, too."

"I think the aroma of your coffee would have lured me here even if it wasn't my day to play storekeeper while you turn into Matt the Miner."

It hasn't lured you over any time in the last nine days. Mattie shrugged. "I'm just glad you didn't forget, what with your schedule lately."

A plate of flapjacks in hand, Aron sat down. "I'm not the only one who's been working long hours." He nodded her way.

"Me?" Mattie shook her head. "I've been lazy compared to you. Nursing the sick, counseling folks, preaching, spending hours with the Underwoods—building." She broke off. Did she sound . . . jealous? She shifted in her chair. "Aunt Lou thinks you aren't eating right."

Aron pointed at the tall stack of flapjacks in front of him. "You're my witness that Aunt Lou has nothing to worry about." He slathered butter between each of the cakes before smothering the tower with molasses. While he ate he talked. Tough times had started people asking questions and listening to some of the Bible's answers. There was even talk of building a church in Deadwood. "And," Aron concluded, "until that happens, Jack Langrishe has offered to let us use his theatre for church services."

"That's wonderful."

"And when the Underwoods heard about it, Kitty volunteered to play for the service."

Kitty. Not Miss Underwood. Kitty. Mattie forced a smile. "Even more good news."

Someone was knocking at the front door. Aron jumped up. "That'll be—" He looked toward the front of the store and smiled. "Right on time." Coffee cup in hand, he went to open the door. Mattie got up and followed, pausing in the doorway just as Kitty Underwood placed a gloved hand on Aron's forearm and smiled up at him.

"Thank you so much for opening early for us," she said.

"Not a problem." Aron gestured toward Mattie. "You've met Miss O'Keefe?"

"No," Mattie spoke up. "We haven't actually met. Not officially, anyway." She crossed to where they were standing and said, "Nice to meet you."

She was answered with a barely disguised look of disdain as Kitty looked Mattie over, staring pointedly at the work pants and boots.

"Miss O'Keefe works a claim up on Deadwood Gulch," Aron said. "A rather *successful* claim." He smiled at Mattie. "And Miss Underwood—"

"—plays the piano," Mattie said. "And will grace the congregation with her talent this coming Sunday."

The girl giggled. She blushed. She covered her mouth with her gloved hand and batted her eyelashes and gushed, "Oh, I'm not very good. But Mama insisted I try. And I'm just so pleased to help out."

I just bet you are.

Miss Underwood glanced Mattie's way. "Do you play, Miss . . . O'Keefe?"

Mattie shook her head. "No. I prospect. And it's time I got to it."

But then she just couldn't resist. Looking at Aron, she said, "Aunt Lou's expecting us for dinner tonight."

"Oh . . . all right. That'll be . . . fine. Great."

Mattie made her escape, blushing furiously as she hurried up Main Street toward the gulch. *Mattie O'Keefe, Aunt Lou said no such thing. You made it up. You LIED. What has gotten into you, anyway?!* What, indeed, but an overwhelming desire to wipe the uppity expression off Kitty Underwood's face. And it had worked.

CHAPTER 18

That ye might walk worthy of the Lord unto all pleasing,
being fruitful in every good work,
and increasing in the knowledge of God . . .

Colossians 1:10

Not being strong enough to do anything else, Jonas kept watch. The day after he left the pest tent, he saw Mattie leave town and head up into Deadwood Gulch. She was dressed like a man, and it wasn't hard to figure out that she was going to meet up with her brother on his claim. Jonas wanted to follow her, but his legs wouldn't even carry him the length of Main Street yet, let alone up the gulch. No, locating Mattie and Dillon O'Keefe on a gold claim would have to wait. He made a camp of sorts up behind the hotel where he'd first seen Mattie, resting during the day and coming out at night to scavenge. Hunger drove him, but weakness reduced him to picking through a bucket of slops set outside by the mammy who cooked for the hotel.

For a while Jonas thought maybe he'd been wrong about Mattie owning that store. She was at the hotel so often, he wondered if she lived there. Or maybe she just cooked for them. But she had the keys to the Garth and Company store and no one else seemed to be around over there. It was a puzzle that he was too tired to solve. He'd been a sniper in the war. He was good at hiding and good at observation. For now, he would be content with watching. He would heal and regain his strength and then—then it would be time to act.

———

Swede's wagonload of cats caused no small stir in Deadwood. Long before the oxen halted in front of her store, folks had begun to follow alongside the lead wagon in her outfit. They pointed and chattered and opined, and a good-sized crowd had gathered before Swede so much as set her bullwhip down.

Her first customer was Slim Danvers, a shy typesetter who worked for the newspaper.

"I-I-I'll g-give you t-twenty-five d-dollars for that one." He was pointing to the prettiest cat of all, a soft gray one with china blue eyes and dark gray nose and paws. When Swede looked doubtful, Danvers reached for the leather bag around his neck. "I c-can p-pay," he said.

"I do not doubt dat you can pay," Swede said quickly. "I vas only surprised dat you vant one at all, much less de most expensive."

The boy blushed. He nodded toward the north end of Main. "D-daisy will l-love it." He swallowed. "Sh-she'll t-take real g-good care of it." He nodded and gulped.

And so began one of the more unusual exchanges of goods between freighters and the citizens of Deadwood. Now that the wagons had stopped moving and the cats had been fed, they'd calmed down considerably. It was no trouble getting hold of the soft gray cat Slim wanted.

Soon after he hurried off up the street with his purchase, the sporting girls of Deadwood descended upon Swede with a vengeance. She almost had to break up a fight when two of them insisted they must have the calico with green eyes. Long before the end of the day, thirty-nine cats had found homes, and Swede was trying not to be smug about it as she walked into the store with an enormous black-and-white female obviously ready to give birth any day.

Tom English looked up from where he'd spent most of the day weighing out payments for cats and going over Mattie's figures in the store ledger and smiled. "Once again, you prove your brilliance," he said.

"I am not brilliant." Swede shook her head even as she cradled the purring cat in her arms. "I only hoped."

"I beg to differ," Tom said, stroking the black-and-white cat. "Keeping the one that guarantees a high return on your investment is brilliant."

"Vell," Swede said, and put the cat down on the counter, where it struck a regal pose, "it couldn't hurt to have more dan one. Aren't ve both sick of mouse droppings in de storeroom?" She reached for an empty box and, taking the last length of hideous cloth off the shelf, arranged it at the bottom before setting the box on the floor. The cat watched but didn't move until Swede walked back to the storeroom and poured a half cup of precious milk into a bowl and set it down on the floor. Instantly the cat bounded after her and began to circle her, rubbing against her legs while it purred appreciation.

"I believe you have won her over," Tom said.

"I vill believe dat ven she stays."

"Why wouldn't she stay?" Tom gestured around. "There's a warm stove, a roof over her head, and a lovely woman pouring bowls of fresh cream."

Swede blushed at the compliment. "Vell, lovely or not, I von't be surprised if she jumps out de storeroom vindow tonight and ve never see her again."

"Are you going to name her?"

"Perhaps it is vise to vait and see."

"If she stays?"

Swede shook her head. "No. To vait and see vat she is like. So de name fits de personality."

"Think I'll call her Cat," Tom said. "That definitely fits."

Swede laughed. She looked around the store and sighed. "It is good to be back."

"Yes," Tom agreed. "It is."

"It vas good to be rescued."

"You didn't really need to be rescued."

"But if I had, you and Freddie vere dere to do it."

"Yes," he agreed. "I hope we always will be."

When Tom didn't look away, Swede didn't know what to do. So she looked back, and her heart thumped even as she scolded herself about her impossible dreams.

Tom finally broke the mood. "Well," he said, and closed the ledger, "if it's all right with you, I'll leave the rest of the ciphering for tomorrow. As expected, Matt the Miner has done a fine job in our absence."

Swede nodded. She pointed toward the upper level. "Eva fell to sleep de instant I laid her down. Ve are all tired." Tom locked the front door. He turned down the lamps. Together they walked toward the back of the store. And just when she was about to say good-night, he kissed her. On the cheek.

"Sleep well, Swede," he murmured, "and welcome home."

Swede stood transfixed while he let himself out. And then she mounted the stairs. But she did not sleep. Not for a very long time.

———

The minx was back at the hotel on Saturday. *With a dog.* Ah well. He could handle a dog. He'd just have to be careful about leaving his scent. And he knew some tricks that would throw a dog off the trail. Jonas watched for most of a day, content to see the comings and goings, aware that his strength was returning, albeit much more slowly than he would have liked.

It made him laugh to think of Mattie O'Keefe cooking. The little snip who'd never lifted a hand in any kitchen in all her life was helping a black mammy. And liked it. She *sang* while she worked, the sound floating through the back screen door and up to where he lurked.

For all his weakness, his hearing and his sight were still good. And his appetite was back. Too bad he wasn't strong enough for hunting yet. But moments later, when a Chinaman delivered the carcass of a pig to the kitchen door, inspiration struck.

———

Jonas waited until sundown to pick his way slowly toward Chinatown, passing first behind the hovels in the Badlands. Folks were used to vagrants and drunks hunched against buildings or sleeping it off there, and no one bothered him when he stopped to rest. As for Chinatown, it was the usual collection of laundries and cheap eateries, opium dens and whorehouses. Jonas skulked down one narrow alley after another, shuffling along, keeping his pockmarked hand hidden and his head bowed. It was dark by then and no one noticed that smallpox was among them.

Finally he found the perfect opportunity with two white-haired ancients seated just inside an open doorway at a low table. Each one was picking at a bowl of rice and some other dish Jonas didn't recognize. Once he was certain they were alone, he walked in and, in two quick moves, used his hook to dispatch them. Death was swift and silent, if a little messy. Fortified by a quick handful of rice, he inverted one bowl over the other and took it with him as he made his getaway. So efficient was the attack, so silently did he move, that no one followed.

He barely made it back to camp before collapsing. He slept for a while, but when hunger pangs woke him, Jonas ate rice and whatever it was until he was stuffed. In the morning he congratulated himself on finding a way to survive. Just as he'd learned during the war. Survival was the supreme motivator. He might use the same ploy a few more times. Deadwood had no law, no sheriff . . . and who cared about a couple more or less inhabitants in Chinatown anyway.

He looked down at his arms. Some lesions were dried, but not all. How long, he wondered . . . how long would it be until he could exact his revenge and shake off the dust of Deadwood and reclaim his life?

He savored the thought of finding the O'Keefes, of forcing Dillon to watch while he taught Mattie the real cost of running out on Jonas Flynn. The money she'd taken was almost unimportant now. Oh, it had been the initial reason he'd followed her, but the money paled in comparison to what Mattie had done to him now, what he had become because of her. The money was only a very small part of what she owed him now.

Jonas returned to Chinatown and stole food for three nights in a row, each night carefully choosing his elderly victims, before he had to stop. Who would have expected a powerful young buck with a queue trailing down his back to emerge from the dark with a meat cleaver in his hand?

Jonas had to kill him, too. The shrieks that went up before he'd dispatched all three victims threatened to bring the entire lot of Chinamen down on him. He managed to get away, but barely, and he had to settle for the food he'd stuffed in his pockets before the hulk intervened. There would be no more dining in Chinatown.

He was getting stronger, but he wasn't ready to take action against the O'Keefes yet. For one thing, he didn't know enough about Mattie to plan the perfect moment. He knew she was friends with the mammy. And, interestingly enough, with the idiot who'd offered to care for the bay gelding all those weeks ago. The kid was something of a hunter, it seemed. He'd delivered game to the mammy several times while Jonas watched.

The return of the freighters to Deadwood explained what Mattie had been doing with the keys to Garth and Company Merchandise. She'd been working there while the couple who owned it were gone. *Some couple.* Swede's man was so thin he'd break in half if she ever took a swing at him. She hadn't mentioned a husband when Jonas was following the freighters to Deadwood, but then she hadn't really said much of anything to him. The blond-haired child was charming, but already becoming a burden to her mother. As they all did, sooner or later. It was, Jonas thought, quite a menagerie. He still couldn't figure out their exact connection with Mattie beyond her minding the store, but he would. He had all the time in the world.

And so he continued to watch.

———

Mattie paused outside the Langrishe Theatre building long enough on Sunday to read the chalked sign. The play *The Banker's Daughter* was scheduled. Nightly performances, it said. She stepped inside, lingering to the right of the door as she listened to the congregation sing.

Kitty Underwood had spoken the truth when she'd said she wasn't very good on the piano. No one seemed to notice, though. " 'Amazing grace, how sweet the sound that saved a wretch like me. I once was lost but now am found, was blind but now I see.' " She didn't think that was quite the way she'd sung it for Bill's funeral. No matter. The meaning was the same. She couldn't help smiling at the way she'd learned that hymn. They'd had a customer with a habit of singing hymns when he was drunk, and he was drunk a lot.

When the hymn was finished, everyone seemed to know to sit down. Swede and Freddie were up front, as was Aunt Lou, wearing an enormous hat with a long black ostrich plume curving elegantly along the crown. The Underwood women were wearing hats, too. Mattie was fairly certain Kitty's bonnet had been on display in the Berg sisters' store window only yesterday. It was a red and black version of the blue and lavender one Mattie was wearing right now. As she slid into a chair right inside the door, Mattie loosened the bow at her throat and slid the bonnet back off her head.

Just as Aron got up to speak, Justice padded through the door and came to her side. There were a few chuckles in the back rows, but no one said anything, so Mattie patted his head and pointed to the floor, hoping he would lie down. Which he did, but then he quickly lifted his head, sat up, and stared at the door. His tail thumped, and when Mattie looked about, Tom English was standing there looking nervous. She waved him over.

"You new at this church thing, too?" she whispered. He only nodded as he removed his hat and sat down. Mattie noticed that he hid his hook under his hat. She'd have to tell him that it wasn't really an issue anymore. The hook was simply part of who Tom English— an admirable man—was. In Tom's case, the hook didn't matter.

Aron welcomed everyone and had the Langrishes stand up so he could thank them publicly for the use of the theatre. He looked up at the canvas roof and said, "And, Lord, if you'd hold off any rain until I'm done preaching, I'd be grateful." And everyone laughed.

"Now, why didn't I think of praying on opening night?" Langrishe quipped, referencing how everyone who'd attended the inaugural performance at the theatre had come away drenched to the skin when it stormed and the canvas roof stretched and leaked.

Aron's sermon topic was once again about hope in the face of disasters like smallpox. The only hope for *this* life was to focus on the *next* and get things right with God, he said. The only way to get things right with God was to put ourselves in the place of the thief on the cross, to realize we had nothing to offer, to put our faith in Jesus.

As usual, Aron stopped talking abruptly—long before he'd brought his talk to a proper conclusion, as far as Mattie was concerned. Kitty Underwood sashayed back over to the piano and there was more singing, but Mattie and Tom didn't stay for that. Mattie had to take Justice out before he did his business right there in the middle of a church service, and as for Tom, he said he had to get back over and open the store. They both slipped out unnoticed. At least that's what Mattie thought.

————

"I know ven de snows come to Dakota, Mr. English." Swede lifted her chin and glared down at him. "I need no lectures from you. Ve vill be fine and back into Deadvood by de end of October. Or maybe first of November." She paused. "Either vay, ve vill be fine."

Tom had been sitting behind the counter with the ledger open before him doing sums, and he'd just mentioned that maybe Swede should consider forgoing the last supply run of the year. "I didn't mean to lecture you," he said gently. "I only meant to suggest."

"If dere is much snow once it starts," Swede said, "ve vill need much more of flour and other staples dan ve haf. Much more of *everyting* to keep from running out."

Tom disagreed. "Not if we close the store when supplies get low. If we do that, there would be plenty for—"

"For who? Are ve now to make a list of who goes hungry and who does not? How does dat show kindness to others? Did Aron's sermon yesterday mean noting to you? Is dat vy you left so soon?"

Tom stood up and, placing hand and hook atop the counter before him, said quietly, "Let us not turn this into a religious discussion. I was only raising a hypothetical situation. Your family would *not* go hungry." He closed the ledger book.

"I promised Mattie I vould bring de tombstone. And it vas not dere last time. But it *vill* be vaiting for me ven I reach Sidney dis time. It is promised to me, and I have promised Mattie, and I vish to see her pleased vit the marking of her brother's grave before de vinter. Already he has been buried too long and no marker."

"Mattie would understand. And I don't think you should go."

Why was he being so *obstinate*? He had never been this way

before. She loved him for his gentleness. For his not minding Garth's name on the sign. For the way he didn't push to take over. They had been true partners. He had never acted as though a woman knew nothing. *Until now.* It was a part of Tom English she had not seen, and one she did not like. Not one bit.

"Of course she vould understand. Dat is not my point. It is not right to disappoint ven I can avoid doing so. And I can avoid it. De oxen are strong and I vill make de load lighter. It von't take so long. But I am going. I must."

"Have you considered Eva—and what being caught in a storm might mean for her?"

It was the straw that broke the donkey's back. For all her hard labor and all her fears about how Eva was being raised, for all her guilt over the countless miles her precious child had spent virtually locked in a makeshift cradle and getting rained on . . . she had done her best, but her best was not enough, and now to have Tom point that out . . . and hint that she might let her stubbornness endanger Eva! How could he say such a thing?

Whether it was anger or hurt, the emotion filled Swede's eyes with tears. "How dare you say such a ting to me, Tom English! How dare you hint—" She could not continue. And she could not look at him. She marched toward the stairs.

"I didn't mean it that way. You're a good mother, Kat. A wonderful woman. I—"

At the base of the stairs, Swede whirled around and pointed at him. "Hush. You hush now. Never did I tink dat you vould do dis ting, Tom English. To say such things to me, ven all I vish from you is—" She bit her lip to keep from speaking further. It was too embarrassing to face him with these womanly emotions rolling over her common sense. And so Swede turned and ran up the stairs to the room she shared with Eva, and if Eva had not been napping at that moment she would have slammed the door. She did not cry, but she sat on the edge of her bed, her arms crossed, muttering to herself. "Vonderful voman? Hmpf. You tink I am vonderful, vy don't you—"

Kat? Had she heard correctly? Had he just now called her Kat? Swede stood up and crossed to the door. She reached out and had the handle in her grasp. But then reason won out. She imagined Tom English down below, closing up the store and turning down the lamps. She heard his footsteps as he headed for the back door. Was it her imagination, or did he just now pause at the base of the stairs? Closing her eyes, Swede waited. Listened. Hoped. But then came the sound of the back door closing.

Swede took a deep breath. She retreated to the bed. Lying back atop the patchwork quilt, she stared up at the ceiling. Presently she closed her eyes. *Hush, now. Just hush. Hush and sleep and tomorrow . . . get the oxen yoked.*

CHAPTER 19

. . . the Lord seeth not as man seeth; for man looketh on the
outward appearance, but the Lord looketh on the heart.

1 Samuel 16:7

*P*raise be to God. Swede traced the letters in the simple white
stone.

Dillon Patrick O'Keefe
Born June 6, 1854
Died May 1, 1876
Beloved Brother
They'll give me a welcome the warmest on earth,
All so loving and kind full of music and mirth,
In the sweet-sounding language of home.

The words blurred as Swede remembered Mattie singing that
song. She'd called it "Mist-Covered Mountains" and said she and Dillon had often sung it together. Taking a deep breath, Swede stepped
back. She nodded at the baggage handler who'd unwrapped it for
her. "Load it onto de second vagon, please," she said. "Dere is much

hay in de bottom for cushioning. Ven you have it in place, fill dat vagon with hay."

"All the way?"

"Yah, sure." Swede nodded. "All de vay." She didn't think it was going to snow, but if it did, she would not be caught on the prairie without a way to feed her oxen. In spite of what Tom English thought, she was not foolish.

———

Finally. He was strong enough to take action. It had taken most of a month, but none of it had been wasted. He had grown wise in the old ways of hunting and hiding, remembered many of the tricks from his days in the war. He hunted in Deadwood for food, and it was easier than he expected it to be. The mammy left her kitchen unguarded at times. Once, Jonas had slipped in and taken an entire ham back up to his camp. It made him smile just to remember the next few days of good eating from that one act of thievery.

He hadn't planned to be camped out for this long. The nights were getting cold. Sometimes in the night when the dried leaves rattled in the wind, it woke him. Such a strange sound compared to pianos and laughter, glasses clinking and dice rolling. The memories made him homesick. Once back in Abilene, he would never leave.

But first he would follow through with his plan. The very next time Mattie headed up the gulch he would prowl along the rim that ran high above the gold claims, and she would never even know she was being followed. He would finally solve the mystery of why he hadn't seen Dillon in town. Having located the claim, he would plan a little surprise for them both. A *re*prise. He chuckled to himself. Mattie O'Keefe would regret ever stealing a penny of his money, and she would especially pay for cutting him with that ring and for being the cause of his scars.

———

The delay in Sidney was no one's fault. It simply took longer to load all the freighters' wagons this time because when Red Tallent realized Swede was hauling hay against an early storm, he decided the rest of the wagons should follow suit, and that meant waiting for the ranchers to haul hay to the depot. It also meant some creative loading to accommodate the hay and still haul everything expected in Deadwood.

It was October 1 before the supply train finally left Sidney headed north for Deadwood. Swede had purchased some pelts to line Eva's cradle, and while she waited for the other teamsters to load their hay, she laced one together into a kind of bunting. For herself, she would make do with a couple of furs sewn together at the shoulder the way Red Tallent did it. And a fur hat and mittens, too. There was just enough left to line her boots.

Oh, but she was stiff when she wakened in the morning these days. How she longed for the warmth of the feather comfortable and patchwork quilts on her own bed in the room she shared with Eva above Garth and Company Merchandise. She never suspected that the simple matter of having a room and a bed of her own would change her attitude toward the trail. Of course if she let herself think about it, she realized it wasn't just the longing for her home that had changed her attitude about the trail. It was Tom.

She had barely said three words to him after their fight, and yet he had kissed her on the cheek before she left town. That made two kisses. For the entire trip from Deadwood to Sidney, she had battled thinking about those kisses. Finally she was able to think more clearly about things. But it wasn't just the time on the trail that had accomplished that. It was pondering that day back in Sidney when she'd seen herself in a mirror.

She had only meant to buy a new bonnet for Mattie O'Keefe. As a way of saying thank-you for all her work at the store while Tom and Freddie were gone. But when the shopkeeper—a nice woman named Mrs. Johnson—insisted that Swede try it on herself, she submitted to one moment of feminine pleasure. A moment that was either a terrible mistake or a clarification of reality, depending on how one chose to see it.

"There now," Mrs. Johnson said, and tilted the mirror just so. "See how nice you look? Those yellow flowers are the perfect accent for your lovely blond hair."

Yellow might accent her hair, Swede thought, but nothing could hide the fact that a once pleasant-looking Katerina Jannike now looked more like a weather-beaten man than a woman. Quickly, she looked away from the mirror and handed over the hat. "Please to write on de package, *To Miss Mattie O'Keefe.*"

"Package?" Mrs. Johnson asked, even as she held up a fine leather hatbox, "or traveling case?" She raised the lid to show off the purple velvet lining.

Swede didn't hesitate. "Put a tag on one case for Miss O'Keefe, if you please, and if you have more, I vill take five."

"Wise woman," Mrs. Johnson said with a smile. "The ladies of Deadwood will buy you out in no time."

Swede didn't bother to explain her intent to sell all five hatboxes to the Berg sisters upon arrival. She only nodded as she glanced back into the mirror one last time. *Remember what you see here when next you have foolish thoughts about you and Tom English.*

———

Jonas needed a mirror. People still turned away after one glance. Could it be that bad? He was feeling better now and tired of skulking around like some animal. The pest tent had been taken down. He couldn't be the only former inmate who'd stayed in Deadwood. Surely he wasn't that much of an oddity. But he hadn't run into any of the other patients—except for one hideously scarred sporting girl staggering around behind Al Swearengen's place. She was drunk, and Jonas could understand why. A creature like that might as well take a gun to her head and end her misery.

An idea took shape. The mammy would likely have a mirror in her bedroom next to the kitchen, and she always went to church. Jonas smiled to himself. She'd never even know he'd been there. And on his way out, he'd help himself to whatever was cooking for lunch. He laughed aloud. Maybe he'd even leave a little gold dust from the bag he'd taken off that body. *Gold dust on a saucer on the table.* Now, that would give old mammy something to wonder over.

———

"Just let me put my hat in my room, and we'll have us a fine Sunday dinner," Aunt Lou said as Mattie and Aron followed her into the hotel kitchen. "I'm so glad the two of you said you would do this. I declare, Mattie, you have been up at that claim of yours so much lately I thought maybe you'd left Deadwood."

"It hasn't been that bad," Mattie said with a laugh. "I have been busy, though. Trying to sink another hole to bedrock before the ground freezes." *And counting my gold. I'm rich, Aunt Lou!*

"Well, you just—" Aunt Lou's hand paused in midair as she reached for the elaborate pin anchoring her hat in place. She stared into her room, then leaned against the doorframe groaning, "Oh no . . . not my best quilt . . . oh *no . . . no . . . no . . .*"

Aron stepped up to peer over her shoulder. Mattie joined them, and that's when she saw the devastation. Someone had reduced Aunt Lou's room to shattered glass and shredded cloth. She slumped down onto the edge of her cot, frowning as she looked up at where the mirror used to hang. Motioning for Mattie and Aron to step into the room, she pointed to the back of the door. "What *is* that?"

Aron frowned as he examined several deep gouges in the wood.

"And there," Aunt Lou said. "And there." She pointed at the rips in the newspapers covering her walls.

Mattie turned in a circle, pointing out gouge after gouge. She ran her finger along the marks in the top of the old bureau in the corner and shivered. "Who would do such a thing? The whole town loves Aunt Lou."

"It seems there's at least one person who don't," Aunt Lou said. Looking down at the hat in her hands she smiled. "Well. At least he didn't ruin my favorite hat." She forced a laugh. "And he isn't gonna ruin my Sunday dinner with two of my favorite people, either." She stood up and motioned for Mattie to follow her into the kitchen. "Come along, Miss Mattie. We're all hungry and"—she waved around her—"sitting here ain't gonna change what's been done. I got one of my fattest hens all ready to—" She stopped in midsentence. "Now, what on earth . . ." She looked around. "It was right here." She motioned to the shelf just above her worktable in the corner.

"What? What was right here?"

"A pie. An apple pie. And now—look at this." Aunt Lou pulled a saucer down off the shelf and stared at it. She held it out for Mattie and Aron to see the pinch of gold dust right in the center of the white saucer. "Now, who steals a pie and *pays* in gold dust?"

"Is anything else missing?" Aron asked.

Aunt Lou made a quick tour of the kitchen and pantry. "I had a nice roast all ready to slice for the lodgers' lunch. Had it in this crock, covered with a towel." She held out an empty crockery bowl.

Mattie gazed at Aron. "Who destroys a woman's room, steals food, and then leaves payment?" She lowered her voice. "This isn't just someone who doesn't like Aunt Lou. This is a *crazy* person who doesn't like Aunt Lou. A crazy person with a *weapon*."

Aron nodded. He glanced at Aunt Lou. "Is it all right with you if I ask around a bit? See if I can learn anything?"

Aunt Lou shrugged. "Whoever done this had to have made some noise. If no one came when it was happening . . ." She paused. "Ain't nobody cares about a few things that belong to an old black woman."

"I care," Aron said.

"We both do," Mattie agreed.

"Then you do what you got to do," Aunt Lou said even as she tied on her apron, "and I'll get us a meal ready." She busied herself lighting a fire in the cast-iron stove.

Aron headed out the door, hesitating long enough to say to Mattie, "Lock this door until I get back. And keep your Colt handy."

———

The mirror . . . Jonas swore abominations, he cursed the Almighty above and the demons below . . . he raged and wept, and still, what he'd seen in the mammy's mirror would not fade from memory. When he closed his eyes, it was there in his mind, that hideous, pockmarked, scarred, splotched thing that had once been his face.

Ravenous, he tore at the stolen roast with his teeth, not caring that the juices soaked his beard and stained his shirt. What did it matter? He looked like an animal out of someone's nightmares . . . he might as well live like one.

The little witch . . . the gorgeous, unscarred, plotting, scheming, violet-eyed minx. It was her doing. All of it. If she hadn't stolen from him, if she hadn't cut him, he could have let her go. But a man in his position couldn't let something like that go unpunished. He had to come after her. And if it weren't for her . . . if it weren't for her . . . He raged. He wept . . . and, exhausted, he finally slept.

When he woke, Jonas had a new clarity about what would happen now. Before, his revenge had been of a general nature. He would have frightened both O'Keefes and gotten his money back. He would have made them beg. The punishment would have been painful, but Mattie would have healed. Even if she was scarred, he would have made sure it would be a hidden reminder. Like the scar on her arm. Something no one else would ever need to know about. A little secret just between the two of them.

No more. Now his rage was purified. In the white heat of his own destruction he had gained a new clarity of purpose. Now he would not fail. He would kill Dillon O'Keefe, but only after he'd made him watch as he introduced Mattie to the same fate she had dealt him. As he was scarred, as his life was ruined, so would he scar and ruin her. Perhaps he would start with the brother. Or the dog. He would work up to Mattie. And then . . . oh, then.

Jonas began to sharpen his hook.

———

The freighters were two weeks out of Sidney when it began to snow. Swede had been watching the sky and feeling nervous for two days, willing the thick gray clouds away, reminding God that it was only mid-October even as she cracked her whip and tried to make Lars and Leif move faster.

"Looks like we're in for an early one," Red Tallent said that night when they'd made camp. He lifted his cat down off his shoulders, where it seemed to be content to spend the greater part of every day, and set it in Eva's cradle. Eva patted it gently—a skill learned after only a few warning scratches—and the cat lay across her lap and began to purr. Red puffed on his pipe thoughtfully. "Snow never lasts long this time of year," he said. "Nothing to worry about."

Swede agreed. But she still worried. She just didn't like the look of those clouds. And neither did any of the other freighters. Together they all decided to push through instead of resting their teams at noon the next day. Swede hated doing it, but this time she agreed with the others. They must hurry.

For one full day, flakes skittered through the air and clung to the tall grasses in the sloughs. It wasn't much of a snow, and the temperature didn't drop below what was normal for that time of year. Everyone breathed a sigh of relief around their campfires that night and everyone slept well—although not as long as usual. They were up and moving a little after midnight, reasoning that with the hay in their wagons the load was lighter and it was reasonable to ask more of the oxen.

The great beasts lowed their protests, and it took more than the usual amount of cracking whips to keep them moving for that long day, but if Red Tallent's calculations were correct, they made twelve miles. And that was good. They had passed the halfway mark now. No one mentioned going back to Sidney. They would stick together. They would be fine.

And then it was not fine at all. On day eighteen out of Sidney the clouds seemed to gain substance and the wind picked up. The oxen protested to the point that, although she hated doing it, Swede was forced to tickle their backs with the whip.

"I am sorry," she shouted into the wind, "but you must move now and move fast or you vill end up as dinner for stranded freighters, and ve do not vant dat." The oxen pulled. They strained. The wagons rumbled. And the snows came.

At least it was not a blizzard. *Not yet.* And Red was right. Usually at this time of year, even deep snow did not stay. After all, it was only October. They would be fine. It wasn't so cold. Thank God she had purchased these pelts . . . and the hat. And Eva . . . sweet Eva was warmed with a rock Red Tallent had found and hefted into the fire last night, then wrapped with rags and placed in Eva's box.

"You take care of my Goldie now, little one," Red had said earlier in the day as he deposited the yellow tabby next to Eva.

"Go-dee," Eva said, and patted Goldie's head.

There was not a blizzard that day. No, the blizzard came in the night. They hadn't unyoked the oxen, but fed them where they stood and melted snow for drinking, so when the wind began to howl they would be ready. Ready to make two circles this time, one to be a corral for the oxen, and the other to give them shelter until they could build their own.

It took most of the night to erect a kind of hogan, supported on one side by Swede's wagon. They packed snow between the bottom of the wagon and the earth until it was a solid wall, blocking out the wind. Inside the shelter, they dug out what they could, and the rest they tamped down. One of the older men had spent time among the Indians and directed them to bank snow around the bottom rim and up the sides of the canvas. Then Red built a fire inside. They'd all been picking up buffalo chips during the day in anticipation of just this moment. Together, the dozen teamsters huddled beneath their makeshift shelter, prepared as best they could be to wait it out.

As the forced joking and the tall tales of past challenges and storms ended, Swede took Eva in her arms and settled beneath her own pile of hides and worn comfortables.

"Go-dee," Eva demanded.

"Shh." Swede nuzzled her cheek. "Goldie is vit Mr. Tallent. We have each other—and de varm rock. Goldie helps Mr. Tallent stay varm." Presently Eva's breathing evened out. She began to snore softly. Swede lay awake listening to the wind, haunted by Tom English's voice asking, *Have you considered Eva—and what being caught in a storm might mean for her?*

CHAPTER 20

For their feet run to evil, and make haste to shed blood.

Proverbs 1:16

W*hat in the world?* Mattie started awake. Something cold pressed against her cheek. Whimpered. And she chuckled. "All right, you little beggar." Lifting the comfortable, she invited Justice into bed. He settled next to her and said thank-you with his pink tongue. "You're welcome," she said, and stroked his black fur. "I just hope you don't snore."

Justice didn't snore, but in the predawn hours Mattie woke again, this time because of the cold. She shivered as she crept out of bed and stoked the fire in the small stove. It was going to be miserable prospecting today. As she made coffee and huddled by the stove, Justice wriggled out from beneath the covers and went to the tent flap.

"All right," Mattie said. "I hear you." When she untied the flap she let out a gasp of surprise. The world had changed overnight and was now frosted with a thin layer of snow. *Snow? It's October.* How could there be snow?

"Good mornin'!" boomed Fergus McKay from where he sat by

273

a raging campfire near the McKays' tent. He gestured around him. "Beautiful, isn't it?"

"Beautiful?" Mattie called back. "It's *cold* is what it is!"

Fergus looked surprised. "You think *this* is cold? Oh, Mattie, m'love. You are not going to like winters in Deadwood Gulch."

With a shiver, Mattie ducked back inside. Donning as many layers as she could, she made herself a pile of flapjacks. The only good thing about the snow was that it was Saturday morning, and Aunt Lou was expecting her in town to help with her baking. And in Aunt Lou's kitchen, with the huge iron stove going full blast, it would be warm.

Aunt Lou. As Mattie headed down the gulch after breakfast, she thought back to the day they'd come in from church to discover the destruction of her room. Aron said the people he'd talked to since then seemed concerned, but there was little he could do when not a single hotel guest seemed to have heard or seen anything. Someone mentioned getting a glimpse of a vagrant lurking around the hotel, but no one thought that meant a thing. Vagrants didn't leave gold dust in saucers.

Aunt Lou's response to the destruction still gave Mattie pause. She had repapered the walls of her room and mended the comforter. She'd bought a new mirror and, with Aron's help, sanded the back of the door until it was smooth. And she sang. She sang when she cooked and she sang when she cleaned. She sang about a world of troubles and crossing Jordan and saints marching.

Mattie didn't understand it. "How can you be so . . . glib?" she'd asked one day.

"I don't even know what *glib* is, honey."

"Unconcerned," Mattie explained. "You just don't seem worried."

"No reason to worry. I lock my door at night, and beyond that I just leave it to that great big guardian angel watchin' over me. He's done a real fine job for nearly sixty years now and I don't expect he's gonna quit anytime soon."

Mattie didn't understand it. But she admired it. In fact, she longed to feel the same way. When she expressed the longing, Aunt Lou nodded. "I know, child. I know. Aunt Lou longs for you to have it, too."

"So . . . how do I get it?"

Aunt Lou smiled. "You quit tryin' so hard to earn it, and you just accept the gift of what Jesus done for you. You take the free gift of His forgiveness and salvation and then you're in His family. And the rest will come."

"I can't," Mattie said, touching the Colt in her pocket even as she choked back unexpected emotion.

"I know, child, I know." Without warning, Aunt Lou had pulled Mattie into her arms, and for a moment, Mattie had closed her eyes and just let herself be loved.

———

Aron was lingering over Aunt Lou's coffee when Mattie and Justice stepped into the hotel kitchen. "Brrrrr," she shivered. "It's good to be where it's warm."

"Now, where's that pup?" Aunt Lou asked. "I've been keepin' him a nice ham bone just for today."

Mattie nodded outside. "He seems to think the snow is *fun*. At least in the daylight. The little hypocrite begged his way into my bed in the middle of the night. Now he can't get enough of chasing around in it."

"He's treed a squirrel or something," Aron said and they all paused just long enough to listen to Justice barking.

"I don't think so," Mattie said. "That's a pretty serious bark." Frowning, she stepped to the door and peered outside. "Justice!" she called. "Aunt Lou has a treat for you! Come!" The barking continued until Mattie had called three times. Finally Justice bounded down the embankment behind the hotel. Mattie looked down at him. "What's out there, boy?"

"Nothing worth missing a ham bone for, apparently," Aron teased.

"Phew," Mattie said, wrinkling her nose. "Nothing like the aroma of wet dog in a kitchen." She reached for a towel. Presently Justice was settled beneath the kitchen table happily involved with his ham bone, and Mattie and Aunt Lou were hard at work while Aron drank coffee. Mattie hummed as she worked and barely noticed when it began to snow again. But she did notice that Aron Gallagher seemed in no hurry to leave.

———

By the time Aunt Lou and Mattie had fed the hotel guests dinner and begun to make pies, the snow was falling so hard they could barely see the chicken coop out back.

"You best plan on staying in town tonight, honey," Aunt Lou said, and Mattie agreed.

When the last dried-apple pie was out of the oven and the last dish washed and ready for use the next morning, Mattie bade Aunt Lou good-night and made her way to the back door of Garth and Company. Tom English was still there, hunched over his ledger at the small table in the combination storeroom-kitchen.

"Decided to be a weak woman and wait this storm out here in town," she said, wiping Justice down and then hanging the old buffalo coat she'd bought from one of the miners on a hook by the door.

"Wise of you," Tom murmured as he looked outside.

"You're working late tonight."

"Not working so much as worrying."

Mattie looked around. "Where *is* Freddie, anyway? This is no night for that boy to be out hunting."

"Oh, Freddie will be fine," Tom said. "He's got little hidey-holes all over this area. He took me hunting once, and we got caught in a downpour, but we were sitting by a warm fire in a little cave almost before either of us got wet." He paused. "It's not Freddie I'm concerned about."

Mattie looked back outside. "You think it's doing this down South?"

"As far as I can tell this *came* from that direction."

She sat down at the table. "I see."

"So," Mattie asked after a few moments of silence, "what do freighters do when they're caught in a storm?"

Tom shook his head. "They weather it. They don't have a choice."

"I remember Swede telling me that a couple of the men she usually freights with used to live with Indians. They'll know what to do." Mattie reached over and patted Tom's hand. "She'll be all right. They won't let anything happen to her."

He sighed. "Not if they can help it." He looked out at the snow again. Shook his head. Finally, he stood up. "Well, I believe I've proven a man can't worry snow away, so I'll be going." He nodded toward the stairs. "It'll be really cold up there. If it were me, I'd bunk by the stove down here tonight."

Mattie agreed and took his advice.

———

Justice barking at the back door brought her fully awake on Sunday morning, her hand at her gun. When she heard Tom's key in the door lock, Mattie hastened to stoke the fire in the store. When she returned to the kitchen, she saw that Aron Gallagher had come in with Tom and was already setting the coffeepot on the stove.

Mattie looked in question at him. He smiled and shrugged. "There's going to be another rescue mission. Only this time it's just Tom and me and a string of mules."

"You're going after Swede and the others," Mattie said.

Aron nodded. "There's no way to know if they're all right or not, but Tom just can't stop worrying." He winked at her. "Mostly about the baby, to hear him tell it."

"How can I can help?"

"Pack supplies," Aron said, his arm sweeping toward the store. "Canned oysters. Meat. Anything that will travel well."

"Aunt Lou and I baked a dozen loaves of bread yesterday," Mattie said. "I know she'd be glad to—"

"I'll go get it," Tom said, and left without another word.

Mattie and Aron went into the main store and began setting supplies on a counter. "Is this—are they in serious trouble?" she asked.

"No way to know," Aron said, "although I'm inclined to believe they all have enough experience on the trail to weather it fairly well for at least a few days, and this time of year it should warm up again before too much longer."

Mattie blinked back tears. "I just can't believe God would let anything happen to Swede or Eva."

Aron didn't give her the answer she wanted. "His ways are not our ways" was all he said.

"That's not very comforting."

"Actually," Aron said as he packed a saddlebag, "it can be very reassuring. Who needs a god they can understand—or order around, for that matter?"

Mattie worked for a few minutes before blurting out a question. "How do you live with the things you don't know about God?"

Aron smiled without looking her way. "By clinging to the things I do."

Mattie recited the litany of things she'd heard in his sermons. "Hope. Eternity. God plans. God knows. God allows. God permits. All for our good and His glory." She didn't try to keep the mocking tone from her recitation.

"I'm glad you've been listening. That's a good start." He paused. "I just hope you take things past the list you just repeated."

"Aunt Lou says faith just gets dumped on a person."

Aron chuckled. "I suppose it does sometimes."

"Well, that's probably what it's going to take if I'm ever going to change what I think of preachers and sermons." She glanced at Aron and hurried to correct herself. "Present company excluded, of course."

"Thank you. I'll accept that as a compliment, especially coming from a woman who my friend Tom says has a highly developed manure detector."

Aron and Tom had talked about her? What did that mean? Mattie climbed a ladder sitting in front of the shelves and began handing down canned meat. As she descended the ladder, Aron took her arm. She'd reached the third rung from the bottom when he grasped her around the waist and lifted her down.

"Thank you," she said. Feeling her cheeks burning, she hustled toward the kitchen. "You and Tom should have a big breakfast before you head out into this."

And they did.

————

It might be snowing, but it was Sunday, and with the weather against them, miners descended on Deadwood with a vengeance. By noon Mattie had heard gunfire at least twice and endured a tittering visit from the Underwood girls, who came over because they were concerned that the reverend was in ill health because church had been canceled. When they heard what had happened, they sighed with admiration and promised to pray for the "victims."

"I don't think there will be any victims," Mattie said, more harshly than she'd intended.

"Of . . . of course not." Kitty Underwood blinked. "I didn't mean—" She took a deep breath. Mattie was grateful when the two girls fluttered their way out the door. Let them bother someone else.

Of course, once they were gone the silence in the store was almost as annoying as the Underwood sisters.

Worry descended. After a fruitless attempt at distracting herself with shelf-dusting, Mattie decided that if Kitty Underwood could talk to God, she could, too. Maybe it wouldn't be a prayer exactly. Aunt Lou and Aron had said God was always planning and permitting and allowing and all of that. So maybe a little reminder wouldn't hurt.

Clearing her throat, Mattie spoke aloud, "So Aunt Lou says that you give people faith. Well, I've never had any, but Freddie and Swede do. And Aunt Lou and Aron do. And they're good people and you know I care about them." She paused. Gulped. She had said it aloud. She cared about Aron. "So. I guess you being God and all, that's no news to you, is it? The thing is, it would be a very bad winter if these people I care about, if they weren't all right. Especially Eva. *Especially Aron.*" Had she said that part about Aron out loud or not? Her voice wavered as she concluded, "And I think it's already been a hard enough year for me. Don't you?" She swiped at a tear. "So I hope you don't mind listening to someone like me. And if you decide to dump some faith on me sometime . . . I wouldn't mind."

Mattie O'Keefe, what have you gone and done now, praying to a God you aren't even sure listens . . . and falling for a man of the cloth.

———

Freddie came limping into the store along about suppertime that day.

"You're hurt!" Mattie exclaimed. "What happened?"

"Nothing much," he said, shrugging out of his fur coat and holding his palms up to the stove. "I slipped is all. My ankle hurts. It's not broken or anything. The snow made it slippery. I stopped at your claim and you were gone. And I slipped."

"Get your boot off," Mattie said. "Let me see it. We might have the doc take a look at it—"

"It's all *right*, I said. Where's Tom?"

"Tom and Aron put together a supply train and headed south." She hastened to add, "They weren't sure the snow would be all that heavy further south, but—"

Freddie interrupted. "You don't have to make up a story. I saw the storm come in from the south. It's already been down where Mor is." He pressed his lips together for a moment, then he smiled. "But I prayed. And she'll be all right. And Eva, too. You don't have to worry."

Looking up into Freddie's calm blue eyes, Mattie wished she had faith like that.

————

He knew. Knew everything he needed to know. And just when it all came together, just when he had a plan . . . snow. Jonas cursed the snow as he shivered by his campfire on the ridge above Mattie's claim. Dillon must be mining somewhere else. Or dead. That was still an unanswered question, but everything else . . . he knew.

Her claim was paying. He'd seen her take nugget after nugget out of the ground. But he'd never seen her go to the bank. Not once. Which meant the gold was hidden somewhere on the claim. Likely in the tent. Now that he knew she didn't own that store in town, he was convinced she also still had most of the money she'd taken from him. He would get it back. She didn't own the general store and she didn't really work at the hotel. Oh no. Mattie O'Keefe had made *friends* in Deadwood. She'd even started going to church. It was all so touching. And it was all going to be so short-lived.

The key to it all was the simpleminded boy. He and Mattie had some kind of bond. He hunted for her, and it was obvious from the way she acted when he was around that she cared about him. Of course, she probably cared about the mealymouthed preacher, too, what with his perfect face and smile. But Jonas's plan would be easier to work using the simpleminded boy. He would be easy to snare.

It was time. Jonas despised the snow and hated the cold, but it was proving useful, for the preacher and Swede's husband had left with a mule train that morning. Jonas grinned in anticipation. This was going to be fun.

CHAPTER 21

The soul of the wicked desireth evil.

Proverbs 21:10

It was quite comfortable, really, sheltered inside of what was essentially a snow hut with a canvas roof. The roof was slanted, so the snow had not accumulated, and there was no threat that it would fall in. The hard-packed snow stacked all around at ground level ensured they were out of the wind. Eva, her little face and sweet hands barely poking out of her fur bunting, was sitting atop a bedroll playing pat-a-cake with Red Tallent while others played cards. One of the boys had a mandolin. He played amazingly well. Being caught by an early snowstorm was not at all the terrifying event it could have been.

The snow had stopped, praise be to God. Finally. After three days. How they would fight their way through the drifts that must be awaiting them, Swede did not know. How long it would take to get back to Deadwood, she could not know. But the grip of fear that had kept her awake at night was gone.

The freighters crept out of their shelter to check the other corral and see how the oxen had fared. Swede praised God again when

Red Tallent returned and reported, "They're fine." He scratched his chin. "But we ain't going anywhere until some of it melts. Some of us walked up ahead a mile or two, and the drifts are just too deep. It's just as well," he added. "We'd all be snow-blind by evening if we tried." He smiled at Eva and chucked her under the chin. "What d'ya think, little one, can you handle another day or two camping with old Red?"

Eva giggled. Swede sighed. So much to be thankful for, and yet, it was going to be awkward when she finally pulled into Deadwood and had to face Tom. What was it they said when a person had to admit they had been wrong? Eating . . . something. A bird. Yes. She would have to "eat crow" the next time she saw Tom English.

———

It was the closest Aron Gallagher had ever come to thinking he was actually hearing God's voice. The notion kept repeating in his mind, over and over and over again, that he should pray for Mattie. He'd been praying *about* her for quite some time now, but this was different. This wasn't about his attraction to her. This was . . . just different. Such a strong inner pull that he'd literally turned around in his saddle and looked back over his shoulder toward Deadwood. Apparently more than once, for Tom suddenly asked what was wrong and did he think they were being followed.

"No," Aron said. "It's not that. It's just—" He couldn't explain it, because he didn't understand it.

Pray for Mattie. Pray for Mattie NOW. And then . . . *Pray for Freddie. Pray for Freddie NOW. Pray . . . pray . . . pray.*

Aron prayed.

———

Back in her kitchen in Deadwood, Aunt Lou had just leaned over the soup pot to taste the stew she was serving for supper when she thought of Mattie.

"That child," she said aloud. "Needs the Lord so bad . . . likes that preacher so much . . . and jus' can't see her way to either one."

Pray for Mattie. Pray for Mattie NOW.

Aunt Lou frowned. She put more salt in the stew and then crossed the kitchen and went to stand out on the back stoop. She gazed toward the rim of the rocky wall that rose behind the hotel. She thought about Mattie's claim. But Mattie was watching the store again. She'd be over for supper any moment, and maybe Freddie would join them tonight. Maybe he'd bring them some nice fat rabbits from his hunting expedition the last couple of days.

Pray for Freddie. Pray for Freddie NOW.

Aunt Lou shivered. She stepped back inside. And she prayed.

Something's not right at Mattie's claim, Freddie thought. There was smoke coming out of the stovepipe, but Mattie was down in town minding the store again while Tom and Aron took supplies to Mor and the freighters. She wasn't coming back up here until tomorrow. That's what she'd said. *"I'll head up there on Monday just to check things over, but if the snow hasn't started to melt, I won't stay."*

Freddie didn't know why she even had to go up there at all. Winter was here. Probably she had to get more gold down to where she could keep an eye on it. There was something funny about Mattie and her gold. She didn't talk about it very much. Freddie believed that probably meant she had a lot of it. People around here were that way sometimes. They didn't talk about it in case someone might steal it. Which was smart, but in Mattie's case Freddie just wished she would put it in the bank.

Once he almost sneaked into her tent when she was at Aunt Lou's just to see if he was right. But his conscience bothered him and he knew that was God saying he shouldn't do it. So he didn't. But still, he knew there was something funny about Mattie and her gold. And now there was something funny going on at her claim tent. But she said she wasn't coming up here until Monday. He'd better check things out.

Freddie adjusted his string of rabbits and squatted down, thinking. For a long time he studied the footprints leading from the McKays' claim up to Mattie's tent . . . but not back. He smiled. That was it. Finn or Fergus—or maybe Mr. McKay himself—had been so drunk last night they didn't even know they were in Mattie's tent instead of their own. It was sort of funny in a way—but sad, too. And it wasn't right. If Mattie came up here and one of them was in her tent, she might shoot them like she'd shot Brady Sloan. And that pistol she kept in her pocket wasn't loaded with just rock salt, either. Freddie stood up. He would help Finn or Fergus or Mr. McKay get back to their own tent and put out the fire.

Leaving the string of rabbits on the ground, he stood up and limped to the tent flap. "It's Freddie," he called out. He reached through to untie it. It wasn't tied. Which just proved how drunk they had been last night. It was a wonder they had gotten a fire going at all. At least they weren't frozen to death in there.

"I'm coming in," he proclaimed. "I'll help you get back to your own—"

Pain. Darkness.

———

On Monday morning a flustered Mattie decided that she and Freddie were going to have to have a talk. He knew she wanted to go up to the claim this morning, and he'd promised he wouldn't go far to hunt and would be back in plenty of time to watch over the store while she was gone. But she'd waited and waited, and still no sign of Freddie. And now, not only was she frustrated about being behind schedule to get up to her claim, she was worried for Freddie. It wasn't like him not to keep his word. Frustrated, Mattie changed into her mining garb. At least the sun was bright and the snow was melting. Thank God.

God. She'd been thinking about God a lot lately, especially when she was alone. It was as if the idea just kept coming up whether she was with people who talked about Him or not. As far as she could tell, she wasn't any closer to believing in Him. Still, the *idea* of God didn't result in resentment over her list of unanswerable questions. Instead, she had been pondering what Aron said about accepting the things he couldn't understand about God by clinging to the things he did.

This morning, as Mattie let Justice out and prepared her own breakfast, a new idea came to her. Maybe faith was like gold mining. She couldn't see how much color existed on her entire claim, but she believed there was more because of the gold she had seen. Maybe that was what Aron had been talking about. You started with a little bit of faith and trusted for what you couldn't see. The problem was Mattie couldn't seem to conjure up even a nugget of trust in God—at least not on behalf of herself.

She had come to think God probably did have an interest in her friends. Aron and Tom had been gone for a week now, and she had tired of worrying about them and started talking to God about it and felt better for it.

A bark at the back door announced the return of Justice, and when she let him in, she was almost happy to see how muddy he was. Mud meant melting snow. And melting snow meant warmer air and improved conditions for Tom and Aron and the freighters. They might have to slog through mud, but mud wasn't life-threatening. Mud, she knew Swede could handle. Heading into the store, Mattie perused the calendar, counting days, trying to anticipate when everyone would be back.

"Well, Justice," she said aloud, her finger on today's date, October 30, "if everything was going smoothly, I would be expecting the freighters to pull into town somewhere around November third. I'm thinking the snow has added at least a week. And if it gets too muddy . . ." She paused and smiled down at the dog. "What do *you* think?" Justice danced around the kitchen, his tail wagging.

By the time Justice and Cat had been fed, and she'd had her second cup of coffee, Mattie felt better about things. Freddie had just been delayed by the snow. He'd turn up sometime this morning, and if she left now, she wouldn't be gone long.

"So what do you think, Justice?" she asked abruptly. "Can I hire you as a guard dog? Will you keep the bad guys away from the store while I check on things at the claim?"

When Justice barked, Mattie nodded. "Actually, I think you will." The pup was gangly, but he was big, and his bark had changed from the yapping of a pup to a deep "woof" that made people watch him carefully.

She made two signs that read *Back soon. Beware of Dog* and hung one at each door. Pulling on her buffalo coat, Mattie prepared to leave. "You be good now," she said to Justice. "And I'll see that you get a nice ham bone as pay for guarding the place."

After securing the lock, Mattie slogged through town and up toward her claim. She might not have made any progress toward God in recent days, but she had made a huge decision about people. It was time to start trusting. She was going to listen to Tom and Aron, and starting with half the contents of one of the bottles in her cache, she would deposit her gold in the bank. Over the next few weeks she would gradually bring more into town until it was all locked up—equal amounts in each of the three banks in town. She hoped that dividing it up that way would keep most of Deadwood from knowing that Matt the Miner was rich.

The concept of wealth had already presented new things to ponder. She could go anywhere, but there was no place she wanted to go right now. She could buy a business, but she honestly liked prospecting. She could build a church, but it seemed like a person who went around building churches should probably be a member, and she wasn't ready for that. She still had too many questions about God. Aron might be able to live in that space he talked about between things he understood and things he never would, but she wasn't ready to do that. If God was God, then why didn't He just show himself in a way that people couldn't ignore?

He does that, Mattie. He does it all the time. Just look around you. The sky . . . the stars . . . the moon . . . and the changes in people when they finally give in. She could almost hear Aron saying those very words. He'd even told her once that perhaps she should pray the same way someone else who met Jesus once did. "Lord, I believe. . . . Help my unbelief." So far, even though she'd said the words a couple of times, nothing had changed beyond a very tiny understanding of faith as it related to gold mining . . . and the absence of the grudge she'd held against God for a long time. Now, in place of the grudge, she felt . . . almost hopeful. As she headed up the gulch, she began to sing.

———

Staring down at the string of rabbits lying on the ground, Mattie frowned. She glanced toward her tent at the thread of smoke ascending from the stovepipe. The rabbits were frozen stiff. Freddie would never just drop game like that. . . . Not unless . . . Her heart racing, she ran toward the tent, slipped, and almost fell.

"Freddie! Freddie, are you all right?"

A moan . . . *Oh, Lord . . . he's sick. He hurt his leg again . . . he—*

In her panic, she forgot to unbutton her buffalo robe. Her Colt was there, tucked in her pocket and of no use at all as she stepped inside to find Freddie lying bound and gagged on her cot. Her heart in her throat, she stared at the drifter who was seated atop her supply box with a shotgun aimed at her. Tattered clothes, scraggly, greasy hair, a face that was one mass of scabs and healed-over pox, hideous scars and . . . oh . . . no . . . *God, please . . . no.*

"Hello, Mattie," Jonas Flynn said as he brandished his hook. And smiled.

CHAPTER 22

Deliver me from my persecutors; for they are stronger than I.

Psalm 142:6

"Y ou must be hot, dressed in that," Jonas said as he pointed the shotgun at her coat. "Take it off. Slowly. I assume you still keep the Colt tucked in your pocket?" He swung the shotgun barrel toward Freddie. "He's not dead. But that could change, should you choose to be foolish right now."

Trembling, Mattie pulled off the coat. "It's here," she croaked, and turned so he could see her pocket. "I'll just pull it out and—"

"Hold it!" Jonas barked, and turned the gun back on her. Mattie froze. He smiled. "All right, dear. Now suppose you take it out, very carefully, and just toss it outside. Toward the edge of the claim, where the snow's the deepest."

When she'd done it, he nodded. "Good. Good girl." He saw Mattie glance to where Freddie lay. "Ah . . . I see. You're worried about your new brother. How sweet. Where is Dillon, by the way? That's the one thing I don't know yet. It'd be a shame for him to turn up while we're having our little chat."

"Dillon's gone," Mattie said. "He died before I even got here."

Weakness would only encourage the worst in him. She'd learned that long ago. And so she forced herself to look him in the eye when she answered. "I never saw him alive after you ran him out of Abilene. Happy?"

"Tsk, tsk, Mattie"—he shook his hook at her, a teacher scolding a student with an iron finger—"bitterness isn't a very attractive quality." He pointed his hook at his own face. "See what it's done to me?" He laughed. A hideous sound. "But I digress. Tie the tent flap open before you sit down beside your young friend, my dear. Your neighbors won't be a bother, and we're going to be a while."

Neighbors . . . what had he done to the McKays? Her hands trembled as Mattie obeyed him. *Please. God. Please help. Send someone.* Once she was seated beside Freddie's still form, Jonas chuckled. With the morning light streaming into the tent, his ravaged face and tattered condition were even more shocking. He would have been pathetic were it not for the searing hatred in those pale blue eyes.

"Dear, sweet Mattie. You forget how easily I can read your face. After all, I'm the one who taught you all about faces. Ironic, don't you think, in light of what you've done to mine?" When she frowned, he explained. "If it weren't for you, I would still be in Abilene. If it weren't for you . . ." He ground out the words at first, but as he moved along the litany of things Mattie had done to him, his tone intensified until Jonas was dancing just at the edge of self-control.

Let him scream at me, Mattie prayed. *If he screams someone might hear . . . someone might come.* But Jonas broke off abruptly, and when he spoke next, his voice was quiet. Sinister. Deadly. He shook his head. "Poor Mattie, I'm afraid no one's coming to help her." He nodded toward the McKays' claim. "As to your concerns for your neighbors, I've dispatched them with a special concoction. Drinks around the fire with a nice old codger who remembered the homeland was just the thing." He affected a brogue. "Yous never saw the like of it, sweet lass." He sighed. "I dragged them off to bed, where they'll stay for . . . oh, long enough for you and me to finish our business."

He gestured toward Freddie. "Now, Freddie was a bit of a challenge. I knew he wouldn't drink with me. So I had to knock him out. Happily, I was still able to pour enough of my special brew down his throat to ensure he won't be a problem, either." He smiled. "So you see, Mattie, we've plenty of time to get reacquainted." He tilted his head. "To reestablish the boundaries. To, shall we say, negotiate."

"Negotiate?"

"Yes. My terms for releasing your friend. Maybe even for letting you live." He cackled. "Who knows? Anything could happen up on Mattie's Claim." Spittle flew from his lips as he talked.

He might not kill Freddie. God, he said he might let him go. Tell me what to do. Tell me what to say. How can I save Freddie? She reminded herself again that emotion would only fuel Jonas's propensity for diabolical creativity. She touched the place on her arm where a hook-shaped scar remained as a souvenir of the night she'd learned that begging Jonas never earned mercy. And so she begged heaven. *Help me. Help me. Help me.*

Calm washed over her. Lifting her chin, she spoke. She sounded calm. Free from fear. "I'll do whatever you want. But Freddie has nothing to do with you and me. He's never hurt anyone. He shouldn't have to suffer for my sins."

Jonas licked his lips. "I see you've acquired a new vocabulary— no doubt from that preacher you've been spending time with." He echoed her words. " 'He shouldn't have to suffer for my sins.' Hmmm. That's very sweet." The slit in his face curled up in a hideous smile. "Mattie has a soft spot for the village idiot." He winked. "You shouldn't play your hand so soon. You've shown a weakness I can exploit. I taught you better than that. Didn't I?"

He leaned forward and once again his voice dropped and the words ground. "Didn't I teach you well? Didn't I take you in and feed and clothe you? Delectable food. Silk and velvet. The finest gowns. And for that"—he touched his hook to the cheekbone she'd cut with her ring—"you gave me this."

The scar was no longer evident amongst the furrows clawed by smallpox, but Mattie knew what he was talking about. "I didn't mean to cut you," she said. "I only wanted you to keep your promises to Mam. To give me my money and let me go."

"Ah, now we're getting to the heart of it," Jonas spat out. "The *money*." He swiped at his mouth with his sleeve.

"Three hundred dollars was a pittance compared to what you said I'd earned." A plan was forming in her mind. "But if this is about money, I can give you as much as you want."

"Really?" He leaned back and rested his hook atop the shotgun. "Tell me, Mattie, exactly how much money do you think it will take to give me a life back . . . to restore this?" He turned his face from side to side, jutted out his mottled chin, mugged as if he were posing for a photograph. When she was silent, he nodded. "Yes. You're right. There isn't enough money in the world. And as for the money you took, three thousand was considerably more than you'd earned, even if I was going to agree to what the ledger said."

Mattie frowned. "I don't know what you're talking about. I took three *hundred* dollars. And that's all. I even left the ring behind."

He shook his head. "Now, now . . . lying's a sin. You're making me very angry."

Her mind racing, Mattie thought back to that night. She replayed it aloud. "I was afraid you were going to kill me for—" she pointed to his cheek—"for that. And so while you were gone getting it stitched up, I grabbed a wad of bills out of your dresser drawer and ran. There was no plot to rob you. I didn't even know how much it was until I got to the train station and counted it. Three hundred and forty-two dollars." She remembered it clearly. "Think about it, Jonas. Why would I lie to you now?" Suddenly she knew. She gasped, "I think I know what happened."

"This is proving to be even more entertaining than I'd anticipated. Please continue."

"I ran into Flo when I was leaving. Literally ran into her. I was in such a hurry I didn't see her on the stairs. We almost tumbled down them, but she grabbed the railing and I-I just kept going. But she had to know I was running." She swallowed. "Think about it, Jonas. Flo had every opportunity, and you know how she hated me." She paused. "She'd stolen from you before. I remember the night you caught her rummaging in your room." Even now that memory made her shudder because of what Jonas had done next.

When Jonas said nothing, Mattie continued. "Is she still working for you?" She saw the answer in his eyes. "When did she leave? Was it right after I did?" He didn't answer. Didn't have to. "Oh, Jonas . . . you followed the wrong girl." She could tell he was pondering it. Somewhere in the far reaches of whatever logical mind he had left, he had to know it was true.

And then, as quickly as she'd deduced the truth about Flo, Mattie realized she'd made a mistake. Jonas was already blaming her for everything that had happened to him, and now she'd convinced him that he'd followed the wrong girl. As the truth of what she was saying hit home, a new level of rage flickered in Jonas's eyes, rage fueled by despair and a sense of hopelessness. She spoke up. "Three thousand dollars doesn't begin to cover it, does it? I can give you more. Just say how much."

He snorted. "You're missing the point. This isn't about the money anymore. It's about betrayal. And ruination. It's about what *you* have done to *me*."

"I didn't mean to hurt you. Dillon and I just wanted a different kind of life. That's all. It wasn't about you. We just wanted to be on our own." She kept talking, soothing, trying to appeal to any sanity that might still exist inside the wounded brain. "But that's the past. You said we would negotiate now. Let's negotiate."

Jonas swung the barrel of the rifle toward Freddie. "I'm getting bored." His finger locked on the trigger.

Dear God, he's mad. . . . What can I do? . . . What can I do? An answer came, and the instant it dropped into her conscious mind, the calm returned. "You can have it all," she said.

"All of . . . ?"

"All of Dillon's gold. All of mine." Jonas's finger moved away from the trigger. Her heart pounding, Mattie said, "This claim is rich. It's been paying out for months. No one knows because I've kept it all right here." She patted the cot. "It's right here and you can have it *all* in exchange for Freddie's life." She forced reason into her voice and prayed she sounded convincing. "You could buy a new place. A *palace*. A man's face doesn't matter if he has enough money. You taught me that, and you know it's true. I can make you richer than you've ever dreamed."

But how will he get away? The solution came immediately. "You can take the McKays' mule. I'll help you load the saddlebags. No one in town will come looking for me, Jonas—not until you've gotten away. They all knew I was planning on working the claim today. They knew Freddie was coming with me. You can be far away before anyone even finds us."

He smiled. Leered. Chuckled. "You'd do that? Just to see old Jonas gone from your life?"

"I would *owe* you my life," Mattie said. "And Freddie's." She shrugged. "It would be a fair trade."

He was thinking about it. Considering. Finally he said, "Let me see it."

She nodded. "It's beneath me. There's a cache under the bed. We'll have to move Freddie."

"Well, aren't you the clever one."

"Not me. It was Dillon's idea. I was here for weeks before I found it. But I've added to it. I've added a lot."

"How much?"

"Let me show you."

He stood up and pressed his back against the canvas wall, gesturing with the shotgun. "So show me."

"You have to help me move Freddie."

"Oh, I think you can figure out a way to do that. Just move slowly. It would be a shame to have to kill him now, just when you and I are considering a satisfactory conclusion to our negotiations." He smirked.

Somehow, Mattie managed to roll Freddie off the cot. His prone body barely fit in the space between the edge of the cot and the little stove. She had to reach over him to lift the bedframe and prop it up. She pointed at the iron plate. "Can you see that? I have to slide that over."

"Then slide it."

She did. And waited.

"Surely you don't think I'm going to be stupid enough to bend over that hole. Bring up whatever's in it. And if there's a gun hidden down there, pull it out first, where I can see it." He pressed the barrel of his gun to Freddie's temple. "And rest assured that in the time it would take you to take aim, I'd dispatch poor Freddie here into the next life."

With trembling hands, Mattie lifted the bottles of gold out of the cache. When they were lined up along the earth, Jonas surveyed them with a smile. "Well, now. How about that. Matt the Miner has done well. Very well."

She pointed to the leather bag around her neck. "You can have this, too. The snow's melting fast. You can get away without leaving much of a trail. I know you can do that, Jonas. You were a sniper in the war. You know how to do things."

"Not *everything*." His voice was terrifying.

With all the emotional strength she could muster, Mattie looked up at him and said, "I'll help you get away."

He chortled. "Oh yes. That's a wonderful idea. That's just what

Jonas wants. Another taste of the same witch who ruined his life."
He spat at her. "I don't want *you*, Mattie. I want to *destroy* you. I
want you to pay for what you've done to me. Not just once, but over
and over again."

"Then take me with you. You can finish with me . . . later." *Just
let Freddie go.*

He was thinking it over. Thank God he was actually thinking
it over.

"Go get the mule," he said. "And no screaming for help." He
pointed the gun at Freddie again. "Hurry."

Mattie scrambled to her feet. Her hands were shaking so badly
she could hardly get the beast bridled and saddled. When she finally
did, it didn't want to follow her up to her claim. Jonas stood in the
doorway watching. Laughing. "I'm getting tired of waiting, Mattie," he sang out.

Slipping in the snow, she tugged desperately on the bridle.
Please. God. Jesus. The mule took a step. Then another. Finally they
were at the tent. Mattie loaded the bottles into Dillon's old saddlebags. Once they were in place behind the saddle, she turned back
to where Jonas waited. She risked one glance toward where she'd
tossed her gun, and with a loud shout, he was on her, screaming,
"DON'T—EVEN—THINK—"

He grabbed her shirt-sleeve with his hook and yanked her back
inside the tent, throwing her down on the cot with such force that
it knocked the air out of her. As she lay there trying to catch her
breath, he leaned down to touch her cheek with his hook. His breath
stank. He stank. She met his eyes for a moment before glancing over
at Freddie again.

Jonas sat back. "You really do care about that boy, don't you?"
His voice gentled. He crooned her name, and then his face changed.
Something about the light in his eyes . . . how could they look
more evil? And yet they did. Mattie shrank back. *Help me help
me help me.*

Abruptly, Jonas stood up. "On second thought, there's a better way to hurt you now than a little encounter with a hook. Better, even, than making you come with me." He straddled Freddie's unconscious body.

It was too much. "No!" Mattie screamed. "Please, Jonas, please . . . God. *NO!*" She charged him, but he tossed her aside. Her head hit the corner of Dillon's storage chest. Just before the darkness overcame her, she saw Jonas lift and aim the shotgun . . . heard it go off . . . and she cried out to God one last time.

———

"Mattie? Mattie, wake up." Someone was cradling her head in his hand, patting her cheeks gently. "You need to wake up now."

Mattie opened her eyes, but she didn't believe what she saw.

"You look like you've seen a ghost. Here, let me help you sit up." Freddie lifted her upright. He handed her a tin mug. "He said to give you water when you woke up."

"He? He who?" She blinked and looked around the empty tent, squinting against the sun streaming in through the open flap.

Freddie sighed. He motioned for her to drink. "Drink."

Mattie drank. She felt so . . . odd. She kept looking at Freddie . . . remembering . . . trying to make some sense of where she was and what had happened. Hadn't she seen Freddie . . . heard . . . She began to cry.

"Shhh." Freddie patted her shoulder. "It's all right now. Shhh."

"You . . . He . . . I heard . . ." she blubbered.

"I know," Freddie said. "There was a terrible man here. An *evil* man. He hit me on the head and then he made me drink something." He looked around. "But he's gone now and he won't be coming back. The angel said so." Freddie shrugged. "At least *I* think he was an angel."

"Angel?"

"Yes. When I woke up the bad man was gone. You were laying

299

over there." He gestured toward the place where she'd fallen when Jonas threw her. "And there was another man untying me. He didn't have wings, but he said, 'Don't be afraid,' and he put his hand here." Freddie spread his palm across his broad chest. "I felt so much better after he did that. And then he said not to worry about you or the McKays or anything. And you're all right, aren't you, Mattie, and so are the McKays. See?" He pointed out of the tent.

Mattie leaned over then, and peering outside, she saw that Freddie was right. All three McKays were hard at work on their claim. She started to get up. "I owe them for a mule. I should ta—" Her hand grasped the edge of the canvas running along the open flap, but she didn't take another step. The mule was tethered to the same tree the McKays always used as a hitching post. Frowning, she looked back at Freddie. "But—"

"I told you he said not to worry. He said the mule would come back soon and it did. He said you would be all right and you are. So we won't worry." He turned to leave, motioning for her to follow. "But we should get some help and go after that bad man so he can't hurt anybody else. I wish Deadwood had a sheriff but someone will know what we should do now. Maybe Mr. Underwood or Mr. Langrishe."

"I . . . I . . ." Mattie crossed to the supply box and plopped down. She took a deep breath, realizing Freddie was right. Jonas was clearly mad. He couldn't just be allowed to escape. What might he do to someone else? *And why can't Aron be here to help us?* She forced herself to nod. "Yes. We should get help." But she just sat there, trying to make sense of things.

Freddie smiled. "You don't believe there was an angel, do you?"

Mattie shook her head. "But that doesn't mean I don't believe *you*." She smiled up at him. "If there's one thing I know—and I don't know very much right now—it's that you wouldn't lie to me."

"It's okay." Freddie patted her shoulder. "Angels are hard for people to believe. It's sort of like gold mining."

She looked up at him. "Gold mining?"

"Well," he said, gesturing toward the creek, "you can't see how *much* gold there is, but you've seen some and so you believe there's more. We can't see God. Or angels. But after today—" He shrugged. "God will dump more faith out. You'll see." He grinned. "The angel said you'd want to know that."

"Know . . . what?" Her mind reeling, Mattie could barely choke the words out.

"About gold and mining and God dumping out faith." Freddie motioned toward town. "We should go now. If we hurry and get help I bet we can catch the bad man before it gets dark."

CHAPTER 23

Give thanks unto the Lord, call upon his name, make known
his deeds among the people. Sing unto him, sing psalms unto him,
talk ye of all his wondrous works.

1 Chronicles 16:8–9

They had been back on the trail for nearly one full day. "Leif! Lars! Pull harder, you beautiful, strong, bellowing, hungry beasts! Pull harder and faster, and I vill give you de best hay I can find and maybe retire you to pasture up nort." Swede cracked the whip above their heads. The snow was melting quickly, and the problem of deep drifts had been replaced by a more familiar one—mud. Everyone wanted to make as many miles as possible before the thaw created more. And everyone wanted to see Deadwood. But no one as much as she did.

She had made up her mind. She would apologize to Tom, because he had been right and she'd been wrong. And then she would end their partnership, for she had finally come to understand what was at the heart of much of her unhappiness of late. It was Tom. To see him every day and talk over the business together and then to go to bed alone and wake up alone with this horrible yearning in her heart for more could not go on. There were men who could look past tanned faces and calloused hands and thick waists. Garth had been such a man, and she longed for another. A gentle man like Tom. *Not LIKE Tom. You want Tom.* He loved Eva and had befriended Freddie. He fit into their lives like a cog in a wheel, but he wouldn't want to be part of her life in any other way.

Swede cracked the whip above her team and began again the singsong litany that would keep them moving up the trail. Her voice cracked a time or two, and she swiped at a tear now and then, but as she walked along and breathed the fresh air, she called upon God to help her, and she began to feel better. At least she had decided what she must do. At least she would no longer dangle between reality and hope. Swede sighed. She had survived a broken heart before. She could do it again. With God's help.

Toward evening of the second day back on the trail, riders appeared on the horizon. They were moving slowly, and as they came close, Swede could see it was only two, with what was probably a string of pack mules. *Miners giving up and going home.* She paid no further attention until it became obvious they were going to intercept the line of freighters. Her first thought was of the shortage of food and how there wasn't really enough to share. Her second was to repent of her selfishness. And then there was another thought, as she realized who the riders were.

She felt a brief rush of something akin to panic as she looked down at her worn apron, her men's work boots, her skirt . . . all of them splattered with the mud of the trail. And her hair . . . she'd slept in yesterday's braids and simply tied a scarf over her head before putting on her bonnet today. Ah well. It was of no consequence. She had already decided how to think about these things.

With a prayer for strength, Swede shoved the bonnet back off her head and watched as Tom English and Aron Gallagher approached. They paused to talk to Red Tallent for a few moments before riding up the line toward her. It gave her time to pray. She had the time, but no words, and so when Tom and Aron rode up she was grateful that Eva waved and screeched, "Ta-ta!"

Tom dismounted and went to Eva, kissing her soundly and laughing when she tugged on his nose. "You're all right" was all he said as he looked at Swede.

"Yah, sure." Swede pointed toward the third string of wagons ahead of her. "Jake knew vat to do. He vas vit de Indians once, and he showed us how dey banked up de snow around tepees. Ve vere varm and safe. Never in danger." She shrugged. "As you can see."

"Short on food?" Aron Gallagher had remained in the saddle.

"A little," Swede admitted. "But ve share among us. It vould be all right. Now it vill be better." She forced a smile even as she thrust her hand into her apron pocket and brought out her pipe. It calmed her nerves to smoke, but then she thought better of it and put the pipe away.

"Well," Aron said, "I'm going to ride back up and make arrangements with Red about how to handle distributing the supplies we brought."

Tom handed him the reins to his own horse, clearly intending to walk with Swede.

Presently she cracked the whip and got the team moving, self-conscious about everything she did. As soon as the train was moving again, she said, "I am sorry for de vorry I have caused and for de time I have taken from your duties."

"Mattie's minding the store," Tom said. "Other than the one day a week so she can work the claim, Garth and Company is open as usual."

Swede nodded. She cracked the whip and called out to Leif

and Lars before saying, "Mr. English, I have someting to discuss vit you."

"And I with you," he said. "But not here. Not like this." He paused. "I expect Red will agree to having Aron and me ride ahead a few miles and make camp so we can share supplies with everyone."

"I imagine so."

"So I'll see you in camp in a few hours," Tom said, and waving to Eva he loped to catch up with Aron and Red.

———

She could not wait. It had to be done. And so, at the midday break, Swede rushed through tending her team, took Eva in her arms, and hurried to where Tom and Aron sat, drinking coffee and talking to some of the other freighters.

"Mr. English," she said. "May ve speak now?"

Tom nodded and got up. He followed her to the opposite side of her string of wagons. And then she could not do it. "I have brought Mattie her brother's gravestone," she said instead, pointing to the crate in the middle wagon. "It vas vaiting. As I expected."

"She'll be happy to see that," he said as they walked toward it. "We had snow in Deadwood, too," he said. "But I expect we'll have a couple of days of good weather yet. Between Aron and Freddie and me, it shouldn't be a problem to get it put up." Brushing away the layer of cushioning straw, he nodded. "It's a fine stone. Mattie will be pleased."

"Yah, I know she vill." She took a deep breath. "And as to de store—I am tinking dat perhaps you vould vish to have your own." She had expected to see relief on his face. Instead, he seemed unhappy.

"Are you *firing* me, Katerina?"

"No, no. I yoost tink you vould perhaps radder to haf your own business vare you are making de decidings and vare you don't must to ask another's opinion." She blushed furiously as her English reverted nearly back to Swedish. She was so nervous. Close to tears.

Tom frowned. "I didn't expect to get fired over a little fight."

"Is not about disagreement. Is—" Oh, now. This was not what she had wanted to happen. Not at all. Eva was whimpering, and she herself had to swipe at a tear. She gulped. "Ven a man is partner—business partner—vit voman, people make assumption. Dey . . . You . . ." She sighed. "People might tink you and I . . . Vell, I know is silly, but perhaps is better for you—"

"I'm sorry, but I have no idea what you're talking about."

Must it be this way? Must she be humiliated as well as brokenhearted? So be it.

Swede lifted her chin. Now she was angry. He was being cruel, though he probably didn't know it. Men were so stupid sometimes. "I am hardly beautiful voman. I verk hard, and I am not ashamed, but I also know dat men—except for Garth Jannike, who was God's gift to me—men yoost do not care for vomen like me ven dey haf Mattie O'Keefes and Kitty Undervoods about." She was really crying now. "And so I am tinking dat ve end our partnership, and you open your own store, and I vill haul for you as before, but den you vill not be associated vit me and mebbe you could—"

"Excuse me," Tom interrupted. "Give me the baby."

"Vat?"

He held out his hands, and Eva readily went to him. With Swede trailing a ways behind, he carried the baby around the string of wagons to the campfire and plopped her into Red Tallent's lap. He said something to Aron Gallagher and to Red. And then he walked back to her. "Now *I* have something to say."

"You don't have to say—"

"And I would like it very much if you would hush now and let me say it."

Swede put her hands on her hips. It was going to be another fight. Ah well. So be it. Not all partnerships could end peacefully.

307

She had hoped— But she never finished that thought about her hopes, because they were replaced with entirely new ones as Tom English took her in his arms and kissed her. On the lips. In front of all the freighters. Who whistled and hooted, and Tom didn't seem to care one bit.

When he finally let her go, he stood back and said, "Now, we'll have no more talk about Katerina Jannike's deficiencies," he said, "because I love her. And she is about to become my wife. If she'll have me."

———

Mattie stepped to the edge of the cliff and peered down at the tangled end of Jonas Flynn's life. She shivered. When she reached out, Freddie was there to take her hand.

The men who had helped track the mule this far stood at a respectful distance.

The story was laid out for anyone with eyes, told in the pattern of footprints that showed a man dismounting up here and walking ahead and a mule backing away. How or why the struggle had been allowed to continue to the edge of the precipice, and how Jonas had been dragged over the edge were details no one would ever know. But the man who'd ridden away from Mattie's Claim on a pack mule laden with gold was nothing like the intelligent business owner who'd first come to Deadwood in search of a runaway. Madmen often ended their lives in inexplicable ways.

"I'll climb down and get the gold back for you," Freddie said.

Scanning the ragged edges of the canyon, Mattie gulped. "I can't see how."

Freddie pointed to the opposite canyon wall. "You see that spot right there by that fallen tree?" When Mattie followed his gaze and nodded, he explained. "That's one of my caves. I know the way down there. It won't be that hard."

Mattie sighed. And then she wondered. She looked up at Freddie.

"Do you think you could bring *him* out?" She shuddered and repeated the words she'd learned from Aron Gallagher. "Some might think he doesn't deserve it, but I'd like to see he has a decent burial."

"I'm strong," Freddie said. "I can do it."

―――――

Freddie kept his word, and on the Friday after Jonas's body was found, Aron, who'd arrived back in town along with the freighters the previous day, read a simple service at Jonas's grave. After the amen, Mattie laid pine boughs on three graves—Dillon's, Wild Bill's, and Jonas Flynn's. She lingered at Dillon's while Freddie and Aron waited for her. She bowed her head and murmured, "I don't know if you do things like this, but just in case you do, could you let Dillon know that it's over . . . and I'm all right. I'm not afraid anymore. I have new friends and—" She was afraid to give words to the rest of her feelings about the people in her life. She waited another moment before turning her back on the graves that represented her past and, lifting her chin, walked toward Aron and Freddie and whatever future God had in store.

―――――

On the evening of Saturday, November 18, 1876, Jack Langrishe's theatre was aglow with candlelight. The aroma of pine emanated from both the evergreen wreaths lining the walls and the wood shavings sprinkled over the scrubbed board floors. A capacity crowd had filled every available chair long before the scheduled time for the evening's special production, but no one minded waiting. There was always news and gossip to share in Deadwood.

Finally the reverend Aron Gallagher, clad in his new suit—provided by the Berg sisters—stepped onto the stage. He was accompanied by two people: the beautiful Miss Mattie O'Keefe and the dapper, but somewhat nervous, Mr. Tom English. The crowd was instantly quiet, except for a blond-haired angel sitting on Aunt Lou's lap, who screeched "Ta-ta!" and made everyone laugh.

When Kitty Underwood went to the piano and struck up a tune that would only be remembered as "something highbrow," the crowd rose as one and turned toward the back of the theatre. What they saw made them draw in their collective breaths.

Katerina Ingegaard Jannike was not the most beautiful bride anyone had ever seen. Her face showed the effect of years of wind and sun, and it would ever be so. But her straw-colored hair fell to her waist in a golden cascade that glimmered in the candlelight, and her elegant pale-blue gown made her eyes shine. Her hands clutched an artful arrangement of evergreen bows with pinecones wired in. As she walked toward the stage, the similarities between mother and the son who proudly escorted her up the aisle were unmistakable.

No, Katerina Ingegaard Jannike English was not the most beautiful bride folks would ever remember seeing. She was, however, the happiest.

———

Freddie hung the sign his mor had printed on the front door at Garth and Company Merchandise and locked the door. *Closed*, it said. *Happy Thanksgiving*.

"Dat's good, den," Swede said as she donned the fur-lined coat her new husband—who was always such a gentleman—held for her. Together the new family crossed Main, navigating their way through and around drifted snow toward the Grand Central Hotel and the celebration Aunt Lou had planned for the six folks she had taken to calling her "Deadwood family"—Swede and Tom, Eva and Freddie, Aron Gallagher, and Mattie O'Keefe.

Once everyone was seated, Aunt Lou rose from her place to speak. "Now, this is just what I like. A table overflowing with love." She looked to Aron. "If you don't mind, Reverend, I would like to thank the good Lord for what He has done among these folks before you do the honors of carving the bird."

"Please," Aron said, and bowed his head.

"Dear Lord," Aunt Lou began, "we have so much to say. All of us here at this table came to Deadwood for different reasons. Mattie came hoping to reunite with her brother, Dillon, only to find that he was already with you. But you gave her a new brother in Freddie, and a baby sister, too, with little Eva, and you gave her a family in us—if she will have us. So we thank you, Lord. I don't know if Tom English came looking for a wife, but you gave him a good one, and ain't that just like you, Lord, giving folks blessings they don't even know they got coming. Thank you. And Swede came with a broken heart and you filled it all the way up. Thank you, Lord." She paused and sniffed the air. "And now, that turkey Freddie shot for us is about to burn, so we will thank you for it and promise to thank you some more yet today. Amen."

Swirling snow kept Mattie in town through the first few days of December, and although Freddie insisted he didn't mind spreading his bedroll on the floor by the kitchen stove, Mattie decided to accept the Berg sisters' offer to rent the tiny room at the back of their shop. She divided her time between working in Aunt Lou's kitchen and Swede's store, and treated Freddie to an almost daily supply of cinnamon pinwheels courtesy of Aunt Lou's pie-baking lessons. The more it snowed, the less inclined Mattie was to climb back up to her claim. She told herself that had nothing to do with the frequency of Aron Gallagher's visits to Aunt Lou's kitchen.

The telegraph arrived in town, "heralding a new era for our fair city," according to the *Pioneer*. Mattie smiled when she read the article, thinking of Dillon's "hell's front porch" description of the town and wondering what he would think of Deadwood now.

In mid-December, Mattie was dusting the china on display at

the store when Aron stomped in. Removing his hat and shaking the snow out of his coat, he said something about the wind picking up and the temperature dropping before adding, "Freddie challenged me to a no-holds-barred game of checkers tonight."

"Sounds like the beginning of a long night," Mattie said with a smile. "Freddie's very good at checkers."

"Very good," Aron agreed, "but *not* unbeatable." He glanced around. "Where is he, anyway?"

"He just let Justice out," she said, and laid the feather duster atop the counter. "They should both be back in any minute. I'll get some water on for coffee." She paused. "You *do* want coffee?"

"Coffee would be great," Aron said. "The newlyweds gone somewhere?"

Mattie could feel herself blushing. "Only upstairs. As soon as Eva turned in." She headed for the storeroom-kitchen as Aron began setting up the checkerboard. Freddie and Justice came in, and the dog galumphed to Aron's side.

"You sure this dog isn't half horse?" he joked as he stroked the broad back.

"I wish," Mattie replied. "It'd make getting up to my claim so much easier."

"Well, I'm glad you're staying in town through the worst of winter," Aron said. He didn't look up as he added, "It gives us all less to worry about and makes the town so much prettier."

Mattie curtsied. "Thank you, Reverend Gallagher. Keep it up, and you'll earn a piece of the mince pie I made with Aunt Lou today."

Aron chuckled. "It makes the town prettier and more civilized. And did I mention prettier?"

"I think you're real pretty too, Mattie," Freddie piped up.

"That does it, gentlemen. Two pieces of pie with coffee coming up." Mattie headed for the stove.

Mattie had barely finished tidying up the kitchen when Freddie, after beating Aron two out of three games of checkers, stretched and announced—rather loudly, she thought—that he was ready to turn in for the night. She bade him good-night and accepted Aron's offer to walk her to her room at the Berg sisters' shop, but before she could grab her coat off the hook by the door, Aron asked if they could talk for a bit.

"I'll heat up the coffee," he said.

"And I suppose you could force yourself to eat yet another piece of pie," Mattie teased.

He shook his head. "No—just coffee's fine."

"Am I in trouble?"

"Of course not," Aron said. "I just"—he set the coffeepot on to heat while he talked—"I just wanted to ask you about something Freddie told me the other day." He motioned for her to sit down at the table, then pulled out a chair for himself and sat down. "Something about an angel appearing up at Mattie's Claim."

Mattie looked away for a moment. She swallowed. "I see."

His voice was gentle. "I'm a little surprised it took all this time to learn exactly how terrible that experience was. Freddie said you'd both agreed not to say much about it, but he had some questions for me. About angels, mostly." When Mattie was still quiet, he said, "It seems Freddie wasn't completely unconscious the entire time. He's remembering more as time goes on." He cleared his throat. "You made it sound like that day was more about robbery than anything else. Which would be frightening enough if that was all that happened, but, Mattie—"

She interrupted him. "It's not exactly the kind of thing a person wants to relive."

"No. I suppose not." Aron got up, poured coffee, and set steaming mugs on the table before them. "I apologize if this is upsetting you. I just wanted—"

"If you're upset about some conspiracy to hide the truth, that's not why I asked Freddie if we could avoid repeating the gory details."

She was surprised when tears sprang to her eyes as she thought back to that day.

"No," Aron said, shaking his head. "That's not it at all. I just wanted you to know . . ." He reached across the table and took her hands in his. "I just wanted you to know how glad I am you're both all right. And how sorry I am you had to go through something like that—with or without angels in attendance."

Was it her imagination, or was he fighting off tears? "Thank you," Mattie said. It wasn't until her palms were warming around a steaming mug of the strong brew that she spoke again. "So—what did you tell Freddie? What do you think?"

"About?"

"Angels. Miracles."

He thought for a moment before saying, "I've never personally witnessed a miracle. I suppose most people would be inclined to think Freddie was . . . exaggerating."

"That's the main reason I told him we should keep the details of that day to ourselves." She looked down at the table as she murmured, "People probably get put in asylums for telling stories like that. And Freddie . . . Freddie gets made fun of enough already."

"I know what you mean." Aron sat back in his chair. "We don't ever have to talk about it again if you don't want to." His blue-gray eyes stared at her intently. "I only brought it up because when I realized how close I came—we all came—to losing you . . ."

Suddenly she *did* want to talk about that day. To have him know how it had impacted her. "I prayed," she blurted out. "Up there. That day."

"You must have been so terrified."

She shrugged. "I was at first. But then . . . it changed. I prayed and it changed." She paused. "It wasn't even a real prayer. All I could think was *help me help me help me.* No *heavenly Father*s or even an *amen.* But the minute I threw those words up, this unbelievable calm just . . . descended." She shook her head. "And even though

I was in the middle of the worst thing I could imagine happening, I had such an uncanny sense of . . . peace." She frowned. "Do you think that was God?"

"Of course it was God," Aron said. "He answered the thief on the cross. He answered me. Why wouldn't He answer you?"

She swallowed. "There's something else. I was really getting caught up in the gold." She stared into her coffee. "In spite of all your sermons warning against it. Anyway, that day, all I cared about was Freddie being all right. The gold didn't matter. Nothing mattered but my sweet friend." She choked back tears. "You know, right before that happened I told God it would be all right if he wanted to dump some faith on me." She looked across the table at Aron. "You were part of the reason I did that."

"I was?"

She nodded. "Seeing what faith did in you made me wish—" She paused. "Both you and Aunt Lou have something I don't. Didn't, I guess I should say. Lately it seems like maybe God *has* dumped some faith into my hard head." She looked straight at him. "Does it work that way?"

Aron smiled. "You mind some preacher talk?"

"I think I'm asking for preacher talk."

"All right, then. There's a verse that speaks to what you're asking me. It goes like this: 'For by grace are ye saved through faith; and that not of yourselves: it is the gift of God: not of works, lest any man should boast.' What I understand that to mean is that our salvation comes through faith. And that not only is the salvation a gift, so is the faith. *Both* come from God."

"So God *does* dump faith on people."

Aron chuckled. "Yes."

Mattie smiled. "I think He's done it to me. Actually, I think he did it before whatever happened between Freddie and his angel. I can't really say when, but things I knew in here," she said, tapping her head, "started making sense here." She put her hand over her heart.

"Dumping's good," Aron said.

"Yes," Mattie agreed. "It is."

As December went by, the snows piled high and the temperature dropped. Mattie completely gave up the idea of wintering on her claim. She climbed the gulch once a week and played at prospecting just enough to "prove interest" should Ellis Gates and company decide to challenge her right to the claim, but otherwise she continued dividing her time between working at Garth and Company and cooking with Aunt Lou. It became common knowledge that if you needed the preacher, the first place to look was wherever Mattie O'Keefe was hanging her hat.

Mattie was sweeping the store one day when the back door opened and a tree walked in. At least that was how it looked, for Freddie was entirely camouflaged in a mass of evergreen. "Mor says we're having a true Christmas this year," Freddie said, his face beaming with joy as he clomped toward the front of the store and leaned the tree against a counter while he took off his coat. "Can you help me set it up?"

Mattie and Freddie spent the next hour trimming bottom branches away, melting enough snow to fill a bucket with water and bracing the tree inside the bucket until finally a bona fide Christmas tree graced the front window of Garth and Company. That evening, Swede and Mattie and Aunt Lou gathered around the storeroom table with paper and scissors, creating ornaments and a paper chain garland for the tree while the men played checkers. It was, Mattie thought, as close to a perfect evening as she'd ever experienced.

On Christmas morning moonlight reflected off the deep snow outside Mattie's window at the Berg sisters' shop and provided just enough light for her to see that Justice was at the door wagging his tail at whoever had just awakened her by knocking on the door. Throwing a blanket across her shoulders, Mattie climbed out of bed and padded barefoot across the cold floor to stand beside Justice. She opened the door to see footprints in the snow and a piece of paper weighted down by a rock. With a glance in either direction, Mattie picked up the note and closed the door. Lighting the lamp at her bedside, she read, *Have coffee brewing at the store. Aron.*

"He has coffee brewing," Mattie grumbled as she looked down at Justice. "I think I'm being summoned. Should I go?" Justice gave a low yip and wagged his tail.

"You just want to go out and play in the snow," Mattie said. "You don't *care* that it's twenty below, do you?" By way of answering, Justice scratched at the door. "All right, all right," Mattie said. "Coffee with a handsome preacher. I guess there are worse ways to spend Christmas morning."

Whatever Mattie had expected to find at the store, this wasn't it. He'd lighted the candles on the tree. Just for her.

"I got permission," he said softly as he put his open hand at her waist and guided her closer.

"It's . . . breathtaking," she said.

"No, *you* are breathtaking."

Mattie turned to look up at him.

"Merry Christmas," he said. "Do you like my surprise?"

She nodded. "And . . . you. I like you."

He chuckled. "I was honestly hoping for a little more than *liking.* But I'll settle for *like.* For now."

She swallowed. "Maybe I lied."

"About what?"

"Just now. I mean I *do* like you, but . . . it's changing."

He cupped her face in his palm and traced her jaw slowly, ending at her lips. His eyes never left hers. "You can't lie if you're gonna be a preacher's wife."

Mattie took in a quick breath. "Wife?"

He nodded. "I love you, Mattie. Will you marry me?"

Closing her eyes, Mattie leaned in, wrapped her arms around him, and murmured, "I will."

"Thank you, Father," the handsome preacher said. And they kissed in the golden light of Christmas morning.

Give thanks unto the Lord, call upon his name,
make known his deeds among the people.
Sing unto him, sing psalms unto him,
talk ye of all his wondrous works.

1 Chronicles 16:8–9

More From Bestselling Author Stephanie Grace Whitson

The chance of a lifetime…a handsome cowboy… and Buffalo Bill's Wild West
When Irma Friedrich is offered the chance to live her dream, she takes it. But nothing is ever free, and she soon finds that the price of living your dream isn't always what you think.

Unbridled Dreams by Stephanie Grace Whitson

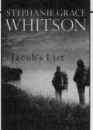

Unaware of any family problems, Jacob Nolan creates a list of adventures he wants to experience before college graduation. But his parents receive a wake-up call when tragedy strikes. Jacob's list won't be completed the way he envisioned, but God has His own redemptive plans for the Nolans.

Jacob's List by Stephanie Grace Whitson